IMAGINE ME GONE

ALSO BY ADAM HASLETT

You Are Not a Stranger Here

Union Atlantic

IMAGINE ME GONE

A NOVEL

ADAM HASLETT

HAMISH HAMILTON
an imprint of
PENGUIN BOOKS

For their support during the writing and editing of this book, the author wishes to thank Ben George, Amanda Urban, Simon Prosser, Nicole Dewey, Amity Gaige, Minna Proctor, Jon Franzen, Nancy Haslett, Julia Haslett, Robert Millner, David Menschel, Jenna Chandler-Ward, Andrew Janjigian, Melissa Rivard, Mark Breitenberg and, most especially, Daniel Thomas Davis. For the provision of space and time thanks to the American Academy in Berlin, the MacDowell Colony, the Aspen Writers' Foundation, Adrienne Brodeur, Jennifer Coor, and Susan and Ben Baxt

HAMISH HAMILTON

UK | USA | Canada | Ireland | Australia
India | New Zealand | South Africa

Hamish Hamilton is part of the Penguin Random House group of companies
whose addresses can be found at global.penguinrandomhouse.com.

First published 2016
001

Copyright © Adam Haslett, 2016

The description of the historical episode recounted on pages 299–301 is drawn from Greg Grandin's *The Empire of Necessity*

Set in 11.73/17.35 pt Sabon LT Std
Printed in Great Britain by Clays Ltd, St Ives plc

A CIP catalogue record for this book is available from the British Library

HARDBACK ISBN: 978–0–241–20121–3
TRADE PAPERBACK ISBN: 978–0–241–20122–0

www.greenpenguin.co.uk

Penguin Random House is committed to a
sustainable future for our business, our readers
and our planet. This book is made from Forest
Stewardship Council® certified paper.

For Tim

Perhaps all music, even the newest, is not so much something discovered as something that re-emerges from where it lay buried in the memory, inaudible as a melody cut in a disc of flesh.

—Jean Genet

IMAGINE ME GONE

Alec

As I stepped out of the cabin, whiteness blinded me. The snow-covered yard glistened under the full sun. Icicles lining the roof of the shed dripped with meltwater. The fir trees, which had stood motionless and black against the gray sky, appeared alive again, green and moist in the fresh light. The footprints that Michael and I had made on the snowy path were dissolving, fading into ovals on the flagstone. Beneath our tracks in the driveway I could see gravel for the first time since we'd arrived. For weeks it had been frigid cold, but now had come this December thaw. I wasn't certain what day it was, or what time, only that it had to be well after noon already.

Across the road stood the young lobsterman's truck. Brown water seeped from the icy muck caked to its undercarriage. The red tarp covering his woodpile showed through a dome of melting snow. Up the slope, on the roof of his little white Cape, smoke rose from the chimney into the sheer blue.

I had to call my sister. I had to tell her what had happened. Hours had passed already, and still I had spoken to no one.

I began walking toward the village. Past the summer cottages closed up for the season, and the houses of the old retired couples with their porches glassed in and their lights on all day behind chintz curtains. In the deep cold this walk had been silent. But now I could hear the brook as it ran down through the woods, and under the road, emptying onto the rocky beach. I could hear the squawk of gulls, and even the trickle of water at the foot of the snowbanks, each rivulet wiping clean a streak of dried salt on the pavement.

I wanted to hear Seth's voice. I wanted to hear him describe his day, or simply what he had eaten for breakfast, and tell me about the plans he was making for the two of us for when I returned. Then I could say to him that it would be all right now, that we could be together without interruption. But I hadn't been able to bring myself to call him, either.

As soon as I spoke, it would be true.

I walked on, my coat unzipped, no hat or gloves, almost warm in the sun. My sister would be up by now out in San Francisco, riding the Muni to her office, or already there. My mother would be running errands or meeting a friend for lunch, or just out walking in this fine weather, imagining and worrying over Michael and me up here in Maine, wondering how long she should wait before calling us again.

At the intersection with the main road that led down into the village, I came to the old Baptist church. The high rectangles of stained glass along its nave were lit up red and orange, as if from within. Its white clapboard steeple was almost painful to look at against the brilliance of the sky. I wondered if the lobsterman and his wife came here. Or if he had come here as a child with his father, or his grandfather, or whether he went to church at all.

The sound that he'd made, chopping firewood in his driveway, it had grated on Michael. The slow rhythm of the splitting. It had brought Michael up off the couch, to the dining room window, to watch and mutter his curses.

4

Why couldn't that sound do that again? I thought, in the waking dream of the moment, the unreal state of being still the only one who knew. Why couldn't that sound summon Michael once more? Needle him, scrape at his ears. Why not? What kind of a person would I be if I didn't at least try to call him back?

I turned around and started walking fast in the direction I had come, along the strip of road that dipped to the shoreline, up the little rise onto the higher ground, driven by the chance to begin the day over.

At first I thought my mind must be tricking me as I made the turn and saw the lobsterman—he was only a couple of years younger than I was—coming down his front yard in his Carhartt jacket and ball cap. I started jogging toward him, thinking he would disappear if I didn't make it to him in time. But instead he halted a few yards short of his driveway, and watched me approach his truck. When I reached it I rested a hand against the tailgate, steadying myself.

In the month we had been here, neither Michael nor I had spoken a word to him.

We stood there a moment, facing each other. His arms hung straight down at his sides. His bearded face was strangely still.

"Can I help you?" he asked in a slow, wary tone that made of the question a species of threat.

I gestured with my head, toward the cabin. "I've been staying over there."

"Yeah," he said. "I've seen you two."

Come nearer, I wanted to say. I needed him close enough to hit. Or to fall into his arms.

"Something's happened," I said, aloud, for the first time. "It's my brother."

Closer. Please come closer. But he didn't, he stood his ground, squinting, uncertain of himself and of me.

5

Michael

Hello. You've reached the voice mail of Dr. Walter Benjamin. I am currently out of the office. If you are one of my patients, please leave your name, a very brief message, and your telephone number, even if you think I already have it, as it may not be handy. I will return your call as soon as possible. Please note that I am out of the office on Fridays, Saturdays, Sundays, Mondays, Tuesdays, Wednesdays, and Thursdays, and that any messages left on those days will be returned on the following Monday.

If this is an emergency, and you have gone on holiday by accident with your younger brother, in the hope that you might finally tear your eyes away from the scenes you have been fixedly contemplating your entire life, but find instead that a storm blowing in from paradise has become caught in your wings, so that all you can see is the wreckage of the past piling up before you, one single catastrophe, with no future, then please hang up, and contact my answering service.

Finally, if this is about a refill for a medication you require in order to survive, and you have some concern that your request may not reach me in time, and it seems likely that the words you are about to speak into this machine will be your last, then please know that you tried very hard indeed, and that you loved your family as deeply as you could.

I

Margaret

We're bound to forget something in the rush. I could pack only so much yesterday with taking Alec to the doctor to get his stitches out, Kelsey to the vet, and stocking up for the trip. But I did all I could, and at least John helped Alec and Celia pick out their books when he got home from work last night. Come hell or high water, we leave at eight thirty sharp. John drums it into the children. He turns it, like everything he does with them, into a game: You'll be left behind if you're a minute late and we won't come back for you! When he parades through the house and calls out, Time to go, they'll grab what's at hand, assuming I've got the rest, and race for the car to compete over the backseat and the bucket seats, Michael and Celia opening another front in their roving war, Alec running behind toward another defeat at their hands. If he's not included he'll whine to quash their fun. Departures speed all their wants and fears, this one most of all: summer vacation, two weeks up on the water in Maine, in a borrowed house.

The babysitter has agreed again to feed the rabbits, the guinea pig, the bird, and even Michael's snake, which requires her to dangle defrosted mice on the end of a stick. Of the menagerie, only Kelsey comes with us, most unruly of all, and object of the children's keenest ridicule and devotion. Their untrained mutt of a mascot, who plows through window screens and shits on beds, though I still love her through their eyes.

For the long drive I make them surprise boxes, which I hold back until we're halfway there, giving them something to look forward to and buying me a half hour's peace once they're doled out. The shoe boxes are full of license-plate games, peanuts, and oranges, a little Lego set for Alec, a book for Celia, and a music magazine for Michael. I have to finish putting them together now before they come downstairs or the effect will be lost, and I manage it just a minute before Alec appears in the kitchen asking, What's for breakfast?

He's followed by Michael, who walks straight up to his little brother, squeezes his upper arm until Alec cries out for him to stop, and says, "Mom's in a preparatory mode which means Dad will cook and he only cooks Viennese eggs so that's what's for breakfast, you little thing."

Michael and Celia both treat Alec as akin to Kelsey on the evolutionary scale, a reliable entertainment when properly goaded.

"That hurt," Alec says, clutching his arm, but Michael's not listening. He's at the radio changing the station, flying over news, violins, shouted ads, Dolly Parton, and rock ballads, up the dial and back down again three or four times before he settles on a disco song, his favorite music of late.

"Please," I say, "not now."

"We can't listen to any more baroque music. It *enervates the mind*. We need a beat."

Where does a twelve-year-old get "enervates the mind"? From some novel he's reading, no doubt. Beguiled by the sound of the phrase, he'll repeat it for a week before latching onto the next one. He tries them out at the dinner table, usually on Alec, who at seven has no recourse that doesn't confirm his siblings' conviction that he's stupid. "I believe you have delighted us long enough," Michael said the other night, as Alec tried explaining how the teams worked on field day at school. Michael waited a diplomatic second or two before glancing surreptitiously at John and me to see how we'd reacted to his bon mot. Alec kept on about sack racing, until Michael once more pinched his arm.

"Not now," I say, so he turns the dial back to whatever it is Robert J. Lurtsema is playing this morning on WGBH, and opens the screen door to let a wheedling Kelsey into the yard, following her out.

The sun's been up more than two hours already—5:17 this morning, a minute later than yesterday—and is already well above the tops of the pines. Finches and sparrows flutter in the square of the birdbath, which sits atilt in my bed of marigolds. It's a rather ugly object made of coarse concrete, and it looks forlorn in winter holding askew its dome of snow, but this morning with the splashing birds making its water glisten it's a perfectly pleasant part of the mild shabbiness of the place—the barn with the collapsed rear roof that we have to constantly remind the children they're not allowed to play under, and the gently crumbling brick patio, where I've got the morning glories blooming up the drainpipe, their petals crinkled like linen around their dusty yellow centers.

Kelsey has lit off down the path into the woods—that'll be another fifteen minutes—but Michael's declined to follow, instead stopping at the station wagon, where he's stepped onto the bumper, and, holding the roof rack, is bouncing the car up and down on its rear wheels, as if it were a beast he could coax into forward motion.

John appears spiffed up in one of his jaunty summer outfits, Bermuda trousers, a canvas belt, a blue Izod polo, ready to captain our seafaring adventures. It's nothing to the children that the house on the mainland and the house on the island and the boat we use to go back and forth are all loaned to us by a partner of John's, that we couldn't possibly afford this on our own, not two weeks of it, not a hundred-acre island to ourselves, and mostly it's nothing to me—a happy gift that we happened to have been given three years running now, a place I've come to love. It's just that not knowing if we'll have it, or when we'll have it until what seems like the last minute reminds me how provisional, how improvised our lives here are.

This isn't the town we were meant to live in, or even the country, and it's not the place we want to put the children through school. We lived in London and had Michael and Celia there for a reason, because that was John's home. And it's where he wants to return. Living here as long as we have is a kind of accident, really. He was sent to Boston on a consulting assignment for what we thought would be eight months, so we rented this house down in Samoset up the street from my mother, in this town we used to come to in the summers, where she moved full-time after my father died, a house it turned out some carpenter ancestor of mine built back when the whole family used to live around here.

Then John's firm in London went out of business. And here we were. Lots of space for the children to play in. Their grandmother three minutes away, which has its pluses. So John looked for a temporary job, while our furniture stayed in storage back in England. He found one, then another, and then one potentially more permanent in this new business of venture capital, and the life we'd assumed we'd have—urban, with his friends, and the parties—stayed on hold one year after the next, for eight years now, the presumption we'll return always still with us, up ahead in the distance. Which can leave me feeling in limbo. Though most often, like this morning, when the children are happy and the weather is fine, I don't want to think too much about it.

Behind the wheel, John wears his tortoiseshell sunglasses, completing his summer look. He's a showman when he's on, capable of great largesse. In his sunny moods the winningness flows like water from the tap. He prefers Ellington to Coltrane, Sinatra to Simon and Garfunkel; likes to dance in the living room after the kids have gone to sleep, and find me across the bed in the morning; and he knows he'll never stop working or earning, because his ideas for new ventures are that good and there are that many of them, such an easy multiplication to perform. And lately I must say he's been fine, not overbrimming, but more than half full. Steady at work, and he comes home in time for dinner and to see the children, and plays with them on Saturdays and Sundays in the yard, mowing paths in the field for them to ride their bikes on, and clearing paths in the woods, and really it's fine, however different it may be from the gin-drinks parties at the house on Slaidburn Street, off the King's Road, and his glittering eyes and well-dressed friends, and so much of that time in London before our wedding.

I knew him naively, then. He wasn't raised to be understood in the way people think of relationships now. He grew up in the old world of character as manners and form, emotion having nothing to do with it, marriage being one of the forms. Which isn't to say he doesn't love me. He's just British about it. I think when he met me he realized he might be able to escape some of that, in private at least. In his eyes, I had that American openness he admires, though in fact by coming to London I was escaping my own old world of coming-out balls and the matrons of Smith College. We were meeting in the middle, I suppose.

"At least we all speak the King's English." That's what his mother said to no one in particular at the dinner table the first time I visited his parents, outside Southampton. She was apparently less appalled at my accent than she'd expected to be. His father had installed a putting green by the side of the house, where he spent most of his afternoons before coming in for a supper he preferred eating in silence. At breakfast, there was the tea cozy, and cold toast in a rack, and at Sunday lunch mint jelly with the dry lamb, and in the evening being asked if I planned on taking a bath. John was and is his mother's favorite, the oldest, who went to Oxford and into business and wears good suits and understands there are proper and improper ways of going about things, all of which he plays up when he's around her, keen to reflect back her image of him.

I had a job at a library, out in the suburbs. I'd get up early to catch a train to Walton-on-Thames and then the bus along the high street to the red-brick Victorian fortress, where I'd stamp and shelve books all day, and then reverse the journey, riding back into the city on half-empty trains running against the commute.

A few months ago I read Mailer's *Armies of the Night* and it reminded me of what I had missed being away from America for most of the sixties, reading about the violence from overseas and hearing about it from my friends, always at a remove. There was one passage that stuck with me. After the posturing speeches followed by the melee at the Pentagon, once they've all been arrested and are being driven out to Virginia in buses in the dark, everyone quiet, Mailer writes it's in motion that Americans remember. Maybe he could have dropped "Americans" and just said "people." Either way, it struck me as true. If you think of memory not just as looking back but as being aware of time and how it passes and what the passage of it feels like, then there is something about being in motion that does cause it. Through some sleight of mind, physical forward motion makes time seem visible. Which causes me to think that maybe the unnatural speed of cars and jets actually creates nostalgia. Because the simplest way to block out the strangeness of time passing before your eyes is to fix it in place, to edit it down to monuments or potted plants.

Like, I suppose, my rides on those nearly empty trains back from Surrey in the early evenings, already dark in winter, passengers across the car visible in reflection on the glass—a fixed memory I carry now as a stand-in for the more particular instances of wanting badly to see John, to be done with the courtship so we could live together and see each other every night as a matter of course.

Or like all of this coming to me now in the car after I've handed out the surprise boxes and earned a lull in the children's impatience for a while, with the windows down and the salt air rushing in on us. Remembering being at a packed, loud party at the flat with John's roommates, everyone in ties and dresses, on the evening that the fire engines appeared at the building, and we all had to scurry down the four flights of stairs with our sloshing glasses, John running back up to grab his jacket in case the press appeared to cover the impending blaze—a jest to prevent the good cheer from dissipating on the sidewalk, which worked, keeping the laughter going until we got the all-clear and clambered back up to keep drinking.

It was almost grave the way he kissed me in the beginning. His nerves showed like they never did with friends; with them, words were the only currency that mattered. The contrast seduced me as much as anything. The American boys I'd dated in college and immediately afterward brought their offhand confidence into the bedroom, where it struck the same slightly false note that it did in company. John might have wanted to be that smooth, but with me he couldn't manage it. Which I've always decided to take as a compliment. And then, as if he'd betrayed himself in the dark, he'd up the gallantry the next day, appearing at my door with a picnic basket and a borrowed car and driving us into the countryside, where even if no one was around he still wouldn't try to touch me, as if it proved something about his character. I fell in love watching him do that. I knew the starkness of the difference between his *savoir-faire* and his wordless, heavy-breathing grasp in private owed something to his never knowing exactly where he stood with me, because he couldn't interpret me as easily as he could an Englishwoman. By the same token, I couldn't help wondering if my being an outsider in his world was what drew him most. Which could make me skeptical of him, parsing his words and deeds for signs that he'd noticed or appreciated something about me other than my foreignness.

It was all part of what kept up a sense of mystery between us at the start. That tension of not knowing but wanting to know. You'd think that after seventeen years of being together and three children and moving together from London to a small town in Massachusetts, this kind of mystery would be dead and gone, the ephemera of early love washed out by practicality. And much of it is. He doesn't charm me anymore. I see how he charms others, how far his accent alone goes in this country to distract and beguile, but it's not the kind of effect that lasts in a marriage. And I am certainly no escape for him anymore, not in the simple sense of being a departure from familiarity. We fight. We disagree. He indulges the children to curry favor with them, suspending my bans on this or that, leaving me to stand alone as the enforcer. I resent not knowing when or if he'll decide the time has come for us to go back to Britain, and I resent that it depends on his work. Not all the time, and not that I can fault him for it entirely, but I'm not quiet about it when it gets to me. Like when I'm rummaging through old furniture in my mother's garage for dressers or side tables because the ones we bought together after our wedding are sitting in storage an ocean away and he doesn't want to ship it all here since maybe we'll be returning soon.

And yet there remains mystery between us. What I want to say is that we still don't know each other, that we're still discovering each other, and of course because it's no longer the beginning it isn't always, or even mostly, a romantic proposition—the not knowing, the wanting to know—but there is the wanting. Certainly there are times when I think maybe it's one-sided, that he knows just about all of me that he cares to, and that I'm the one who's still deciphering, which can be its own source of resentment.

Whatever it is, it's not about nationalities anymore, or his family or mine. It's what all that stood in for at the beginning without my realizing it. At least until his episode shortly before our wedding.

That autumn of '63 after our engagement I could tell something was getting to him at work because whenever we met up he'd be more distracted than usual and have less to say. He was the fastest-talking person I'd ever met, that is before Michael started talking, and in the right mood I could just sit back and listen to him go on about the complacency of Harold Macmillan or the latest news in the Profumo affair, he and his friends interrupting and talking over one another, dashing and clever and well oiled with drink. I'd think of my friends who'd gotten married, junior or senior year, to men just like the ones they'd grown up with, headed now to Wall Street or law school, some of them already with three- and four-year-olds, and I'd think, Thank God! I'm not a doll in the house of my mother's imaginings. I got out. And far.

But during that October John's clock began to run more slowly. It wasn't dramatic at first. He didn't talk much about his work but I imagined it was some pressure there that was tiring him out, making him less inclined to spend evenings with friends. He just appeared let down, that was all. Harold Macmillan resigning as prime minister was the sort of thing he would usually have been reading and talking about furiously but he showed barely any interest. It was the evening Kennedy was shot—evening in Britain—that I thought to myself something must be the matter with him because when I appeared at his flat in tears he hugged me and sat me down on the couch and tried to calm me, yet it didn't seem to have reached him at all. I didn't expect him to cry—it wasn't his president—but it was as if I'd told him a distant uncle of mine had expired, obliging him to pat me on the shoulder. It was unnatural.

Three weeks later I sailed back to New York for Christmas. I stayed just under a month. We wrote several times a week. Daily bits and pieces but lots of fond things, too. There were some particularly ardent ones from him—as strong about how he loved me as he'd ever said or written before.

I didn't understand what his flatmate was saying when I called the day I got back to London and he told me that John had been admitted to the hospital.

"Has he had an accident?" I said.

"No," he said. "But perhaps you should call his parents."

I phoned right away. His mother handed the receiver to her husband with barely a word. "Yes," he said. "We were rather hoping all this business was done with. His mother finds it most unpleasant."

I had nothing to prepare me. John sat in what looked like an enormous waiting room with clusters of chairs and coffee tables, all those waiting being men, most of them reading newspapers or playing cards or just gazing through the filmy windows. His face was so drained of spirit I barely recognized him. If he hadn't moved his eyes I would have thought he was dead.

The room got only northern light and the shades were half

pulled. It just made no sense to stay in that tepid, dingy atmosphere so I said, "Why don't we go for a walk?" I had to leave there to plant my feet back in reality, and to bring him with me.

Of course it wasn't that simple. It turned out this wasn't the first time he'd been hospitalized. His second year at Oxford he'd had to leave for a term. Since then—almost ten years—he'd been generally fine. He'd been the man I'd met. Now, utterly unlike that person, he barely spoke. He just held my hand as we walked through Hyde Park, the ghost of John in John's frame.

He had to rest, he said. He was tired. That was all. But I knew that couldn't be it, or was only half true. Being the pushy American, I made an appointment to see his doctor. This was most surprising to the staff, "But all right then," he would speak with me.

I remember the man's blue checked cardigan and square glasses, and his thick black hair brushed back with Brylcreem. I couldn't tell if the room where we met was his office or just a space for meetings off the ward. The books on the shelves were arranged in desultory fashion and there were no diplomas on the walls. But he seemed comfortable and settled there and offered me a smoke before showing me to the couch. He sat opposite and attended mostly to the tip of his cigarette, which he flicked frequently against the rim of the sea-green ashtray nestled in its tarnished brass stand.

"He's doing reasonably well," he said, glancing upward with a slight nod of the head, hoping perhaps that would settle it.

"But why is he here? Can you tell me that?"

"How long have the two of you been together?"

"A year and a half."

He thought about this for a moment, as if deciding how to proceed.

"There's an imbalance," he said, crossing his legs and resting the hand that held the cigarette on his knee. He wore cuffed wool pants and brown leather brogues. He must have been twice my age. Between the absence of any white lab coat and the slow, considered pace of his conversation he struck me as a professor more than a doctor.

"You could say his mind closes down. It goes into a sort of hibernation. He needs rest and sometimes a bit of waking up, which may not be necessary right now, but which we can do if it becomes so."

"And it's happened before."

"Yes, it would have done."

"And that means it'll happen again?"

"Hard to say. It could well do. But these things aren't predictable. Stability, family—those things help."

I think that's when I was closest to crying. I hadn't spoken to anyone about what was happening. Not more than to mention and excuse it in the same breath, to say that all was well. But in that room with that man whose English kindliness undid something in me, I suddenly felt afraid and homesick, and probably I did cry for a moment. "We're supposed to get married this spring," I said.

He tapped his cigarette again against the lip of the ashtray, then slowly changed the cross of his legs, his shoulders and head remaining perfectly still. He pondered my statement for such a long time that I wondered if he'd heard me. Then he looked up with gentle eyes and asked, "In that case I presume you love him?"

I nodded.

"Well, then, that's as it should be," he said.

I went to the ward in Lambeth every afternoon and we took a walk together, even if it was raining. The light in that room was a kind of malpractice. I never saw or spoke to the doctor again.

It was hard to get information from anyone. Asking questions wasn't the proper form. It was the same way a couple of years later when I gave birth to Michael at St. Thomas's, everyone perfectly pleasant but with nothing but blandishments to offer.

John stayed on the ward for a month. His father visited once, his mother not at all (John was perfect, and she wanted nothing to do with evidence to the contrary). I don't know what he told his roommates or managers, but it wasn't that he'd been in a psychiatric hospital. Often during that month I didn't know which was worse, his dark mood or the shame and frustration it caused him. And he didn't want to talk about the particulars with me.

I decided not to tell my parents. And certainly not my friends, because they would only worry. My sister, Penny, I did confide in, but swore her to secrecy. In an odd way I felt closer to John. I was the only one who visited regularly, and though it was a strain to be making decisions about a wedding when he barely had the energy to read the news—having to wonder what kind of shape he'd be in by then—there was something about those walks in the park, perhaps precisely because he didn't talk a blue streak as he usually did, that added a kind of gravity to being in love with him. I'd always wondered before if the mystery that made the beginning of romance enthralling necessarily had to vanish, or if with the right person it just lasted on. I couldn't have imagined the answer would come in this form, so tied up with trepidation and anger at him for disappearing, in a sense, leaving me with this remnant of himself, but there it was, a mystery deeper than I had guessed at. All his animation and verve could vanish like the weather and stay lost, but then somehow, after six weeks or so, return with such self-forgetting that he didn't see anything strange about how blithely he led me by the arm into a car showroom to look at MGs, and then took me out to lunch and a bottle of wine, as if nothing had ever happened.

In the fifteen years of our marriage, he's never gone back to a hospital or come anywhere close, in fact. He's never had to stop working, or gone nearly so low as he did that fall. He has moods, and occasionally a stretch of a few weeks when I notice his energy flagging, and I don't suppose I'll ever be able to rid myself of the worry I have then, that it will all get much worse. Which is part of what keeps the mystery between us going. You could call that perverse. Fear playing that role. But it's not only fear, and what's hard to explain is that the fear is also a kind of tenderness. I'm the only one who knows in the way I do that he needs someone to watch over him. At the worst moments, when the children are tired and the house is a mess and I see from the pace of his walk up the drive at the end of the day that he's at a lower ebb, it can seem no better than having a fourth child and I want to walk straight out the door and not come back for a month. But most of the time it's not like that. I may not be able to tell what he's thinking, but he reaches for me. And the excitement from the beginning fills me again at those moments. I don't see how it could if I understood him through and through.

Seventeen years together. Three children.

And here we are, the five of us, floating up Route 1 in this boat of a car, the children beginning to scramble again in the back: Michael calling out additions to his list of a hundred names for Kelsey ending in *ator*—the eviscerator, the nebulator, the constipator—all of which she answers to from the bucket seat, yelping in response, having ears only for the tone of a voice, causing Celia to climb over the backseat to protect her from Michael's mockery, while Alec stands up behind his father's seat and reaches his hand around to play with John's double chin, asking how much longer it's going to be, all of them their father's impatient children.

I'm the only one who doesn't always want answers. John

may never articulate his questions, but they are with him, a way of being. And the children want answers to everything all the time: What's for breakfast, for lunch, for dinner? Where's Kelsey? Where's Dad? Why do we have to come in? Why do we have to go to bed? Some days the only words I speak to them are answers, and reasons I can't answer, and instructions in place of the answers they want.

The questions won't stop up here, but once we're on the island and the three of them are spending most of the day playing on the rocks, or in the boat with their father, or traipsing up and down from the porch to the tide pools and back with their crabs in tin saucepans, the salt water and sun will wear down the edges of their nervous energy, and now and then I'll get to be with myself long enough that when they come back, or I spy them going about their business, I will actually *see* them for a moment. Which ordinarily I don't. Sight isn't really my sense of them. They're touch and sound. I can look at pictures from just a few years ago and barely recognize them. But the day starts and ends with their voices and bodies. John is something else. There are parallel worlds. Apparently science says so now, too. I didn't know it until Michael was born. Now it's obvious. I was reading a novel the other day and some character said, "We live among the dead until we join them," something portentous like that, dreary, and I thought, Maybe, but who's got time for the dead with all this life, all these lives, all jumbled up?

We arrive at the little blue clapboard cabin in Port Clyde in midafternoon and go to the general store to order the propane for the morning and buy groceries. John wants us to get up early again tomorrow to get out to the island as soon as possible. He'd go this evening but by the time we got the house sorted out and the food put away we'd still be making beds by oil lamp. And besides, the children like this mainland cabin too, playing on the granite boulders that jut from its sloping lawn, dashing up and down the aluminum bridgeway that runs over the tidal flat to the jetty. I watch them at it as I get supper ready.

They sense, without noticing, the new world about them, the salted air, the clear light we don't get farther south until autumn, the brightly painted lobster boats reflected in the rippling mirror of the bay. These are not things to pause over for them, the objects at hand always being what matter most—the chain Michael can put across the bridgeway to try to block the others from coming down, the bushes they hide behind, the tall grass they climb through, which will have Alec and Michael wheezing soon enough.

After supper, Michael and Celia are allowed to stay up for another hour reading. Though he has a room to himself at home, Alec doesn't like being on his own when he imagines the other two are still conspiring together somewhere in the house. But tonight it's okay because his father's telling him a story. John never reads them books. He makes the stories up. I don't have the energy at the end of the day for that, or his invention. He makes a ghost out of tissue paper, a king out of a wooden block, and Alec will be quieted to the point of trance, by the story, but also because his father's attention is pouring over him, and only him, like the air of heaven. And when John leans down to kiss him good night, Alec will reach up to feel his double chin again, chubby and warm and a little scratchy, and he'll be content in a way I can never make him because I am never the exception.

I disappear for twenty minutes into Ford Madox Ford's *The Good Soldier* while John does the dishes, fighting past my initial irritation at all the class nonsense and how no one will say anything of significance to anyone else because it's simply not done to be *explicit*. Like in James or Wharton. Those novels where you're screaming at characters to go ahead already and blurt it out, save us a hundred pages of prevarication. But my pique wears off and I sink into the allure of the Ashburnhams at Nauheim, idling on the notion of how someone could so distort his life around an obsessive love, when John comes in having forgotten the dish towel still over his shoulder, and looks across the disarray of the room for the newspaper somewhere in the tote bags. He wouldn't be able to remember where he stowed it to save his life. I reach into the side pocket of his briefcase and hand it to him.

"Did you call Bill?"

"Yes, we're all set," he says, already scanning the headlines, settling into the chair opposite me beneath the standing lamp.

I'm pleasantly tired enough to trust he got the dates right when he spoke to Bill Mitchell. Why it couldn't be settled a month ago I don't understand. I just have to assume we have our two weeks (they arrived a day early one year and we had to check into a motel). John's absentmindedness is chronic and infuriating. Whereas I remember the dates for everything. It's embarrassing actually to admit how much I still store in my head: our first visit to John's parents (April 5, 1963), the day he bought his Morris Minor (March 10, 1964), and on and on. I remember the anniversaries of these events too, but I don't mention them to people because unless it's a birth or death or wedding I get quizzical looks, as in, Why have you bothered to retain such trivia, why does it matter? (I tell the children instead; they have no idea what I'm talking about and don't really listen, but nod anyway before asking their next question.) It was sixteen years ago last month, for instance, that John appeared unannounced on my doorstep with a car already packed with food and wine and drove us all the way to the Highlands, to a friend's house he'd been loaned for the weekend.

John's friends' houses. That's where we spend all our vacations.

Upstairs, Celia has fallen asleep with her book propped on her chest. She rolls over without opening her eyes when I lift it from her hands. Michael's still sitting up against the headboard reading his novel, his feet wriggling beneath the blanket. It takes him forever to wind down. Alec and Celia have simpler batteries that burn through and fade. But to Michael this is a new bed and a new room, even if he's been here three summers in a row, and all the driving and running in the yard aren't enough to still him. In a few days, out on the island, he'll unclench a bit, getting into a rhythm closer to the other two, but never entirely. He's seen me come in but keeps reading, his teeth biting softly at the inside of his cheek. I run my hand through his thick black hair, which needs a cut—it's coming down over his eyes and ears—and start feeling for ticks. He turns his head away.

"You already did that."

Alec is so easy to touch. He never doesn't want to be touched. Celia's ten now and beginning to notice she lives in a body, so touch is getting more complicated, no more clasping at my leg, more pushing and pulling and long looks. But with Michael it's been fraught from the start. Babies are scrunched little creatures, but then they splay flat on the crib or floor. Except Michael never quite did. Like a little old man, he remained almost always hunch-shouldered and bent at the waist. He slept blessedly well but when he did cry, holding him rarely helped. I didn't understand. That's what a mother was supposed to do, hold her crying child. I thought maybe it was my inexperience, but then Celia came, and then Alec, and picking them up when they cried was like throwing a switch: the wailing ceased. And then I knew the difference. Celia's and Alec's discomforts were creaturely and fluid; they passed through them and were gone. But holding Michael had always been like holding a little person, who knew that his feeding would end, who knew that if you were picked up you would be put down, that the comfort came but also went. Without knowing what it was, I'd felt that tension in his little groping arms and fitful legs, the discomfort of the foreknowledge. Was I more skittish in my touches and kisses because I sensed my ineffectuality? I can't say. With children, everything's already happening and then over with. It happens while you're trying to keep up and gone by the time you arrive at a view of things.

"We're getting up early tomorrow," I tell him. "You should turn out the light."

"But I'm not tired," he says, still without looking up from the page.

I'm sitting beside him on the bed, my arm over his shoulder. That I should notice the position of my body to his at all—that's the difference.

"What are you reading?"

"Thomas Mann. He's German. But it's set in Venice. Have you ever been there?"

"Before I married your father."

"Did it smell?"

"Not particularly. Do you like the book?"

"I only just started. *The poet of all those who labor on the brink of exhaustion.* That's not bad."

"Is that all you brought?"

"No. I've got the one on machine code." A tiny-print tome he's ordered direct from McGraw-Hill about computers or the numbers in computers. It's Greek to me. But there's another boy at school who's interested and he doesn't make friends like the other two, so I'm all for it.

"Five more minutes, all right?"

"Okay, okay," he says, turning the page, rendering me superfluous.

Downstairs, John has poured himself a glass of Bill Mitchell's Scotch and moved on to the business section. I must make the children's lunches for tomorrow, I think, until I remember there's no school and so no rush.

Suddenly, my eyes are brimming with tears. I wipe them away. John hasn't seen it. "Spend time with Michael," I say. "While we're up here. Take him on the boat, the two of you. Or pack a lunch and take a walk. Will you?"

"What's the matter?" he asks, not looking up from the paper.

"Nothing's the matter. He'd never ask for it. Any more than Alec would stop asking. Are you listening?"

"Yes," he says, meeting my glance now. "That's fine."

"Would you get me a glass of that?"

"This?" he says, holding up his highball, surprised.

"Yes."

He goes to the sideboard and pours me a drink.

I sip it on the couch beside him while he reads a while longer. I've seen him at the mirror when he doesn't see me, glancing at the strands of gray at his temples, trying on the notion that they make him look distinguished, a state he's always aspired to, tinged with the fear that he hasn't accomplished enough yet, that the gray means nothing more than getting older.

I should ask him about the meetings he had this week, about the possible new investors in the fund he's been trying to raise for over a year now, if he's still worried about how long they'll commit for, or, rather, still worried as much. He needs to be asked. He won't talk about it of his own accord. He imagines that if he can contain it inside himself its resolution will be contained as well. That everything will work out—his upbringing distilled into a superstition.

He puts the paper aside and leans toward me and we touch

30

foreheads. Sometimes this is prelude to a kiss, other times it's just its own little respite. Giving up effort, letting in the drowsiness which isn't yet sleep coming on but is the body gaining on the mind.

"Thank you," I say, combing my fingers through his hair.

"For what?"

"For this. For bringing us here."

He kisses my cheek. However nervous he was at the beginning about our lovemaking, he's always been gentle. I suppose some women would find this boring. I don't. Perhaps because most times between us feel like the overcoming of an unlikelihood, as if I was unsure if it would ever happen again and now here it is, happening. Finding him is such relief.

Celia

We'd already bought the lobsters from the lobsterman off the side of his boat, and the island was already in the distance when Dad turned the sputtering motor off and the little cloud of gray smoke that came out of it each time it stopped floated by me, filling my nose with the smell of gasoline. He tipped the propeller out of the water and took the key from the engine, putting it into the pocket of the pink pants I wished he wouldn't wear, and the boat stopped going forward against the waves and began to rock back and forth between them instead, like the logs we sometimes saw floating out beyond where the waves broke against the shore. Up the side of each wave and down the other, the boat moving farther out, away from the island. Dad lay down in the bottom of the boat, using one of the life preservers as a pillow. He closed his eyes and spoke to us like he did when he was taking a nap, with no expression on his face. All right, then, he said, imagine something happened and I can't drive the boat and you can't start the engine. What do you do now? Alec said, Why can't you start the boat? And Dad said, Imagine me gone, imagine it's just the two of you. What do you do? There weren't any boats around or much wind but the water made its own noise and the house was

32

too far away for anyone to hear us if I yelled. I asked him if this was some kind of test. But the way he plays games is to be really serious about it, like it isn't a game, which makes the games he plays with us more exciting than anything else because everything matters the whole way through and you never know what's going to happen. It's never boring. Is it a test? I asked him again, and he just said, Imagine I'm not here. What's happening? Alec said. The back of his red life preserver came up above the top of his head because there weren't any small enough for him. When he had put it on the first time, Michael said he looked like an albino rabbit in a Soviet body cast, which made Dad smile and Alec cry because he didn't understand. What do you *think* is happening? I said. We have to figure out what to do if Dad is gone. It's like a safety drill at school. I don't want to, Alec said. Can you sit up now, Dad? But Dad kept his eyes closed and didn't say anything. He can take a nap anywhere and it was even possible he was actually already asleep. The lobsters in the canvas bag next to him were trying to get out but couldn't fit more than a claw through the knotted handles. We have to row, I said. If there's no engine, we have to use the oars. I picked up the one nearest me. It was long—much taller than I was—and heavy. I had sat between Dad's legs before and held both oars with his hands over mine so I knew how it worked but I needed both hands to lift one oar and when I put it over the edge of the boat, the water grabbed it, sliding it almost out of my hands, and I had to pull it back in again. Then I remembered they were supposed to go in the little metal horseshoes that hung on the chains either side of the middle bench. I told Alec to take the little horseshoe hanging on his side and put in the holder. For once, he did as he was told. When I got the oar in the holder, I put just a bit of the paddle in the water so it wouldn't get pulled down in again and I moved it back and forth. That's not how Dad does it, Alec said. You're doing it like a girl. In the direction the boat faced I saw only water and sky ahead of us and I had to turn to make sure that I could still see the island, which I could, but it looked even farther away than a minute ago. Dad, she can't do it, Alec said, shaking Dad's ankle. Get up now, *please*. We have to do it together, you little whiner, I said, or it doesn't work. I pulled my oar in and moved across the bench to pick up the other one. Here, I said, showing him how to hold it. Use both hands. Start out in front of you and then pull it toward you. You have to make sure it's in the water but not too much. He put his little freckled hands on the handle and sat there pouting. I slid back to my side—you're never supposed to stand up in small boats because you might lose your balance and fall—and put my oar in the water. Now put yours in the water, I said. We have to do it at the same time or it doesn't work. He put his paddle in the water but then he pushed the handle forward, which would make us go backwards, and because I wasn't looking at mine it splashed water and clanged against the side of the boat right next to where Dad was lying. His expression didn't change at all, like he really was asleep. It wasn't fair that he was doing this with Alec and me instead of me and Michael because if Michael had been here, even if I had to tell him what to do at least he'd be strong enough to use the oar and we could have moved the boat. But Alec was just too little and he was a crybaby. I don't want to play anymore, Dad, he whined. She doesn't know how to do it. Open your eyes, Dad. He's not here, I said. You can't whine to him because he's not here, didn't you hear him? We have to make the boat move, so stop whining. I showed you how to do it. You have to hold it out in front of you first and then pull it back. Don't be such a weakling. Just put it in the water and pull it toward you when I say go. We put our oars in and I said go and then the wave coming toward Alec's side lifted his oar out of the holder and it went into the ocean. Get it! I shouted. He tried but his arms were too short and I had to slide over again, tipping the side of the boat just a few inches from the water, and by then another wave had gone under us, taking the oar with it. I could see it a yard away and then more. Alec started sniffling. He shook Dad's leg again but Dad didn't move or open his eyes. It was hot in the sun and it hurt my eyes to look at the water because the light on it was blinding white. I looked back and we were getting farther away from where we'd been when Dad waved down the lobster boat and farther away from the island too. It was so unfair of him, leaving me with the crybaby. I lifted my oar out of the holder and crouched up to the front of the boat onto the little thin bench where you'd normally get wet from spray. This is what Dad did when there was fog and we were getting close to landing. He'd turn off the engine and row from the front, one stroke on one side, one stroke on the other, poking through the mist to find the jetty. He could do it sitting down, but I had to kneel on the bench to get high enough for the oar to go in the water. At least I could see the house from here so I knew what direction we should be moving in but it didn't do any good because mostly all I could manage was to keep the oar in my hand and not let it get sucked down by the weight of the passing waves. After a few minutes of kneeling like that, rocking from side to side, looking into the water, I began to feel seasick. I turned around and sat on the bench to try to make my stomach feel better. Alec was crying. He crouched on the floor of the boat next to Dad and shook his limp arm back and forth. He's not here, I said. Though now that I'd given up I knew the game was almost over.

Margaret

"You're *contemplating* something," Michael says, watching me from the top of the steps, holding his computer tome down at his side. He's thin as a beanpole, which is only more apparent in shorts and a T-shirt. It's one of the reasons he's unhappy at school, being teased for it.

"Am I?"

"You're staring fixedly into space with an expression of mild bemusement. That's how people are described when *ruminating*."

"Where's your father?"

"He's *mucking around* in the boat. He took Celia and Alec."

"Why didn't you go?"

He glances over the shimmering water, ignoring my question. "What are you *cogitating* about?"

It's been a week and John hasn't spent ten minutes alone with him yet, and now he's gone off with the other two. Michael plays with his brother and sister some, but fills most of his hours with reading and sketching out his elaborate parodies, the latest one being of our local newspaper. I found it on his bedside table this morning. The *Pawtucket Post-Intelligence: Local Family Goes on Holiday by Accident, Returns. A special joint-investigation with the 700 Club, plus weather.*

In my generous moods, I think John just forgets what I've asked him to do, and, being freedom-loving, thinks the children should all do as they like, but at other times my frustration intuits that it's more than absentminded. He doesn't know what to say to his elder son; it's sticky and awkward, and he'd just as soon glide over it, flicking the switch from treating him like a child to treating him like an adult who can teach himself how to cope with the world. John was sent to boarding school at eight. He's enlightened enough to believe that was and is a form of organized cruelty, but having gone through it himself, some remnant of the fear of being associated with weakness remains lodged in his gut. Michael gets the silent brunt of it, Celia and Alec none at all.

"What about Sand Dollar Beach?" I say. "We haven't been there yet."

"Are you suggesting a *divertissement*?"

"I'm suggesting a walk. It'll be cooler in the woods."

"Cooler, but treacherous in the event of a hurricane."

"Come on," I say, "let's go."

He puts his book down on the bench and with a pensive look of his own passes by me into the house. They're polite, my children. We've raised them to be polite. It never occurred to us to do anything else. It's not the British relegation of them to silence in the presence of adults. But manners teach them the forms of kindness. The way to greet a stranger, and eventually how not to make a scene over every little feeling because there are other people to consider. Overdo it and it will stifle them. I don't think my mother ever stopped to wonder what good form costs a person, because the cost could never be greater than someone having a poor opinion of her. It could never exceed the failure to live up to the standards of propriety. John's mother is more hidebound still, appalled that we don't better contain the children's energy. She told John it's my American influence. She blames me for her

37

son being in the States, as if I'm the one in control of where we live.

We didn't discuss raising our children differently than we were brought up, it's just a natural softening, I suppose. As if Celia would ever be a debutante, even if we had the money; it's absurd. Of course I want others to think well of my children but they already do and through no great labor of mine. It's just a matter of pointing out what's rude and what's the proper way to thank a person, and the importance of imagining yourself in someone else's shoes, that's all. John spanked Michael and Celia when they were much younger, and he's spanked Alec two or three times, but it was only when they lied or refused repeatedly to obey. And now with the older two it barely arises. They've learned how to behave. We're not a formal family, but we set the table for meals, and we eat meals together, and they have to ask to be excused when they're done. I suppose some people would consider it dated. I should encourage their whims in case they are the seedlings of genius. But that doesn't make sense to me. Whatever they do, there will be other people around and they'll have to converse with them and be polite. I want them to be happy. That's the point.

At the trailhead, Michael holds the branches of the blackberry aside for me as he leads the way through the overgrown stretch of path up the slope and into the trees. The beach is twenty minutes away, which is perhaps too far a round trip when I should be getting supper ready, but it's good to stretch our legs. He's talking about Mr. Carter, the man he got his king snake from, but the breeze carries every other phrase out of earshot. I stay close enough not to lose track entirely.

Last night it rained and the mushrooms are out—I should know their names but I don't. There are the perfectly white billowy balls, like bits of solid cloud floating over fallen branches, and the creamy clusters with brilliant orange tips massed on the sides of rotting stumps, and those extraordinary zigzags of brown crescents wending their way up the bark of the older trees like staircases for the Lilliputians.

It's amazing how many thin young pines and spruces strive to reach the sunlight lavished on the mature trees, and how many of them lie fallen like oversize matchsticks on the forest floor, the ones that didn't make it, hosts for the lichen and moss, food for bugs.

We climb up and down the steps that Bill Mitchell cut into a giant Douglas fir that must have fallen years ago across the path and now has ferns growing in its opened seams.

I wish Michael enjoyed the wonder in all this more, but his asthma has taught him to be cautious of the outdoors, or of too much running in the field behind our house, and even of the winter cold, which can set off an attack.

"... where he keeps the iguanas," he's saying as I come up beside him, now that the path has widened, "with the little stream running through his downstairs, he says he's thinking of getting a small crocodile if he can build a big enough habitat, but he's not sure, because it would take up the two spare bedrooms."

John met David Carter a few years ago when he came to a minority entrepreneurs' forum. If I remember rightly, he wanted to expand his pet business, and John tried to convince his partners to invest. They didn't, but John stayed in touch, and he took Michael over to see the reptiles. One day, without consulting me, they brought back a four-foot-long black king snake. I could hardly say no given Celia's rabbits, Alec's hamster, the birds, and Kelsey. Michael has never given it a name, which seems right somehow. It's apparently a constrictor, not a biter, but if that is meant to reassure me, it does not. He takes good care of it, mostly, cleaning its terrarium in the playroom, feeding it those awful dead mice, but he did leave its sliding door open a slit one night, and it got out, somehow making its way up into his bedroom, leading to a terrible commotion when he woke to use the bathroom and placed his foot on it. I didn't mean to yell at him the way I did, but the whole thing was too awful.

"If he got the crocodile," Michael continues, "then he'd have a complete collection, or almost with the boa and the python, and the monitor lizard."

"He doesn't let you get close to those other creatures, does he?"

"It doesn't *matter*," Michael says, swatting at ferns with a stick. "They're tame."

We walk for a minute in silence.

"I think he's sad," he says. "I think that's why he keeps so many pets in his house."

"I wouldn't think reptiles made the best company."

"Did Dad want to help him because he's black?"

I'm not sure how to answer this. I don't know why John's taken an interest in getting minority businesses started. It may have begun through the Small Business Administration, some advantage to that sort of investing. But if so he's carried it well past that: a Hispanic magazine in Chicago, a restaurant chain started by a black football player. It's a fair amount of what he does. If he were American, I suppose you'd say he was lending a hand in the next stage of civil rights, supporting black ownership, and maybe that's what he's doing—we don't talk about it—but because he's English that doesn't seem the best way to describe it. He's not caught up in that particular history. I'm not sure what the draw is, though I'm all for it, certainly.

"I suppose your father enjoys his company," I say. "I'd say that's mostly why he wanted to help him."

"I think one of the reasons he's sad is because he's black."

"Don't say that, Michael. You mustn't say that. There's no reason someone should be sad because of what race they are. It has nothing to do with that. Doesn't he live on his own? That could make anyone lonely."

"That's not what I mean. I don't mean that being black makes him sad, like he doesn't want to be black. It's something else."

"What has he been talking to you about?"

"Nothing. The snakes."

"Well, I think you must be imagining it, then. People aren't lonely because of the color of their skin."

He *ruminates* on this awhile as we enter the meadow. Half of it is covered in shade, and it's in the shade that the buds of the wild primroses have begun to open, their heart-shaped yellow petals peeling away from the stamens. Caterpillars feast on the seeded heads of the milkweeds. Butterflies flutter in the high grass. We have a field behind our house in Samoset, but not so lovely and secluded as this.

Michael seems to take no notice at all of where he is.

"If you were a slave, you'd be depressed," he says. "And you'd be terrified."

"What are you talking about? Mr. Carter runs a business. He lives in a perfectly nice house. I hope you don't say this kind of thing to him. He could be quite offended. He has nothing to do with slavery. Where did you get that idea?"

"You can't say that. His ancestors, they were slaves."

"Michael: What has he been talking to you about?"

"Nothing. I told you."

"So you're just dreaming all this up on your own?"

"Never mind. You don't get it."

This is one of his new refrains: *you don't get it.* I suppose I should be used to it coming from my children. And I would if I thought the phrase meant for Michael, as it already does for Celia, an attachment to a world of peers. But when Michael says it to me it's not because he's caught the first hints of adolescent

41

cynicism from some commiserating friend. He's referring to something else, something he sees alone. It's not just I or his siblings who don't get it.

The ground slopes down from the meadow and a few minutes farther on bits of clear sky show through the gaps in the trees as we approach the cliff above the beach. It's a sharp drop-off, thirty feet or more. The way down is to the right, along the angled sheet of granite running from the trees to the ocean. It's lined with cracks, amazingly straight and parallel and sealed with some kind of black magma however many thousands of years ago. Boulders sit on it like old men keeping watch for returning ships.

The beach itself is small, just a clearing in the rocks, really, with hard-packed sand, where a flock of plovers skitters through the thin water of the retreating waves. Farther back, the sand is dry and powdery, strewn with seaweed and driftwood. This is where we've found the sand dollars the last couple of years, which the children put in the saucepans and buckets they collect the crabs in, furnishing their little aquariums with other inhabitants of the sea.

Michael, eyes down, writes in the sand with his stick. He's only a few inches shorter than I am and a year from now he'll be my height, and soon enough taller altogether. He doesn't know what to do with his new body, how to sit or stand, which is why he never stays still, hiding in constant motion. Or it's partly why, the rest being his ceaseless brain. His limbs twitch in response to it, more bother than pleasure, let alone athletic joy. A whole dear, unknowable creature, molting before my eyes. And if in that strange little office off the ward of the hospital in London the doctor had said to me, No, you might want to reconsider what you're getting yourself into, you might want to put the marriage off, if he hadn't asked me if I loved John, the unthinkable would be possible: Michael wouldn't be here at all. His name loses meaning

42

when I repeat it too often to myself, but I have no other word to designate the mystery of him, my firstborn. There's something illiberal about the way infants are thrust into the hands of people who have no idea what they're doing, who can only experiment. It's unfair, he had no choice.

"Aren't you going to look for sand dollars?"

He keeps writing, giving no indication that he's heard my question.

"What does that mean?" I ask, coming up behind him to read what he's scrawled in capital letters: YOU MAKE ME FEEL MIGHTY REAL.

"It's a lyric. By Sylvester. You don't know Sylvester?"

"Is that disco?"

"That's an understatement. But, yes, you can call it disco."

"You like those records so much. Why don't you ever dance to them?"

He rolls his eyes and walks away toward the far side of the beach, scraping a curving line in the sand behind him. He's at that turntable of his hours a day with his headset on but he never does more than move his head back and forth. It seems a pity to me that he doesn't take physical pleasure in it the way we did, and sometimes still do, with our music.

"We're going to move back to England," he says, still facing away from me. "Dad's going to move us back there."

Something in the tone of his voice brings me to a halt. It's been cracking lately, dropping down a register at the oddest moments and then skipping back up into his boyish chirp, but these words come out complete in his new lower range, a sound from his chest, not his throat, and he utters them in a perfectly matter-of-fact way. Most disconcerting of all, he says them slowly, and he never speaks slowly.

"What are you talking about?" I say. "Did he tell you that?"

It wouldn't be beyond John, in some abstracted mood, to mention such a thing, thinking aloud to the children with no cognizance of where it might lead their own thoughts. If it's true, I'll wring his neck—to hear it from Michael first.

"Well, did your father say that? Answer me."

He turns around at my raised voice and shakes his head.

"So why do you say it?"

"Why are you angry?"

"I'm not angry. I just want you to tell me why you said that."

"Because it's true."

He's got John's black hair, his hazel eyes, the same pale complexion. It's clear as day they're father and son. Which is only natural. But why, then, staring at this utterly familiar face, stilled now by something invisible, something new but very old—why is it that I am so terrified?

Celia

When Dad got us back to shore, Michael was waiting for us on the jetty. He told Dad that Mom wanted to see him. Dad went up the wooden steps to the house, and Alec and I followed Michael the other way, out onto the rocks. Michael started running, skipping from rock to rock. I kept up, watching his feet and following his jumps, avoiding the slippery edges. Alec called from behind for us to wait. Michael slowed down but kept going toward the point that we couldn't see past from the house, the point where the shoreline turned onto the open ocean. When he got to a big flat rock just above the spray he stopped and stared out at the waves breaking onto the boulders. Alec caught up to us and immediately went down closer to where the spray was blackening the gray stone and then scurried up again each time just before it landed, looking back at us to see if were watching him.

Brother Sun, Sister Moon, Michael said, and I agreed. Alec said he didn't like that game, but Michael and I started searching for the right little nook or cave in the rocks, and Alec came after us, saying we should look for crabs instead. We found a good spot with a flat bottom and a little overhang from a bigger slab of rock above it. It was shaded, almost like a real cave. Okay, get in there, Michael said to Alec, who complied, sitting cross-legged and fidgeting with the stones he'd picked up. Who am I? Alec asked. You're a monk, Michael said. This is where you live. Who are you guys? That doesn't matter. You don't know us yet. What am I supposed to do? Alec said. You live here, you little fidget-buster, Michael said, squeezing Alec's arm. You live here and think about the sea. Alec said, I don't want to. Tough, I said. Why do I always have to stay in the cave? Alec said. Because you're the monk, Michael said. We have to find you. Just stay there and don't look what direction we're going, okay? Shut your eyes. Alec closed his eyes and Michael and I ran across the smooth rock up along the tree line, going on like that for a while until we were well out of view of where we'd left Alec. The waves were bigger here and the water was loud, slapping against the rocks, then rushing off them as the waves drained back into the sea, showing all the seaweed and barnacles on the sides of the boulders, which disappeared again when the throat of the next wave rose up and covered them. It was getting later in the day but the sun was still in the sky.

Look, I said. Down on a broad rock just above the spray line to our right three seals were basking. They look dead, Michael said. They're not dead, they're sleeping. We climbed diagonally down toward them. Not too close, I said, they'll wake up and go back in the water. Their skins were gray and brown and green and a little bluish too, all the colors mottled together, and they had huge dirty white whiskers and snouts that were wet like Kelsey's. The biggest one was huffing and snoring. Do you see the blubber on that thing? Michael practically shouted. We could harpoon it and harvest its body fat for fuel, that blubber whale! His voice said he wanted to squeeze it like he squeezed Alec's arm, squeezing the fat till it almost hurt.

I think they are protozoan, he said. What does that mean?

Very old. Ancient. They were here before humans, living off their own blubber. Michael liked that word, *blubber*. He said it all the time, even if there was nothing blubberish around. We squatted down and watched them. Every few minutes one of the seals would raise its head, look over its shoulder at us, and then lay its head back on the rock. Eventually the middle one started rubbing its snout against its flank.

Do you think we'll be late for supper? Michael asked. Maybe, I said. How long have we been here? he asked. A few minutes, I said. No, on the island. I don't know, I said. Do you think we have a week left? he asked. I don't know. Do you think we have ten days? Maybe.

He asked questions like this a lot but I usually didn't answer because I didn't really get them. It was just Michael saying stuff, asking things Mom ignored too, but that sometimes he convinced Dad to answer, which he'd do by asking more questions of Michael.

A harpoon would wake those puppies up, he said when I didn't answer. Alec would have laughed and squealed at that, egging Michael on, but I didn't. Michael stood up and walked in an arc around to the other side of the seals, keeping his distance. A minute later I followed him and we squatted down again, this time in the shade. A big wave doused the heads of the seals and they jostled themselves back from the wetness like big lazy dogs with no legs.

Mom and Dad are going to argue tonight, he said. How do you know? I just do, he said. Mom's going to get angry at him. She always gets angry at him, I said. No she doesn't, that's not true, he said. Yes it is. She gets angry at him after we go to bed. Not every night, he said, she doesn't do it every night. Besides, all couples have arguments. Mom told you that, I said. *All couples have arguments*. Mom told you that. So what? he said, that doesn't make it not true.

Down the shoreline from where we'd come there were black cormorants on a wet rock. Some stood perfectly still with their necks folded back. Two had their big wings wide open drying in the sun, which made them look a little scary, like giant bats. None of them seemed to notice any of the others, like each bird was the only one on the rock. Out a ways seagulls flew in big circles above a lobster boat headed back toward the harbor. I still didn't understand how they could stay up in the air that long without resting.

Michael tossed a pebble onto the tail of one of the seals but it didn't notice. Don't, I said. He lobbed another that landed on the biggest one's back but it didn't react either.

Don't!

They'd heat Cleveland for a week in January! he exclaimed. He said that kind of thing all the time to his one friend, Ralph, our babysitter's younger brother, and Ralph made strange noises and piled on more, like, They'd heat Nova Scotia for a year! and they'd keep going like that. Alec tried to join in but he didn't understand how it worked so he was never funny. I understood, but they didn't like playing with a girl. Stop it, I said, and he threw the rest of his pebbles away down toward the water.

What did you do in the boat? he said. Dad made us pretend he wasn't there, I said. Michael had started taking small shells out of a tidal pool in the rock, drying them on his shirt, and arranging them in a straight line at his feet. I picked some up and added onto the line until it stretched in front of me too. Do you think it's three weeks before we go back to school or a month? I don't know, I said, why? I just want to know, he said. Once the line stretched a few feet on either side of us, he started removing shells until it looked like a white chain with missing links. A fine spray in the wind was making my face damp. I'm hungry, I said, let's go have supper. The seals had backed themselves onto all dry rock again and weren't moving at all, not even their heads.

Michael didn't want to return to school, that's why he was asking about it. Ralph was his only friend. Usually he didn't get upset until a few days before we started, not this early, when we were still on the island.

He stood up and looking down at the seals said, Protozoan mammals beached like giant, animate pork loin. Then he started back along the rocks up by the trees and I followed him.

I hate you guys, Alec said when we reached the cave again. But we found you, Michael said. That's how the game ends. You're Saint Francis of Assisi praying here until your palms bleed. I don't get it, he whined. Who are you? I'm Saint Francis as a younger man, Michael said, and Celia is his friend Clare, who cares for lepers. I hate you, Alec said, standing up and running out over the rocks ahead of us.

I knew Michael had to be right about the argument that would come later because Mom didn't say anything about us being gone or even ask where we'd been. In the kitchen, Dad had the extra cheerfulness he got with us when Mom was angry at him. He let us each drop a lobster in the boiling water. He had to hold Alec so he'd be high enough not to get his hand splashed. Their black antennae whipped back and forth against the sides of the pot before disappearing.

Mom told us to clear the saucepans with crabs in them off the dining room table, and we put them on the floor by the door to the porch, a whole collection, fifteen or twenty, different sizes and colors. They were all alive and seemed happy enough. Kelsey sniffed at them but didn't like the way they moved.

The invigilator is hungry, Michael said, petting her flank.

After supper Alec did his hyperactive-playing-then-crying sequence, and Dad took him up to bed, and he screamed that it was unfair. Mom had left the dishes for Dad to do and was reading a book by the dim yellow light of one of the oil lamps. We each

49

had our own (except Alec) to carry from room to room and another by our beds. You turned up the oil-soaked canvas wick with a key on the side and, once you'd lit it, placed the curvy glass cover back in its metal holder. It was hard to make out the different shades of color in the Brueghel puzzle with it, but I didn't feel like reading so that's what I did until we played Boggle, and Alec came down again whining, and Mom said it was time for all of us to go to sleep.

After a few minutes I could hear the two of them through the floorboards. Mom started in her loud whisper. Totally different from her normal voice, faster and much more intense. I could make out some of her words but not all. Dad responded quietly like he usually did, in a much lower voice. I couldn't make out any of his words, just the flat tone that didn't change, which wasn't how he normally talked either. Mom said something about furniture, and *God bless it,* which is what she said instead of swearing. Dad didn't make any response to that. And then Mom's voice got louder. You're just going to sit there? You're not going to say anything!

I was lying on my side and I wrapped my pillow around my head so it would cover my other ear but I could still hear her: It's Michael who tells me! I ask a thousand times and I have to learn about it from the children! Dad said something I couldn't hear, low and quiet again. Whatever it was just made her angrier, which didn't seem fair, that every time he spoke she got angrier. And then what? she shouted. Another year, another two years, and all our lives, mine and the children's, hanging on whether you talk these people into doing what you want them to do? Goddamn it, John! she shouted. It sounded like she hated his guts.

My door opened and I heard Alec sniffling. Why don't they stop? he said. My blood was pumping in my ears as loud as when I held big seashells up against them. Just go back to bed,

I whispered. But he was crying now, not the whiny give-me-attention crying but scared crying. He never went into Michael's room when he got upset like this, only into mine. He was standing at the edge of my bed now.

And you sitting here not saying a damn word! she yelled. You think it's my fault! You think I'm being unreasonable! This isn't how people live. It's a fantasy!

Why won't they stop? Alec sobbed. Shut up! I whispered. Just be quiet. Dad said something short in the same flat, low voice.

Before Mom could start yelling again, I ripped off my covers and ran down the stairs into the living room, and shouted, Stop it! Stop it! I'm trying to sleep!

Mom was standing over the couch above Dad. She wheeled on me, her eyes wide with fury. Dad only moved his head to look at me. His face was pale and had no expression. Alec stood on the stairs behind me, still crying. Christ! Mom said to Dad. Look what you've done now!

Stop it! I shouted. He didn't do it! You did! It's not fair!

Oh, good Lord, she said with a sigh. This is nothing for you to worry about. Really, Celia. You don't need to worry. Take them upstairs, would you? she said, and Dad stood up and walked toward me, holding his arms out to pick me up, but I was too big for that now, which he didn't even seem to remember, so instead when he got closer his arms went down onto my shoulders, and he turned me around toward the staircase.

All right now, he said, as calmly as if he were napping and wanted us to be quiet.

Why do you yell at him, Mom? I said.

That's enough now, Celia, really. Please. Just go upstairs with your father.

I shook his hands off my shoulders and stomped back up the steps, pushing Alec ahead of me. Down the hall, Michael was peeking out from a crack in his door, which he closed as soon as we reached the landing.

Get back into bed, Alec, Dad said, I'll be there in a minute. He followed me into my room holding one of the oil lamps, and waited for me to climb into my bed and pull the covers up and then he sat on the edge of my mattress, facing the shaded window, so that I could only see the side of his face in the light of the lamp, which he'd put on the bedside table. My heart was beating fast and I knew I wouldn't be able to sleep for a long time. He reached his big hand down onto the side of my head and ran his fingers through my hair and over my ear until he had the back of my head in the palm of his hand. His thumb rubbed against my temple.

Why do you let her yell at you like that?

Your mother's upset. She'll be all right.

I didn't want to, but I started crying a little as he rubbed my scalp. But why are you always arguing? You think I don't hear you, but I do.

He looked away, his shadow flickering on the wall behind him and across the ceiling above. He held my head, but didn't say anything. His shadow seemed darker than no light at all, because when there was no light there was nothing to compare the darkness to. I had stopped crying. I wanted him to say something more. But he just rubbed my head, staring at the white grain of the shade, and then he patted me on the arm and rose to leave.

Michael

August 27

Dear Aunt Penny,

Greetings. I hope this letter finds you better off than we are. Our journey is proving to be a rough one. It started with the town car Dad had hired to drive us from his friend's house in Armonk to the West Side piers breaking down on the Henry Hudson in ninety-five-degree heat. You can imagine how frazzled Mom was! The minutes to sailing ticking by, steam billowing from the engine, the five of us and the de-fibrillator on her leash standing on a little wedge of road at the top of an off-ramp sweating like heifers. It took them forty-five minutes to send another car but we made it to the pier in time. As you know, Mom has been driven to distraction waiting a whole year to move since Dad announced his plan last summer, but she held him to his promise that we'd travel by ship. She so wanted us to experience the way she used to go Europe as a young woman, and certainly we were all very excited about it.

I don't know when you'll receive this letter. We're now on day four of our eight-day crossing to Southampton but I haven't figured out how their supposed "daily mail" system works (it hasn't exactly been a priority, for reasons that will become clear). But I know you're always curious for news of the family so I wanted to bring you up to speed. Unfortunately, as we were on our way to dinner the first night, Mom tripped on one of those raised metal door-jambs that I guess are meant to keep water from rolling in off the deck (not all that effective, as we've learned). If it had been a simple stumble I think she would have been okay, but she got her other leg caught up too and was whipped down onto that metal flooring pretty hard. The ship's doctor threw around a lot of vocab—"fractured tibia," "subluxated knee," "contused femur"—but I don't know what any of it means. Basically, I think she broke her leg. The cast sure makes it look that way, together with the pulleys it's raised up with. Suffice it to say, Mom is basically out of the picture. We visit her when we can but there's been a lot else going on.

For one thing, Alec is currently missing. We lost him at a lunch buffet the day after Mom's accident and haven't been able to find him since. Weirdly, the crew isn't all that responsive, even to Dad, who as you know isn't shy about demanding things from service people. They say it's a big ship, this kind of thing happens all the time, and that he'll find his way back to our cabin eventually. It is true that there are plenty of couches in the lounges for him to sleep on and that he'd have no trouble feeding himself with all these dining options. And as long as we assume he hasn't fallen overboard, how far could he really have gone? Still, it's been forty-eight hours now and I can tell that Dad's miffed by it. Obviously, we haven't told Mom. That's the last thing she needs, trying to heal her shattered leg. Celia said Alec's probably just trying to get attention and that the best thing is to ignore him and let it blow over.

I more or less agreed with her, at least until yesterday morning. I don't know if you remember how you left that long message on our machine about transatlantic crossings during hurricane season, and then sent Mom that clipping a couple of days before we left about the cruise ship in the Caribbean that got slammed by a huge tropical storm, resulting in several fatalities, but let me just say: you were right. They can talk all they want about their radar and stabilizers but as you've probably read in the paper already, Esmeralda, that category 3 that grazed the Outer Banks and then hung a right into the North Atlantic a few days ago, well, it reached us at about six a.m. yesterday. They canceled breakfast and told everyone to remain in their cabins, probably because they wanted to prevent people from vomiting on the upholstery in the common areas. Through our porthole Celia and I watched the gale-sheared mountains of water carve valleys beneath us before striking the ship and covering the glass entirely, like we were in an aquarium, the waves crashing onto the deck high above us, sending us onto the listing floor along with the luggage knocked from the closets.

I won't lie. It was a rough day. Dad took it all in stride, telling us stories about sailing as a boy to the Isle of Wight in choppy seas. He said there was no chance of us sinking, just a bit of broken china and a lot of sick passengers. In point of fact, a female honeymooner *was* washed off the stern, though her husband's spinal injury from that same incident wasn't nearly as serious as first reports suggested. Of course we thought about Mom in the infirmary, swinging from her pinioned leg for all we knew, but they'd powered off the elevators and we weren't about to climb six flights to check on her, or on the deregulator, who's boarded in the kennel up by the funnels. Frankly, I am more worried about Alec now that someone definitely *has* gone overboard. Still, Celia and I were vomiting all day and it turns out there's only so much you can worry about when you're vomiting.

That said, yesterday probably sounds more dire than it was. The worst of the storm passed to our west and by nightfall the skies had cleared and the temperature dropped a good twenty degrees. We ate up the week's worth of snacks we'd brought with us (no dinner service) and went to bed early.

It wasn't until this morning that I finally had time to sit down and write you this letter. I haven't seen any small craft coming up alongside the ship and certainly no helicopter, so I'm not sure exactly how it's supposed to get posted but I wanted to try to get word to you one way or another. Whatever you do, don't worry about us. We've got another four days to Southampton, and they promise to be much calmer than the last four. Meantime, everyone here sends their best.

Yours,
Michael

August 29

Dear Aunt Penny,

As I wrote the day before last, not sure when this will reach you, but I know you'll be keen for an update so am stealing a few minutes here in the casino to toss off this missive. There's no sign of Alec yet, though Celia is pretty sure she saw him from the promenade deck exiting the pool area after breakfast. On the whole, though, things on the ship are getting back to normal since the storm.

And you're never going to believe this! Guess who's on board? Guess who I'm sitting just three one-armed bandits away from right this very second? Donna Summer! I am not even kidding. It turns out, unbeknownst to me—why Mom and Dad didn't have the wit to tell me months ago, God only knows—she is the main stage entertainment for the crossing! I can't imagine how much dough they had to drop to get her (maybe she gets a free cabin?) but whatever they paid is worth it.

The evening shows are twenty-one-plus, but it's dark and crowded by the entrance and last night I managed to squeeze in undetected and stand behind a dormant food cart. Needless to say, I've listened to her records more times than I've had hot dinners. I must have worn down a dozen needles on "MacArthur Park" alone. I packed five of her cassettes for the trip (the other twelve are in the crates). As you no doubt already realize, she is the avatar of an entirely new dispensation, machine-driven but secretly brokenhearted. I am convinced she is aware of this but tortured by it. "This monstrous, monstrous force." That's how she described her career to *Rolling Stone*. "This whole production of people and props that you're responsible for, by audiences and everything that rules you until you take it upon yourself to be a *machine*. And at some point a machine breaks down." She's all carved up by ears and eyes like mine. I'm part of that monstrous force. And I can't help it. The music is salvific.

So there she was, live, in person, in the same room as me, in dazzling white sequins and bloodred lip gloss and metallic-blue eye shadow, her upper lip and nose flaring slightly heavenward, just like on the album covers (did you know she grew up in Dorchester?), and her long painted fingernails wrapped tightly around her wireless black mic. That audience of luxury-craft pikers had no concept of her larger significance. They were just there to digest.

I don't know how closely you followed the controversy over her first American twelve-inch, "Love to Love You Baby" (Oasis/Casablanca, 1975), but you may remember that's the one the BBC refused to promote and a bunch of U.S. stations wouldn't play because of the moaning sounds she made on the track, which simulated—maybe you'll think I'm too young to say this—climax? Apparently, when she recorded it (Musicland Studios, Munich, May–June 1975), she asked for the lights to be turned down and sang the lyrics lying on a sofa imagining herself as Marilyn Monroe. Hard to confirm, obviously, but it makes sense when you hear that cooing-whispering tone in the first few verses—she did it live, too—and then those throaty ecstatic passages that whipped the scolds into a flurry.

As of this writing, she is sitting about six feet from me feeding a slot machine, dressed in a nautical-themed outfit of white cotton pants, a navy linen blazer, and the largest sunglasses I've ever seen (it's pure Halston). She's with this tricked-out Italian guy with an Afro and a handlebar mustache and sunglasses almost as big as hers, whom I believe to be none other than *Giorgio Moroder,* her producer and collaborator, who at this point you'd have to say is really one of the fathers of disco.

I have no urge to talk to them, though. What would be the point? They could have no conceivable interest in me as a social matter, and all I could say is what they already know: that they are changing the course of history. When she sang "Love to Love You Baby" last night it left me weak-kneed. And yet even that did little to prepare me for her encore, "Our Love." Are you familiar with that particular assault on the soul? It's on side four of *Bad Girls* but didn't get much radio play until a few months ago when they released it as the B-side on the "Sunset People" twelve-inch ("Sunset People" itself is anemic, just a bloodless, dialed-in glorification of LA nightlife, not one of their better outings). But "Our Love" is epochal. Short of nailing this letter to a copy of the twelve-inch and sending the whole thing COD, I don't know how I can do it justice. That plaintive opening line is enough to cripple a water buffalo. *Dropping you this line to give you peace / And to set your weary mind at ease…* People think disco is shallow, that it's plastic and heartless, but they fail to hear the depth of its sadness. What else forces you to move and weep at the same time? When Moroder strips away all the effects at the one-minute mark, leaving only the drum track, and Summer's voice hardens to belt out the chorus, insisting their love will last forever, over and over, twelve repeats, you can't help but hear the lie in it. Of course it won't last. And yet still she wants to give us peace, to set our weary minds at ease. Could a person ever not want that? And the bubbling, alien synth that comes in at the end? That whipping, chemical torque? That is the sound of what's to come. There's not a dance floor from Rotterdam to Tokyo that isn't stretching that track to the breaking point. It's the most important twenty seconds on the album. In two years, you won't have to go farther than a fire-department bake sale to hear that beat sampled into every white pop-radio hit you can shake a dollar at.

Seeing her live was a jackhammer to the frozen sea within me. I stumbled out of there higher than a mule on a horse. Which is when I saw Alec down at the far end of the promenade. It turns out he'd had a rough few days himself. Apparently, he'd been abducted by a child-prostitution ring down on deck 3. English, Russians, and he thought maybe Dutch. He was about to be sealed in a crate and smuggled to a Soviet resort on the Black Sea when he managed to secrete himself on the bottom of a curtained tea trolley that rolled him into the kitchens. I was obviously taken aback. Transshipment to Sebastopol would have been a suboptimal outcome for Alec. As I understand it, sex slavery is pretty much a nightmare. But what it makes me wonder is, Is there anything that *isn't* happening on this ship?

Please don't mention this last episode to Mom or Dad. They've got a lot on their minds at the moment, and we're doing our best not to worry them with anything further. Alec says he'll steer clear of deck 3 from now on and stay out of the casino during the afternoon hours when they allow minors to play slots. We told Celia but she said Alec was making it up. She's currently reading a nine-volume biography of the Brontë family and doesn't like to be interrupted.

I guess the lesson is, wherever you go, life follows you

60

there, hunts you down, and abducts you (just kidding). We're only two days from landfall in England, where Mom can be transferred to a tertiary-care facility. And on the last night of the crossing Donna Summer is performing again!

Come visit us soon!

Yours,
Michael

September 7

Dear Aunt Penny,

I was expecting to be writing to you from England by now but it turns out our trip has been extended. Dad, as you know, is a bargain wizard, a master at traveling in style for a fraction of the going rate. But this time he's really outdone himself. About a week ago, scanning the horizon with my binoculars for the tip of Cornwall, I saw a bunch of islands off the port side, which in due course I was able to identify as the Azores. This certainly explained the "heat wave"! For days, passengers had been complaining about sunburn and doffing their evening cruising jackets like hookers. Everything got damp and no one felt like moving. The crew was initially circumspect, saying only that we could look forward to a big surprise. But by the time we had dropped anchor somewhere in the Gulf of Guinea, people wanted an explanation. The captain came on the PA and said that every once in a while Cunard tacks on a tropical excursion as a way of thanking their loyal customers. There would be no extra charge, he said, and free champagne.

At least for those still on the ship. It turns out Alec's brush with that syndicate down on 3 is only the tip of the iceberg. At first, it just seemed like fewer people were coming to dinner, and we figured the heat had sapped their appetite. It made sense that the oldsters would keep showing up owing to their greater sense of form. As far as the tropical excursion went, we basically just sat parked in the baking sun. So the whole marketing angle got bogus in a hurry. I've been going down to the rec room every morning after breakfast to play video games, and two days after we'd dropped anchor, when I swung the door open I saw something peculiar: a row of naked guys in their teens and twenties lined up against one wall, with their wrists bound. At a stretch, I suppose it could have been some kind of gay event that they hadn't put on the public schedule. That might even have explained the two crew members wiping their bodies down with baby oil. But if this was some kind of affinity group, why were so many of them crying? I was too embarrassed to tell anyone about it, especially Dad, so I just stopped going to the rec room.

But what really set off alarms for most people was seeing that first lifeboat head for the coast loaded with naked men yoked at the neck. That, I think, was the proverbial "wake-up call." Turns out this puppy is a full-on white slaver! And quite a cargo it has.

Being late to Southampton was one thing. But there seemed no excuse for this. And the captain's explanation—that the shipping company had a contract with the U.S. government to deliver extradited criminals to Gabon—struck many of us as thin. Just how many people did the U.S. regularly extradite to Gabon? And even if they were criminals, didn't they at least deserve some protection from the sun? At our table, the Milfords said they were going to ask for a complete refund (including taxes and fees) and were considering circulating a petition. Sally Milford says Cunard has gone seriously downhill. And of course Mom is disappointed, not only that she's still in traction, but also that our experience of an Atlantic crossing has been so different from her own earlier trips, of which she has such fond memories. I've seen Dad get high-handed with plenty of hotel employees, but this time he really went off on the purser, who was the highest-ranking officer he could reach. He told him he knew a member of Cunard's board of directors (not true) and that those responsible for exposing passengers to this ugly business would be held to full account.

But let's face it—those were the salad days. We were still getting three meals and dessert. Our waiter, Lorenzo, was still putting a flower on Celia's cake plate every evening and the whole waitstaff sang their nightly happy birthdays and anniversaries. At least until half the diners had contracted dengue fever! Mom got kicked out of the sick bay like a two-bit malingerer to make room for that afflicted horde. But what really stank, literally, is that the ship's sewage system got backed up—something about a broken pump—which meant we couldn't flush the toilets anymore. They said they would send crew members around to slop them out at least once a day, but like a lot of their representations, this proved false.

Those lifeboats leave every few hours now packed with butt-naked passengers slickened up like competition weight lifters, chained from neck to toe, and they come back empty. Celia thinks the larger ones are being sold for blubber, while the fitter ones are likely to enter the agrarian sector or be traded on into the interior for other goods. She said she read about it in *National Geographic*. I told her that was impossible, that whatever was taking place here must be part of an underground economy. But she said no, she'd definitely read about it, and that the most common fear was cannibalism but that this was a racist stereotype. At worst, people's fat was harvested for fuel, not food. Which was probably why none of us had been taken yet because we were too thin.

The truth is, I think Mom's really pissed. Which always makes me nervous. I want to find a way to calm her down but sometimes she just gets in a state and there's nothing I can do to end it. It's scary.

Of course, she's not the only one. The Milfords are fit to be tied. If I sign that petition of theirs calling for the captain to resign one more time I'm going to be had up for fraud. It's all they talk about at dinner. They strike me as the kind of overwrought liberals who are glad for the opportunity to finally be outraged at something actually happening to *them*. I guess some people just want to drag you down with their obsessions so they don't feel so isolated with them. But is that really the adult thing to do?

We've certainly gotten to know couples in the neighboring cabins better than we might have otherwise, like Jim and Marsha Pottes from Harrisburg. Jim says our situation reminds him of the Battle of the Bulge, though Marsha says *everything* reminds him of the Battle of the Bulge, and what does that have to do with slavery anyway? I like her. She's always got an ice bucket of Lipton tea going, and she wears these one-piece jumpsuits that she doesn't even realize would probably get her into Studio 54 if she rode in on a gazelle. But mention the

Milfords to Jim and Marsha and they just roll their eyes. Sure, lashing Sally to a bench on the sundeck yesterday and horsewhipping her until she bled from her flank and then leaving her there, exposed to the sun, was harsher than necessary. But Jim's point was that Sally's not about to be rowed to the coast and sold, and so maybe she ought to just butt out now and then. Rome wasn't built in a day (he says that all the time, too).

Suffice it to say, between one thing and another, the social atmosphere on the ship has taken a hit. I see fewer people shopping in the jewelry store or getting their portraits taken, and I think some of the couples who got hitched on the crossing are wishing they'd just gone ahead with land-based weddings.

I have to run, though. Time for this new daily group exercise thing that the captain has us doing. More soon, I promise.

Yours,
Michael

September 19

Dear Aunt Penny,

This trip bites! Now Mom's got that Marburg virus, *the same one you were obsessed with last year!* She's doing her best to stop the bleeding, but man is it a DRAG. Our situation is getting ridiculous. It seems that we'll be parked here until virtually everyone has been auctioned off. And it's not just the lifeboats now, either. Canoes, Boston whalers, a whole slew of small craft show up and barter with the crew, taking passengers right off the port-side service entrance. There are at least three other cruise liners anchored near us doing the same thing. Weird, right?

A few days ago a bunch of people just began to say, "Fuck it," and started jumping off the ship. The Potteses' tablemate Jill Sinclair jumped after her husband kicked it with the dengue (the ship doesn't have a morgue so it's all burial at sea, though I have to say the ceremonies have been getting progressively less elaborate). According to her husband, Mrs. Sinclair used to be a decent swimmer. Though apparently not good enough to outrun a shark herd. It was a full-on nature special. That gave some folks pause, though not everyone. It's gotten to the point where the captain felt it necessary to order the crew to put up nets all around the edges of the ship, to prevent people calling it quits. I suppose it's a public-health intervention of sorts, but I have to say it doesn't offer much comfort.

To my shock, Celia has actually stopped reading about the Brontës, so she's more available now, but still it's getting pretty grueling. And she's right: cannibalism *is* the biggest fear, followed by what are presumably less-than-ideal labor conditions in Angolan mines. Lots of people are saying it must be one of those African famines that has made this business a runner, but that's just ignorant because the famines are usually in Ethiopia, and I don't see how white tourists could be cheaper than rice. Truth be told, there's not a lot of blubber left on these cruisers. Between the dysentery and whatever slop they're buying in off the coast to feed us, they should advertise the trip as a weight-loss clinic. Alec is back down to twenty-three pounds, which has Mom out of her mind with worry. I just try to remind her that she needs to focus on her own bleeding. Alec will fatten up in no time once we get to England.

I told you about the mandatory exercise, right? I'm guessing it's not Donna Summer's favorite contract clause, singing some of her finest work to the remaining five hundred passengers crammed onto the stern pool area while the crew shouts through bullhorns for all of us to dance. And yet she brings to these performances something remarkable. I'd give my front teeth for a recording of yesterday's rendition of "On the Radio." Its opening piano and strings have always hovered between LA session-music schmaltz and the prelude to a tragedy, only to be redeemed by the purity of her voice in that first verse. But yesterday she reached higher still, a longing as clean as elation. *Someone found the letter you wrote me on the radio / And they told the world just how you felt...* By the time the beat came in, I could have sworn I saw tears in her eyes. Her makeup was running, like the mascara on many of the ladies in front of her, who still put their faces on each morning even though their clothes and luggage have been confiscated. They're not the best dancers and can be quite lethargic, but yesterday I saw many of them close their eyes and begin moving their hips in time not to the drum machine but to the rhythm of her words.

When she reached the middle verse, that pool deck might as well have been the Paradise Garage at two a.m. on a Sunday, minus the gay and black people. She had that crowd of sun-charred crackers dancing like jackrabbits. They tripped on their chains but just got right back up again.

After this morning's session ("Dim All the Lights" and "Bad Girls" followed by a "MacArthur Park" that left even the weary crew in tears) I passed a suite on 9 whose door had been left ajar, and there Donna was, kneeling at the foot of the bed, praying. I was more ashamed than ever to be dressed in nothing but my underpants. At any moment, her bodyguard would return from his toilet break and hustle me off. Still, something about the image of her at prayer arrested me and I couldn't help watching.

At this late date, I suppose there's no reason not to tell you that I have in fact (forgive the confession) "pleasured" myself a number of times to "Love to Love You Baby," and not only to the drum track, but also to visions more particular to the artist herself. Apparently, she's always considered herself plain and been highly self-conscious concerning her physical appearance. When I read that I felt closer to her, if only because I'm the same way. As I was peering at her through the slit in the door, Giorgio Moroder opened it wide and started at the sight of me. "Buzz off," he said in an Italian accent. I didn't think. I just reacted. "You're the greatest producer of our age," I said.

This took him aback, and for a moment he didn't seem to know how to respond. He too had been shackled in leg irons. His striped linen pants were soiled and ragged. He asked me how much of his early, solo work I knew. All of it, I told him. *That's Bubblegum, That's Giorgio* (Hansa, 1969). Not exactly a seminal bubblegum album, but that's not the point. Somewhere in there he was hearing what would lead him to the Moog synthesizer and the revolution in the sound of modern life, to a music that mirrors to an almost frightening degree the frictionless surface of commercial culture, but reminds us that it's still human beings who are condemned to live in it, caught in the undertow of its melancholy. And so his first work, I told him in all honesty, is interesting in the way Picasso's early academic realism might be to an art historian. He handed me a towel to cover myself and invited me into their suite.

He shut the bedroom door to give Donna her privacy and then told me this gig was like nothing they'd ever done before. "Bullshit," he called it. He's been bribing an officer to send telegrams to everyone in LA he can think of to try to get them airlifted out of here, but he suspects the messages are never sent. Donna apparently has a heart condition which is acting up. She was supposed to be in the studio five days ago, and her voice is at the breaking point. We talked a bit about Munich in the mid-seventies, the dilemma about whether to sign with Geffen, and how Donna wanted to move toward more of a rock sound on her next album. I wanted to tell him that they couldn't control what they'd started, that the beats would only get faster and the synth more gorgeous, but this seemed presumptuous. I was worried the door might open and Donna might appear and I would be ugly and dumbstruck. So eventually I excused myself, and hustled back down to our cabins on 5.

To be honest, Aunt Penny, I'm not sure what will become of us now. We thought it was bad when Dad got shackled to Jim Pottes two days ago, making sleeping awkward for everyone, and then Dad woke up with Jim's corpse locked to his ankle and wrist, dead with the Marburg that Mom presumably gave him. We lost half the morning cleaning up all that blood and mucus (except that little fidget-creature, Alec, who said he had a headache). I'd planned to do so much reading on this trip, and have got to practically none of it. In any case, at the rate the crew's expiring I guess they'll need someone to sail this puppy north again, so maybe I'll have a chance to catch up then.

In the meantime, be well, and know that while this move of ours has turned into a major bore, the five of us have our eyes fixed on one another like cement. Someday soon you'll come visit us in England at our new house and we'll all have a good laugh about the crazy turns life can take.

Yours,
Michael

Alec

The downstairs bathroom had a cork floor and one of those strange electric towel racks. There was a bathtub but no shower. To flush you had to pull a chain hanging from a water tank up the wall. The sink was high and tiny. But no one could see you in the bathroom, it had no window, which made it safe. And it was warm, too, unlike every other room in the house, and brightly lit.

I sat on the toilet until my legs went numb, but still nothing came out. Being there that long, my legs tingling, it was as if I had the power to see through the door, out into the front hall, and onto the driveway and the little lane that Michael called twee-to-beat-the-band, and beyond that through the other houses to the center of the village we'd been living in almost two school years already, into the weird English food stores, the butcher and the greengrocer, and the newsagent. Sundays were the only times I got to wear long pants here, because it was the only day I didn't have to go to school, and long pants were for the upper-form boys, the ones with pubic hair.

The lined gray wool of my trousers lay crumpled around my ankles. When the numbness started to hurt, I got up from the toilet and stepped out of them. All I had on now was Michael's silky white shirt, which felt like someone touching me. I unbuttoned it and let that slink to the floor, too. I put the footstool in front of the sink and climbed up to look at my bare self in the mirror, and then I leaned forward and flapped my penis up against the glass.

Have a good look then, you little wanker, Linsbourne had said in the showers after games. I'd been staring at his without knowing it. Everyone looked at me, and I looked down at the gray soapy water puddling by the drain.

But here with the door locked no one could see me bobbing my penis up and down with the handle of my toothbrush, or running naked in circles around the bath mat. I touched my bare legs to the curves of the towel rack, and the radiator, which burned, and my stomach to the knob of the linen closet. Then I got bored and went over to the door.

I took the knob of the sliding-bolt lock between my thumb and finger. The lock was stiff and hard to use. Mom kept saying that. You had to press it until your fingers hurt. She kept telling Dad to fix it. I pressed hard enough to feel the little pain on the pad of my thumb. But not enough to shift it open. Which excited me again. One hard push and they could open this up and discover I was naked.

I knocked on the door. Then I stood very still, and listened, not breathing. Nothing happened. I knocked again, more loudly. I heard footsteps. Mom coming into the front hall.

"Who's in there?"

"It's me. The lock's stuck. I can't get it open."

"Just push it a little harder."

I pressed the knob again, enough to feel the prick of the little pain.

"It's too tight," I said. "It won't move."

"Well, then find something to push it with. The handle of the plunger or something."

I did as I was told, crossing the room, naked, getting the plunger, and scraping the wood of it against the metal loud enough for her to hear.

"It won't go," I said.

"What's the matter?" Celia asked, coming down the stairs.

"He can't get the lock open."

"Why, because he's too weak?"

"*No*," I called through the door. "Because it's stuck."

"Well, push it harder."

"He's tried. I knew this would happen. I told your father."

Kelsey bashed her tail against the bottom of the door, excited by our voices. I heard Michael passing through from the living room.

"Alec's trapped himself in the toilet," Celia told him.

"I keep saying he's the fortunate one," Michael said. "But no one believes me."

"That's not helpful," Mom said. "I have to check the meat. Could you two help your brother, please?"

"Just open it," Celia said. "I need my barrette."

"I can't," I said, my cheeks burning, a strange light-headedness lifting my body until I almost floated there just a few inches from them, the door the only thing covering me.

"What are the conditions like in there?" Michael asked. "Are you well provisioned?"

"You're just encouraging him," Celia said, walking off toward the living room. "Leave him there and he'll come out."

But Michael stayed. He sat in the creaking wicker side chair by the hall table. I heard the drawer open, and a moment later the end of a black shoelace appeared under the door.

"What's this?"

"You could tie it to the bolt and pull."

I pressed my bare back to the wall and slid down it until I was sitting cross-legged.

Michael had hated his school as much as I hated mine, at least in the beginning. He'd cried about it, even though he seemed too old to. I listened at night from my bedroom, to Mom telling him it would be okay, that he would meet people and it would get better. That was when the two of us had still played together with Kelsey on Sundays, steering her into the same room as the white Persian cat that had come with the house, so we could watch them fight. But now Michael usually went into Oxford to go record shopping instead. And during the week he didn't get home until suppertime, and always studied afterwards.

"Where's Dad?" I asked, fiddling with the shoelace.

"In bed," Michael said. "Where, of late, he is wont to be."

"Why does he sleep so much?"

"I guess because he's tired," Michael said. "Very tired. Apparently unemployment will do that to you."

"What do you mean?"

"He picks you up from school, doesn't he? Did he ever do that before?"

Dad had started coming to get me from school in the last month, in the blue Skoda wagon. On the way home, on the straightaway of the country road, he'd speed up to eighty or ninety miles an hour, and then shift the car into neutral and turn the engine off. We'd swoop into the valley, freewheeling through the open fields, seeing how far we could get, if we could make it all the way to the pub at the bridge, until we were going only a few miles an hour and cars behind us were honking and passing.

"He's not still *in* there, is he?" Mom said, agitated now. "This is ridiculous. Where's your father? Michael, get your father."

I leaped to the sink and put my clothes on. And then went to the door, and was about to slide the lock open but I didn't. I waited. For Dad's footsteps on the ceiling above me. For the sound of him moving in their bedroom. He would have to get up

74

now. He'd have no choice. And then I heard him on the stairs, and heard his voice just on the other side of the door.

"Alec?"

"Yeah?"

"What's the trouble, then?"

"The lock. It's jammed."

He walked out of the hall without saying anything and came back a moment later, and I heard a scraping at the base of the door, and saw the tips of a pair of pliers. But they wouldn't fit through the crack. He got up again and returned with a smaller pair, which he slid through to me.

I clasped them to the knob and scraped them along the metal.

"You have to squeeze," he said.

I stopped the scraping and made a little grunt. "It doesn't work," I said. "It's still stuck."

"For God's sake," Mom said, charging back in. "The food's on the table."

"Open the fucking door," Celia said.

"You will *not* use that language," Mom said.

All four of them were there now, and Kelsey, too. Dad didn't say anything.

The blood was pumping in my ears.

"That's it, then?" Mom said to Dad. "You've got nothing else to offer?"

"Alec," he said. "Step back, step away from the door."

"What are you doing, John?"

"I'm going to break it down," he said.

"No!" I said. "Wait, let me try again." And I grabbed the pliers, biting the steel with them and yanking the bolt across.

John

From the clearing in the woods, I can see down through the spruce trees to the river, where a long slab of rock parts the slow-moving waters covered now in morning shade. The rock is mute and still in the encroaching summer heat. It has the in-human patience of objects. A reminder that mineral time does not care for sentiment, or life. Every human thing, a ruin in waiting. On a planet that is a ruin in waiting. Which says noth-ing about divinity, one way or the other. I only know that this trial is what has become of my sliver of time.

My great return to Britain was a great failure. There was a reces-sion. Purposeful risk was a hard enough sell to my complacent countrymen. The declining market made them more cautious still. I did what I had told all the entrepreneurs I ever trained not to do: moved my family before I had sufficient commitments. These, at least, are some of the excuses Margaret encourages me to give myself for what happened. That is, when she is not eaten up by fear and rage at the fact that she and the children have been uprooted twice now: first to go over there, to retrieve our furniture from where it had remained in storage, to settle the children in English schools, and then less than three years later to retreat back here to America. Because of me. Because I was fired by my own partners, told they couldn't afford my debilitation any longer—at the firm I had started. Back here to a different town and different schools, everything new again. Walcott, west of Boston. Because at least here, a man whose business I had helped to start pitied me sufficiently to offer me a job. Which itself couldn't possibly last, and didn't. Eighteen months of work, and then the suggestion that I go part-time, and then, a few months ago, the end to that, too.

Against the monster, I've always wanted meaning. Not for its own sake, because in the usual course of things, who needs the self-consciousness of it? Let meaning be immanent, noted in passing, if at all. But that won't do when the monster has its funnel driven into the back of your head and is sucking the light coming through your eyes straight out of you into the mouth of oblivion. So like a cripple I long for what others don't notice they have: ordinary meaning.

Instead, I have words. The monster doesn't take words. It may take speech, but not words in the head, which are its minions. The army of the tiny, invisible dead wielding their tiny, spinning scythes, cutting at the flesh of the mind. Unlike ordinary blades, they sharpen with use. They're keenest in repetition. Self-accusation being nothing if not repetitive. There is nothing deep about this. It is merely endless.

I taught my children how to handle themselves on the water, how to step in and out of a boat, how to row, how to steer an outboard and tie knots, and when I had the chance I showed them how to sail. I taught them how to ride their bicycles, and in the country, in Samoset, I cut paths in the field for them to ride on, and built them a tree fort. And back in Britain, for the two and a half years we lasted there, I showed them castles and Roman walls, and taught them what history I remembered from school. You could say that I fathered them as I was never fathered, but that sounds awfully American and psychological. My father did what his time expected of him without complaint, and I have no bitterness toward him. We weren't meant to know each other and we didn't. He didn't plant the monster in me. It's older than him, and far savvier. He worked for his family's shipping business in Belfast, and when he turned thirty he became their agent in Southampton, where he met my mother. He saw his family through the Depression and the war, and ensured that his children were properly educated, and throughout it all he spoke very little, which was no deprivation given that I'd never known him to behave otherwise. It's easy to make too much of fathers, I want to say.

A few months ago, a fog blinded me, thicker than ever before. I slept in the monster's arms. I felt its breath on my neck, its scaled stomach rising and falling against my back, its head and face invisible as always. I couldn't pretend anymore to Margaret that I was working. The children receded into noises grating on my ears. I stopped moving. Weeks went by indistinguishable one from another. I could smell the rot of myself, my armpits, my breath, my groin, as though the living part of death had already commenced, the preliminary decomposing, as the will fades. In Dante and Milton hell is vivid. Sin organizes the dead into struggle. The darkness bristles with life. There is story upon story to tell. But in the fog there is nothing to see. The monster you lie with is your own. The struggle is endlessly private. I thought it was over. That one night the beast at my back would squeeze more tightly and I would cease breathing. What remained of me hoped for it.

But it didn't happen. Through the window by the bureau I saw the leaves of the Japanese maple and the roof of the house next door and clouds stretched across the sky. Particulars began to return. Dust in the sunlight. The weave of the carpet. The very things which earlier harbingered trouble by threatening to derail my attention and distract me from the through line of a conversation were now, strangely, signs of mental animation: the registering of color, the sharp delineation of objects against their grounds. I got out of bed. Talking seemed nearly impossible but I started eating again with the family. Margaret was exhausted but still she made sure to cook a meal most every night. I noticed again how oddly beautiful my children were, even amid the moroseness I had imposed on the house. Celia's black hair shone in the buttery light of the sideboard lamp and her enormous eyes coursed with anger at the stifling fact of me and her mother. And Alec—uncannily already my height, always trying to keep up with his sister, measuring his opinions against the force of hers, guileless yet acting at the same time (perhaps his acting is what makes him guileless). I can't imagine I was ever that young, not so unguardedly. He looks at me out of the corner of his eye, unsure of who or what I am.

And then there is Michael's empty chair. He came back with us from Britain, but he couldn't stand it here. Or maybe he couldn't stand me. Simon, a friend of his from the comprehensive, said he could go back and live with his family to finish his last year of school, and eventually we consented. Of course it made sense. If I hadn't created such a wreck of things he wouldn't have been so miserable. The fact is, his being gone makes it easier. It's harder for me to look at him than at the other two. When he was little he tripped on the stairs in Battersea and hit his head. It wasn't a serious injury and Margaret didn't ring me at the office. But around that time, midmorning, I got a terrible headache, bad enough that I left the building to get some air. Walking in the park, trying to shake it off, I sensed something had happened to him. When I rang Margaret I didn't mention that I already knew what she had to tell me, because I didn't want to disturb her.

Michael was quiet and very thoughtful as a boy. There were times when he had the air of a mystic about him, as children sometimes do, as if he were staring calmly into the nature of things and had the wisdom to know there were no words for it. But more often his prescience spun him into worry. Was there enough petrol in the car to get us to his grandmother's house? Did we have enough time to make the train or would it leave without us? What if the water boiled over when his mother wasn't watching? What if the policemen didn't know where to find the criminals? His questions had no end and no answers sufficient to mollify him. I didn't mind. Then he became old enough to realize his questions were childish and instead of asking them aloud, he turned them inward. We stopped having the conversations where I explained simple things to him. School, which made him so unhappy, took over, and whenever I tried to protect him from it, like speaking to a classmate's parents about how their child was teasing him, I only made it worse. Now he's taller than I am, thin as a rail, and he talks as fast as can be, not questions but endless invention, his imagination running out ahead of him, to make sure everything stays in motion, that he doesn't get stuck.

A few weeks ago, the first night that I ate with Margaret and the children again, Celia kept scrunching her napkin on the table beside her, clenching and unclenching. When I told her to put it on her lap, she shouted at me that she would do what she wanted. Margaret slammed her utensils down and said if we didn't stop it she would leave the table. But the next night was a little better. Michael wasn't there to distract his brother and sister with laughter, but still, it was better.

Being up and about again, I started taking these walks. I wake early and bring Kelsey, who runs off the leash once we reach the woods. The cool oxygen of the plants and trees before the sun has dried them feels like a balm to my lungs. I've always preferred the woods in America to the woods where I grew up in Hampshire, which I can never help knowing are the hemmed-in exception to towns and villages and farms. New England is the other way around: a series of clearings in a forest. Keep walking north, and the clearings will shrink, until there are none. I don't meet other people here, and that's what matters. My mind can rest. Which is when my situation becomes obvious. There is no getting better. There is love I cannot bear, which has kept me from drifting entirely loose. There are the medicines I can take that flood my mind without discrimination, slowing the monster, moving the struggle underwater, where I then must live in the murk. But there is no killing the beast. Since I was a young man, it has hunted me. And it will hunt me until I am dead. The older I become, the closer it gets.

It's midmorning by the time I cross back over the river and follow the path into the field at the end of our street, which is saturated now in the July heat. The grass is intensely green, the scrub-apple trees by the road past blooming, on into their pure summer verdancy, along with the rhododendron and the lilac, their flowers gone, their leaves fat with sun. The air smells of the fecund soil—the flesh covering the skull of the planet, the muck from which the plants rise, busy in the mindless life of heat. Celia and Alec were drugged with sleep when I left the house, as they always are, and I didn't want to wake them. In summer, I can't be sure of their whereabouts, but last night at dinner I paid attention, and got a sense of where they would be today.

Turning before I reach the house, I carry on into the center of the town. It's quiet. Kids are away at camp or on holiday. The shops have bins and tables of merchandise out on the sidewalk and signs announcing sales. A few skateboarders sit glumly on the bench under the awning of the ice cream store watching the cars move slowly past. Across the street a woman smiles at me and waves enthusiastically and I nod and wave back, though I have no idea who she is. A mother of one of the children's friends, in all likelihood, someone I've met at the school or in a driveway picking up Alec or Celia. I look away and keep walking lest she cross the street and begin speaking to me. In another time, I would have hooked into the aggression of her good cheer and doubled it up until running into her became an event with a momentum of its own. I've lived vicariously at times off that birthright of the American upper-middle class—their competitive optimism. It's what I loved about working in this country. *What are your plans? How's the project? How's business?* When I left university in Britain, we didn't have entrepreneurs. We had managers and industrial relations. Meeting someone at a party led to the circumlocutions designed to tease out where you'd been at school, one's accent having made one acceptable company in the first place. In America, I flew all over the country talking to people about their wildest ambitions and they were always delighted to see me, even if I could promise them nothing. Calling them back a year or two later, after my partners and I had raised a fund, and telling them

I wanted to help them create what they'd been dreaming of was a heady feeling. But that was a lifetime ago.

Back then, in Samoset, we rented a house for three hundred dollars a month. We had a secondhand station wagon, a vegetable garden, enough money that Margaret could stay home. Alec used to gallop up the street to meet me as I was walking back from the bus. He'd take my briefcase and carry it with him across the front lawn and around the house, where Michael and Celia would be playing in the tree fort or in the barn, and they'd come rushing over to push through the back door ahead of me, calling out to their mother that I was home. In the summer, we'd eat outside on a picnic table left by the previous tenants. I'd moved the table over toward the edge of the woods, onto a mossy square of concrete, and from there you looked back across the circular dirt drive to our octagonal house, white clapboard with a black roof and brick chimney. Margaret's great-great-grandfather had been a carpenter in the town, and it turned out he was the one who had built the place for a Methodist minister. There had been an enthusiasm for the design among members of the Spiritualist movement. Having no right angles, the octagon was said to leave no corners in which evil spirits might become trapped. In the evening, with the windows illuminated, it resembled a squat lighthouse sending its warning in all directions. When the children were full and drowsy and had ceased their play I'd sometimes pretend with them that the house was haunted and tell them stories about the people who had gathered there a hundred years ago to speak with the dead by candlelight. Michael didn't want to listen, pretending he was too old for ghost stories. Margaret would say, You'll frighten them before bed, but Alec and Celia would squeal to me, No, no, keep going. I told them how the neighbors would come and join hands in the dark listening for the voices of their departed relatives, who would appear in our very living room and speak of the life of the dead. Alec clung to my side, Celia became very fixed and still, peering into the trees behind us, long after Margaret had cleared the table and Michael had gone off to his room, the three of us there together under the full-laden branches of the oak, surrounded by the hum of crickets. I sensed their tremendous need for me in those moments—for my voice to go on, to carry and protect them from everything that encircled us. And I did protect them. I told them they were safe because their mother's ancestor had built our house so that no ghosts would ever stay, that all the frightening things that might ever have happened were long in the past and couldn't possibly reach them now. Then I'd put Alec over my shoulder and take Celia's hand and walk them into the house and up to their beds.

Walking past the cemetery of the Congregational church, I cross the street into the grocery-store parking lot. It's barely half full and baking hot. Through the glass door at the rear of the building, I can see the row of three cash registers. And there's Alec, leaning against the steel rim of one of the narrow black conveyor belts, talking to Doreen, a heavy smoker in her late sixties with a dyed-red bouffant and heavy jowls. Whenever I come into the store she tells me how much everyone loves Alec and she herself is clearly charmed by him, by how polite he is and how well he listens. He has a slightly precious manner for a fourteen-year-old, almost courtly. He asked me last year if he should take metalwork or theater, and I told him he'd meet more interesting people in the theater class. Which may be part of the reason for how he holds himself now, I suppose—the acting he's been doing. But his formality he gets from his idea of me. He's the only one born in America, the only one of the three who was excited when we told them we'd be moving to England.

I've never watched a child of mine strain to be an adult before. Michael and Celia have done it in private, away from my view, though their mother says I'm the one locked away from them, and I suppose I can't deny that. But here is Alec now with his chin ever so slightly raised, nodding with judicial solemnity at whatever Doreen is pattering on about, while one foot taps rapidly on the linoleum floor and he holds his hands down at his waist, picking discreetly at his cuticles, his attention fixed on her. Something she says causes his eyes to widen in surprise, and he shakes his head, feigning indignation. And then his hands are out at his sides, he's leaning forward, gesticulating with great vigor, and Doreen rolls her head back, laughing. Alec smiles, delighted by what he's just said and the response it's getting. The young actor with the audience of one. I find it almost repulsive. The overweeningness of it. Is this what I have bequeathed him? Doreen turns back to her register, and starts passing a woman's groceries down the belt for Alec to bag.

All three of my children have jobs and more or less pay for their own things. Still, I don't know how much of our situation they understand: that there is only debt. Their mother would never tell them, but she yells it at me at night. And though Celia has given up, Alec sometimes knocks on the living room door and pleads with us to stop fighting, and then the liquid in my skull becomes so heavy I can barely keep my eyes open, wanting so much for it all to go away—the tight air, the words contracting like muscle over bone. Alec pushes the woman's grocery cart to her Volvo, but it's only as he's skating it back across the parking lot that he sees me off to the side and comes to a halt.

Business being slow, they don't mind him taking his lunch break early. We walk down toward the town hall. I have no destination in mind and he doesn't ask for one. It's ordinary for us not to talk when we're alone together, which isn't often. He's become prehensile, stretched up on spindly legs. He could probably bathe more than he does. He's in that larval stage, the damp, pained shedding of the child's body. This is what boarding school is for. To store them away during years like this, so they can suffer without the embarrassment of their parents watching. And much good that did you, Margaret would say. He's fiddling with his fat little Swiss Army knife, picking out each blade and tool, folding them back down again, then fanning them out at different angles.

"I'm hungry," he says.

We keep going past the Catholic church and the police station and the semi-detached white town houses set back from the road. There are free tables visible through the window of the diner; at least it will be cool inside. I spent a lot of time here last fall with a legal pad drafting letters to investors for what I thought might become a new investment fund. Tradesmen and retirees are the people who frequent the place. Not the young mothers or men on business meetings. The food's too greasy and the inside not clean enough. The owner, a Latvian fellow who sat with me one afternoon and spoke for two hours about his life in the Soviet navy, waves from the kitchen. The smells from the fryers are unusually heavy. They fill my head and lungs, leaving me slightly nauseous. I notice the dandruff on Alec's shoulders as he hunches over the laminated menu. He is asking me if I heard his question. The waiter is standing by our table. No, I tell him, what's your question?

"Is it okay if I get the chili and a Monte Cristo sandwich?"

Afterwards he will want chocolate cake. In restaurants his mother tries to save small sums of money by ordering the cheapest thing on the menu. Which I've always considered defeatist.

"What are you getting, Dad?"

"Nothing," I say, "I'm fine."

The beast isn't in Alec. I have no way of knowing this for certain. He's too young. Maybe I just don't see it and don't want to. But in his eagerness to please there is such squirming energy and a kind of literalness. He's up on the surface of himself opening outward, even when he's embarrassed, perhaps particularly so then, because he finds embarrassment so painful he'll do anything to get off the spot. He's a bit of an exhibitionist, too. As a toddler he used to walk naked into our bedroom and stand there, biting his lower lip and smiling. There's a photograph of him at my brother-in-law's house at Christmastime when he's four or five standing at the top of the back stairs with his trousers down asking for help in the bathroom. Who the drunk was that took the picture before helping him, I forget. Never such things with Celia, and certainly never with Michael. Being the youngest, that is part of it. He understood the rules from the point of view of someone who got to break them. They were provisional, and with wile, they could be set aside. And then eventually I would have to give him a spanking and he would weep. But his sullenness never lasted. He was too impatient. And still is. Impatient to be older. He eats his sandwich with his mouth open.

"Are we going to go back to Maine ever?" he asks. "Like, this summer?"

"I don't know," I say, and I can tell from the way he stops chewing for an instant and glances at me that he suspects there is something wrong with me again, though what that means to him I have no idea. I am, after all, out of bed and here with him now. And I am all he has ever known. I heard him once through the door of his room boasting to a school friend that his father had his own company and made all the decisions himself and traveled all over the world. My strange American son, who doesn't close his mouth when he eats, but is otherwise so well mannered.

"Celia earns more money than I do," he says. "And she just makes salads at the restaurant. But she gets better tips. So I think maybe I should ask for a raise. I saw the assistant dairy manager's paycheck and he makes eight forty-five an hour, I get six twenty-five, but I still work the dairy case when he's not there. Don't you think I should ask for a raise?"

"You should visit your grandmother in England," I say. "She's mentioned that to you, hasn't she? You coming there to stay with her sometime?"

"There's nothing to do at her house."

One day he'll go. She won't tell him the story of her own father, or the one time I met him—by accident, in a shop in Southampton—because for her it wouldn't be proper to discuss such unfortunate things. Which makes me think that I should tell him.

My mother never mentioned my grandfather because he'd divorced my grandmother, which was unheard-of then, and taken his sons with him. He'd gotten rich several times and always wound up broke, though how I'm not sure. The day I met him would have been sometime in 1946 or '47. My mother and I were in a queue at the bakery, waiting for bread rations. She gripped my arm and I looked up to see her staring in guarded terror at a man with a gray-brown mustache, dressed in an expensively tailored suit and bowler hat, who had stopped beside her.

"Hello, Bridget," he said. "You look well. And who is this?"

For a moment, she said nothing. I thought the man had offended her by being familiar. But then, in an oddly low tone, very unlike her usual voice, she said, "This is John. John, shake your grandfather's hand."

It was the first time she'd seen him in twenty years. He waited with us in the line and then came back to the house for tea. He told us he was living in London, and that he had come down to Southampton for the day on business. I remember how he sat with his legs crossed in the wingback chair by the fireplace, with his gold cuff links and polished brogues, his body very much at ease, as if he'd run into an old friend and was visiting a house he knew well. Each time he took a biscuit from the plate he gave me a little smiling nod. After half an hour of pleasantries and inter-mittent silence he checked his watch and said he had a train to catch. On the doorstep, he kissed my mother on the cheek and tipped his hat to me. "Very glad to meet you, John," he said, and then he was gone.

Given that he was a stranger, his sudden brief appearance didn't much matter to me. But the sight of my mother perched on the edge of the sofa as the two of them spoke—her jaw tightened, her eyes wide and unblinking, her body rigid as a post—quickly and quietly destroyed the illusion of her perpetual sameness, of her having always been my mother and nothing else. She suffered for alien reasons, caught up in times I could never reach. I'd under-stood that people put on various manners: the soldier's perpetual joking; my teachers' punitive zeal; even my father's brusqueness, which suggested everything was an interruption, could seem an act. But my mother had always been actual life, not prejudice or adap-tation. She was the way of knowing anything to begin with. Until that afternoon. Air raids hadn't frightened her. She would shoo my brother and me into the reinforced room, get the little bag of food from the cupboard, and tell us to sit under the dining room ta-ble while she and my father sat in chairs nearby, only occasionally whispering to each other. Her voice didn't change then. It simply became more efficient. But here was an elderly gentleman having tea on a Saturday morning in our sitting room who could make her very speech and body foreign to me.

We didn't talk about his visit once he'd gone. I presume she told my father about it, but not in my presence. It would have happened eventually, the revelation of her partialness, that she might need something, that her need could be a burden, but it came so suddenly and so starkly. I forgave her everything I had ever blamed her for and tried to love her more without saying anything. She lives on her own now in a pleasant market town outside Southampton, in a comfortable little brick-house development that my brother found for her. To the children she is Granny with the good dark chocolates and the strict table manners. She will blame Margaret.

"You didn't say if I should ask for the raise," Alec says.

And in *my* children's eyes, how long have I been partial? How long have I been a burden?

"Why not?" I say, but my words have no life to them, and he knows it.

His cake has arrived and is already gone. He scrapes at the last smudges of icing. "Mom said you were better."

His straight brown hair falls at a slant across his brow. I could reach over the table now and touch the top of his downturned head. The beast is a projector too, every day throwing up before me pictures of what I'm incapable of.

The little agony of stillness is ended by the appearance in the diner of a boy whose name I should know; he's one of Alec's friends—Scott or Greg or Peter. I'm facing the door so I see him first. He waves and comes over to our booth. Like most of Alec's friends, he's dressed in dark, secondhand clothing—a black suit jacket and paisley shirt, both several sizes too large. When they're together they look like a group of young hobos. If it's meant as some kind of class transvestism it doesn't much work; the air of the costume gives it rather the opposite effect, of boy actors affecting a pose. He and Alec greet each other with elaborate

90

nonchalance. Yet I notice Alec is blushing. Something about the moment is making him nervous. He trips over a question about whether Scott or Greg or Peter is getting together later with others, and the boy, who's greeted me with an upward nod of the chin, as if he and I were convicts meeting in the yard, replies to Alec with what I think he means to be a sardonic comment, but which instead comes off as a mixture of daffy and cruel. It's a reference I can't follow, about someone being lame.

He perches on the banquette beside Alec, who looks most uncomfortable now. They're like harlequins, the two of them, young and droopy-faced and strange. As a little boy Alec would wake me from my naps by climbing up on the bed and rocking back and forth until I grabbed him and pulled him down on top of me, and then I'd take a coin and grasp it in my fist and he'd use both hands to try to pry my thumb loose and get at it, and everything between us then seemed as I thought having children would be, and as it had never quite been with Michael. I want to break Alec back down to that, to wipe away all this tentative foolery, just for today. And say what to him? Do what? If I ever had the care of his soul, I don't anymore. I gave it up ten times over by not getting out of bed, by lingering in the basement and letting him find me there, staring at a wall. I may have been all he knew for a time but he's been old enough for a couple of years now to measure me against others. My trousers don't fit me. I have to cinch my belts to the last notch. Soaping myself in the bath, I can feel the softness of my flesh where my muscles once were.

"I'm going record shopping with Brad," Scott or Greg or Peter says; he's ordered a milk shake without asking if we are staying, and sucks on it noisily. Alec's desire to go off with him on his expedition is all the more obvious for how he tries to hide it, saying Michael's probably already got whatever albums they're looking for. But if he didn't have to go back to work shortly, he'd be out

91

the door with him. At their age, I wore a blue uniform and spent my idle time avoiding the cruelty of prefects. Excitement was the purchase of candy at the tuckshop. They have more merchandise in their rooms than we had in our house. Still, I'm glad he knows nothing of that world. I pay at the cash register, wave good-bye to the owner, and eventually Alec and his friend trail after me onto the blazing sidewalk.

My family will never know how they saved me. Margaret, maybe, but not the children. When I turn back Alec is looking almost beseechingly at his friend, who seems oblivious to the attention he's receiving, as he kicks a pebble down the pavement, loping with an ostentatiously casual gait, the cartoon of a rock star, all flounce and droop. I have the passing urge to visit upon him some deprivation to see how his elaborate manner would fare in less bountiful circumstances but more than being angry at this little customer, I realize that what I really want is for Alec to stop paying him such mind. After we've passed the town hall, he finally takes his leave, and Alec walks up beside me again, reluctant and clearly deflated as we climb the hill back to the grocery store.

"Remind me who that was."

"Sam," he says, sounding practically disconsolate now. All this is wrong. Our time can't end like this. "Come on," I say, "let's walk."

"My break's over. They'll get mad at me."

"I'll tell them—I'll explain it." I'm already leading him to the other side of the street, the cars halting to let us cross. The sun burns directly above, the buildings giving no cover. I don't know where we are going. Shards of light from the glass and steel of parked cars burn at my eyes. A little farther on we reach the footpath that shadows the brook—a strip of parkland winding through the town behind backyards and playing fields. I head onto it, making for the shade. I've never adapted to the climate here. Summer is an oppression.

"What are we doing?" Alec says.

He's trailing many steps behind me now. I think that of all of them, he will manage the best. His born selfishness. His impatience. The way we spoiled him. I stop and wait for him to catch up.

"My break's over," he says again, pausing a couple of yards away, kicking lightly at the grass. "I have to go. What are we doing here, anyway? Why'd you come to the store?"

"I wanted to see you."

"Why are you acting so weird?" he says. "Can't you just stop?"

There is nothing I can say to him now that isn't murder. But I have to try. "Sam—he seems like a nice fellow," I say, though I don't believe it. It's just that Alec will have friends, and I want him to know that. People he can rely on. People to spend time with.

"What are you talking about? You don't even know who he is. Just stop, *please*, will you?" He looks as mortified as if the two of us were onstage together naked.

I can see in his eyes how hard he's trying not to pity me. This is what I do to them. Over and over. And then, like Alec's face now, their faces become the mask of the beast, used by it to torment me. My voice used to protect Alec, the way I invented stories for him. Protecting him from the ghosts. Now I'm the spirit trapped in his house.

He's turning to go, upset and fed up. I walk over to him, to put a hand on his shoulder, but he ducks out from under my touch and hurries back up to the street.

The deepest shade is beneath a maple further along the path. I lean up against it, sitting on the grass. The water of the brook is clear to the sandy bed. *These beauteous forms / Through a long absence, have not been to me / As is a landscape to a blind man's eye / But oft, in lonely rooms, and 'mid the din / Of towns and cities, I have owed to them / In hours of weariness, sensations sweet...* That first time I went into hospital, during university, I remember being glad Mr. Gillies had made us memorize poems at school *... that blessed mood / In which the burthen of the mystery / In which the heavy and the weary weight / Of all this unintelligible world / Is lighten'd:—that serene and blessed mood / In which the affections gently lead us on,— / Until the breath of this corporeal frame / And even the motion of our human blood / Almost suspended, we are laid asleep / In body, and become a living soul.* The words meant nothing to me as a boy. They were just a rhythm. Jumbled up with Gilbert and Sullivan and "Onward Christian Soldiers." But after the treatments, I would come back to my room bruised across the chest from my convulsions against the restraints, and for several days I wouldn't be able to recall much of anything except passages of music and those stanzas. They became the way I measured time. By bringing back that earlier world, assuring me it had existed, and thus that when more time passed things might be different still. And so I began to piece together the meaning of the phrases. That the motion of our blood could almost stop, our bodies be laid to sleep, but somehow the soul be kept alive. Simply by the things we saw and heard, in any given moment. It was a report from the inside of another person's head, someone who'd been in lonely rooms, who'd lived through hours of weariness but knew a path back to life. Which is what I found then. Returning to my college, being with friends, having happiness. I'd seen the monster, but I didn't recognize it because I was young and had never encountered it before. Why should I think I ever would again?

In the Royal Signal Corps, I met Peter Lorian, and when our

compulsory service was done we got an apartment in Chelsea together with two other friends and started having our parties. Where a few years later Margaret appeared. In her green satin dress and long dark hair, tall and slender. No woman had ever looked at me as directly as she did. I couldn't stop trying to charm her because I wanted her to keep looking. And she kept blushing at my attempts, but laughing too, which made the difference, because then I could keep going, and we could acknowledge the game for what it was, and forgive each other for playing. It's what let us fall in love. That we could laugh together.

These bits of poetry float back to me again now, and they still measure time, but cruelly.

It's no use resisting this heat. My shirt is soaked, the sweat has seeped into my shoes. But I mind it less. There's nothing of my person to protect anymore. The simplicity of this is a great relief. An empty stomach and throbbing temples are no more personal than a bank of thriving weeds, or the mirage of asphalt melting in the distance along the bridge. Such distinctions are made of tension, and the tension is melting. Why fight? The inanimate world has such unimpeachable wisdom: no thought.

"Where in Christ were you? It's three o'clock." Margaret's stricken voice comes at me across the front lawn before I even reach the walk. "I just drove all the way out to the restaurant to pick up Celia and the manager tells me she didn't show up today. No sign of her. None. Are you listening? I've had it. You understand? You need to get in the car and go over there to the Schefers'. That's where she'll be, with that Jason."

I suggest maybe she's at the track. Margaret explodes, shouting that school has been out three weeks! There is no practice! Arguing is pointless. Her anger spreads in too many directions, and I am the root of it. She has lost me already. But she refuses to know this, and the refusal drives her mad. It galls her that I gave us so many years and so much life together unmenaced, and then simply no longer could. Before, she had a choice. To break it off or go forward. Now she has none, any more than the children do. I don't even provide money enough for food and clothing. They're put on credit cards.

"I'll go," I say. "Give me the keys, and I'll go."

Mrs. Schefer lives on Raymond Street, up behind the post office. Her house is one of those split-level Colonials with brown siding and a garage cut into the hillside. A circle of large white pines blocks out most of the sunlight. A girl of ten or eleven answers the door and says that her mother is not there. I tell her I'm looking for Celia and she says she hasn't seen her, and that her brother is out as well. There is a television on in the background. The girl has peanut butter smudged at the corners of her lips. "Celia's pretty," she says. "Are you her dad?" I am, I tell her, and ask if she knows where her brother might be. She has no idea but says he sometimes stays with their father on the other side of town. It strikes me as negligent to leave a child this age on her own, but who am I to judge?

It's not because Celia missed or skipped work that Margaret wants me to find her. It's because of Chris Weller. A few months ago, when I was deep in the fog, we were woken one night well after midnight by shouting in the front yard. A boy, clearly drunk, was yelling up at Celia's window, "Give me back the fucking ring, give me back the fucking necklace." Then he started knocking loudly on the front door. He was waking the whole neighborhood. Margaret shot out of bed and went to the window. Celia came running into our room. "Get up!" Margaret yelled at me. "For God's sake, get up!" I swung my stone legs to the floor and pushed with my arms to bring myself to my feet. "What the hell is going on?" Margaret demanded of Celia. "I don't know, I don't know," she said, failing to hold back tears. I'd never seen her so terror-stricken. "You need to go down there," Margaret said to me. "Go out there and tell that idiot he needs to be quiet and he needs to leave."

I stood there mute in front of the two of them as they waited for my response. The boy kept hammering at the door. I couldn't do it. I couldn't go down those stairs and cope with it. It was as if the boy's fist were hitting my chest and it was all I could do to stay upright. My wife and daughter gaped at me, appalled. "The police," Celia said desperately, "we can call the police." Margaret told her not to be ridiculous, that it would cause a scene; we weren't going to have flashing police lights in front of our house in the middle of the night. "Where's the jewelry?" she said. "Do you have it?"

Celia stopped crying then and went stony-faced. I saw the change happen. It took only an instant. She turned from us and left the room. Margaret and I followed, standing on the upstairs landing as she went into her bedroom and put on a pair of trousers, and then walked down the stairs on her own, to open the front door and confront that raging boy. As if we weren't even home.

That was the last of Chris Weller. But not of Celia's dating. Now there is Jason, with whom Margaret thinks she's using drugs of some sort. Apparently when she comes home late her eyes are bloodshot and she doesn't want to speak with her mother.

The little girl told me the name of the street her father lived on, where Jason might be, and she said the house was white, but that doesn't narrow it down. There are no people out in their yards to ask. Stopped at an intersection, I see someone who I think might be Jason glide past in an old gray Audi, and follow him around the corner to another split-level Colonial with an unused flagpole mounted over the front door. He notices me pulling up behind him. I was expecting a lout like Weller, one of those oversize American high schoolers. But this boy's face is more blurry than aggressive, his cheeks covered in an adolescent attempt at a beard and his brown curls flopping over his forehead. "Oh, hi," he says, to my surprise, for I have no recollection of ever having met him. When I tell him I'm looking for Celia, he says he dropped her at the track, and from his hapless eyes I can tell that he is adrift, afraid he's been caught at something but unable to focus sufficiently to defend himself. He isn't Celia's equal. He doesn't have her will. Whatever she's doing, it isn't at his bidding. He asks if something is the matter, if there is some kind of emergency, and I want to say, What business would it be of yours? But I can hear the concern in his voice, and I realize he spends more time with my daughter than I do. Margaret wants me to interrogate him, to find out what they get up to. But it's too late for that. All of that is far away. It's Celia I need to see.

I find her at the track, running sprints along the straightaways in front of the empty bleachers. It's even hotter now than at midday, the afternoon haze pressing against the field. I open the gate and step onto the oval. She's wearing shorts, a sleeveless shirt, and a bandanna round her forehead. She's running away from me, and so doesn't see me at first. When she comes to the end of her sprint, she pulls up and rests her hands high on her waist, leaning her head back and heaving for breath. I'm past the goalpost and well onto the field by the time she notices me at a distance of fifty yards or so. She bends forward, palms to her knees, still huffing.

Neither of her brothers is the least athletic, but Celia's played on teams since grade school: softball, field hockey in Britain, volleyball, track. She's kept it up through both our moves. For years, there has always been a practice to drop her at or pick her up from.

She jogs back down to the starting line as I approach, staying focused. I watch as she crouches into position, raises her knee, and then leaps into the lane again, arms swinging, chest forward and head back, shooting past me and over the finish line, jogging from there around the bend before turning once more to walk back to the start. Her breath's still rapid when she reaches the steps of the bleachers where I'm standing. Every inch of her skin runs with sweat and her face pulses red.

"I told Mom I didn't need to be picked up from work. She's checking on me."

She takes a towel from her knapsack and wipes her forehead. It's no surprise that boys are attracted to her. There's a precision to her good looks, a fierceness even. That, and the way she carries herself, with a confidence bordering on aloofness. Which I suppose she got from me. An earlier me. And what do I do now? I steal her confidence back, day by day, cheating her of steadiness and care. Of the three of them, she sees me most clearly, which makes it harder for her because she isn't protected by distraction. Michael has never been able to bear the tension, so he disappears into other worlds. And Alec is too young to conceive of the situation independent of himself. But Celia's ways of coping are already the adult ones: discipline, drinking, the search for someone else to love her.

She's explaining why she didn't go to work, and how irritating it is that her mother is monitoring her, but none of it matters and I don't really listen. Which of course she notices, getting more irritated still. Once she's gathered up her things, we walk together across the field.

Being beside her, close enough to sense the heat flowing from her body, I'm momentarily astonished at her existence—this child of mine. How narrowly we all avoid having never been. Yet even if the knife of chance did happen to cut her into being, I have the passing terror that it isn't so simple, that in these ultimate matters time is collapsed into a single moment in which you are forever in danger of having the knife tilt the other way, as though, if I am not careful between here and the parking lot, I might go astray and she will be canceled, stolen back by not-being, like a thief grabbing her through an open window. But we make it to the car, and she tosses her bag over her shoulder into the backseat and puts her feet up on the dashboard.

I take us along Green Street past the dense thicket of the nature preserve. When I miss the turn toward the house, she asks where we are going, and I mumble something about the other route, carrying on under the rusting railroad bridge. We drive on in silence for a while, the motion of the air through the open windows offering some relief from the heat.

"How come you don't have to be anywhere?" Celia asks. "Do you still work for that company?"

There are only woods now on either side of us. The evergreens are thick and the shade between them dark. It is a long, straight stretch and there is something mesmerizing about the lines of the trees reaching out toward each other in the middle distance. She is thinking of Roger Taylor's firm. He is the one I had to ask for a job when we moved back. I had helped him start his consulting company a decade earlier. He gave me an office and a salary. And it lasted those eighteen months before he politely suggested it might make more sense for me to go part-time, which turned out to mean occasional projects, and eventually none. Margaret says he is ungrateful. The ending of it is so small to me, next to the defeat of leaving Britain in the way I did, that I have trouble thinking about it much.

"Did you hear what I asked?"

"I don't work there anymore. The fact is, I've let you down. All of you."

"You just missed the other turn," she says.

I say I'll go back, but she says it's okay, she doesn't mind. I suppose she's in no hurry to get home. The road winds toward the less inhabited side of the lake. We pass the entrances to two or three mansions, the only houses out here, hidden away up the hillside. I sometimes get this far on my longer walks with Kelsey. It's the first really quiet place I discovered when we moved here, a beech forest mostly. I pull into a turnout, where the road comes close to the water, and I switch off the engine. A gap in the stone wall leads onto the path around the lake. From here you can see across to the wooded shoreline of the college campus, and the two brick towers stretching above the trees, thunderheads gathering behind them.

"You haven't let us down," she says flatly, looking away into the woods. She is being kind. As she was raised to be. To strangers and relatives and those to whom it is good to show care. That is what it has come to. She doesn't believe anymore that I'm strong enough to bear her complaint or frustration. And I can't blame her. If she let herself love me, she'd be furious. So she shows me kindness instead. "Did you want to take a walk?" she asks. "Is that why you parked?"

It's impossible, what I'm trying to do. To say good-bye without telling them I'm leaving.

I follow her across the edge of a meadow, through a patch of swampy ground, and then back under the cover of the trees, as we reach the first point along the shore. Her form is marvelous, the supple muscles of her legs, the gentle curve of her spine, her strong shoulders rolling back, her head balanced. I held her hundreds of times as a girl, tossed her shrieking above her bed, caught her in my arms. I've felt the weight of her head on my chest and the warmth of her body under the shelter of my arm. But her body has never struck me as quite the miracle it does now. It seems almost enough to live for, that she came from me and is part of me, and yet as soon as I think this I know again how selfish that is, and disordered, for a parent to need so hopelessly a child still so young.

"I broke up with Jason," she says over her shoulder, turning only far enough for me to hear her. "If that's who you and Mom are worried about. That's why I wasn't at work. I had to talk to him." This business of teenagers having personal lives—it's alien to me. I've never known what to say. "You don't have to worry about me, though," she says. "They're not going to fire me. I still have a job." Taking an offshoot of the path, she leads us to a log bench facing the water and perches at the far end of it, leaning her forearms down on her knees. The air has gone still between the peak of the heat and the break of the rain to come.

"I'm sorry you have to work," I say, "that there isn't more money. I know your mother and I don't talk to you much about my difficulties. It's a kind of sickness. When that other fellow came to the house this spring, when he was shouting at you, I wanted to help. But I couldn't. And that isn't fair to you."

It's not until she sits up and wipes her eyes that I realize she's crying. My words are like knives; they cut into the people I love. It will be worse if you touch her, I think, a worse lie. But I ignore this thought, shifting down the bench to put my arm around her—my daughter—and as I do, she weeps openly, pressing her face against my damp shirt.

I am a murderer. That's what I am. I am a stealer of life.

A patch of water on the far side of the lake wrinkles under a new breeze, ruffling the black mirror to a scaly gray that shimmers dully under the gray sky. Peter Lorian has a house in the

Highlands of Argyll, and standing at his front windows you can see the weather traveling over the hills from the Irish Sea, the bands of rain filling the valley and then the loch and then the fields in front of the house, all before the first drops arrive. You don't get such views without elevation but here on the water's edge, the sky and the expanse before us are big enough to see clearly the first motions of the storm: the branches of the trees on the far shore swaying like congregants to a hymn, the gray scales flashing now over the lake. The wind reaches us, cooling the slick of moisture on my face and neck. Celia sits up and wipes her nose. The dropping air pressure seems to slacken the pressure in my head. The whole static atmosphere is coming to life. A roll of thunder echoes in the distance. If it passes off to the south, this may be all we get, a stirring of the elements. We sit for a few minutes in the churn, looking onto the water. The clouds darken and take on a bluish tinge. And now the real wind arrives, carrying leaves and pine needles into the air, making a racket in the trees. We walk back along the path, me in front this time. As we cross the meadow, it flashes before us in the glow of lightning, thunder cracking the air. Loud, heavy drops are slapping our shoulders as we reach the car. We roll up the windows, which steam over almost at once. It sounds as if the roof is being pelted with stones. Sheets of water stream down the fogged windshield. The worst storm I was ever in happened aboard a sailboat in the middle of the English Channel, caught in a squall that nearly capsized the boat, and though Celia and I are perfectly safe here and mostly dry, the force of the rain releases some tiny fraction of that adrenaline that comes with fear of death, and I manage a sigh, so gladdening is the momentary sense of balance between me and the world, the violence everywhere now, unleashed. Celia asks what's the matter. I tell her it's nothing.

When the rain lets up to a shower, I turn on the engine and back the car onto the road. By the time we get home, the sky is nearly clear. The early-evening sun is bathing the side of the house, where the storm has soaked the shingles.

Margaret has made the four of us a cold supper. We sit at the dining room table with all the downstairs windows open. There's a reason I try to be away from here as often as I can. The worst of the fog may have lifted, letting me see again, but it's in the most familiar objects that the beast still nestles, exuding itself from the caned rocking chair in the corner, the one that Margaret and I bought together in Southampton, and from the fluted-glass lamps on the sideboard that her parents gave us as a wedding gift. It pulses in the watercolor of the old octagonal house that hangs above the sideboard, over Margaret's shoulder, as she passes Celia the bulgur salad and Alec the plate of bread, and it slinks onto the table between us, its head invisible as always but its body breathing, everyone straining to behave as if there were only four us here, eating supper together on a summer evening.

"Aren't you going to take some food?" Margaret asks, unable to hide her impatience, holding her knife and fork rigidly against the table, waiting to start, which is when I notice that all the dishes are at my end and my plate is empty. A few months ago, I overheard her describing to a friend on the phone the exhaustion of trying to get me out of bed in the morning, how her energy for the day was spent before breakfast.

"I asked for the raise," Alec says, interjecting himself to protect me from his mother's ire. "The manager said she'd think about it."

I take some salad and bread so they can begin their meal. A moment later, the phone rings. Celia starts up from the table before the first bell has ended and strides into the hall to answer it.

104

"It's Michael," she calls out. "He wants you to call him back on their number."

"It's quite late for him," Margaret says, standing up from the table. She carries the phone into the living room and closes the door behind her as Celia takes her seat again. The two of them miss their older brother—they laugh less without him—but they would never say it because they know he wasn't happy here, and that he wanted so badly to go back.

They eat quickly and then excuse themselves, bringing their plates into the kitchen. Margaret is still on the phone. I stay at the table for a while, feeling the cooler air drifting in through the screens. Above the hydrant at the foot of the drive, the street lamp flickers on, casting a pale oval of light onto the pavement. Crickets sing in the bushes. Through the wall behind me, I hear Alec leaping up the stairs, then Celia following more slowly, muttering something about him staying out of her room. These sounds don't grate anymore. They flow back into me now, ordinary once again.

There's a click of the latch to the living room door, and Margaret calls out my name. "Here," she says, handing me the phone. "He's got his literature A level tomorrow, and he can't sleep. God knows what this call is costing." She walks away, back to her meal, and I close the door between us.

"Dad?" he says, and I know from the strain in his voice that the words have already been streaming out of him to his mother. It's been a relief having him gone. Margaret never let up about what I wasn't doing, how I didn't make time for him, or speak to him like I should to an eldest son. But it was never what she thought—some hesitancy or lack of nerve on my part about his reaching puberty and adolescence. I wouldn't have talked to him about that in any case because he wouldn't have wanted it any more than I did from my father. Our silence wasn't about that.

"Yes?" I say.

"I can hang up now, if that's better, I know it's expensive."

"You spoke to your mother about your exam."

"Yeah."

"No use fretting about it." I want to say more, to say, You'll be fine, in the long run, you'll be fine, but I don't believe it, not as I do about the other two.

"I know, I know, you're right, it's just that I couldn't read everything in time, not closely enough."

This is the thing: He isn't calling about his exam. I don't want to know this, but I do. He's calling to be reassured about something he can't put into words yet. I glimpsed it in him when he was young, but told myself, No, don't imagine that. Children have stages; he'll change. Then the words started running out of him in a torrent, and I knew they were being chased out by a force he couldn't see. What was I supposed to say to Margaret? That I see it in him?

"I'm sure you've studied more than I did," I tell him. It is dark outside now. The light from the kitchen lies square on the unmown grass.

I will leave him more alone than anyone.

"If we don't get into a university," he's saying, hurrying to fill the silence and prolong the conversation, "Simon and I decided we're going to move to London together. He's got friends who already have a flat, and he thinks it would be easy for us to get jobs."

My son in London as a young man. It's hard for me to picture.

"You should talk to your mother about that."

"You wouldn't mind—if I didn't get in anywhere?"

I tell him that he will. "It's late," I say. "You should get some rest." He agrees, reluctantly, wanting to stay on the phone. "How are Celia and Alec?" he asks. "Are they okay?"

I'm reminded I haven't answered only when he says, "Dad? Are you there?"

"Yes, I'm here."

He senses the trouble. He knows it is there. If I could only take that part of him with me, to spare him. But I can't. And so, unlike the others, it's as if he is following me, and won't let me go.

"It really is late with you," I say. "You'll be fine—with the exam. You're a good writer."

"You think so?"

"Yes."

"Okay, then," he says. "I guess I'll go."

"Good-bye, Michael. Good luck."

"Okay, Dad," he says. "Bye."

Later, lying next to Margaret as she sleeps, I sense a tingling in my feet and ankles and up into my calves. It is the opposite of numbness. My muscles are awake, my blood moves freely. This halo of warmth creeps over my knees, easing space into the joints, letting the bones of my thighs settle into the mattress. It lingers over my belly, and my gut goes slack, unclenching the muscles at the base of my spine. My lower ribs rise with my breath up off my stomach, stretching the skin from navel to sternum, arching my back. It feels as if my lungs have doubled in size, allowing me to swallow air in great gulp-fulls. My shoulders fall back, my throat opens, the tingling warms my jaw and scalp and then moves through into the folds of my brain, releasing it away from my forehead, letting it rest against the back of my skull. Thus it is that the beast passes out of me, to hover in the darkness above, faceless still, but quarry now, its hours numbered.

I get up before dawn, rousing no one but Kelsey, who lifts her head from her blanket in anticipation of her walk, and then scampers toward where the leash hangs by the back door. I pat her on the head, and leave her there, getting what I need from the tool drawer, and going out the other way, through the front door, closing it quietly behind me. Outside, in the charcoal light, it is blessedly cool, as if the fever of summer has broken. It's still too dark to make out the far side of the sloping meadow at the end of the street. The dew-covered grass blends into the trees silhouetted against the barely brightening sky.

It is the fallow field next to my parents' cottage, where I played in the tall grass; and the field behind the octagonal house, where I cut paths for the children to ride on; and the hillside in Scotland where I walked with Margaret; and the woodland meadow on the island in Maine. All of these are given back to me now, the landscapes of my happiness, returning in this damp calm, limpid and flooded with life.

I cross the street and walk into those fields. There is just a tinge of blue emerging between the branches. The shadows at the edge of the woods are retreating. At last, I have the beast out in front of me, out in the open. I sense it trying to run, to flee ahead of me into the woods. But the long night is ending, and there is nowhere left for it to hide. Not in my children's faces. Not in Margaret's stubborn love. Not in all my failures. There is no cover left for it on this terrain. I know its paths too well. Through the tall pines and down along the riverbank. Across the footbridge, and up through the spruce trees to where the ground levels out. I've come here so often trying to escape this monster. But now it is the one sapped, and limping. And I am the hunter. In the clearing overlooking the bend in the river, we come to a halt. The first rays of dawn pierce the gray light of the forest. I sit on the pine needles, up against a fallen trunk.

Invisibility. That is its last defense. That I won't have the courage to look it in the eye. *You wretch!* it cries, desperate for its life. *You selfish wretch! Leaving them with nothing!* But it is no good. It is my prey now.

The razor opens the skin of my wrist almost painlessly. Blood runs down my palm, and along the length of my fingers. My head rolls back, and I gaze upward.

And there it is: the face of the beast—my face—human after all.

II

Michael

HAROLD J. BUTTERWORTHY, MD (psychiatry)
PhD (neuroscience), MPhil (geology)
MFA (metallurgy), BFA (dance)
BA (algebra)*

Patient Intake

Name: Michael
Date of Birth: January
Primary Care Physician: Mass General
Current Therapist: Walter Benjamin
Therapist's Phone: No longer in service

What are the problem(s) you are seeking help for?
1. Fear
2. Trembling
3. Individualism
4. White supremacy

---

* board certified

What are your treatment goals?
1. Ordinary unhappiness
2. Racial justice

Current Symptoms:
Yes

Personal Medical History:
Yes

Family Medical History:
Let's not pretend either of us has time for a complete answer here. In brief, Dad didn't make it; Mom's never taken a pill in her life; Alec had an ulcer early on, when they were still fashionable, but has since transitioned into the back-pain industry; and I'd guestimate Celia's chronic fatigue peaked out around '94 somewhere in the Bay Area, though she still has Persistent Annual Lupus Scare Syndrome (PALSS) and Cryptogenic Abdominal Rash Syndrome (CARS). As for my grandparents, all four suffered from Eventual Death Syndrome (EDS).

Have you ever been hospitalized for nonpsychiatric care or surgery?
On Christmas Eve 1992, I came down with a self-diagnosis of esophageal cancer requiring what amounted to an overnight stay in the decongestant aisle of a twenty-four-hour CVS in Medford.

Please briefly describe your educational background:
The usual grade-school misery. Though a boy named Ralph eventually befriended me over *Star Trek* and the music I played him. Funkadelic's "America Eats Its Young," for instance. When I heard George Clinton ask, *Who would sacrifice the great grandsons and daughters of her jealous mother by sucking their brain until their*

ability to think was amputated by pimping their instincts until they were fat, horny, and strung-out in her neurotic attempt to be queen of the universe? Who is this bitch? (read: America), it struck me that our fifth-grade curriculum was somehow incomplete. I thereafter spent every nickel of my allowance on funk. This being 1978, there was a lot to catch up on: Curtis Mayfield, Gil Scott-Heron, everything by James Brown. I listened to records in every spare hour, including while I did my homework, and on my headset after I'd "gone to bed." I couldn't be certain what it meant to "Give Up the Funk" or "Tear the Roof Off the Sucker" or why Parliament would title an album *Mothership Connection*. But I had my first secret joy at knowing that beyond the veil of the apparent, meaning ached in the grain of music. A joy accompanied by my first intuition that black people might know a thing or two about the need for that meaning—history being the culprit. The only affective correlative of such history I had thus far experienced being the queasy feeling I'd get in my stomach watching my grandmother show extra politeness to black people on the rare occasions she encountered them, in order to make very clear that she was not affiliated with those terrible, other white people who hated and mistreated them, success being when a black person smiled back at her, acknowledging her politeness and her goodness, thus completing the blameless circle of liberalism.

As for high school, moving overseas and returning less than three years later didn't much help. Nor the premonition I had that second autumn we were back in Massachusetts, in the woods where my father later disposed of himself. My family has an unfortunate habit of taking walks: my father by upbringing, my mother by faith in the medicinal quality of fresh air, Celia because of an idiopathic athletic streak, and Alec, as ever, in affectation, dolled up like some child earl, all tweed and Wellingtons. My mother was the one who nettled me into compliance, nagging me to abandon my station at the turntable and accompany, on that particular day, Celia and my father on a walk with the deracinator, who scurried off her leash like a giant swamp rat in heat. It was a Sunday afternoon in November (don't ask me for a nature description; there were trees, a path, etc.). We got to some kind of clearing. I was bored and hoped we would turn around soon. The fornicator had vanished down a landscape feature. Celia had gone after her. My father sat on a fallen tree. A general pause set in.

The horror was brief, a few seconds. Flayed bodies swarmed in front of me in a bloody, contorted mass. I looked up and away trying to evade the menace, but it was pressing down from above, filling the circle, thriving on its own gore. Years later, when I came across the paintings of Francis Bacon, and saw those innards turned outward but still alive, it struck me that the man understood. As in his *Three Studies for Figures at the Base of a Crucifixion*, with those mouths agape at the end of nearly human limbs, testifying not to physical suffering but the bleeding of the mind. At the time, however, I just went cold, my mouth dry as chalk. And I knew evil was seeded in that place, waiting to bloom.

I don't particularly believe in a spiritual world, other than music. I'm a materialist to the bone. But I had the overwhelming sense of needing to escape whatever it was that dwelt there. I hoofed it home like a ghost from its enchanter fleeing. I couldn't sleep that night or the next. I watched my father and Celia for signs that they had sensed it too, but they behaved as if nothing had happened.

For months, I'd been pleading to be allowed to go back to England to finish my schooling with my friends. Now I had no choice. I had to get away. I stopped asking about it and just called my friend Simon, who said I could live at his house, and then I told my mother and father I would be leaving after Christmas. To my surprise, they no longer protested. In fact, they seemed relieved. I realized their previous resistance had had nothing to do with me. They just didn't have the organizational wherewithal to cope with my demand. As soon as I lifted that burden from them, they folded like a cheap umbrella. And so I left them there, my family, without ever warning them, without ever telling them what I'd seen. Left them to face it on their own. An act for which I've never been able to forgive myself.

To go and live with Simon and his family in a damp stone house back in Oxfordshire, just up the road from Fairford Air Base. I was given a spare bedroom overlooking a paved courtyard. The return to the States had put me behind on my A levels. On Saturdays, Simon and I went record shopping in Oxford, but otherwise we mostly slept, went to class, and studied. I found no pleasure in speed-reading Thackeray, but there you have it. I had to fly through those ballroom scenes on jet skis.

It wasn't until spring that I went to get my hair cut in the village and met Angie. She worked in a little salon next to the greengrocer, just two chairs, a wall of mirrors, and a waiting bench, with a sink at the back and photos of soft-punk hair models in the window, like head shots for the Human League. The day I went she was the only stylist there. We had the place to ourselves. As soon as she put on Gloria Gaynor's "I Will Survive" and began singing along with it, I knew we had things to discuss. That track may have started as a monster gay-club hit, but Angie sang it as though it were a personal anthem, nothing camp about it. She was beautiful. Right away. A slight, African-American woman between the hopelessly sophisticated ages of twenty-five and I don't know what, with freckles under her eyes and across the bridge of her nose. She had three earrings in each lobe and a metallic blue bandanna wrapped around a cascade of Jheri curls. I asked question after question, and she answered them freely, her hands cupping my head, tilting it this way and that as she clipped. She'd grown up and gone to school in Cleveland. That's where she'd met her husband, who was a jet mechanic at the air base. They'd been stationed in Turkey, then Germany, and now Fairford. This was the first place she'd been able to get a job of her own, which was a good thing too, she said, because her husband was in the habit of cheating on her with what she called "native women," and she'd asked him for a divorce.

Was it the Sister Sledge / New Order mix tape that I brought her on my second visit that transformed me in her eyes from a client into a living subjectivity? Maybe. All I know is she didn't complain about my returning every three or four days to get my bangs trimmed, with ever deeper and more challenging compilations in hand. She didn't know Kraftwerk, or for that matter any German industrial music. It was when I suggested she give Einstürzende Neubauten a whirl that she said, "You're cute." That evening, Simon insisted she must have meant it in the diminutive sense, as you would speak to a child, not a prospective lover. But he hadn't been there. He hadn't seen her smile.

When I dropped another cassette off the next day, I enclosed a note asking if she would go on a date with me. I suggested we go to Oxford, imagining she might feel awkward being seen with me by the locals. I envisioned us holding hands on the night bus back to Carterton, perhaps with her head resting on my shoulder. I would absorb all her suffering, leaving her weightless, and free to love me. We had never touched, and yet she had already voided all of my worries but one: when I would see her next.

After forty-eight hours, she still hadn't called. Desperate, I tried to make another appointment, but her colleague said she was booked up and couldn't see me. That night, after the salon closed, I slipped another tape through the mail slot, this one starting with Joy Division's "Love Will Tear Us Apart," along with a note apologizing for being too forward, saying I understood she might need time, given that her divorce wasn't final. It was three days later, on a Saturday evening, that Simon and I saw her at the pub. She was with one of the other girls from the salon. I could tell she was trying to ignore me. But after she'd had a few drinks she relented, nodding hello from their table in the corner. Simon told me that I was crazy, that she was an older woman, and still married. Simon had a girlfriend, and they seemed to like each other, but I could tell from hanging out with them that he didn't feel for her what I felt for Angie. They enjoyed each other, but they were still individuals. Their love hadn't obliterated the quotidian; it hadn't rid them of their workaday selves. That's what Angie and I were capable of. She and her friend didn't protest when I dragged Simon over to sit with them. They made us buy them drinks. Angie was tipsy but not drunk, and she didn't move her leg aside when I touched it lightly with mine (of such miracles, strung endlessly together, true happiness is made). We talked about the deathly boredom of the Cotswolds and how Simon and I were going to move to London. When the publican barked last call, her friend said she hadn't realized how late it was, and had to dash. Simon wisely did the same. Which left the two of us. She was taking the bus back to the base, she said. I asked if she would let me walk her to her stop. The thin fluorescent light that filtered through the scratched plastic siding of the bus shelter wasn't strong enough to reveal her expression as we stood there watching the drizzle wet the pavement. And so it was with extreme trepidation, braced for rebuff, that I put a hand on her shoulder and leaned down to kiss her gently on the lips. But she closed her eyes and let it happen. After a moment she even put her hand to my arm, giving me the passing sense that I had a physical body.

Whatever psychic bandwidth I had for A levels vanished. I could think only of our future. I had curated my mix tapes for her with great care, but now they took whole afternoons. I needed to keep impressing her with my taste but demonstrate at the same time how much emotional experience we already shared. Those tapes were the line of flight out of the trap of language. Through the incision of music we could know and love each other much, much faster.

Each time I went by the salon to give her my latest cassette, she would thank me, take it quickly, and tell me she had a customer and couldn't chat. I'd go every evening to the pub, risking the ire of Simon's parents, and stay until closing, power-reading *The Mill on the Floss* by fake candlelight, waiting for her to appear. And on the nights that she did, she and her friend would sit with me again, kidding me about my exams, drinking more than I ever could, and Angie would let me walk her to the bus stop, and if no one was around, I got to kiss her, and sometimes hug her, too.

And yet to my consternation, she refused to let me take her on a full-on date. She kept using her husband as an excuse. But contained in each refusal, by the implication of her tone, was the one acknowledgment that counted: sooner or later we would see each other again.

I don't know what most people mean when they use the word *love*. If they haven't contorted their lives around a hope sharp enough to bleed them empty, then I think they're just kidding. A hope that undoes what tiny pride you have, and makes you thankful for the undoing, so long as it promises another hour with the person who is now the world. Maybe people mean attractiveness, or affection, or pleasantness, or security. Like the nonbelievers in church who enjoy the hymns or go for the sense of community, but avert their eyes from the cross. I feel sorry for them. They are dead before their time.

As it happened, I didn't do so well on my exams. Angie's husband attempted to reconcile with her the week they started. I pleaded with her to go with me on the bus to Oxford, just for a single afternoon, and finally she relented. The day before my Modern History A level, I took her to the Debenhams on Magdalen Street. I had seen a fitted silk shirt in a catalog that Simon's sister got in the mail, and I wanted to buy it for her, but she was crying intermittently and didn't want any gifts. If you go back to your husband, nothing will change, I told her. He'll keep you close for a while, and then cheat again. He wants to retain you for your physical beauty, but anyone can appreciate that. We're on the threshold of something much greater. I may have confused her when I said our worlds could end as soon as we joined, but I meant only our life-worlds as separate subjectivities, not a material end. She told me I read too many novels, and led us out of Women's Tops back onto the sidewalk.

Though it was expensive, I had made a reservation for tea at Browns. But I could see now that this was completely wrong and stuffy, and that what we needed was alcohol. The pub we ended up in turned out to be full of university students, shouting at each other over the blare of Depeche Mode's "Shake the Disease." I got us drinks. After half a pint she seemed calmer. Which is when she said it was time she cleared something up. She thanked me for being kind to her over the last few weeks, but said that I had gotten the wrong idea. She shouldn't have kissed me, she said. It had been a mistake. It wasn't my fault, she added, she had let it happen. At which point, she reached into her bag and handed me back all my cassettes.

In retrospect, I suppose the cruelty of the gesture may have been her attempt to cauterize the wound as she inflicted it. I only knew that she was delivering me into purgatory, between the irrevocable hope of being with her and the death of life without her.

It was the next morning that Simon's mother woke me early to say I had a phone call. I went down to the kitchen in my pajamas and stretched the phone cord over to the Aga to warm myself. It was Peter Lorian, my father's oldest friend, calling to say my father was dead. I asked where they had found him. He said in the woods. I was to meet him at Heathrow the next morning. He'd made reservations for the two of us to fly to Boston. He said he was terribly sorry, and that I would need to take care of my mother now. We hung up, and I went back upstairs to sleep another forty-five minutes before it was time to come down for breakfast. When I told Simon and his family the news, they looked appalled.

I was at the doorstep of the salon no later than nine thirty. It was an hour before one of Angie's colleagues eventually appeared to open the shop and told me I had better buzz off.

Have you ever had an EKG?
Alas, no.

How many caffeinated beverages do you drink a day?
What I have always found most comforting about these forms is
the trace of hope I get as I'm filling them out. How they break
your life down into such tidy realms, making each seem tractable,
because discrete, in a way they never are beyond the white noise
of the waiting room. You get that fleeting sense that you're on the
verge of being understood, truly and fully, and for the first time,
if you could just get it all down in black and white before the re-
ceptionist calls your name.

Please briefly describe your work history:
My first legit employment began in the fall of 1985, after Dad,
when I moved to London with Simon, as we'd planned. Z80 machine code was much in demand at the time, and I happened to
have picked it up as a youth. I got a programming job at a small
firm stocked with early video-game fiends who spent their off-
hours disassembling Ataris. Later, during my various periods of
under- or unemployment, my mother would say, Why not go back
to computers? You were so good at them. But she hadn't experienced the conditions I was working under, conditions I knew
would be the same wherever I went: the stupefying lack of humor,
the wretched taste in music, and all that unforgivable clothing.

Of this last item, I should say, it wasn't just my colleagues' ignorance of peg-legged jeans or the use of eye shadow in club dress.
Trends come and go. These boyos were ignorant of the entire
canon of twentieth-century menswear, of the precepts laid down
by masters like Montgomery Clift and the emperor of Japan.
Rules as precise as the laws of British prose. You could violate

them for effect, but only if you understood them. Which meant seeing how the lines of architectural modernism had been recapitulated in wool and linen, softened only by the heraldic color and pattern of accessories. The members of Joy Division likely weren't meditating on Frank Lloyd Wright when they took the stage in Manchester but those flat-fronted black cotton trousers and narrow-cut shirts didn't come from nowhere. Peter Saville, who designed Factory's records, understood it perfectly well: the iconic weight of black and white balanced against the release of splendor, in this case the dark magnificence of the music itself. Which might describe the tension of Protestant affect more generally: all guardedness and restraint until the eruption of an unextirpated beauty wakes us for a moment from the dream of efficiency.

The point being, my cubicle mates at NextFile couldn't make it through a London club door to save their lives. I *had* to make it through those doors because of what was being played on the other side: early Chicago house, or some of the most sublime dance music ever recorded. Frankie Knuckles, Marshall Jefferson, Jesse Saunders—Roland drum-machine royalty. White-rock homophobia may have killed disco on American radio play but the arc of history bends toward justice. They could burn Diana Ross records at a White Sox game, but on the south side of Chicago four-to-the-floor beats rose from the ashes and got stretched onto ten-minute loops by DJs sampling the heaven out of classic disco. The ubiquity of its traces may render it invisible today, but early house had the power of all original art, to reveal the structure of the present: the body on the rack of the electronic, the mind on the rack of the virtual. And it didn't just lay the structure bare, it gave a body a means to metabolize it, making the new relentlessness as human as dance.

Repurposing historical forces of that size required the power of volume, i.e., a sound system that shook your rib cage, whose subwoofers slapped air to your brow with every beat of the kick drum. Music thick as a hurricane. When the world wants to kill you, sometimes inoculation requires killing little bits of yourself. In this case, your eardrums.

But in London at the time, if you weren't wearing at least a thread or two by Vivienne Westwood, you couldn't get past the velvet rope. As Boy George later recalled, a dandy working the door at Taboo off Leicester Square once held a mirror up to a lager lout and said, Would you let *yourself* in? So I did what was required. I quit NextFile and got a job as a shop assistant at Browns (London clothier, not Oxford restaurant), hawking everything from Katharine Hamnett to Yohji Yamamoto. Chambray shirts to die for. Linen pants cut to break your heart. My sartorial standards may have peaked at nineteen but they peaked high. With the store discount and a kebab diet, I could afford to attire myself well enough to pass through those yearning crowds like Marcel into the salon of the Duchesse de Guermantes. Doormen would pick me from the back of the crowd on my shirts alone. Inside Taboo or Pyramid Night at Heaven, or the less discriminating Delirium, I'd order a beer to have something to hold on to as I stood at the edge of the dance floor. I didn't know anyone at the center of the scene, where the drugs circulated and the outrageous posed, and I didn't particularly want to. I just needed to be in the hurricane, in that storm blowing in from paradise, pushing skyward the wreckage of James Brown and George Clinton and the Jamaican dub masters and, yes, Giorgio Moroder and the German industrialists, and all the forgotten producers and DJs who kept the ideas and the vinyl coming, vanishing mediators of a culture considered too throwaway to chronicle. Or perhaps it's simplest just to say, in the words of Mr. Fingers, intoned in the cadence of King:

In the beginning, there was Jack, and Jack had a groove.
And from this groove came the groove of all grooves.
And while one day viciously throwing down on his box,
Jack boldly declared,

"Let there be house!"
and house music was born...

And in every house, you understand, there is a keeper.
And, in this house, the keeper is Jack.

Now some of you might wonder:
Who is Jack, and what is it that Jack does?

Jack is the one who gives you the power to jack your body.
Jack is the one who gives you the power to do the snake.
Jack is the one who gives you the key to the wiggly world.

Or words to that effect. Which might leave you with the impression that I danced. In fact, I never did. After the annihilation of love, I still consider the dance floor the best cure for individualism. But if I'm honest, I can say this only from a certain remove, because I was never able to pick up that key to the wiggly world. The music shook my chest and slapped my face, but I could only sway my head, standing at the edge of the pool, watching the deep end throb. My mother, who finds many things to be a pity, found this a pity. Wouldn't you enjoy it? she asked, plaintively, hoping as always for the absolution of a remedy. She might as well have asked why I didn't swim the English Channel. Where my mind goes, my body has never followed.

I didn't want to leave Britain. Things made sense there for a couple of years, living above the vegetable shop with Simon out in Manor Park with no central heat and the fetid kitchen. I didn't mind the bus ride to the station past all the depressing little terraced houses with their chintz curtains and grubby hedges, or the overground to Liverpool Street through the blackened warehouses, or the long night buses home after the clubs let out, with the yobs' vomit streaking under the seats. I was invincibly dressed, after all. Plus, no one asked personal questions. Not even Simon. Mom could send postcards mentioning the upcoming anniversary of my matriculation to nursery school in Battersea, asking if I'd been by the old building, but her wistful calendrics were an ocean away. If it hadn't been for my shitty exam results I might have gotten into Goldsmiths or Bristol at the beginning of my sojourn, and stayed on. But higher education was a class necessity, and as it happened there were things that I wanted to study. So after putting it off to stay a second year in London, I applied to American colleges. Alas, grade inflation hadn't reached the UK, and American admissions officers took a dim view of my comprehensive-school Bs. I ended up with six rejections and a job at a bakery in Walcott. After ten months living with my mother and Alec in the house, a time now blessedly voided from my memory, I got off the wait list and into Boston College.

In London, those who didn't make it past the club doors may not have worn Vivienne Westwood, but most had at least heard of her. They read *NME*. They read *i-D*. It was generally understood that

127

music and rigor weren't unrelated. But not so much at BC. Well-cut linen just didn't have the same profile. More Led Zeppelin. More Michelob. My work-study job in the rec room drained my serotonin faster than a producer snorts coke. To say nothing of my roommate from Westborough, a "tool" dressed most days in stone-washed jeans and a Guns N' Roses wifebeater, with whom I was forcibly housed in a sub-brutalist tower sided with gravel. He hadn't read Celan *or* Hardy. *Death in Venice* or *Middlemarch*. Contemplating his interior life was like staring at a velvet knockoff of an Agnes Martin painting. You needed dental work before long.

What it turned out the place did have, however, was a kick-ass radio station, run chiefly by adult aficionados who had nothing to do with the undergraduate rabble. I managed to talk my way into a weekday two to four a.m. slot. This was at the dawn of techno (at least in Detroit). The listening public, i.e., the dozen or so people who tuned in to my show, needed acclimation to something like Derrick May's oracular "Strings of Life," a seven-minute syncopated piano riff looped over a barrage of pop synth and high hats kicking at 128 bpm. Putting this revolution in context required playing songs that most straight musicheads—indulging at that time in the Beastie Boys—considered fey to the hilt, like, say, Ultravox's "Vienna." Electronic music has long suffered this prejudice in favor of the four-piece band and the lead singer. As if to break up that nuclear family of rock was to burn the flag. But if we can't wring spirit from the technical at this late stage, we might as well just donate our bodies to science and get it over with. The machines have to be made to matter. Not on their terms. On ours. They have to be worked back into human longing. And that's what Atkins, May, Saunderson, and the others were doing. Their pastures weren't the Lake District or Woodstock but the darkened basements of suburban Michigan.

After a couple of weeks, people began calling the station and asking, What is this stuff? The future, I told them, it's the future. Listen and be thankful. Not to me, or some genius artist hero, but to the scene producing the sound—the collective witness to life in the shadow of the faded industrial base. Mostly they just wanted to know where they could get their hands on the vinyl so they could start spinning it.

It's hard to say exactly why I dropped out the fall of my junior year. The architecture obviously wasn't helping. Nor was my third roommate, a Zionist Patriots fanatic who'd failed to get into Brandeis. The vicious tedium of classes with jocks. A general brownout. Cement in the limbs. I've since read about Norwegian reindeer that simply stop moving in winter; they call it arctic resignation. The added blight being that the only place I had to resign to was the house from which I'd fled for the UK in the first place, the house I'd already been forced to retreat to once before. My mother was something of a Norwegian reindeer herself during this period, still trudging back and forth to her job at the Walcott library that she'd begun the winter after my father died. There was a low metabolic rate all around. At least the bakery took me back. I walked there at five most mornings to put the bread and pastry in the ovens. As far as employment history goes, this developed into something of a bright spot. Because I was the first to arrive, I was able to commandeer the kitchen boom box and before long had salvaged several local high school Deadheads. One went so far as to shed his tie-dyes and sweats for pleatless pants and used button-downs. I was at least appreciated.

Because I never told the station manager that I'd dropped out, I was able to keep my radio show, and that January I noticed a schedule change announcing the slot after mine would now feature ska and early dub. Naturally, my curiosity was piqued. What DJ had come forward to fill the only spot deader than my own with grooves that demonstrated such an advanced sense of where dance music on both sides of the Atlantic was headed?

I first saw Caleigh through the glass of the booth. She was hefting a crate of twelve-inches across the lounge dressed in an oversize black turtleneck, baggy purple cords, and black boots, a getup which, properly fitted, wouldn't have been out of place in London, 1965, or Oakland a decade later, but which on her looked like a thrift-shop effort to obscure how slender she was. She was tall too, nearly six feet, but seemed keen to hide the fact, walking with her shoulders hunched and her head dipped, as though trying to move as invisibly as possible through the room. She wore no makeup or jewelry and had her hair pulled back flat off her high forehead. None of it was enough to disguise her beauty. That she would try apologizing for it only lifted it out of the realm of mere physical chance into a kind of moral grace.

I put on an extra-long final track and came out of the booth to ask if she needed help carrying her records in. She made no response, as if she weren't the person to ask. I gestured toward one of the crates at her feet; she didn't protest. The plastic grips were still warm from the touch of her fingers. "I love early dub," I said. "You can get lost in it." She nodded, looking straight at me for the first time, for only a split second, her enormous cat-like eyes driving stakes through my feet into the carpet like a Roman soldier nailing a thief to a cross. When a half smile lit her face, and she said, "Yeah, I guess you can," there seemed nothing left but the question of where we would spend the rest of our lives together.

I stayed and listened to every record she played. As I did the following week. She barely spoke between sets, practically whispering her playlist into the mic, using only the recorded PSAs, her demeanor strictly divorced from the frenzied energy of the tracks she spun. Obviously, I had to know more. After that second show I hazarded an invitation for her to join me for an early breakfast. By some miracle she agreed. We ate at a Dunkin' Donuts in Cleveland Circle. She ordered tea and a plain, and offered the briefest of responses to my questions. Though I did manage to get out of her that she'd gone to high school in Houston, that her father was Nigerian and her mother Sri Lankan, and that (like me) she had no friends at BC. She was, moreover, studying black Anglophone poetry. Maybe when she told me this last fact I shouldn't have reached quite so quickly into my messenger bag to read her the Audre Lorde quote I'd highlighted the day before— "The principal horror of any system which defines the good in terms of profit rather than in terms of human need, or which defines human need to the exclusion of the psychic and emotional components of that need—the principal horror of such a system is that it robs our work of its erotic value, its erotic power and life appeal and fulfillment"—but then I couldn't help myself. We were meant for each other even more deeply than I had first understood. When I put the book down, she looked at me skeptically, as if I were a cad feigning interest for seduction's sake. "Why do you read Audre Lorde?" she asked, unconvinced. But when I replied, "Who *doesn't* read Audre Lorde?" she laughed for the first time, and I was able to breathe again, knowing this wouldn't be our last meal.

Should the fact that we bonded that first morning at Dunkin' Donuts over the work of a radical lesbian feminist have tipped me off that Caleigh would one day date women? You could argue that. But even if I'd known, I wouldn't have done anything differently. I needed her too fiercely.

One of the troubles with reading Proust while living at home with your mother because you're too depressed to be in college is that the experience simultaneously aggrandizes and hollows out your fondest hopes for love, leaving you both more expectant and already defeated than most people are into. "One can feel an attraction towards a particular person," MP allows, which I sure in heaven did for Caleigh, "but to release that fount of sorrow, that sense of the irreparable, those agonies which prepare the way for love, there must be—and this is perhaps, more than a person, the actual object which our passion seeks so anxiously to embrace—the risk of an impossibility." A sweet impossibility to goad the heart higher. Albertine's lesbianism may be a filigree of Marcel's imagination, trumped up to fend off boredom and the suspicion he doesn't actually care for her, but Caleigh's turned out to be the real, impossible thing.

But all that wasn't until later. In the beginning, I just organized my life around her as I had organized my life around Angie, though we had so much more to talk about that there wasn't any question of not seeing each other every day. I arrived at her dorm room midafternoons, after I'd finished my bakery shift and made the trip into Chestnut Hill. If she wasn't there, I'd write a note on her door and wait for her outside. She'd lead me upstairs without saying much, and we'd start playing records, and I'd read aloud from Gide or Baldwin or Angela Davis as she lay on her bed with a hoodie pulled over her head, rolling her eyes at my oracular tone, chiding me more gently for what I cared about than anyone ever had. Her base state was one of melancholy. She read poetry but ignored her other assignments, sleeping ten to twelve hours a day. I pressed her again and again to reveal every detail of her past to me, but she divulged very little on that score. I had to piece together the internal exile of her high school years, when she was nearly as alienated from the black kids, who saw her as an immigrant freak, as she was from the white kids, who saw her as just black. About her vexed parental relations, she offered little more. All I could make out from stray comments and the occasional overheard phone call was a serious-minded Nigerian businessman who wanted his daughter to study a subject more practical than literature, and a somewhat morose Sri Lankan woman who hadn't bargained on Texas. The only two subjects she was the least bit voluble on were music and her sense of being inadequate. Whatever portion of our afternoons and evenings that I didn't monopolize describing how beautiful she was or reading aloud to her, she filled telling me I was just infatuated and that she was clumsy.

But while she insisted on disagreeing with my estimation of her, she wasn't at all scared of my feelings the way Angie had been. She seemed, instead, to accept them as you might a physical disability. I was allowed to say constantly how much I loved her, and to complain about any delay or skipping of visits. She listened patiently to my descriptions of all that mesmerized me about her, and after protesting that she possessed none of the qualities I ascribed to her, she would reason out with me how I might cope with such a powerful need, as though counseling a friend with romantic troubles. If I had been a testosterone case, I suppose I might have found this condescending, but it struck me instead as deeply kind—for her to bear the debilitation of my love, and even to care for me in the throes of it. I could have talked about nothing else, but occasionally she would put a stop to it by changing the record, and we would both lie back and travel together over the peaks and valleys of those endless dub tracks carved into vinyl by King Tubby and his descendants, the occasional lyric echoing down the trenches of bass so deeply you couldn't make out the words, only the longing behind them.

As time went on, her generosity toward me extended to hugging. I would sit next to her on her bed and she would put an arm around me and let me rest my cheek on her shoulder. I don't need reminding how pathetic this seems, to be pitied in this way for what you want and can't have by the very person you want it from. If I'd managed the tidy, maturational career of a bildungsroman protagonist, I might have suffered all this for a while, and then chucked passion aside for functional reciprocity. But Angie and my early days with Caleigh were no obligatory errors of youth; they were the blueprint. You can diagnose me all you like, and no doubt you will, as Celia and Alec never cease to, pointing out the doomed aspect of obsession, the anxiety it feeds, the supposedly genuine intimacy it precludes. And given my many years of experience in this field I can throw in for free whatever pathology you choose to make of a romantic and sexual attraction to black women by a white man who studies slavery and its legacy in the U.S. But you will come up with nothing that I haven't thought or worried to death already. Which is one of the reasons I fill these forms out in such detail. The only relief comes in describing it.

That first physical contact with Caleigh, that first hug, wiped out whatever vestigial dignity or restraint I had managed to maintain. I wept. And not a few smiling tears of relief, but open sobbing. And still she held on to me. She said later that she kissed me then not out of pity but because my weeping made her want to kiss me. If she hadn't already been my best and perhaps only friend, I wouldn't have believed her, but she's never dissembled. She doesn't have the energy for it, and she isn't trying to get anywhere, so she has no reason to lie or manipulate people. It's one of the upsides of avoiding ambition.

Thus the answer to the question of a "real date" that had tortured me with Angie came in the vanishing of the question. With Caleigh's first kiss, that full fount of sorrow opened up: my wretchedness had never been so entirely relieved, even if it returned with a vengeance as soon as our kissing ended. She forgave even my shuddering awkwardness in bed. Being naked with her was terrifying. I couldn't see how everything I did wasn't a prelude to rape. My thoughts were unacceptable; my body jerked like a spastic dog; I did everything I could to make sure I wasn't hurting her and was still certain I was hurting her. It was best when she closed her eyes and I sensed there might be pleasure for her I couldn't touch or see, some thing or place hidden back inside her where she could go in my presence, if only alone. Then, at least, I didn't feel purely selfish. It's so easy to mock the earnestness of men who actually believe in feminism rather than simply pretend to for advantage, as if trying to step beyond a history of violence is a dweeb's sickly riposte to not getting enough. I wanted to love her, and to be as kind to her as she already was to me. She says she's never regretted that we had this period together, and I believe her.

There was nothing luxurious about those first months, no panning shots across a clothes-strewn floor leading to the couple naked atop the sheets. Even with as abject a lover as I was, she shied from displaying herself, hurrying instead into the shower when we were done, staying there for long stretches and emerging fully clothed. Her most comforting intimacy was ceasing to use my name and calling me Flipper instead. I had never earned an endearment before, and though its etymology was a mystery to me, I felt chosen each time she used it.

When at the end of the school year she needed a place to stay for the summer, naturally she moved in with me and my mother. She'd absconded with one of the college's vacuum cleaners and derived some odd comfort from vacuuming our living room rug several times a week. My mother was attracted to the vacuum (unlike ours, it worked), but also wary after Alec, already a college freshman living with Aunt Penny in New York for the summer, characterized it as stolen during a rare home visit. It was the first new appliance to reach the household in years; its shiny yellow casing gave it the appearance of a probe sent from an advanced society to gather data on primitives. Caleigh wanted us to present ourselves to my mother as friends, which should likely have been another tip-off, but it defused awkwardness, so I was all for it. "Your friend likes vacuuming," my mother would say to me when she got home from work. "She's been at it again." Having a guest clean the house might once have offended her sense of propriety, but she didn't have it in her to make more than a token protest.

Once Caleigh had moved in and I no longer had to worry if I would see her every day, it began to dawn on me that she wasn't just melancholy, she was about as depressed as I was, if not more so. But again, she didn't want to talk about it. It doesn't matter, she kept saying, which was a decent stand-in for her general approach to the world: all obligation was a chore, romance was a fraud, most days hurt, and the only real relief was music. We did read critical race theory articles together, and bemoaned the racial amnesia that hid the decline of black life-worlds behind endless civil rights hagiographies. So that was something. Truth be told, her depression was a comfort, giving me hope we might stay together awhile because there was so much it turned out that I needed to comfort her about.

In August, my mother went away to visit friends and Caleigh and I had that cursed house to ourselves. The month was one long heat wave. My mother didn't believe in air-conditioning for herself or others, so in my bedroom at night, we'd place a fan a few inches from the mattress and leave it on high. At the bakery, several employees fainted quietly by the ovens. When I got home from work Caleigh and I would sprawl out in the living room, sweating like catfish, distracted even from our own misery, listening to nothing more taxing than ambient house. Celia or Alec would call now and then to check in, and I'd hear about her summer living in Berkeley, or his friends in New York. They'd gotten into colleges with better financial aid, where people drank less Michelob and listened to less Led Zeppelin, and where professors had seminars in their living rooms. I wouldn't say that I resented them yet because I mostly just worried about how much pain they were in without knowing how to help them. But when they called, it did remind me, as if I needed reminding, that I was living in the house where I had once left them, my younger siblings, to fend for themselves, while they had somehow contrived more permanent escapes.

It would have been appropriate, even natural, I guess, if while I was there I'd dwelt on my father, but I had very few recollections of him and didn't think about him much at all. This despite the fact that I had been seeing his old psychiatrist, Dr. Gregory, for some time already. I obviously couldn't afford to pay him, but he'd never lost a patient to suicide before and was apparently guilty enough about it to ignore my nonpayment of his bills. He sent them, I threw them out, and on we went. Celia, asserting her newfound wisdom as a psychology major, said this was clinically unsound, but then she had more resources than I did, and tended toward self-confidence. His office was on the second floor of a small mansion on Marlborough Street in Back Bay. I sat in an upholstered leather chair in the middle of what must once have been a living room, Dr. Gregory's cherrywood desk placed between two floor-to-ceiling windows with their long sashes and miniature balconies straight out of Edith Wharton, though he didn't dress half as well as, say, Lawrence Selden in *House of Mirth*. No suits cut on the bias. No unstructured linen. It's strange what people do and don't do with their money. I would never have known he was a Midwesterner or a Methodist, but my mother used to accompany my father to his appointments and she'd gathered this intelligence early on (for her, a visit to a medical professional is first and foremost a social call). I talked to him mostly about psychoanalytic cultural criticism, theories of mass trauma, and occasionally my vicious bouts of panic that Caleigh would leave me imminently for a woman. He was a good listener, Dr. Gregory, and rarely interrupted me.

Perhaps also because of his guilt about my father, he had a quick draw with the prescription pad. This has proved fateful. At some point he introduced the term *anxiety disorder* into our discussion, and suggested a small dose of Librium, prn. When I told him it didn't do much more for me than a Benadryl, he wrote me a script for something he described as "slightly more potent."

I remember my first dose of Klonopin the way I imagine the elect recall their high school summer romances, bathed in the golden light of a perfect carelessness, untouched and untouchable by time's predations or the foulness of any present pain. As Cat

138

Stevens wrote, *The first cut is the deepest,* though I've always preferred Norma Fraser's cover to the original (the legendary Studio One, Kingston, Jamaica, 1967). Stevens sings it like a pop song, but Fraser knows the line is true, that she'll never love like that again. Her voice soars over the reverb like a bird in final flight. The first cut *is* the deepest. I've since learned all about GABA receptors and molecular binding, benzos and the dangers of tolerance, but back then I knew only that I had received an invisible and highly effective surgery to the mind, administered by a pale yellow tablet scored down the middle and no larger than an aspirin. There is so much drivel about psychoactive meds, so much corruption, bad faith, over- and underprescription, vagueness, profiteering, ignorance, and hope, that it's easy to forget they sometimes work, alleviating real suffering, at least for a time. This was such a time.

I took my first pill as soon as I filled the script at the CVS in Copley, a few blocks from Dr. Gregory's office. By the time I'd reached Newton Centre on the Green Line, I couldn't stop smiling. The kind of big, solar smile that suffuses your whole torso, as if your organs are grinning. Soon I began to laugh, at nothing at all, pure laughter, which brought tears to my eyes, no doubt making me appear completely insane to the other passengers. But happier I have rarely been. For that hour and the three or four that followed, I was lifted down off a hook in the back of my skull that I hadn't even known I'd been hanging from. Here was the world unfettered by dread. Thoughts came, lasted for whole, uninterrupted moments, and then passed away, leaving room for others. The present had somehow ceased to be an emergency. In fact, it seemed almost uneventful. Down the tramcar a gaggle of high schoolers snickered at my lunatic ways and I wasn't even ashamed. It was as if their derision moved too slowly through this new atmosphere to reach me with any force. I neither envied nor despised them. Who was I? Steve McQueen? When I saw my used Cutlass turning into the parking lot at Woodlawn—Caleigh coming to pick me up—I waved to her sitting behind the wheel. She too looked at me like I was a sociopath. Since when do you wave? she said. Since I found out you could tear down the Berlin Wall with a Q-tip.

Dr. Gregory had told me to take one pill in the morning and one before bed. I slept that night like a baby lamb on sedatives, and woke unafraid. Morning after morning this miracle repeated itself. I began to run experiments. I would summon my worst fears—that I would never get back to school, that I had already ruined my chance to do my larger work, that I was a burden to Caleigh, that she didn't love me even as a friend but put up with me only because she was depressed and needed company—and I would dwell on each in turn, summoning the images that came along with the fears: being stuck in the house forever, Caleigh living thousands of miles away in love with someone else. And yet, lo and behold it, I couldn't worry. I imagined this terrible future, I rehearsed the story lines, but my breath wouldn't tighten, and thoughts moved through me as frictionlessly as a weather report.

I told Caleigh she had to try it, but when I dosed her one morning after breakfast she fell into a six-hour coma, and woke with a hangover, cursing me. Turned out she didn't have an anxiety disorder. That was the thing about Klonopin: it didn't just void my anxiety, it diagnosed my state like the X-ray of a fractured bone. The muscles of my face became so relaxed I expected to look in the mirror and see a basset hound. I'd never known a body could be so free of tension and still remain upright.

That fall I went back to school. I read by the hour, wrote papers, sat exams, and initiated my listeners into acid house. Caleigh and I spent all our time together, in our rooms, at the radio station, in the library, I imploring her to enter therapy, she resisting and putting me off, though still allowing me to make love to her. If I had hoped that my guilt about sleeping with her might dwindle with time, I was wrong. It only intensified. It wasn't just about being a man who might repulse her, or cause her pain. It was being white, and yet free to touch her, to kiss her lips and breasts, to put my finger inside her, when twenty minutes earlier I'd been reading aloud from Andrea Dworkin or Sojourner Truth. This didn't stop seeming wrong. I tried my best to focus solely on her pleasure, to ignore myself entirely in deference to her. But the political isn't so easily banished. Yes, I wanted to abdicate myself, to give up my own person, because why else be in love if you can't leave yourself in the dust? But it was more particular than that. Soon my deference had morphed into something more loaded: the desire to physically reverse racial privilege by becoming her slave. Where else could this transposition occur with any real force but in the trauma of sex?

One night in bed that spring, too consumed by the urge not to confess it, I whispered words to this effect into the porch of her ear. "Oh, Flipper," she whispered back. "What do you mean? Some plantation thing?" My horrendous silence allowed the implication, Yeah, maybe, inverted? She placed her long fingers on my cheek and brushed my hair back with her other hand, as you might pat a child's cowlick. She loved me enough by then, if only as a friend, not to be shy in my presence. For that, I'll always be grateful to her—that she showed me who she was. "I get it," she said. "I do. But not for us, Flipper. Not for us. Okay?" She shushed the stream of apologies that came out of me for even asking, holding a finger to my lips, and then, to my amazement, raised her head up off the pillow and kissed me.

So I kept that longed-for defeat in check, not wanting to trouble her, holding it at bay as I have ever since. It would be much tidier if the negligible chipping away I've done at the edifice of white supremacy issued purely from a concern for justice. But the fact is my life has been all caught up with black women (romantically, I would have been a *lot* better off as a lesbian of color, that's for sure) so there's no use pretending to some fiction of principle. I never would have kept up my work if I hadn't seen up close the depression and self-hatred that the women I've tried to be with have suffered but not wanted to discuss. To think that their states of mind have nothing to do with politics or history would be as pitiably ignorant as imagining that my pining for them—their bodies and mothering care—isn't likewise haunted.

I realize I'm going on here a bit in answer to the question on work history, it's just that listing dates of employment doesn't really get at what I've been up to. My real work began during that first reprieve of Klonopin. Caleigh had met a woman named Myra, a grad student at BC who TA'd one of her discussion sections. They struck up a conversation after class one day and had coffee a few times. Myra had grown up in Atlanta, gone to the University of Chicago undergrad, tended bar in Boston for several years, and now DJ'd at an all-women's night in Central Square once a month. I could tell by the way Caleigh looked at me out of the corner of her eye whenever she mentioned her name that she was testing me to see how I would react. It is a measure of the power of benzos on the virgin mind that I could listen to Caleigh, who meant everything to me, talk about having coffee with this woman and not end up hospitalized for jealousy. She clearly wanted permission. She had forgiven me my terrible need for her. She had let herself be swayed by my devotion, and eventually persuaded by it. She'd even forgiven me my guilt for desiring her. What was I going to do now? Stand in the way of what she was trying to tell me she wanted? Just a few months earlier, my ambient dread and my obsession with her had been so entwined I would have been reduced to pleading and threats. Instead, I found myself bewildered at the equanimity of my response. It struck me then, for the first time, how unethical anxiety is, how it voids the reality of other people by conscripting them as palliatives for your own fear. For a moment there, I was able to step outside that, to hear what she wanted to be.

When Caleigh suggested that the three of us form a reading group to make up for the paltry offerings in African diaspora studies, it seemed like a perfect solution, a way for Caleigh not to have to choose between us. Myra was wary of me at first, knowing Caleigh and I were still sleeping together, and finding it hard to believe a white man could have much to contribute to discussions of black life. I didn't blame her for this. But with Caleigh to vouch for me, she eventually came around, and the three of us spent our first month reading that giant of postcolonial psychiatry, Frantz Fanon. Not the world's leading feminist, but you could fit on a postcard what he didn't get about the psychic half-life of colonialism. On his advice, so to speak, we surveyed the more recent clinical-psych literature for studies on the treatment of black patients (shockingly, there wasn't much). But I did come across the study that helped set me on my path.

A British psychologist working at a clinic in Manchester had written a paper about his treatment of black teenagers with recurring nightmares of slavery. Some dreamt of being confined to the holds of ships amid the withered and dying, others of being publicly stripped and lashed. One boy, who evinced no particular knowledge of black history, had a recurring nightmare that he was being hung from a lamppost and dismembered. It was the transcripts that got me. The author had excerpted them in an appendix. One of his subjects, in language replete with Mancunian slang, described seeing blood run down his chest and realizing it was leaking from the cuts inflicted by the iron collar around his neck. Not knowing what to make of the phenomenon—none of the boys knew each other and they attended different schools— the psychologist had interviewed family members to see if there were stories of enslavement among ancestors that might have been passed along in family lore, giving rise to the boys' nocturnal fantasies. But he found no such pattern. What the boys did share were symptoms of depression, which, as the author noted, were not unusual among black teenagers, though few came in for treatment. It was the press of these particular nightmares that had driven them over the barrier of pride and stigma to seek his help.

The oddity of it all—kids from the Midlands, not the old Confederacy, the uncanny exactitude of their descriptions—would have been memorable enough. But what lodged in me was an observation that the author himself made little of. Toward the opening of the paper, as he was describing the boys' working-class social milieu, he mentioned in passing that each went regularly to clubs and that all were avid music fans. Alas, he didn't get their playlists. But given where and when they'd grown up, it wasn't hard to guess what they'd been hearing on the dance floor— and it wasn't white punk. It was house and early techno, with some Kraftwerk and New Order thrown in. Of course, there were thousands of kids listening to the same stuff at the same time whose sleep went untroubled by the Middle Passage. And yet it turned out that what these kids had in common wasn't great-grandmothers from West Indian plantations but black American dance tracks. No one doubted that the agony of slavery haunted generations of spirituals and gospel. Why not the latest twelve-inch? These boys weren't listening to Mahalia Jackson sing about how she got over, but somewhere in the cut the same ghosts were being shaken loose. There was no empirical conclusion to draw from any of this, as if you could measure the pain in music. But spending my days reading the history of lynchings and race riots, and then playing my records at the station, I kept returning to the image of these boys dancing and dreaming through some dark repetition bigger than any of us.

I suppose, then, you could say that our little reading group was a success all around. Caleigh and Myra got to spend lots of time together, and began hooking up that spring. And I got the assignment that weighs on me still—my real work—to get down in words what doesn't live in words. To track ghosts by ear.

Have you ever taken any of the following medications? If so, when, for how long, and what was your response?

Luvox

The trouble being that, after that one blessed year, the Klonopin stopped working. Not overnight, but gradually. I didn't wake up convinced I was dying, just less unafraid than I'd been in the halcyon days. Morning by morning. Until I didn't wait anymore until after breakfast to take the pill, but swallowed it as soon as I woke, hoping an empty stomach would let more of the drug into my system. That Caleigh had stopped sleeping with me and started having sex with Myra is what you could call a contributing environmental factor to my increased anxiety. But Dr. Gregory saw no problem—nor, for shit sure, did I—in simply increasing my dose. I'd responded to it once, why not again? And indeed, it did the trick. The second cut wasn't the deepest, but there was relief in it all the same. I was able to see Caleigh almost every day without crying. And able to let her talk me through the losing of her, just as she had talked me through the loving of her in the first place. With enormous patience, she listened to me describe every facet of the pain she was causing me. How I lay in bed thinking of her with Myra, bitten by envy and loneliness; or about the hours spent listening to the records we'd listened to together, knowing I'd see her that same evening but not be allowed to kiss her. She would hug me, as she had before, telling me it was going to be okay, that she was the unlucky one for leaving me, even if she had to. And she'd assure me again and again that I wasn't as pathetic as I felt, carrying on like I did, needing *her* to be the one to help me through it, and even help me accept her help, against the taunting voice that told me to show some "self-respect" and masculine amour propre when all I wanted was to be in the same room with her no matter what the conditions.

Through it all she kept calling me Flipper, and I called her Cee, and we even added new variations—Flipster, Flimmy, the Flimster, Ceedling, Ceester, Ceemer. It was this more than anything that made me realize with relief that she didn't want to depart our cocoon of affection and commiseration any more than I did, regardless of who was sleeping with whom. It was as if we were becoming childhood best friends, siblings, and an old married couple simultaneously. If she took a trip home or away with Myra, I'd speak to her each day on the phone. We talked as we had from the start about what we were reading and listening to. After a few months, I could even tolerate hearing her speak about Myra, now and then offering her advice on how she could overcome her skittishness about being with another woman. I knew then we would never lose each other, no matter whom either of us became involved with. Our private world was too necessary to both of us to be replaced wholesale with another. I wanted to live with her. I didn't mind if Myra lived with us too. I could be their roommate. It took Caleigh a while to convince me this would be a bad idea. That we could still talk every day, and that it would be easier for me to meet a romantic partner if I wasn't always with the two of them. So they found an apartment in Allston together, and I moved in with Alec's old high school friend Ben.

Which is when this second reprieve of Klonopin came to an end, only faster this time. Celia and Alec have since come to form a dim view of Dr. Gregory, seeing him as little more than a guilt-ridden pill pusher who sedated me to fend off his fear of losing another patient, rather than tackling the issues at hand. But frankly I still consider him a humanitarian. The increased doses are what I asked of him, and what I needed. When a physician ups a diabetic's insulin there's no question of indulgence or rectitude, just a condition and a drug it would be malpractice not to give. Which is hardly to say I have no regrets. I regret that the reprieves kept getting shorter.

Paxil

And it is not as if, in the years following that first blush of benzos, Dr. Gregory didn't try anything new. He would sit in his Eames chair, all mild-mannered and bald, in pleated chinos and a V-neck, asking how I had been, nodding gravely as I answered, and every few months, along with the increase in Klonopin, he'd suggest a new drug we might add to the mix to help dampen the growing general fear.

Serzone

I'd taken to writing music reviews, not for the abysmal pay, but to bring to light the overlooked wonders issued from labels run out of bedrooms from Oakland to Eindhoven, kids sampling their uncles' Run-D.M.C. records into an old-school hip-hop revival, or those unemployed Belgian pranksters turning out tracks hard enough to keep a warehouse of teens dancing till Sunday noon. I never went in for rave culture myself. I was usually in bed by ten. But before it collapsed under the weight of its own promotional shtick and became an ecstasy theme park for weekend punters, it spawned a number of ambient house masterworks that I listen to to this day.

Other than that, I worked in record shops. Not at the chains, which I couldn't stomach, but various independents. I lasted about a year at a place down on Newbury before selling Nirvana albums to Armani-clad foreign students drove me to a storefront in East Boston frequented mostly by local DJs. I got paid even less, but at least the company was tolerable. My student loans had long since come due but I didn't have the money to make the payments so I shoved the envelopes in a drawer to be opened at some point down the line when I'd gotten things sorted.

As long as I was in the store itself, talking to other people about music I believed in, ordering it from distributors or listening to it on headsets, my shakiness was kept mostly at bay. My distracted energy got absorbed into the pace of the tracks themselves or driven into the necessity to convert others to their power. In

148

Walter Benjamin, there is the concept of the *vanishing mediator*, the person or idea that travels between cultures, pollinating one with the other, before disappearing from view, the way black musicians carried blues and rock into recording studios and then vanished from sight and accounting, listening to their invention played out by white bands. If I could sell a hip-hop DJ on a reissued Dolly Parton album or place in the hands of some devoted European Industrialist kid from RISD a Pet Shop Boys aria and make him hear the kinship, then my job for the day was done. I've never made a piece of music in my life, which is another thing my mother considers a pity, but as long as I was inside it, passing it on into others' ears, I wasn't absolutely alone.

Still, afterwards, riding the T back to Ben's apartment on the margins of the South End, wondering if Caleigh would be home when I called her, and, when she wasn't, sitting on the couch with Ben nursing the first of the evening's beers while he got high, I would sense the fear I'd woken with slink back in, accusing me of failing to pay it sufficient mind, mocking the day's respite as an illusion.

Ben, a semiprofessional knitter, had taken me in out of the kindness of his heart and a need for rent money (and also perhaps as a favor to Alec). He ran a tight ship, insisting on extreme tidiness to make room for all his wool and mail-order supplies. He regularly updated the chore regime posted on the fridge, which left me in a state of suspense as to what I would be required to sweep or scrub in any given week. But once he had put down his needles for the day and smoked a joint, he achieved an enviable calm while cooking vegetables for us and watching *Simpsons* reruns. We'd become friends, of the sort men often are, in that we daily confirmed each other's existence but pretty much left it at that.

After ratatouille and an hour of cartoons, I'd try Caleigh again, and if she didn't answer, I'd call Celia or Alec, not to confess in full the shape of the trap, because they had their own to avoid, but just to talk with someone for whom I didn't have to mask my basic state. I knew they wanted to help. They would always ask, hopefully, how my meds were working. I've never stopped wanting to give them at least some reason to think I'm getting better.

Anafranil

There are years it is difficult to account for in retrospect. Most of my twenties, for instance. I can't say exactly when it was that the vinyl shop in East Boston went out of business. Late in the first Clinton administration, maybe? Or how long it took me to find the job at the left-wing call center. We raised money for whatever not-for-profit had hired our shift to rake through old lists of *Mother Jones* subscribers and members of the ACLU who might be talked into giving ten or twenty dollars to endangered fish or gay people. I *can* say that getting paid on commission blew. You'd be soliciting some Arkansas outlier for a Native American higher-ed fund, watching the seconds disappear on the huge digital clock above the supervisor's desk as the person you'd already given up on began explaining how the bills for her fibromyalgia treatment had cleared out her savings and was making her wonder if she'd have to give up her dog, a three-legged rescue with hypertension and hookworms, and you'd want to say, Look, lady, it's through with you, you're terminal, that shit's not improving. But you know what? If you chip in fifty bucks to the college fund, someone not yet down for the count might actually get an education, so stop yakking and pay it forward. I'd like to afford that burrito in four hours and you're not helping. And why did the owner of the call center drive a BMW? Because a bunch of essentially unemployed people managed to suck enough pocket change out of enervated hippies to fund at least one upper-middle-class existence. As for Anafranil, I put up with the tachycardia for a while, but being unable to take a shit more than every ten days proved untenable. Which is a pity given that its eradication of my libido took the edge off missing Caleigh as sorely as I still did.

Celexa

There was a downside to seeing my father's old shrink and never paying his bills, which was that when he eventually stopped returning my calls, I didn't have much of a leg to stand on. His unannounced withdrawal from my care after all this time seemed highly unprofessional given how essential his prescription pad had become to my daily functioning, but I figured he'd spoken to colleagues who'd suggested it was time he extracted himself from such a messy relationship. I could have used a referral, but there we are. I didn't want to ask my mother for the money to actually pay for a psychiatrist, but what option did I have? I was on things you weren't supposed to come off of unsupervised.

The guy I found at Boston City Hospital was only a few years older than I was and wore a wedding ring. I'm against marriage on principle—not love and trust, which I pine for, but the legal entity, given its history—so it wasn't Dr. Bennet's marital status per se that I envied, but the indication it gave that he, too, was one of the elect, enjoying the plenary ease of intimacy with a woman who had chosen him over and above other men. And of course he had a steady income, and all his hair, and that mild-jock physique of the former team-sports player, giving him the air of physical carelessness, that impunity which went along with even the merely passable good looks prized by women for the social capital they offer, and I suppose the pleasure. Which returns us, by the logic of opposites, willy-nilly, to the category of the *loser* or *creep,* that staple of high school which lives on in a youth-obsessed culture, hunting people into middle age—the erotically failed man whose desire is imagined to grow lascivious with embitterment until his loneliness has made him so ugly he's a pervert, beginning then to shade into the monster of the pedophile, subject to the most righteous and violent anger of all, the rage of parents on behalf of their minor children. Which isn't to say that meeting Dr. Bennet "triggered" anything in me, just that I wanted to be sure he wasn't going to bluster his way into some misbegotten get-tough approach and start cutting back on my Klonopin. Luckily, he proved more humane than that. Like Dr. Gregory, he didn't want to subtract drugs, only to add them.

Effexor

When he asked about the work I did, I told him about music as the medium for the transgenerational haunting of the trauma of slavery, and how what I needed most was a research library, a JSTOR account, and three years of postgraduate funding. To be honest, I didn't care about the degree. I'm not an academic careerist. I would have been happy simply with the time to write. But it was hard to get at what needed to be done after eight hours of pleading with white liberals for the habitat of a frog. So I settled for a new prescription. The Effexor plus the Klonopin, combined with the lithium Bennet put me on after hearing about Dad, added up to a minor reprieve of their own, enough in any case to let me focus on applying to graduate school and get started on the reparations work Caleigh and I had been discussing for several years already.

To the extent that people consider the reparations movement at all, which most don't, they think of General Sherman and Special Field Order No. 15, granting freed slaves the coastal lands from the Carolinas to northern Florida, the infamous promise of forty acres and a mule, and so imagine that the modern push amounts to a claim for cash for every living descendant of a chattel slave. Whereas in fact the movement's first demand is an official U.S. government apology and recognition of the injustice of slavery, accompanied by suits against banks and insurance companies whose prior corporate entities profited directly from the uncompensated labor of the human beings they owned. And only then, a congressional allocation of billions of dollars to be spent on institution building to improve the education, health, and well-being of African-Americans generally. After all, the U.S. compensated Japanese-Americans for interning them during World War II, and Germany paid restitution to surviving victims of the Holocaust. That governments should pay for the sins of their past, even if committed by repudiated regimes, is hardly unprecedented. The caustic, knee-jerk rejection of the idea of restitution for slavery is but an indication of why it is necessary. What we ignore only persists.

So Caleigh and I, with Myra's assistance, set to work writing a brief, explanatory pamphlet, our modest contribution to the consciousness-raising effort. I wanted to put an eighteenth-century schematic drawing of the hold of a slave ship on the cover, to show how the ancestors of our fellow citizens had arrived here, but Caleigh favored an early-twentieth-century photograph of a black dirt farmer harnessed to his plow. We ran off five hundred copies at Kinko's, and from then on I always made sure to have a supply in my bag so that when riding the bus or the T, I could spend a few minutes imposing them on my fellow passengers.

153

Lexapro

When I did get around to applying to grad school the year I turned thirty, I was surprised, given how much thought and study I'd put in, to be rejected by each and every one. Being white was probably not an advantage in my chosen field of African-American studies (though, naturally, that is an admissions preference I wholly support, no matter its effect on me). By this time, my roommate Ben had performed the hat trick of meeting a highly intelligent and alluring woman outside of his knitting circles, maintaining his sense of self-worth long enough for them to complete a course of dating, and eventually convincing her, Christine, to move in with us. As the rejection letters arrived weekly through March and April, the two of them didn't know what to say after asking me how my day had been and hearing only another report of canceled possibility. Any more than Celia or Alec did. I'd never felt the least bit competitive with either of them (though Celia's ease in finding a new boyfriend each time she broke up with an old one irked me at times), and I put out of my mind the fact that my sister already had a master's in social work and that Alec had completed his journalism degree, despite being five years younger.

Wellbutrin

There continued, the following spring, to be no rational basis to resent either of them in particular when I got rejected everywhere I applied for a second time. The left-wing phone bank had cut back on staff by then and I was unemployed, which Dr. Bennet was helpful enough to remind me was a major life stressor. As in, justifying of increased doses across the board. Generalized anxiety, that's how he now described my condition. He suggested a support group, which conveniently met just down the hall from his office. Where the support group met that would help me get over going to this support group wasn't clear. But oh well.

I thought fibromyalgia in Arkansas was bad, but there was no telephonic remove from the Gulf War vet who slept curled around his rifle and looked at us as if we were bloody remains, or the woman being charged with child neglect because she could never clean enough to satisfy herself it was safe to feed her malnourished offspring. Our youngest colleague still wet himself at the age of twenty-two. When we weren't hearing about melted corpses on Iraq's highway of death, we could kick back to the tale of a bankrupt lawyer's sixteen-hour odyssey to find a lightbulb in sufficiently undimpled packaging. Someone once said, It's all about the parties you go to. No kidding. The facilitator was into what she called "aversion treatment." The lawyer was instructed to go straight from the meeting to the nearest drugstore, walk to the housewares section, and pick up the first 100-watt bulb his eyes alighted upon. Not so clear that the vet should cluster-bomb downtown Attleboro for a little DIY reenactment, but the woman afraid of her groceries could force herself to cut broccoli right on the counter and then eat it with her little ones. Before my terror at the reality of these people's lives caused me to flee the scene, I got two assignments from the facilitator myself: to leave the house just when I expected Caleigh to call, and to empty the drawer where I put all my unpaid bills and sort them in order of priority, presumably so I could figure out which one to talk with my mother about first. I completed neither.

Remeron

Flummoxed at my refractory symptoms, Dr. Bennet ran me through a complete re-eval, said I needed to stop talking about psychoanalytic theory in our sessions, and put me on enough uppers to cheer a POW. I recall a period of two or three months when my head felt compressed to the density of an anvil strapped to a potting wheel left on high speed in a sun-drenched meadow. It was like getting root-canal work while vacationing in the tropics. Indeed, the experiment came to an end when my stepped-up jaw-grinding caused me to chip a molar. But for a while there I did get out of my room at Ben's a bit more often. I toured the remaining indie record shops on Saturday mornings when the new shipments arrived. It was on one such outing, after many dateless years, that I encountered Bethany. She had a tiny glistening nose stud, and a nearly shaved head, and was flipping through a bin of Aphex Twin. Need I say more?

Celia

Jasper was an Anglophile from Coeur d'Alene. He did his best to monogram everything he owned. Today it was a royal-blue turtleneck with his chosen initials—JHP, for Jasper Henry Philips—done in three-inch brocade letters outlined with sequins and pinned at the breast like a Michael Jackson costume still under construction. So far, he'd avoided the shelters by couch-surfing and squatting. When Michael phoned me at work, we were almost at the end of our session, which Jasper had again idled away with his fantasies, this time of befriending Princess Diana, his all-time-favorite celebrity. I had five minutes left of my weekly effort to find him a job.

I told Michael I couldn't talk.

"What about later?" he asked. "Can we talk later?"

A girl who hadn't shown up in three weeks was waiting outside my door. I had appointments all afternoon. I needed to go running after work.

"I'll try you," I said. "But it'll be later, your time."

"Oh," he said, as if he'd forgotten we lived on different coasts. "Okay."

We spoke twice a week at least, but in the evenings or on

weekends. I was surprised he even knew the name of my agency to look up the number. Something had agitated him; he was calling to be assuaged.

"I'll try you," I said. "I will."

"Sooo," Jasper said as soon as I hung up, "your boyfriend's traveling—and he isn't your husband because you're not wearing a ring. Where is he? Paris, London?"

To help establish a rapport during our first meeting, I'd made the mistake of mentioning I'd lived in England. Now it was all he wanted to talk about.

I suggested we look over the listings together. There were openings for baggers at the Marina Safeway, temp-driver jobs he didn't qualify for because he didn't have a license, a copy-shop assistant position in Oakland, and the usual volunteer stuff, distributing condoms or working at the Meals on Wheels kitchen, what the agency called "community networking opportunities."

I needed him to focus and commit to three applications before our next session. If I'd had an hour with him, I would have asked whom he was spending his time with, if anyone was pressuring him for sex, how he was doing physically and emotionally. But that wasn't my job. I was supposed to prevent him from becoming homeless (which he effectively already was), help him find legitimate employment, and coach him on maintaining whatever support structure he already had, which in his case consisted mostly of asking each week if he'd been in touch with his mother. My older colleagues often didn't bother with parents when a client was no longer a minor, but according to Jasper, his mother had left his stepfather—the person he'd fled from in the first place—so it seemed at least worth a try for him to talk with her, given what his options were.

He stood by the window now, gazing into the alley as if across a rough, romantic sea. "What does your boyfriend do in London?

158

Is he an international businessman? Does he feature those fierce three-piece tweed suits? Or cravats, does he wear cravats?"

I couldn't decide which of my brothers he'd get on with better, Michael or Alec.

"That wasn't my boyfriend," I said.

"Your lover, then."

"Jasper, if you don't apply to anything, I've got to put that in your file, and in a few weeks they're going to tell me to terminate you from services."

"If you lived in England, how come you don't have an accent?"

"Listen—"

"Okay, I'll apply. Just tell me."

"I've lived here more."

"Did you grow up in a house with servants?"

"Where do you get all this?"

He picked up and examined the tape dispenser on my desk as though admiring the facets of a crystal vase. I would have said he was high, but his speech and movements were too precise, his affect too consistent. He was practicing, that's what he was doing, rehearsing for a future life.

"My grandmother said it was the classiest place she'd ever been, and that I would love it there. She had a videotape of Diana's wedding. We used to watch it all the time. People thought she was pretentious, being into all that, so I knew she was onto something, pissing those jackasses off. She left me all that stuff, the books and music and the mugs with the coats of arms, everything she'd bought over there and all the stuff she'd collected. Most of it's at my mom's. But I brought a few things with me."

I pictured him there with his grandmother, on their little island of manners. I wanted to draw him out on it, to hear what it meant to him. And from there maybe get him to talk about his

159

growing up, and eventually about what exactly his stepfather had done that caused him to leave. Jasper was one of the clients who shared something of himself, if only because he desired an audience. Most of the kids I saw were sullen and defensive, and treated me as another scold of the adult world who didn't care what they felt. It wasn't that I wanted to cut him off now, just that our half hour was up. I told him he had to call me with the three jobs off the list he was going to pursue so I could set up the interviews, and that I needed copies of his applications at our next appointment.

"It's true, isn't it?" he said. "People do live in castles there."

"Like ten people, Jasper. Most of them are just normal. They're not that different than here. Really."

"Normal like you? Like college and going to Europe and working here because you feel good helping ignorant people like me? That kind of normal?"

"Our time's up," I said. "I have someone waiting."

"People always get angry when I tell the truth. Happens every time."

On the outbound N Judah that evening I noticed a man in a three-piece suit. Instead of reading the paper folded in his hands, his eyes crept along the bodies of various young women, particularly those in skirts and lipstick, his glance occasionally falling on me as well, curious but uncertain, and a bit aggressive, a bit pissed off, as if I wasn't giving him something that belonged to him.

Jasper's image had stuck with me. Of my boyfriend dressed in tweed, like the suits Dad used to wear. Paul sitting at a big conference table with other men in suits and calling me after his meeting, as I suppose Dad had called Mom. I'd never wanted such a partner, or even been able to imagine why anyone would. Still, getting back to our apartment and finding Paul lying on the couch, reading under a blanket, a glass of bourbon beside him on the floor, I found myself wondering what it might be like if Jasper's fantasy were even a little true.

The drink irked me. It threw his sugar off. Which made it more likely that he would have a low in the night, waking us both. But if it was just one, or maybe two, and he drank them slowly enough and timed his shots right, it might still be fine.

"What's up?" he said. "How was the day?"

The fact that he was flat on the couch suggested his hadn't been exactly fruitful. But then through the open French doors into the kitchen I noticed the sink was empty of dishes, and the cereal we'd needed was on the counter. So he'd been shopping. Which meant that he would make dinner, holding up his end of the bargain we'd struck: if he was going to work only part-time while he wrote his screenplay, he had to do more than his normal quarter share of the domestic work.

"The usual," I said. "I badgered homeless kids to present themselves in a professional light."

He chuckled, and took another sip of his drink. "Well, I finished my second act," he said.

I was headed into the bedroom to change, but stopped in the doorway. "Really?" He grinned with an openness and satisfaction I hadn't seen in him in a long while.

"That's great," I said. "Congratulations."

"It's just a draft. But thanks."

He followed me into the bedroom and watched me start taking off my work clothes. He'd made the bed as well, and put away the laundry. For once, there was nothing to be disappointed in. Which left me with just the feeling of the disappointment itself. I tried to let go of it as I looked for my shorts and sneakers, to shuffle the weight of it off, the semi-constant low-grade suspicion that he was inadequate. That he didn't have enough energy. That I had to provide it for both of us. That I would resent this no matter what else he did, or how well he managed his insulin.

He was standing by the door, smiling, as if his good cheer were nothing unusual. He hadn't gotten his hair cut in a while and it hung down over his forehead, his dark curls set off by his pale, nearly unblemished skin. His boyishness had always been part of his allure. He was thirty-one, two years older than I was, but could pass for twenty-five. The most handsome man I'd been with. And the most ardent. At the beginning. Which had made a difference—his confidence. *I want you.* He'd been able to say that, clearly and aloud, before he knew what my response would be. Standing on the back porch of a triple-decker in Somerville, in frigid air, while the party carried on inside behind fogged windows. He'd put his red plastic cup down before saying it, his arms at his sides, unguarded, looking right at me. I'd had no time to think. When he leaned forward, I took the kiss, and gave it back. I wasn't interested in being seduced. I was too wary for such credulity. But Paul had seduced me.

That was three years ago, back east, when I was still getting my master's, and he was working at the Brattle, spending his mornings on his short film. We'd come out here to San Francisco as much to leave the place we'd both grown up as anything else. We'd found an affordable apartment far from downtown, and jobs that covered our rent, groceries, and student loans. For the first couple of years this had seemed like its own achievement, requiring nothing more. Paul's college friends Laura and Kyle came for long weekends from Boulder, and we visited them in the summer, exploring parts of the country we had never seen. For our second Thanksgiving, I persuaded my mother, Michael, and Alec to fly across the country and I produced the full meal from our galley kitchen, after which the place seemed more like a home.

When Paul drank more than a diabetic should or we argued about petty domestic things, I would employ a kind of preemptive nostalgia, filing the episodes away under the heading *A Couple's Early Years*. This generous retrospective of the present leaped ahead to forgive our moments of anger and doubt, and the occasional day when the frustration and recriminations between us became grinding. It helped alleviate my sense of having been duped into believing Paul would be the person to deliver me from my family, rather than imitate it. And really it was okay, and most often better than that, being the object of his desire, sensing he would never leave me. That we were safe.

In summer, when there was more daylight, I used the track in the park, at the old polo grounds with their crumbling bleachers and weedy track. There, at least, I had a discrete lane and a clear shot. But in winter, I settled for a dead-end street nearby with barely any traffic. It would have been simpler to take up distance running, but I'd never got in the habit, or felt the satisfaction of it. I ran to move as fast as I could, to the point of no more speed to give, not just once at the end of a long run, but over and over in a rhythm: sprint, release, jog back to the line; sprint, release, jog, until my legs gave out and my chest hurt. I'd been timing myself for too long to give up the stopwatch, but I didn't run to hit a number anymore, it just let me know how hard I could still press. There was no audience. I didn't do meets. I wasn't even running against my own best time, though I could have.

I kept it brief, knowing Paul was cooking, bursting hard and early on hundred-yard dashes, and running back to the line faster than my usual recovery speed. I quickened my pace the more tired I got, holding up only for the occasional passing car, or people crossing the street on their way home, a few of whom were used to me now and nodded or waved. The lamps high up the electric

163

poles lit the street in a yellow brightness, no trees to block their glare, just the two rows of parked cars, the wide sidewalks, the barely indented strips of curb in front of the garage doors with the No Parking signs, and the shaded windows above—a couple of blocks of the Outer Sunset never more than Sunday quiet.

Eventually, my muscles gave out, and I got to that deep, whole-body fatigue that made the pain worth it.

These were the moments of the week when my mind was clearest. When the internal nagging stopped, I noticed the air and the sound of the city, and things became simple again.

I wasn't happy. This much came as no great revelation. But my unhappiness had become mired in a routine that obscured the obvious choice, which I kept trying to avoid. I had to quit my job. Kids like Jasper didn't get work because we hit the ratio, as my boss called it, of clients to applications, like hitting a monthly sales figure, all to ensure the state would renew our contract. If they found jobs it was because, mostly without our help, they managed not to feel so shitty about themselves for long enough to actually want a life. And that's what I wanted to be a part of. Their feeling better.

San Francisco was lousy with therapists and social workers, but if I registered with Medi-Cal, and got the agency to give me some of their overflow of counseling referrals, I'd have as many people as I was willing to take, albeit for a pittance. I could make it on my own, if I took on enough clients. And if Paul went back to working full-time.

The fog off the ocean cloaked the lights only a few blocks ahead as I began walking home, and soon encompassed me in a cool drizzle. When I got upstairs, I went straight into the shower, and stayed under the hot water awhile.

Paul had made a vegetable stir-fry with peanut sauce, and, in a rare flourish, broiled chicken to go with it. I asked him about his good day, about how much revision he thought the new act would require, and how he wanted to move forward from here, listening to him think it out aloud, which I knew he found useful, and seemed tonight to even enjoy. I wished he would share these things more with his friends, but he'd always been hesitant about it, and counted on me as a sounding board more than anyone else. I listened for a good while, glad to sense his mood lifting.

At some point, after a pause, I mentioned what I'd been thinking about on my run.

The first thing he said was "When?"

Before I could answer, the phone rang in the living room. Our eyes met, but neither of us moved. We remained like that for a moment, as the phone rang a second and then a third time, frozen in another little episode of our ongoing struggle to control the disposition of each other's bodies. The daily tussle of two people in a small space, opening and closing doors, navigating a kitchen and bathroom, nudging and reaching over and gently pushing, often with affection but often too with this petty resistance.

After the third ring, Paul was the one who stood, and walked into the other room. He told whoever it was to hold on. Then he returned to the kitchen, took his seat opposite me, and, picking up his knife and fork with great deliberation, said, "Michael."

"I told you about her—Bethany—from the record store, the Aphex Twin fan, we had the drink at the Middle East last week, and I called her the next day and we had pizza that night in Kenmore? I told you about it, that we were together for five hours and she told me everything, about just getting out of the hospital, and her parents not wanting to talk to her, but that her mother was sick and she needed to go back to Cleveland to see her, remember?

"It was like we were in a relationship right away, she trusted me that much, and she said she thought she might love me, and I told her all about Dad and Caleigh, and she said she wished I could come to Cleveland with her, but that her parents think everyone she's met in Boston is part of the problem, and that she just needs to go back and get into school there. But then after that, after I talked to you, I've seen her every day since then, except Tuesday—I had a temp gig. And she told me she wasn't going to be leaving right away, which was obviously a huge relief, because she needed to get her rent money together first, so I felt relieved, like we weren't racing toward some kind of deadline.

"Because at that point we still hadn't really said anything official to each other, and we hadn't slept together, because I didn't want to pressure her, she's obviously in a transitional state. And I didn't want to bring her back to Ben's anyway, because then he'd ask questions about her, and I just didn't want to deal with all that. But I did take her home on the T to Allston not last night but the night before. With no ulterior motive. But we were still talking when we got there, and she asked me up to her place, and I did actually end up spending the night, not in her bed, on the floor, on her roommate's air mattress, and obviously I didn't sleep, but around dawn, she did reach out and take my hand, and we actually did end up getting together that night. Or that morning. Which, I didn't even know if that would happen, because she's been mostly with women, but she said I was different, and that she was so glad we'd met, that no one had ever listened to her the way I did, and we went out afterwards for bagels, and spent the rest of the morning together until I went home to get meds. Which was yesterday.

"And then we were supposed to get together tonight in Central Square at seven o'clock, and I called her to confirm but there was no answer. Not for hours. And when I finally got her roommate, her roommate said she was out and she didn't know where she was. Which is when I tried you at work. But anyway, obviously I just went to where we'd agreed to meet, and I waited two and a half hours figuring she was just late, but she never showed up, she just didn't show up. And when I call her roommate's now I get the answering machine—I've left three messages already—but I don't have any other number for her, so I'm thinking of going over there now, but it's close to midnight, and by the time I walk to the T, get over there, and figure out what's going on, I'd miss the last train back, but I don't know what else to do. What should I do?"

Across the street, a young couple with a fancy stroller passed under the streetlight, returning home from dinner at one of the places up on Irving, and it struck me our mother would never have been out this late with a baby.

"You just have to give her space," I said. "You shouldn't go over there now. She probably just needs a day off. You should go to bed."

"I can't go to bed, something's happened. She's been late before, but she's always showed up, and now nothing, which means either she's in some kind of danger, or—and I don't even want to think about this—she's decided to end everything between us, maybe because of something I said that I didn't realize offended her, or she was just lying to me and doesn't care at all, which I just couldn't stand, it would just be a nightmare, so it's not as if I can sleep, but I just don't know if I should go over there now, or if that could make things worse and I should just white-knuckle it until the morning. That's what I'm trying to decide."

"I just said to you that you shouldn't go over there."

"But I can't decide if I should or not."

I could hear Paul rinsing his plate in the sink. He hadn't waited for me, and I didn't blame him.

"Michael."

"What?"

"This isn't about her."

"What do you mean?"

"We've talked about it. The panic, it isn't about her."

"That may be—I'm not opposed to that thesis—but she's the only solution to it, there's no other solution."

"You met her a week ago."

"Yeah. What difference does that make? I'm as in love with her as I've ever been with anybody."

"That's absurd, and you know it is."

"Right, then. Well. I thought at least you'd empathize—being abandoned like that."

"You haven't been *abandoned*. She flaked on one date. She just got out of a psych ward, you slept together for the first time last night, and what is she? Nineteen? And you're thirty-one—"

"Twenty, she turned twenty last month."

I closed my eyes, and saw him there in his room at Ben's, his heart racing like a bird's. He would have already talked to Caleigh about all this for a couple of hours at least, but that wasn't enough. As soon as he'd gotten off the phone with her, he'd dialed my number.

Nothing I could say would help. It wasn't for my advice that he'd called, no matter what he told himself. Tomorrow my mother would phone and ask if I'd spoken to him, and tell me that she was worried about him, about this Bethany woman, and how upset he seemed, as if it were a new and wholly discrete problem. And after that Alec and I would compare notes, gauging together how serious the episode was, to no more fruitful an end than measuring it against our own tolerance for more of the same.

"And she doesn't care about my age anyway, she said so, she said that I understood her better than anyone she'd ever met, and that I listened to her more than anyone. And I don't have any problem with her being twenty. If we really understand each other, none of that matters. We could move in together while she's finishing school, and I can help her with her work, and with dealing with her parents. I think that's the plan, we haven't talked about it fully, but I think she's open to that, and at this point I need that to happen, I can't wait any longer, which maybe it's harder for you to get, being with Paul, but Bethany is perfect—I know you think that isn't possible—and I don't mean she's a perfect human being, but when am I going to meet someone that much younger than me who's willing to share their life with me, and reads James Baldwin? Who isn't Caleigh. She said she wants me to help her with her thesis, and then help her get into grad school. But if something's happened now, or her roommate or someone else—her parents maybe—are starting to talk to her about me, and maybe turn her against me, I have to talk to her, it's the only way. I guess if I miss the last train, I could take a taxi home, I could definitely take a taxi. But you think I shouldn't. That I should just wait?"

My food would be cold by now, but I wasn't hungry anymore. In fact, I didn't feel much of anything but the ache in my thighs from the sprints. The straining to be there for him, to be as close as I could to sitting next to him on the edge of his bed, hooking myself into each phrase and turn of his worry—it gave out eventually, as it always did, into blankness.

Most often, I just started saying, "Uh-huh," agreeing with him however tendentious he got, and after a while I could beg off, having sympathized, if only by ceasing to argue. But tonight he was threatening to leave his room at midnight in a panic, which would only get worse when he reached her empty apartment or her roommate asked him to leave. He couldn't protect himself from the impulse, even if he glimpsed its desperation. And so the only thing to do was wait it out, to stay on the phone talking about Bethany, asking him more about their week together, hearing if not listening once more to his dread fantasies of why she hadn't appeared. Which is what I did.

Long after I had tired of it, so did Michael. Not enough that he wanted to stop talking about her, but a bit. Enough to drain the energy he would have needed to get out of the house.

"I guess I could just wait and try calling her again in the morning," he said, finally.

I told him that sounded like a good idea, and that I hoped he would get some sleep.

"Trouble in paradise?"

Paul stood with his back to me at the sink, doing the dishes. When next we squabbled, he might bring this up, his having cooked and cleaned. He was banking domestic credit.

His question was snide, though not as mean as it sounded. He liked Michael. He enjoyed his company. He just thought that I indulged him. His own sister he spoke to once every three or four months. She had problems, but for whatever reason, they weren't his. Likewise his parents, who were divorced and single. His family seemed, more than anything, incurious about one another. As if they'd known one another well in the past but had moved on now and resented, without saying as much, the need to keep up. It wasn't so terribly unusual. Or, for that matter, pathological. I just simply couldn't imagine it. Having the option to disattend.

"He was pretty worked up," I said. In the cupboard, I found a recycled takeout container and put what was left of my dinner in it for lunch the next day. "Sorry about the meal."

"No worries."

"What I was saying before—"

"You want me to work full-time again."

He said it flatly, without anger or apparent consent. He knew as well as I did that his working more was the only way I could afford to attempt my own practice. At least at the beginning. He'd known it all along. We had discussed it.

"I don't mean next week," I said.

He'd begun to sweep the kitchen floor. I wished he'd just fight me in the open, rather than going quiet, resentment staying crouched in his throat, waiting but never pouncing. But I did it, too. Always cautious, lest an argument break out that we couldn't control.

Later, he took his book into the bedroom and lay down to read. He didn't look up from the page as I came in and undressed. But when I sat on the edge of the bed and put a hand flat on his chest, in peace, he set the book aside and rested his hand on top of mine.

"We can talk about it, can't we? It doesn't have to be right away."

He nodded, passing a hand idly through my hair. This is what I had at the end of the day that Michael and Alec didn't. A person.

I brushed my hand across his stomach until my fingers were just under the button of his jeans.

"I thought you'd already gotten your exercise for the day," he said, his eyes narrowing.

We never used to dig at each other like this on the verge of sex, poking at each other's desire. But I did it now, too, when he approached me. I tested his motivation. It was the means we'd invented to argue over our doubts without mentioning them. We kept making each other prove we wanted each other. Right at the moment of openness, when you didn't want to have to prove anything.

"What's that's supposed to mean?" I said, withdrawing my hand. The most effective response to the smallness of the testing

171

was to shame the other for doing it. If he felt momentarily guilty, he'd go soft again, at least enough to get us started. And once we'd begun, his diffidence would fall away, and I could forget awhile, under the cover of his wanting.

"Nothing," he said, pulling me by the shoulders down toward him. On his tongue, I could taste the dinner I hadn't finished, and suddenly I was starving.

Alec

I stepped off the train at Thirty-fourth Street before the doors were even fully open and dashed for the stairs, reaching the turnstile ahead of the crowd and yanking my suitcase up over the bar as I went. Then I was off, dodging and weaving through the choke of befuddled tourists and the loiterers standing by for Jersey Transit, across the shitty low-ceilinged concourse lined with newsstands and juice shops, pleased with my skill at avoiding collisions by fractions of an inch as I dipped and swung through the on-comers, then took the stairs two at a time up to the gates for Amtrak. There, a giant herd milled under the big board, sheep to the holiday slaughter, waiting to be told which stairway to mass at. My track hadn't posted yet. I pushed my way through, and then down the far staircase, where, by using the lower-level entrances to the tracks, I could circumvent the crush. I'd made it. I wouldn't be without a seat. The rush and relief together left me almost high.

Thirty seconds after the board flapped my track number, I was boarding the train, even as the passengers from DC were still getting off. I grabbed a window on the right side for a view of the water, and put my computer bag on the aisle seat to dissuade anyone from joining me. The herd was staggering in now, filling the empty doubles.

Several minutes later, when the train finally jerked forward, I felt the secret glee of having avoided a seatmate. Then the car door slid open and a straggler, a thirty-something white guy in khakis and a ski jacket, spotted the empty space, and asked if it was free. If I lied, the woman across the aisle would clock my deception no later than 125th Street. I pulled my computer bag onto my lap and, turning to the window, stared past my reflection at the black walls of the tunnel.

As we rolled slowly through the darkness, the energy of hustling to make the train began to subside, letting the events of the day seep back in. The end of the apartment hunt. In the last two weeks, I'd seen nineteen places—the dregs of December—one more lightless and cramped than the next. In desperation, I'd switched to a new broker two days before I had to leave the city. She had shown me another round of anonymous, immiserating rentals, and then without warning or fanfare escorted me onto a chrome-plated elevator and then into a condo with a fully adult bedroom, a dishwasher, and floor-to-ceiling windows facing south across Nineteenth Street. It was like waking from a nightmare to discover I hadn't in fact been sentenced to life in a dungeon. Here was a place I could entertain people, friends, colleagues, even dates. They would see the clean, polished floors, the newish appliances, the generous portion of sky, and they would relax in the safety all this implied. New York apartments either reminded you that you lived in one of the most crowded places on earth or allowed you to forget it.

But she had baited me, this new broker. The place wasn't just slightly out of my price range, it was five hundred dollars a month north of it—plus the higher broker fee. I was in the miraculously clean bathroom—white down into the grouting—

174

stalling for time by pretending to evaluate the fixtures when I heard the front door open. It was another agent. He had two men with him, and he was answering their questions about the building's management. I didn't need to see them. Their voices were enough. I glimpsed right away what would happen. How they would move in here with their curated furniture, their dachshund, their two incomes, their plans for children and a larger place in a few years, erasing me with their domestic establishment like a town car swiping a pedestrian at a crosswalk and gliding on through the light. The elect, as Michael called them. The comfortably coupled.

But this didn't have to be. I could push back. I'd find extra freelance work, take sandwiches to the office, lengthen the schedule of my student loans, pay off less each month on my credit card, buy cheaper groceries, shop discerningly at Banana Republic sales. True, I did most of these things already. But I could do them with more discipline.

I was leaving for Christmas in four hours. When I returned, even the worst of the rentals for January 1 would be gone. I'd be moving my stuff into storage and sleeping on friends' couches.

I got myself out of that bathroom, and, without so much as a glimpse of my competitors, led my broker into the hall and told her that I'd take it. She smiled knowingly, and hurried me back to her office. By the time I'd filled out the application and frozen the listing with a deposit, I was sure I'd miss the train.

Now, passing over the Bronx River in the dusk, all I could think was how impulsive and ruinous my grabbing had been. How I'd panicked, and sunk the money I'd saved for first and last month's rent on a place I couldn't afford. It wasn't until a half hour after Stamford and half of one of the Klonopins Michael had given me that I could bring myself to start the reading I'd planned to get through. Once I started, though, I didn't stop. I zipped through one campaign finance filing after the next, highlighting, circling, typing a stream of notes, going at it like the research was due in hours, not days.

As we reached New London, I finished marking up the pile and had nothing left to do but stare again out the window. The lines for the ferry to Orient Point filled the lot and trailed back onto the other side of the tracks, the travelers in their idling cars reading newspapers, smoking out of the slits of open windows, some napping, others appeasing their children. Above their heads, across the estuary, the naval base was lit from waterline to smoke-stack, a sleek gray sub moored to its giant dock. Off the coast a nearly full moon was rising. My mother would be telling whoever had already arrived to come and see.

As we crept out of the station, I noticed that the woman across the aisle was gone, along with several others nearby, leaving a number of empty seats. I glanced sidelong at the man next to me, thinking maybe he'd move now. But he was reading his book and seemed unaware. There wasn't much to pick out in the dark. Just the sporadic lights of little houses along the water and the occasional cluster of low-slung shops at the railroad crossings of eastern Connecticut and the beginnings of Rhode Island.

When I leaned my chair back I could see my seatmate's profile reflected in the glass. He was average-looking for a holiday re-turnee to the confines of the Northeast, not unhandsome, though carrying a tad extra weight in his face, for which the light beard was maybe a cover, and wearing a slightly dated pair of wire-rimmed glasses—the rims too thick—but he was definitely male and under forty.

Now that I thought back to it, before he took the seat, before he'd even asked if it was free, he had appraised me for an instant. Anyone would, checking for insanity before committing to a journey next to a stranger. But his face had brightened, and he had given me a little nod, which might have been merely relief at the fact that I wasn't visibly crazy, but which it now occurred to me might have been something happier.

Where was the wife? Where was the girlfriend? There were no children. Suddenly, I was hard. Absurd, but involuntary.

He'd cruised me, that's what he'd done, he'd cruised me but I hadn't given him the chance to follow up because I'd been in such a state, and then was working like a fiend. To strike up a conversation now, from nothing, would be awkward. It would lead to facts, which could only get in the way.

I clasped my hands behind my head and stretched my legs. I hadn't intended for my shirt and sweater to ride up off my jeans and expose an inch of my abdomen, but the mild shamelessness of it quickened my pulse (I boasted no six-pack but in this posture appeared reasonably skinny, and was, after all, younger). With my face to the window I could gaze at him with zero risk of being caught in a mistake.

And that's what I did for the next few minutes, occasionally sensing the forced warm air of the train car on my strip of bare flesh. He shifted several times in his seat, crossing and uncrossing his legs, transferring his book from one hand to the other, but in his reflection, at least, I detected no spying in my direction, his attention absorbed by his sci-fi novel. Still cloaked in the immunity of facing away from him, I slouched further in my chair, and, feeling my blood move faster through my chest, reached into my pants to adjust myself. Briefly, of course, with all the crude nonchalance of the frat boy I wasn't, but still a second or two longer than strictly necessary.

And there it was—the darting, avid glance, belying instantly any illusion of indifference. Followed quickly by an exploratory quarter-turn of his head to establish the coordinates of my own head and eyes. And then, most telling of all, imagining me to be ignorant of his inspection as I continued to peer out the window, he blatantly checked me out, head to foot, and rested his stare on the waist of my jeans. My breathing grew shallow, the drug of danger loosed into my veins. He had to see the breathing, the way my stomach and chest rose and fell. There was someone in the seat ahead and behind, making our privacy exquisitely tenuous. Without giving him any sign of acknowledgment, I slid my hand back into my pants and held my hard-on in my fist for several seconds before raising my hand back up again behind my head. That's when he finally looked up into the window and saw my reflection.

Immediately I closed my eyes, blood racing in my head, trying to sense if it was too late, if my ruse of slovenliness and inattention might still be viable. He wasn't *that* cute, after all. I'd guessed right, but had picked a soft target. Which made me pathetic in the eyes of cuter guys—the ones who mattered in the end. This was a flawed and vicious logic, I knew, but I had subscribed to it for so long now that it had a back door past self-forgiveness straight to conviction. I could override my own sneering judgment and keep going—somehow I always did—but the judgment never gave back the share of giddiness and pleasure that it stole. Self-loathing was stingy that way. It kept what it took. But it didn't matter now. The danger had me in its thrall. The ride had begun.

I slid my hand into my pants a third time and held it there. Our eyes met for an instant on the glass, though it was hard to read his expression in the dim and shifting image. If I turned and looked at him now any vestige of intrigue would vanish. I wasn't about to proceed to an Amtrak bathroom. We needed to string this out a bit. So I kept my head averted, and watched him gape as I gripped myself and pressed my wrist against the band of my jeans, exposing just the tip of my cock, keeping alive the fantasy that I was drowsily stretching. The window was high and narrow, cutting his reflection off at the chest, but the downward twisting motion of his shoulder told me that he too was touching himself. Game on. I pressed my wrist harder against my jeans, and another bump of adrenaline heated my face. The passengers ahead and behind were too close for either of us to whisper a thing.

When finally I did turn toward him, I avoided his eyes, staring instead at his hand in his pants. I could have been a boy again in England, in the showers at Finton Hall, stealing a glimpse of the upper-form rugby players, terrified I'd be caught, such was the liquidity of time in the press of the moment. Until we acknowledged each other, he could be anyone at all to me.

He leaned into the aisle, checking for passengers wobbling back to their seats from the café car. Seeing none, he slid his right hand onto my thigh. I closed my eyes again for a second and sank further into my seat.

I loved men. Obviously. But it wasn't just sex. To know for certain, as I did right now, that a man was paying attention to me, to me and no one else—what more was there to want than that? To matter, and know that you mattered.

"Providence, ladies and gentlemen, Providence!"

We jerked our hands out of our pants, leaning away from each other, and the conductor lurched past. I hadn't even noticed the lights of the city. We were already approaching the station. The older woman in front of us got up and began struggling with her bag in the rack.

"Here, let me," the guy whose face I still hadn't really taken in said, leaping up to help her.

"Oh, thank you," she said. "Grandchildren! So many presents!"

The train slowed beside the platform, and the car woke from its slumber. People gathered luggage, others got up to stretch. Someone began listening to music on a headset. I took a sheaf of papers from my bag and pretended to read.

I kept up the pretense all the way out of Providence and into the darkened scrubland of southeastern Mass., as if I'd hallucinated the last twenty minutes, aware that the guy was doing the same, clutching his open novel but failing to turn the page. We'd slipped across the line but couldn't get back over it now without one of us declaring himself.

At last, the conductor came on the loudspeaker and announced Route 128.

"This is me," the guy said, in a quiet, controlled voice. "You?"

"Yeah," I said, and just like that we were back in the spell of the hunt, my derision for his middling looks once more no match for the thrill.

At the station, I followed him off the train, staying three or so yards behind. Up the steps onto the covered bridge. Across the tracks, down into the parking lot. Then out past the other cars to one of the back rows, where he clicked open the doors of a Mazda sedan, and lifted his suitcase into the trunk before taking a seat behind the wheel. I put my bag in the backseat. Willing my hand not to shake, I opened the passenger-side door, and got in. He'd started the car and turned on the heat.

"I'm Gary," he said.

"Alec," I said.

And with that he removed his glasses, leaned over the emergency break, and, unzipping my jeans, took my dick in his mouth. My head rocked backward against the seat and then quickly forward. He had strands of gray at his temples and the beginnings of a bald spot. I looked away to my left. Across the parking lot families milled at the platform, the disembarking travelers finding their rides in the crosshatch of headlights. I closed my eyes and lasted only a minute longer. He swallowed. I zipped my jeans, opened the door, and, grabbing my suitcase from the back, strode toward the station house, searching for the pay phone. By the time my mother answered, the anesthesia was almost complete.

Margaret

Spotting me on the bench by the library entrance, my colleague Suzanne breezes over in her miniskirt, rummaging in her bag for a cigarette. She's wearing red lipstick and too little for the weather. A femme fatale in middle age.

"Filthy me," she exclaims as she lights a Winston, waving her hand to disperse the smoke, her clutch of silver bracelets jangling. She coils one bare leg around the other, tucking her foot hard against her calf, then, arching her spine, exhales up and away into the gathering dusk. "And so it ends," she says with gruff languor, as though we had just struck the set of a Broadway musical, rather than come to the end of a workweek.

She's an unlikely librarian, her flair wasted, if not resented, by everyone but the high school boys and their fathers. Early on, she decided that I was to be her ally against the forces of boredom and small-mindedness. I was too tired to resist. She was one of the first new friends I made after John died, she and my neighbor Dorothy, and I'm still thankful for them both. Suzanne and I are by now the two stalwarts of the Walcott town library, the aging single lady and the widow.

She is always quick to note the disproportionate enthusiasm

of the male trustees for our younger female coworkers, and about that she has a point. It's not what men say or do to you. It's what they say and do for other women, and not you. The little questions and compliments, the daily recognitions. It took me a while to understand the subtlety of it, the way invisibility works at my age. I suppose it shouldn't have surprised me that couples who'd known John and me together didn't call as often after he died, but it did. I thought it was owing to the manner of his death at first, the awkwardness of the subject, but really they were just more comfortable with other married pairs.

The job's been good for me that way—meeting new people for whom I'm simply a colleague, nothing more complicated than that.

"Come to Kanty's with me," she says. "You never come."

It's the restaurant where she entertains the bartender on Friday evenings, and drinks more wine than she should before driving home. Luckily, I've never had a taste for alcohol in any quantity, or else I might have been tempted by it.

I tell her I'm waiting to be picked up. "Celia and Alec came back early this year—for my birthday."

She turns, stomps her high heel in mock indignation, then lights into me for giving her no notice. "I would have had a cake and a card! What is it with you? You're getting a cake on Monday, be sure of it."

"Don't be silly," I say, recognizing my car as it enters the parking lot.

"No," she says. "It's no use protesting. You will be feted whether you like it or not."

It's Celia who's come. I'd expected one of the boys. She flew in only this afternoon. As soon as I close the door and wave goodbye to Suzanne, Celia puts the car back in gear and we're off, no chance for a quick half-hug over the emergency brake now that she's got her eyes on the road.

"Sorry if I'm late," she says. "Michael didn't remember what time we were supposed to get you."

"Oh, don't worry. How was the flight? Is Paul with Michael at the house?"

"No. He'll be here in a few days."

"I thought the two of you were flying together."

"Well, it turns out we didn't."

I'm not supposed to ask about these things. I never was.

She looks older than a year ago, more serious still. She's cut her hair short, and as usual wears no jewelry or makeup. Not that I do myself much, or ever encouraged her to, but the lack of it is somehow more severe on her. I sometimes wonder if she's trying to avoid the attention she gets from men. But if I said such a thing she would roll her eyes and sigh. They all sigh, my children. It's their most frequent response to me.

She asks me how work was. I tell her I'm just glad to be finished through the holiday. "I wish you could stay for longer," I say.

"I told you, it was hard to find someone to cover me even for this long."

These people she sees have such problems that I worry about her, that all their woe comes to rest on her shoulders. But she gets impatient with me if I mention it over the phone. She could have done any number of other things, but I've never pretended to give her professional advice. Not like her father would have. And she's never asked for it.

In spring and fall these back roads to the house are full of color and light, but at this time of year the ground is muddy or snow-covered, and shrouded now in the early dark. In January, it will be twelve years that I've been doing this drive. It's where I cried in the beginning—in the car. I suppose because I knew the crying could last only so long, that I'd be arriving home soon and would have to account for myself to Alec and Celia. That was

184

back when I was forgetting everything—keys, bills, what to get at the grocery store. And much of what happened too, apparently, because those years are still a blur to me.

Everyone said not to make any big decisions right away. Continuity, that's what the children needed. You might regret a rash move. Which I understood. But there was the mortgage, and the town taxes, and the credit card bills we'd run up during his illness. That Walcott would hire me twenty years after I'd last worked in a library was a miracle. Still, we'd bought the house on John's salary, not mine. My mother had left my sister and me a small bequest, and Penny helped out now and then. But I was often at the end of my tether, not sure if I had enough in the bank to write another check. And Celia was a good organizer, she always has been. She'd sort through bills and call the credit card people if I'd fallen behind, arranging for smaller payments. She seemed to take to it naturally, without my asking her. But it was lousy of me, I'm sure, relying on her like that. I know now that she resented it, having to take care of me when we were all still reeling. I know that isn't why she went to California, but she is the only one of them who's gone so far.

"You saw Michael, then," I say. "How did he seem to you?"

"I didn't know he had a beard."

"Yes. I'm not sure it suits him."

"He seemed okay. Not worse."

"Still no word from Bethany."

"Yeah, I'm aware of that."

"It's such a pity about Caleigh."

"Mom, she's a lesbian. And that was years ago."

"I'm just saying. They still like each other so much."

I think everyone's a bit bisexual and it seems a pity to be strict about it if people get along. But I'm sure that's naive. They're all very sophisticated, my children, and quick to point out when I'm not.

"Did you see Mercury last night?" I ask. "It was such a clear sky here, and it was so bright. It's closer to Earth than it's been in thirty years, we should go out and look later, you probably don't see it as well from the city. We're supposed to get snow this evening but then it's supposed to clear up. I was hoping we'd get out to the Allens on the twenty-seventh, they've invited all of us, and I know they'd like to see you. Drew's back—I told you he's engaged, didn't I? They met in Peru on some kind of hiking expedition. Samantha's her name. It's all quite sudden, I think, but in any case, she'll be there, too. You'd like to come, wouldn't you?"

"Come where?"

"To the Allens'."

"Maybe. I'll have to see."

Whenever she and Alec come home, no sooner do they get in the house than they're on the phone making plans to be elsewhere, with friends. It's been like that for years. There's no use complaining, but then, they're here so infrequently.

"Well, I know they'd like to see you."

"What day is that? Our appointment is on Tuesday."

"You didn't tell me that."

"I told you I was going to make an appointment, and that's when he could do it."

"Well, I'd have liked to have known."

She accelerates into the turn onto Garnet, tilting me toward the door.

"I didn't think we had a big schedule," she says.

It's Celia's idea—her professional estimation, I suppose—that the four of us should go and speak to someone together. I don't have a huge amount to say, but if it helps the three of them, I have no objection. I will go along and receive my criticism. It's just a shame it has to be straight after Christmas.

186

They've chosen the new restaurant down from the inn, and of course it's far too expensive. Eight dollars for a salad. Sixteen for pasta. I could have made a perfectly good meal at home. There was no need to be lavish. Michael has no money for this kind of thing, which means it will be all the other two, and I can't let them do that. A New Traditional Grill, it calls itself, oak banquettes gleaming under brass lights, the kitchen on display behind a glass barrier, not a stitch of fabric to absorb the diners' voices rising over the music and clatter of pans.

Trying to be heard over the din, I tell the waitress I'll have the soup, which produces a chorus of sighs.

"It's your birthday!" Alec practically shouts.

"I had a big lunch. I'll just have a bite of yours."

The waitress and I exchange a smile. She seems like a friendly young woman.

"Order an entrée," Alec instructs, "and we'll get a bottle of wine. What kind of wine do you want?"

"A bottle?" I ask.

Michael rolls his head back on his shoulders, as if praying to the heavens, which he certainly isn't.

"We'll need another minute," Celia says.

It's so good to have them all here, and I don't want to argue, but it makes no sense to order food I don't want.

"You like fish," Alec says. "Get the grouper."

Eighteen dollars. He's like his father: spending as if he has the natural right to live now as he plans to later.

"I'm fine. Maybe I'll get a dessert."

"You can't make her eat," Celia says with cool fixity.

"It's dietary martyrdom," Michael says. "It has a long pedigree."

"Don't be ridiculous. I'm just not that hungry. Let's not spoil it, let's just have our meal, can't we?"

We reapply ourselves to the menus, the moment passes, and Michael asks Alec if he thinks he's becoming identified with the white-male power structure now that he works for a national news magazine. "Purely at the level of the psychic," Michael says, as if clarifying. "I'm not saying you're a reactionary. As such."

"I'm a researcher and I edit news summaries," Alec says. "And my boss is a woman."

"Right," Michael says. "But is she a radical feminist?"

"She's a features editor. She's not radical about anything."

When the waitress circles back to us, I'm allowed my soup.

"But would you say—again, at the level of the psychic— that the life-worlds of the people you work with are constituted at least in part through an identification with the structures of wealth and power they report on?"

"I'd say they're underpaid and distracted, and most of them are political junkies."

"I'm not talking about electoral politics."

"Why? Because you think they're irrelevant?"

"I wouldn't say *irrelevant*. They're obviously central to the fantasy of nationalism—"

"I'll have the stuffed chicken," Alec says.

"I told you Alice Jolly went to Vassar with your godmother, didn't I?" I ask Alec, not certain if I remembered to or not. The three of them glance at me dumbfounded, as if braced for the outburst of some insane relative at Thanksgiving. "Alice Jolly, she's married to Arthur Jolly, the man who edits your magazine. She went to Vassar with Ursula. Didn't I tell you that?"

"What does that have to do with *anything*?" Michael says.

"I just thought it was quite a coincidence."

188

"That's precisely what it *isn't*," he says, at which point I give up.

As usual in such places, the portions are obscene. Michael's pork chop could feed a village. My soup comes in a bowl a foot wide with an extra basket of bread I neither want nor need.

Alec consumes his food with something akin to lust, devouring it in minutes. His creaturely habits haven't changed since he was a boy, though they are strained now through his more elaborate persona, which makes for a certain tension. It's as though the fever of his adolescence never burned off, but he's desperate not to show it. He wishes he were smoother, and tries hard to be. Which can make him brittle. Difficult not to think that it has something to do with his being gay. The effort to control people's impressions of him.

He was only seventeen, still a boy, when he announced it to me, and yet he did it with such seriousness and finality. When I suggested he might want to keep an open mind, that people often go through phases, he asked if I'd said the same to Michael and Celia when it became obvious they were heterosexual. Which I obviously couldn't say that I had. He seemed greatly satisfied by his rhetorical victory. I know better now than to tell him I worry about AIDS.

"So," Celia says, "just so everyone's been informed, we've got our appointment on Tuesday."

"Is it with a Lacanian?" Michael asks.

"He does family therapy," Celia says. "We're not lying on couches and being told to leave after five minutes. We're not doing theory."

"Isn't that what you studied?" I ask Celia.

"Mom, I have a degree in social work. Michael's talking about literary criticism."

"Not literary," he says. "In fact, I think we need to move away from the text, into the realm of pure affect."

"He's a psychotherapist, okay? He's going to talk to us about the dynamics that have built up over the years."

"The dynamics," I say.

"Patterns," Celia says.

"Which are a bad thing?"

"If you don't want to go," she says to me, "you don't have to."

"No, no," I say, not wanting to upset her. "I'm sure there are patterns. And no doubt they're my fault."

"Case in point," Alec says.

"What's that supposed to mean?" I ask, eliciting another roll of the eyes, as if it's too obvious to explain.

"No doubt I was a wretched parent," I say. "And burdened you all with all sorts of things I shouldn't have."

"Oh, Mom, come *on*," Michael says, "*please*."

"What?" I say. "That's what you think, isn't it?"

Their expressions go blank with patience.

"I should have sold the house and moved us somewhere that doesn't remind you all of the past. Somewhere you wanted to come back to more than twice a year."

"No, you shouldn't have," Alec says. "You like the house."

He has always been the most protective of me, in his way. It's been true since he was young. I remember walking with him when he was only five or six, holding his hand, and his looking up at me and saying very earnestly, "I would die so that you could live." It was one of those preternatural utterances children sometimes make when they first glimpse that things don't last forever. It has always stuck with me, though. He may have been a hyperactive child, and may still be stubborn and overexcitable, but his love is the simplest.

About the house, he's right. It took time, but I am comfortable there now. My first instinct was to leave. The alarm would startle me awake in our bed each morning, and I'd think: He's going to be late for work, you have to get him up. And then I'd see the unruffled covers beside me, and I would feel ill once more, as in that first moment—*John. Never again.* But you can't sustain that sort of thing. It wears you out. Celia and Alec had high school to finish. Michael needed a place to come home to. When Alec left for college—Celia had instructed him to follow her example and apply only to institutions with need-blind admissions—and before Michael dropped out, I thought again about moving, wondering if being there on my own would be too much. But there were the things I liked. The quiet street, with no house opposite, just grass and trees running down to the path along the brook, and the fireplace, which I use most evenings in fall and winter, and the old sash windows like the ones I grew up with, and two healthy pear trees in the front yard.

For the longest time, I didn't have the energy to do anything to the yard. But eventually I dug up the old beds that had gone to seed, and tilled a larger patch in the back for a garden. I cut off the lower branches of the trees that blocked out the sun, and took the evergreen bushes that had climbed up past the windowsills down to their stumps. The garden doesn't amount to anything grand—daffodils, tulips, a few rosebushes, some tomatoes and herbs. But there's satisfaction in it.

Alec, whose chicken is actually quite tasty, explains to Michael how a thirty-year mortgage works, speaking to him like a tutor incensed by the dimness of his charge. He's trying to get through to his brother that I'm still paying for the house, and will be for years, which is why, he says, Michael can't keep relying on me to pay his student loans for him.

"What business is that of yours?" Celia retorts, instinctively shielding Michael, who keeps his eyes on the table. "She can do whatever she wants to. You're obsessed with money."

I'm inclined to agree with her, but I don't say so just now, as it seems unfair to Alec.

"I had an interview this week," Michael interjects. This comes as a surprise. I've heard nothing of it. He usually tells me everything, in great detail. "It's a record distributor. They're not sure they have the money yet. She said she'd let me know soon."

"That's good," Alec says, more softly now, chastened by the news.

He gets so frustrated with Michael. They think that I don't see these things, that I'm distracted or exhausted. But I see them as clearly as when they were little, chasing each other around the octagonal house, shrieking in the yard, Alec forever wanting his brother's attention. Most all of who they are now was there then. They trace themselves no further back than adolescence because that's when they began getting their ideas. But so much of them has nothing to do with all that. They are their natures. Which they'd shout me down for saying.

For dessert, Michael is kind enough to split a berry tart with me; he leaves me most of the filling, and I leave him the crust.

When the bill arrives, I reach for it first, and am astounded by what I see. Michael and Alec had one beer each; there were three entrées, a soup, and two desserts. And yet you'd think we'd emptied the cellar and kitchen. When I dare to express my disbelief, they exhale in unison.

The trouble is that my direct deposit isn't for two more days, and my checking account's off because of Christmas. They should have just let me cook. Michael didn't even finish his pork chop. I reach into my handbag and get out my credit card, but Alec says, "You're not paying."

"Don't be silly, there's no reason for you all to do this. It's too much. Really, it is."

He's counting the bills Celia has handed him from her wallet.

From his messenger bag, Michael produces a ten, which he holds out sheepishly to his brother. Alec takes it without looking up and adds it to the count, which Celia follows from across the table. He puts the cash in his wallet and clicks a Visa down against the bill, closing the plastic folder over it and sliding it to the edge of the table. I'm still holding my card out but he ignores it. I just can't help wishing we'd gone somewhere less lavish. I appreciate their intention to treat me to something, but I'd honestly be more relaxed at home.

We wait in our own little zone of silence while the nice young waitress takes our bill to the register. A moment later she is at our shoulders again.

"So this got declined," she says. "Did you want to try another card? Cash is fine too."

"Yes, another card," I say, holding mine up to her, but Alec has already snatched the bill and tells her we'll need another minute. "Now come on," I say, "don't be ridiculous," but he's left the table, bill in hand, and is headed out the front door of the restaurant into the beginning of the snow.

"Of course," I say to the other two, "there are perfectly nice places that aren't quite so expensive as this."

Celia shoots a glance at me in a clear warning of anger. She's the only one who looks at me that way, who can wither me with my failings so easily. All I didn't protect her from is right there on the surface still, in her shiny black eyes.

"It wasn't my idea," she says. "It was Alec's."

"Did he go to get cash?" Michael asks, as if he materialized at the table seconds ago and has no idea what is transpiring.

"Yes," Celia says.

A woman at the door waiting to sit down with her family glares at us, as if our delay in paying were a purposeful goad to her. I look the other way, at a couple in their late fifties who are eating one table over with a young man in a blue blazer and a young pregnant woman who is either their daughter or daughter-in-law. By the horsey features she shares with the older woman, I'm guessing she's the daughter. I noticed the husband earlier, when we came in, consulting with the waitress over the wine list. John was no expert, but he always chose the wine, and took great care in doing it, which I appreciated, making me old-fashioned, I'm sure.

Alec takes the bill straight to the cashier's podium and disposes of it there. We gather our coats up and follow him into the parking lot.

The snowflakes are small and dry, floating like dandelion seeds over the tops of the cars. They haven't begun to stick and are barely visible on the drive home, even looking for them as I do from the backseat, gazing over the darkened public school athletic fields, where only Celia did much playing, and into the yards of the houses, and across the lawn in front of the town hall, sights I take in now as I never do when driving by myself.

It's inevitable, I suppose, that when they're here I feel guilt for having dragged them back, knowing that they'd rather be getting on with their lives apart from me and this place, and yet their presence is such a comfort, the chance to be able at least to shelter and feed them, no matter how powerless I am to help them out in the world. Even their size is comforting, how they take up so much more space than they used to, their bodies warm and full, a good in themselves, not nearly so fleeting as all their worries.

I've vacuumed the house, tidied and dusted in the hopes Michael and Alec won't be quite so affected by whatever it is in the air that bothers them. None of them seems to notice, but then they've just arrived so I suppose there's no reason they should.

It's Michael who resists the place the most, though he lives the closest and is here most often. It's been true since we first moved here.

From the kitchen, I hear Alec sneeze, followed by the tap and release of Michael opening a bottle of beer. Celia's bag knocks against the spindles as she climbs the staircase.

It's only when they return and I see these rooms through their eyes that I realize how little of the inside I've changed. I did strip off the dried-grass wallpaper in the study and paint over the dining room's drab green walls with a few coats of solid white, but most everything else I've left as it was: a watercolor landscape we were given as a wedding gift still hangs over the couch; the side tables I found decades ago at a stall in Chelsea sit on either side of it, supporting the fluted-glass lamps my parents gave us for our wedding, and which we had in our living room in Samoset. When they're not around I see right through these objects, back to when the five of us were all together.

It's late already, but if I go straight up for my bath, I'll miss the chance to sit with them a little longer, so I fold the paper to the crossword and take a seat by the empty fireplace, waiting for them to settle.

Celia

Mom wheeled on us in the kitchen, crying, *"No! No!"*

We were getting cereal. The trussed turkey sat pale and bulbous on the counter behind her.

"What's the matter?" I asked.

"An *onion!* I forgot to get an *onion!*"

Michael's chest and shoulders crumpled forward in relief at the insignificance of the cause for this year's Christmas-morning panic.

"We'll get one," I said.

"Where, for heaven's sake!"

"The convenience store," I said. "I'll go after breakfast."

"But the *stuffing!*" she said. "The *stuffing!*"

"It's just an *onion,*" Michael pleaded, "it doesn't *matter.*"

"Of course it matters!" she shouted, slapping her thigh.

"I thought we had some," Alec said through the white surgical mask that he wore over his mouth and nose to protect himself from the atmosphere of the house. He pointed under the table, where a red mesh bag of sweet onions lay at the bottom of a terracotta planter beside the birdseed.

"Ah!" Mom called out. "Ah! Thank goodness! When did I get

these? How silly." She bent down, grabbed the bag, and reached for a pair of scissors to slash it open.

"Jesus," Michael said, "that took a week off my life."

"Please, Michael, stop *exaggerating,*" Mom said.

I carried my cereal bowl into the dining room. Alec, still in his bathrobe, had dashed ahead of me and already had the A section spread on the table in front of him. He lifted the beveled cone of his mask off his face in order to feed, leaving it resting on his forehead like a stunted horn. Paul's footsteps padded above the ceiling. He'd gotten in the previous night and was up in my room getting dressed. The jet lag and mis-timed meals would throw off his blood sugar. He needed to eat soon.

"Is something the matter?" Aunt Penny said, appearing in the doorway. She had on her black wool pants and black turtleneck and black cardigan and gray shawl.

"No," Alec said without looking up from the paper. "Everything's fine."

She put on her reading glasses and leaned in to examine the thermostat. "It's arctic in here," she said. "I don't know how your mother survives—I have to turn it up." She was acclimated to her New York apartment where the radiators ran so hot she had to keep windows open in January. She arrived each year with a suitcase full of woolens, girded for battle over the heat.

"Aren't the two of *you* cold?" she asked.

"Not really," I said.

"Christ on a bike!" Michael exclaimed, entering the dining room with a mug of coffee and a palm full of pills. "Where did that come from?"

A tabby cat was rubbing its flank against the front radiator.

"Mom," Alec said, lowering his mask over his mouth and nose, "there's a cat in here."

"It's Nelly!" Mom said from the kitchen. "I let her in this

morning. She's Dorothy's cat from next door, she's perfectly sweet."

Aunt Penny leaned down and began petting the creature. "She just wants to get warm like the rest of us, don't you, kitty?"

"You're *eating*?" Mom exclaimed, looking in on us in alarm. "What about the stockings?"

"Mom," Michael said, "I'm trying to be an adult."

"Oh, come on," Mom said, in a sweet voice now. "I was up till midnight with them."

There had been no interruption in the doing of stockings. We had done them every year of our lives. When the old felt tore, Mom sewed it back up again.

"Yes, we should do the stockings," Aunt Penny agreed.

And so the three of us sat in a row on the couch in the living room and were handed our stuffed red stockings. In each of them were pencils, miniature bars of soap, Kit Kats, lip balm, mints, etc. Deodorant for Michael, a pair of earrings for me, dark chocolate for Alec, and always a clementine in the toe. Mom went into the closet in the other room and got us shoe boxes to put our little presents in. We thanked her for each item as we opened it. She looked on, smiling, saying they were nothing much, just things we might use, or that she knew we liked.

"Oh, there you are," Aunt Penny said when Paul entered the living room, sleepy-eyed in his button-down, V-neck sweater, and corduroys, grinning at the sight of the three of us lined up like toddlers.

We had been set to fly together. But the night before, he had changed his mind. He wanted the two days to write, he said. An unimpeachable excuse, given that I was asking him to sacrifice far more time than that so I could leave my job. Impossible to argue with. But also a dare. Because was I really supposed to believe that his suddenly holding back on coming to be with my family had nothing at all to do with my telling him ten days ago that I was pregnant? Nothing to do with the fact that he'd barely said a word about it since? But it was late, and I was packing—I didn't want to take the dare and open everything up hours before I left.

At least now he was here more willingly. I could tell that much from his relaxed expression, the kind he had after a productive day at the desk, his baseline tension alleviated for an evening. He'd had his two days to himself. He had made his point, if that's what it was. Now he was happy enough to go along with the festivities, to accept my aunt's approval of him as a handsome, marriageable prospect, to laugh with Michael and Alec, and laugh at them, settling himself at a mildly ironic distance from the goings-on. I'd wanted him to step between the others and give me a kiss good morning, but he took a seat by the window, watching us from there.

"Oh, it's *The Messiah*," Mom said, and bolted out of her chair to turn up the radio. "King's College," she added, "they're broadcasting it live." She told us this every year with the same note of excitement. Behind her, in the window, hung the Venetian Advent calendar that used to belong to one of us when we were little, and which she still opened a window of each morning until we arrived, when she said that one of us should do it, for the fun of it.

After stockings, we ate the ritual coffee cake and bacon. Then it was back to the living room for the presents from under the tree. Mom dashed to and fro as we opened gifts, basting the bird, pulling out the good plates, getting the silver from the cupboard. Aunt Penny supplied us with our annual sweaters, hats, gloves, and scarves. Alec complained that he was wheezing despite his mask. It wasn't the cat, he said, it was the mold in the basement. Its spores were everywhere.

Michael's presents to each of us were compilation CDs he'd

burned, Mahler for Aunt Penny, Ella Fitzgerald for my mother, what we ought to be listening to for Alec and me, and a concessionary alt-rock mix for Paul. He did his best to pay attention as we each opened them, but kept circling back into the front hall, to the telephone, willing it to ring, willing Bethany to call. She had eventually offered some excuse for her failure to appear after that night he'd been on the verge of leaving his apartment to seek her out, and they had been seeing each other since, though with enough ambiguity on her part as to their status to leave Michael perpetually on edge. Now she'd gone back to Cleveland and hadn't contacted him in four days, having forbidden him to call her there, given the wrath it might incur from her parents. And once again, he was tortured by her silence.

Soon everyone but Paul and Michael had joined the struggle in the kitchen. Each time my mother opened the oven, Aunt Penny hovered at her side, asking if the juices were running clear, because if they weren't it could be quite dangerous. When the time came, Alec mashed the potatoes, and I sautéed the beans with almonds, and prepped my annual pecan pie. In the final stages, Mom cursed what a furnace the house had become, and threw the back door wide open as Aunt Penny looked on, aghast.

By dusk it was over and Michael had set to work on the dishes. I told Paul I wanted to go for a walk and he consented. The cold air woke me almost immediately from the stupor of the house. I sensed the numbness lifting. I wanted him to put his arm around me, but he walked a few feet away. The ice on the street and the snow in the yards were blue in the fading light. There were no cars out. No sound that wasn't absorbed by the snow. I reached over and took his gloved hand in mine.

"So what do you think?" I said. "Do you think maybe we should talk?"

"Now?" he asked.

As if my pregnancy had been suspended for the holiday.

"It is that unpleasant? Just to talk about it?"

"No," he said, as though fending off the suggestion that he was being evasive.

Neither of us had anticipated this and we certainly hadn't planned it. My diaphragm had always worked before. I was still adjusting to the fact myself. While I hadn't pictured him being over the moon with excitement, I'd imagined it might be the cause for at least a bit of wonder at the prospect. At least a little speculation. Instead, it seemed he'd decided to bide his time until I announced I was having an abortion. Which wasn't illogical. I didn't want to stay home with a baby. He couldn't afford to support us even if I did. There wasn't room for a child right now, not with what we were each pursuing.

"I don't know," he said, slipping his hand from mine. "I guess—I mean—you haven't said much about it. I don't even really know what you're thinking. Maybe I don't want to sway you."

"Well, saying nothing makes it seem pretty obvious what you want, doesn't it?"

His hands were stuffed in the pockets of his peacoat, his shoulders hunched forward. In these passive moments of his, he seemed more like a third brother to me than a boyfriend. Someone to be tended. Even now, in the face of this thing affecting me so much more than him, somehow he was the subject of it all.

We kept going, through what was now nearly darkness, past the black-and-white Colonials, the little Capes hunkered in the snow, the stucco semi-mansion with its drawn shades. I almost never saw lights on here, or people out in their driveways. The neighborhood seemed an abandoned place even when populated. I would never live here again, nor anywhere like it.

I started crying. It had been like this for a couple of weeks now. Tears welling up out of nowhere and running down my cheeks, as if I were a glass filled to the brim, spilling at the slightest motion. I resented the condition: my aching breasts, the stench of food, the back pain and cramping. Paul was fretting over lost freedom in some imagined future, while my body was stealing my mind.

The waterworks brought him to my side again. He put his arm around me, and I leaned in against his chest, furious at needing him.

"I'm sorry," he said. "I should have brought it up. It just seemed like you were ignoring it, too."

"I can't ignore it."

"I know, I'm just saying, it's not like I can really believe it's my choice, even if I did want a kid, and maybe I do, I don't know. But what difference would that make? I'm not the one in charge."

"What does that mean?" I said, standing upright again, away from him.

"What choice do I have? In this, or working more again, or anything that affects our whole lives? If I love you, I have to agree with you. That's the way it's always been. I can see it in Alec. He's the same way. He thinks he isn't in control, but he's controlling everything."

"That's a cop-out. It's bullshit. You think I'm asking you to have a kid? I'm sorry I got pregnant, but I didn't do it alone."

"I really don't want to fight," he said.

"After telling me I'm controlling your whole life." We'd stopped in the middle of the empty street, facing each other. "Were you being controlled having every morning to yourself while I went to work? Really?"

"No," he said, "I'm grateful. I've told you that."

He had that set look to his face, as if battening down the

hatches for some storm of irrationality. In the last three years, being with Paul had allowed me the beginnings of sympathy for my mother. I'd always defended my father in front of her, my father who never wanted to fight. I'd defended him because he seemed weak. But was I supposed to do that again? To defend Paul from myself? *All couples have arguments.* That's how Mom used to explain away her shouting. The difference being that there was no child of mine to hear this. And perhaps there never would be.

"I don't want to argue either," I said. "But I was sick again this morning. You're not the only one not sleeping much right now. I haven't told anyone about this except you. So we need to talk. And not next week, or next month."

"I get it," he insisted, eager, now that I had cornered him, to agree and move on.

Over his shoulder stood the mock-Tudor house my old friend Jill Brantley used to live in with her divorced mother, where she and I used to get high in the attic, like an after-school special about wayward girls and the telltale signs of delinquency. This street—this whole town—was so familiar that I looked straight through it, as if it were no longer a place unto itself but merely an opening onto the past. And holding off the tidal pull of that earlier time, preventing my getting drawn back into the house we had just left, into the family and all its repetitions, was Paul—a separate person, who had never existed here. Unimplicated. Living in the present. Aggravating and noncompliant, but attentive and affectionate, too. Who seemed to keep wanting to be with me.

"We'll discuss it all tomorrow," he said. "I promise. Can we be okay for now?" he said, his eyes gently pleading.

He stepped forward and hugged me, without my asking.

What choice did I have but to believe him?

                    *   *   *

As we were taking off our boots and jackets in the front hall, Alec swept by flashing widened eyes above his mask in a silent warning of drama. It turned out that Michael, in our absence, had broken down and called Bethany's parents' house. Her father had answered. Michael had asked to speak to Bethany. She had come to the phone and told him he was making everything worse. And then she'd told him that it was over. That they could never speak again.

"Maybe you could go up," Mom said to me. "He's in his room."

"You couldn't stop him?"

"There's no need to shout," she said. "We were just here reading. He used the other phone."

We'd been in the house together, all of us, for nearly three days. I'd left for twenty minutes. Quickly absenting himself from the situation, Paul collected his novel from the coffee table and retreated to the wingback chair at the far end of the living room.

"She never did sound terribly suitable," Aunt Penny said, standing over the fire with the iron poker.

I found Alec in the kitchen, vacuuming up a tin of chocolate chip cookies, as though we hadn't already had two desserts.

"What?" he said. "I'm hungry."

"So he just went up without telling anyone, and called her?"

"Basically. He was practically keening afterwards and Mom lost it, started yelling at him. Saying he was being melodramatic. She can't handle it when he gets like that. You may have noticed this," he said, "over the years."

Upstairs, I listened for a moment before knocking on the door.

"Yeah?" Michael called out in a tremulous voice, as if he'd been locked in there for months, and I were the jailer come to free him.

204

He was sitting upright on the bed, in the dim lamplight. Crates of records that he didn't have space for in his room at Ben's sat in the shadowed corners. The harder up he got for money, the more Alec pressed him to sell some of his vinyl. But no matter what bills he had to pay, he couldn't bring himself to do it. The records meant too much to him. The most valuable were the white labels and test presses of the artists who'd gone on to fame, a few with the help of Michael's early reviews. But these in particular he held on to, especially if he thought the artists had sold out down the line. He refused to profit from what he judged to be corporate hype, as if by retaining the better work he could preserve its integrity. I didn't blame him for this the way Alec did. I sympathized with the urge to dissent, in whatever small way, from monetizing everything. As Michael saw it, capitalism had been cruel to our father, giving him no quarter when he was down, the weight of no money and too much responsibility dragging him under. Which didn't mean he hadn't been sick, but that there had been no margin for being sick. I didn't disagree. But I wished Michael could fathom how furious it made him. He seemed blind to his own anger, willfully so. On the few occasions I'd suggested as much, he'd tilted his head to one side and looked at me quizzically, as if I were describing something wholly alien.

"I have to go out there," he said. "I have to see her. I could fly to Cleveland tomorrow. She's just saying we can't talk because her parents are telling her to. If I see her, it'll be okay."

On his lap he held open a half sheet of wrinkled notepaper.

"What's that?" I asked.

"It's her last voice mail to me before she left. I transcribed it. Do you want to hear it?"

"No, I don't."

"Why not?"

Beneath his guilelessness, knowingly or not, lay the accusation that if I didn't listen I too would be abandoning him. This was the disavowal: he could remain innocent of his rage as long as he found a way, however indirect, to channel it through us. "Because you're fixated," I said. "You don't talk about anything else. She's immature. She manipulates you. I get that you're upset. But you can't give your whole life over to her."

"I can't help it, I have no choice."

I could have argued the impossibility of the fantasy, but then out would come the Proust quotes and the diatribes against passionless domesticity. Love was an affliction or nothing at all. In which case, Paul and I were nothing. I had given up years ago on being able to share with Michael what I myself went through day to day trying to be with another person, to ease my flinching against Paul's expressions of love, convinced that what they promised would never last, would vanish without warning and cut me back down to the truth of loneliness. Telling Michael I was pregnant and uncertain what to do? Forget it. His fumbling, anxious response would be worse than his continued ignorance, and would only require me to assure him that I was okay.

He went on about Cleveland, not quite as if I hadn't spoken, but as if it made no difference, talking as much to himself as to me about how he could get a cab at the airport that would take him to a motel, and how from there he could take a bus to wherever Bethany eventually agreed to meet him, spooling out the line of reasoning he would use to persuade her that they had to be together, that nothing else mattered. He sounded like a child insisting on the existence of an imaginary world.

This time, when he finished, or at least paused, I had nothing left in me to add.

"Everyone's in the living room," I said. "You should come down. We could watch a movie."

"What if I'm alone for the rest of my life?" he asked.

I looked away, down at his feet, at his blue Converse sneakers on the old pine-green carpet. I used to come to this room sometimes, after Michael had returned to England and I was alone in the house trying to take care of Alec and my mother. It was the farthest away I could get and still be home. Michael didn't tell me until years later about his premonition in the woods, the one that had driven him to leave. Back then it just seemed he had picked the perfect time to be gone.

I knew by training that my own estimation of how a person would end up in life wasn't the germane thing. Besides, I didn't know how things were going to turn out for Michael. I couldn't predict the future. As a counselor, my job was to make room for fears to be aired, so they could dissolve. That was the professional thing to do. And the kind thing. I was closer now than ever to treating Michael that way, as a case, cutting off what remained of brother-and-sister. But I couldn't. I couldn't kill him like that. For his sake, and for mine.

"You're not going to be alone," I said. "There are lots of women who've been attracted to you. You'll find someone."

He scanned the note in his hand once more, then folded it up and slipped it into his pocket.

"We could talk about it—at our appointment," I said. "It might be good for all of us."

He seemed to brighten slightly at the idea. "That would be okay?" he asked.

"It's whatever we want it to be. Each of us."

"Oh," he said, "okay." He reached for his beer on the bedside table. "Thanks for coming up," he said.

In the living room, Alec was watching a rerun of *Brideshead Revisited*. A young Jeremy Irons ate strawberries under a tree with a blond aristocrat. Mom looked up now and then from her crossword to see how far along the story had progressed. Her gift to her sister this year had been a volume of the Mitford sisters' correspondence, which Aunt Penny perused now by the fire, her legs covered by a blanket. Paul, slouching on the sofa, was still trekking through his Dostoyevsky, the book in one hand, a glass of Scotch in the other.

The family at its leisure.

"Is he all right?" Mom asked, adding without waiting for an answer, "I'm so glad you talked with him. It's all so unpleasant."

"He's not great," I said.

"Is this the *Indian* girl?" Aunt Penny asked.

"No," Alec said, louder than necessary, and without turning from the screen. "She's African-American and has borderline personality disorder."

"Oh, come on now, who said that?" Mom asked.

"I think she did," Alec said.

"Aren't there any women his own age?" Aunt Penny asked. "Women he went to college with?"

"The mixer stage is over," Alec said.

"There's no need to be snide," my mother said.

"I'm not. It's over for all of us. Believe me."

Paul laughed, but stopped short when he realized no one had joined him.

"Well," my mother said, standing up to gather her things before going upstairs for her bath, "hopefully he'll sleep well tonight, and be better in the morning."

On her way out of the room, she stole a glance at her sister, and, confident she wasn't watching, turned the thermostat ever so slightly down. I lowered myself into the armchair she'd vacated and my body collapsed into the springs.

After a few blank minutes, Aunt Penny rose as well, saying she needed to begin preparing herself for "the conditions upstairs."

She too stopped at the thermostat on the way out, turning it slightly up.

"You people are crazy," Paul said.

"Thanks," I replied, glad for the assist. Having made his promise earlier, he'd happily resumed his role as passive observer. Sensing my displeasure, he decided to bow out, saying he was going to read in bed and would see me shortly.

That left Alec and me sitting by the dwindling fire. He'd switched off the television and turned the wingback in toward the room again.

"How are you holding up?" he asked.

"I can't talk to you with that mask on. It's ridiculous."

"You're not allergic to the house."

"Neither are you. Just take it off, would you?"

He lifted it onto his forehead, sniffing at the air like a badger. At least he didn't wear Dad's cravats anymore, like he had in high school, with the woolen pants and the cardigans, that fustian look he'd cultivated to appear more mature than he was. I could never bring myself to tell him that it just made him look gay. It would have been cruel at the time, when the clothes gave him a means to feel superior. Now he wore formfitting pullovers and aged denim, which also made him look gay, though in a more competitive vein.

"Mom's retirement isn't secure," he said.

"What the fuck are you talking about? She hasn't retired."

"That's not what retirement security means. What I'm saying is, she is going to retire in the next five years, and when she does, her income stream will be just enough to pay her bills, but without a cushion. And she'll still be paying a mortgage. That is an insecure retirement."

"I can't talk about this. I just can't."

"Which allies you with her, because that's exactly what she

says when I bring it up. It's like no one wants to even acknowledge the future. Which leaves me to worry about it."

"We should have gone to the movies," I said. "Why didn't we go to the movies?"

Alec picked at his nose, the tag of his new sweater dangling from his wrist like a cheap ornament. I had trained him from late adolescence in basic psychological literacy and so was able to talk with him about more or less anything, including, over the years, the ups and downs of my relationships. All in all, we were about as close as siblings could be. Which meant we monitored each other's responsibility for the family, watchful for any sign of defection, as though we were on a desert island together, each surreptitiously building an escape raft that the other occasionally burned. My cardinal sin was having boyfriends to begin with, because God forbid another family unit arose to threaten the hegemony of the dying colony. His was being younger, and so having required my taking care of him when there was no one else to do it, putting him in the hole, in terms of time served. Now, belatedly, he'd set himself up as the family actuary. It was his attempt to engage at the lowest emotional cost.

Realizing he would get no traction from me on Mom's retirement, he tacked back to Michael, letting me know that Ben had informed him that our brother hadn't paid his rent this month. Michael had been living with Ben, and then Ben and Christine together, for years by now, in an arrangement that had morphed from a stopgap measure in the wake of his breakup with Caleigh into the most constant aspect of his adult life, all, needless to say, without any planning or discussion. Jobs, doctors, romantic crises had come and gone, but throughout he'd remained in that little front bedroom facing Shawmut Avenue on the edge of the South End. I'd long been glad for it because, while it might have overstated the case to call Michael their ward, Ben and Christine had kept him on as a member of their domestic establishment, giving him the daily contact and occasional home-cooked meal he'd otherwise be without. That Alec remained close to them both provided a kind of collective, monitoring intelligence, for better or worse.

"But surprise, surprise," Alec said, "Ben gets a check in the mail from . . . Mom. So it's not just his student loans now, it's his rent. And there's no way she can afford to keep doing that. But whatever! I guess everyone's happy just drifting along."

I zoned out for a bit to the embers of the logs, and he quit his yapping. But only for so long.

"Did I tell you about my trip up here, about the guy who cruised me?"

I shook my head.

"This guy next to me totally cruised me. Seriously. He gave me a blow job in the parking lot at 128. We exchanged, like, three words."

"That's gross."

"Oh my God," he said. "You are *so* homophobic."

"Oh, please. He could have murdered you."

"And that makes it *gross?*"

"It's just a little extreme," I said. "Like maybe you're acting out."

"I thought you worked with Bay Area homeless kids. How is this extreme?"

"You don't prostitute yourself to pay your rent."

"That may change," he said.

"Whatever. My point is, is this really what you want to be engaging in? Wouldn't you rather have a boyfriend?"

He gaped at me, incredulous. In my exhaustion I had walked right into it—the blithe demonstration of my heterosexual privilege in suggesting such a thing was so readily had, when I knew

211

well enough that it wasn't. But here he was, attractive and articulate and employed, and I didn't get why he couldn't find someone else like that in all of New York City. It was half the reason he'd moved there. So why was he exposing himself to these random encounters?

"I'm sorry," I said. "I take it, then, you're not seeing anyone at the moment?"

"No," he said, fiddling with his cuticles.

"Could you stop that picking?" I said.

"Okay—something is clearly up with you. What is it? Paul?"

"No. I'm pregnant."

He glanced from his hands straight into my eyes, testing my sincerity. When he realized it was true, his mouth fell open. "You're shitting me," he said. "What are you going to do?"

"I don't know."

"You don't know? Are you saying you might have a *child*?"

"Well, I'm not going to have a *deer*. You say *child* like it's a disease. You sound like Michael."

"Okay, let's just say, that would be a game changer. Procreation?"

Seeing his reaction, I felt almost giddy, as if all of a sudden my escape vessel was complete, and I'd made it out onto the open water, free at last. What better veto of filial duty than an infant?

Officially, Alec and I were no longer competitive. To be explicit about it would seem petty. But it still squirreled its way into moments like this, when the battle became primal again, and we struggled, pulling each other together because that's what we'd always done to get through, and pushing each other away to convince ourselves over and over that we were more than just functions of a loss.

"I haven't decided," I said, generously, not wanting to scare him any further. "But who knows? Maybe it would be good for all of us. You're the one saying we don't think enough about the future."

This took him a moment to digest.

On the table beside him, next to the fluted lamp with the hexagonal shade of waterfowl, the picture of a younger Dad stared from behind the glass of a studio portrait. He must have had it done for some business venture. Mom had found it in his papers and had it framed. We didn't do family photographs on the mantelpiece or the walls. This was the only one. It occurred to me in a way it hadn't before that my father would have liked Paul. They would have gotten along. Paul would have been able to reassure him that he was a reliable person, trustworthy, an observer of the social contract. Nothing awkward would have arisen. If Dad had been well enough to focus on the fact long enough, he would have been politely happy at news of a grandchild.

"Well, that is a stunner," Alec said.

He had ceased his fidgeting, oblivious to the dull horn of his mask that still poked from his forehead. The house had gone quiet around us.

"I love you," he said. "For whatever it's worth."

Michael

AFTER-ACTION REPORT

Operation Family Therapy
Mission: Enhanced communication / familial well-being
Outcome: Pending

1. After taking cannon fire from a beached dreadnought on Mass. Ave. two klicks east of Central Square (allegiance and origin unknown), Mom continued to operate our down-armored Honda at below regulation speed and ordered the commencement of a routine park-and-destroy mission. The entire unit was placed on alert. Multiple initial space sightings proved false. We tacked south into Cambridgeport, keeping to side streets. Weather was hibernal. Birds were occasional. Eighteen minutes out from rendezvous a viable space was ID'd in front of a deli. Mom was skeptical but maneuvered the vehicle into position.

As she shifted into reverse, a VW sedan driven by an irregular nosed into the designated space behind us. Mom immediately launched a DEFCON 1 verbal barrage, which backfired against the closed windows, causing multiple casualties. Celia was swiftly medevaced to Ramstein Air Base for a laparoscopic frontal-lobe transplant and returned to active duty four minutes later. Others ran for psychic cover only to find the terrain on fire. Fog of war. Following the skirmish, tensions in the little platoon rose. Trying to regroup, Alec commenced a psyop designed to convince Mom that an open stretch of curb downwind of a laundromat ended more than twelve feet from the adjacent hydrant. The operation failed. Mom ordered a higher alert. Celia observed that we had been on one for a decade. Eleven minutes out, Alec suggested we consider PAYING for a garage space. At this point, command and control began to break down. Mom hissed aloud, Who are all these people? I suggested they might be people who lived in the neighborhood. Seven minutes to rendezvous, after Mom had threatened to drop us off and go on alone, an enemy sport-utility vehicle bearing a Dole/Kemp sticker vacated a meter in front of Crate and Barrel. Alec leapt from the vehicle to secure the perimeter and Mom backed our transport into the slot.

2. Unit reached the training facility on time. Decor was South by Southwest (Naugahyde couch, Sierra throw). Vaginal imagery detected in wall hangings. Waiting room ransacked for war loot; none found. I suggested that Mom read *Field and Stream* to kill the additional minute and thirty seconds. Mom nonresponsive. Mortar fire heard from the direction of the Charles River; presumed friendly.

Five minutes after scheduled rendezvous, a woman uni-
formed in Geiger jacket and pearls, presumed hostile, ex-
ited the training office with no visible wounds. Engaging
unilaterally, Alec kneecapped her with a bronze Navajo
sculpture. Body stored in closet. Mustachioed training officer, balding, presumed neutral, then escorted the unit into
a semicircle of modernist sitting furniture. Coffee table,
presumed original, bore a leather, presumed Naugahyde,
box of Kleenex. Unit ID'd itself by rank and serial number.
Training officer's diplomas were too far away to make out;
presumed valid. Training officer, smiling, introduced himself and asked us to call him Gus. Silence. Gus requested
a report from each member of the unit regarding what we
considered our mission to be. Rear Admiral Celia appeared
depressed and drained in these opening minutes of the engagement. PTSD from park-and-destroy mission not to be
ruled out.

3. She nonetheless reported out her sense of our situation:
(1) unit cohesion, and affect of individual soldiers (me), still
questionable years after resignation of the co-commander.
Elephant still in the room. Ghost still in the basement; (2)
retraining required to improve overall performance. Alec
generally concurred. Mom said something about having
nothing against talking. In an effort to get her to elaborate, Gus referred to Dad as her "life partner." Man, was
that a mistake. The phrase grated violently on the brain of
the unit, causing instant suspicion that the training officer
might be a New Age–language infectee, thus unable to survive Mom's judgment and impotent to assist us. Gus asked
what was so funny. It's nothing, Mom said, it's just that I
would never refer to John that way.

4. Mom ordered by Gus to Reeducation Camp Worcester to meet disciplinary standards for therapeutic self-description. Junior members of the unit did not object. Countermanding the instruction, however, Mom ordered a cruise-missile strike from the USS *Passive Disdain,* a destroyer under her command presently operating in the waters off Cape Cod. Camp Worcester reported leveled.

5. Adult acne became general. Scattered reports of giardia, stress fractures, and hair loss.

6. During initial interrogation, Alec informed Gus that he was gay. Celia responded by observing that we were here to discuss things we didn't already know. Resulting friendly fire caused minor damage to decor and fenestration. Mom seen wincing at loss of family privacy. Gus asked if Alec had anything he wanted to say to the family as a whole on this subject. The PFC reported that, yes, in fact, he had kept much of his struggle to himself, in tacit deference to the hierarchy in which Dad's resignation still ranked above all other battle wounds.

7. Records indicated that the little wheezer had come out to Subcomandante Celia first, somewhere back during the Opium War of his middle adolescence. According to later reporting, he had suggested to her he would end up a closet case in light of his ambition to join the Senate (may he be forgiven). Second up was his reveal to Mom (a conversation about which the less imagined the better). Only after he had gone to college did he bring it up with me. I was driving us to the cineplex one summer evening in the Cutlass. He asked if I had met anyone at BC, and

217

if Caleigh was my girlfriend. This came as a surprise, given that he and I never talked about such things, his being his larval, stripling self—boy pretender to the empty throne—and my being generally ashamed. He was single, he said, knuckling bravely through the awkwardness of talking with me about it. And it turned out, he said, looking away from me and out his window, that he was attracted to men. We had just passed the house of one of his high school friends, a precocious fan of Stüssy gear, pretty in a Duran Duran sort of way, whom I remembered him being particularly fond of, and I was saddened at the thought of the little fidget-buster being lonely. I told him that I approved of homosexuality as a counter-hegemonic subject position. That it constituted one of the key sites of resistance to patriarchy, and should be understood as a revolutionary stance. In retrospect, I could have used a more personal touch. He might have wanted something more from me, given the absence of the father function.

8. Moving on, Gus noted that I had yet to describe my own sense of the unit's mission. Searching for cover, I found none. The night before, after Commodore Celia had granted me leave to discuss Bethany in our session, I had stayed in my old room listening to her favorite Aphex Twin tracks, and trying to read a little Althusser. After repeated tries, Caleigh finally answered the phone at her parents' house, where she'd gone for Christmas. To my disappointment, her instructions were to heed Celia's advice: own up already to the hollowness of the salvific fantasy of romance, to its childishness. And take to heart what Celia kept implying: that my lamentation was misplaced, that the loss of Bethany was a stand-in for the older grief, a loss I

was bound to repeat until I let its real object surface. This, of course, was a Freudianism straight out of basic training, and a principle I readily accepted. The problem being that basic training had so little to do with actual combat. My intellectual grasp of my situation never seemed to hold much. Life kept slipping through it. And in life, I needed Bethany. Because she could let me love her now, in the present. And even if doctrine held that this love wouldn't give me back everything I'd lost, what if it did? After Caleigh tired of my resistance, and we said good night, I took my meds and fell into a dream-soaked slumber. I found myself at an auction. A stage, or block, had been erected at the back of a Christian Dior boutique in old Charleston. There, up on the platform, naked and glistening in the spotlight, was Bethany. Some bidders snapped photographs. Others stepped close to appraise the tone of her muscles. White women in beautifully cut dresses made disparaging remarks about the condition of her hair. Meanwhile, on the wall behind her, between two glass display cases of couture gowns, blood ran from the palms of a High Gothic Jesus, skeletal and pale. No one seemed to notice him. I tried taking suits from the rack to cover Bethany, to shelter her from the eyes of the crowd, but the saleswoman told me I had to purchase the merchandise before using it. At which point a hole opened in my chest, and I vomited into the hole, the hot liquid circulating back up through my heart and neck into my head. Bethany crumpled to her knees by the footlights, bowed and silent. All I could do was stand there, failing to save her.

9. Deciding it might be best to skip my dream sequence, I told Gus I concurred with Celia. Airing the effects of the

past was long overdue. As Marx tells us, the tradition of all the dead generations weighs like a nightmare upon the brains of the living. I was all for the discussion of transgenerational haunting. It was just hard to focus at the moment owing to a woman in Ohio I needed to visit.

10. Executing an ingratiation maneuver with a bit of quick jocularity, training officer deployed the phrase *girlfriend trouble*. Tower of Babel. No interpreters in sight. I could sooner have crafted an origami hare from the gold wafer of his melted wedding band than communicate how completely he had misapprehended me. *Girlfriend trouble?* Those pesky ladies it's so hard to keep from bitching at you? Training officer's feminism missing and presumed dead.

11. After thanking us for sharing, Gus briefed us on the rules of engagement: This was not a free-fire zone, we were to limit collateral damage, and leave no one behind. That understood, what, he wanted to know, were present conditions? Mom reported that she was just glad to have us all home. And that she wished I didn't have to take so many pills. So that was helpful. Also, she had noticed that Gus had graduated from Bowdoin, and wondered if he had studied with Maureen Durant-Draper, the archaeologist, who had been a classmate of hers at Smith. She's done a lot of work on Constantinople, Mom said, I don't know if you ever came across her? Junior ranks of the unit slumped, defeated, in their chairs. As you can see, Mom said to Gus, my children are fond of being exasperated. Gus turned to the grunts to ask what bothered us about the mother ship's inquiry. I'm supposed to be more serious, Mom said, an-

swering for us. But we're not here to talk about me, she went on, it's what *they* have to say that's important.

12. Seeing the operation going sideways, Celia redirected us to the core mission. Conversation ensued regarding the long half-life of Dad. I had no objection to this other than my virtually blank memory of him as a person. That Mom should remember her husband made sense. But why Celia and even Alec the Younger should have such vivid recall of him while I, who knew him longest, have trouble even picturing his face I couldn't rightly say. The three of them proceeded to be moved by painful memories. Listening to them was mesmerizing. They cried like they had that afternoon I returned from England to Walcott with Peter Lorian, after Dad died, and I had watched them leaning against each other on the couch in the living room, their grief seemingly intensified at the sight of me. Hearing their collective weeping again in Gus's office, I thought that in the force of their feelings there might be a way back for me. Into the time before I fled the house, before I left them there, blind to the coming evil that I alone had seen. A chance to somehow repent for my cowardice by joining them now. And yet as mesmerizing as their emotion was, it reached me like the sound of a record played low in another room, a world of meaning beckoning me to a closed door.

13. If I had just woken up earlier that morning, Alec was saying to Gus, I could have spoken to Dad, and maybe he wouldn't have left. Dear, Mom said, you can't think like that. And then without warning, Alec was speaking about me, saying how much he worried about my life, how he

221

wished things could be easier for me, and Celia was silently agreeing with him, rocking her whole body back and forth, biting her lower lip, trying not to cry again. Mom put her hand on my knee. It's hard for Michael, she explained to Gus. And it's hard for us to know what to do. Gus looked across the coffee table at me. They seem very concerned about you, he said. How does that feel?

14. There is a point in all wars of attrition when the combatants begin to suspect that their purpose is not at all what they believed it to be, that in fact the war is its own organism, of which they are merely the cells, and that its sole drive is to go on forever. Depending on the hour, the insight either maddens or clarifies, sending you into despair, or clearing your vision by releasing you from the bonds of hope.

15. Time had fled. Our session was ending. In his concluding remarks, Gus appeared genuinely excited at the complexity of the unit's issues. He said there was a lot to work with, and that his office stood ready to complete the retraining if we were willing and able. Afterwards, we went to a Japanese restaurant. Mom asked us what sashimi was. I drank pilsners. The order to stand down was never given. Later, under cover of darkness, we commenced our retreat.

III

Alec

There were no shades on his windows. Lying on his bed I could see across the street to the roofs of the buildings opposite, to the water towers and stovepipes silhouetted against clouds backlit by the moon, a picture of some old New York, a movie-set picture, as if we'd met the old-fashioned way, in a bar, and were a couple of kids who'd wound up here on a drunken lark.

His bed was pressed into the corner, against the windowsill, leaving just enough room for the closet door to open. Above the Ikea dresser, postcards of minimalist paintings and geometric tiles were thumbtacked to the wall. He had gone into the only other room of the apartment to get his computer. It was already two in the morning. An hour earlier and I might have salvaged the following day, but it was close to shot now. Seth was his name.

"What are you doing?" I asked, when he climbed back onto the bed with his laptop.

"I want to play you a song," he said.

A song? How credulous, I thought, at this stage. We'd kissed and helped each other come in the usual imitation of porn—a warming exercise of sorts, trying to clear away the awkwardness of anonymity to see if there might be conversation. We'd been lying in bed awhile now, chatting, which surprised me—that neither of us had balked yet.

His pics had deceived less than most. He'd said he was twenty-eight and he looked about that. For his face shot, he'd employed the standard attitudinal glare, meant to signal languid indifference, a mix of attempted intimidation and reassurance that hooking up would involve no entanglements because he didn't need anything more than that, being otherwise self-contained and perhaps already boyfriended. It was the safest way to go about all of this, conceding nothing of your desire beyond the moment at hand. The jacked-up brain state of skimming pics and profiles and the eventual orgasm—with someone else, or alone if you bagged out and got off to a video clip instead—were narcotic enough to skip you over the grinding moments of outright deception, the encounters cut short at the front door.

"It's a Vanessa Smythe song," he said, scrolling through a playlist.

Sidelong, in the light of the screen, his face was gentler than the image that had got me to click on him. His eyes and mouth had an indefinite quality, a pliancy, which had distracted me as we were getting off. He wasn't, in fact, intimidating. And for a moment I'd hated him for it, for being softer than his ad. Though at the same time it made me curious. His fine black hair needed a cut. He was unshaven, but not, it seemed, for fashion's sake. There was something particular about him, a lack of the usual guardedness. Already I'd stayed longer than I'd intended, and still felt no urge to leave.

"Do you know her stuff?" he asked.

"No," I said. My music had always come from Michael. I'd never developed my own habit of finding new things to listen to. If he didn't share or mention something, it passed me by. For a long time that had meant being effortlessly ahead of the curve as he sent me tapes, then CDs, then audio files of what he was listening to, but he'd done less of that since the whole Bethany episode, which was already five years ago now, and my collection had grown dated.

"Take a listen," Seth said.

The opening notes of a jazz standard filled the little room. A live recording of a piano ambling in a minor key, accompanied by a horn, summoning the ease of some velvet banquette in a '40s nightclub. Then came a woman's low, tentative voice, singing the occasional line slipped in between the motions of the players, as if hesitant to interrupt. I wasn't a big jazz fan, but the tune was pleasantly melancholic. I was trying to let go of how late it was, to give up on tomorrow, and the music helped. A slow beat entered the mix, a snare, then a bass, and eventually a few strings, creating a swirling sound. It was the reworking of a standard, not a classic rendition. When the piano expanded its range the singer seemed to take it as permission to let in more feeling, in the last words of a line, swinging a note, holding it an instant longer than the line before.

Seth had put aside his computer and was lying next to me again. The song went on like this for a while, balancing between restraint and release. I'd expected either a trashy pop hit shared in irony or some aficionado's serious band, but this was neither. The longer it went on, the more I thought Michael would like it. He didn't care who made a thing if it had that particular ache to it. And this did. Whatever safe, old-world reference it had begun with was slipping away now. The opening shyness of the singer had been a feint. Her voice had power, and she knew it.

You're not anywhere else, she seemed to be saying. You're here now, with me, in this room.

As we lay there together listening, Seth, like a nervous kid on a first date, reached over and took my hand in his. It was so un-

227

expected, and so tender, it caused me to shudder. A few minutes ago we'd had our dicks in each other's mouths. We'd kissed and tongued. But all that had been routine. This was different, and riskier. It hinted at intimacy. He was actually touching me. And I was letting him do it.

The muscles of my neck let go, and my head sank deeper into the pillow.

Holding hands listening to a favorite song? As if we hadn't met two hours ago? As if we hadn't both got off like this with strangers who knew how many times before? Did he think he was a magician, that he could just wish the anonymity away?

Whatever the singer was doing now it wasn't cool anymore. Her voice had opened wide, edging toward the point of failure, making it clear she wasn't faking it, that the trouble in the song was her own, that she was in some kind of real danger, which no producer's smoothing edits could save her from. Not that she was crazy. She wasn't letting her audience off the hook that easily, by offering the safety of distance that would open up if she were just to make a spectacle of herself. She was staying close, continuing to bear the weight of herself.

Without thinking, I interlaced my fingers more tightly with Seth's. As though I had traveled back into some younger, more trusting self. When he squeezed my hand, I fell into pure nostalgia. The keen memory of a thing I'd never had. A nostalgia for a moment just like this. As if back when I was a teenager and I'd wanted it so achingly bad, I had met a boy and we had fallen in love, and been together in private ecstasy. And as if, at last, I could mourn the loss of that imagined happiness.

The voice was in full flight now, skipping up and out of any world that could possibly last, into sheer bliss, giving me the ridiculous hope that Seth and I could be together. That he could give me back what I'd lost. Lying beside him, I prayed for it.

228

When I left the next morning, he gave me his number and e-mail and I gave him mine. I walked onto the street I had seen only in the darkness of the night before. Trash cans were lined up at the sidewalk and the cars were double-parked, the pavement wet from an early-winter snow. Men in suit pants and ski jackets with laptop bags over their shoulders and women in tailored suits and knee-length winter coats made their way in silence to the train. Like a college freshman who'd just had sex for the first time, I studied their faces to see if I could detect which of them had come from the warmth of a drowsy morning fuck, who among them were the elect, as Michael called them, and who had slept and eaten by themselves, their mornings spent in the little disciplines of solitude. An absurd perch for me to assume on the basis of one night, as if I were elect now, a giant presumption, but as I joined the sidewalk traffic, trailing with it down toward the sub-way, that was the difference: the spell of the night before seemed for once strong enough to countervail the evidence of the world unchanged.

I'd experienced this before, but only while still drunk. If my high happened to dissipate gently enough, I could sometimes make it back to my shower and bed before the soreness caught up with me. But hooking up most often meant knuckling through a contraction of hope the following morning. A rescission of the pleasures of a few hours earlier. It drew down my workaday armor—the belief in the worthwhileness of ordinary things— leaving me raw and tightened against the rawness. But not this morning. It seemed as if a glaze had been washed from my senses, brightening the sound of the traffic up ahead on the avenue, sep-arating the bus's pneumatic brakes from the bass chug of the delivery-truck engines and the whir and bump of gliding taxis.

I had nothing to read on the subway and I didn't want to listen to music that would displace the echo of the song Seth had played me. I looked at my fellow passengers instead, taking in their shorn, wary affect, the aspiration to undisturbed non-presence guarded by newspapers, gaming devices, books, and headsets. They avoided my open gaze as they would a beggar or lunatic. Normally, I would be full of tiny aversions, or avarice for other people's lives. The absence of all that disoriented me. That I could stand there swaying with the motion of the train, badly late to work, in a state of such democratic calm, almost affection-ate toward my fellow riders—how sappy! But even my cynicism didn't last more than another stop. The heedless goodwill stayed with me all the way home.

By lunchtime, Seth had texted and we had made a plan for dinner the following night. I hadn't dreamed it. Something had happened.

The next evening, he showed up at the restaurant dressed for a date. He had shaved and put on dark fitted jeans and a blue ox-ford shirt. I stood up from behind the table, and awkwardly put my hand out for him to shake. The obviousness of his nerves took the edge off mine. He clearly wanted to be here. And I wanted us to skip over comparing notes on life in the city and dive right back into where we had left off. But that would risk a look of in-comprehension on his face, an indication that I had, in fact, been alone in the moment I thought we had shared. That I was the corny, besotted one who needed to grow up and take it easy. I had picked the restaurant because it was quiet, but I regretted that now, wishing for the distraction of voices and music and waiters squeezing past.

Soon I had fumbled into a question about what kinds of things he designed, falling right into the script of the Internet date

I had wanted to avoid, that face-off across a table stripped of all context and fellow feeling, and supported by nothing more than the mutual assumption of loneliness, a social form that had always struck me as rigged to fail. It didn't matter to me what he designed so long as he would go home with me after dinner.

He talked about graphics and websites. I wanted to stop him and say, Wait, not yet. But I said nothing, and he went on, about album covers, freelance work, and projects of his own. Caught in the train of it now, I asked more questions, realizing as I half listened to his replies that the relief his nervousness had allowed me was being replaced by a sense of deflation. He had put some kind of gel in his hair to keep its mildly disheveled look in place. His lightly freckled skin was scrubbed and moisturized. He had prepared for tonight, he had considered carefully what to wear, trying on different outfits, looking at himself in the mirror, keen to make a good impression. How could this person, who had seemed to have none of this self-consciousness before, take us back to where I thought we had been? Had he just accidentally opened a vein in me through which that song had entered? Did he even register the difference between this moment and that?

He asked if I'd like to share an appetizer, and what wine I preferred. He was tangled up in politeness, which by default I matched and parried, moving on to social autopilot.

I wanted the evening to start over. I wanted to whisper something suggestive in his ear as soon as he arrived, preserving the mystery by ushering us back through the curtain again into the vaguer, richer world of romance. None of this disastrous self-reporting, this checklist discovery of "things in common."

He asked about my journalism, and I retailed a few stories about the more colorful characters, and the excesses of the political fund-raising I covered. It was easy to impress people from outside that world with the extremity of it, trading on the insider-erism my reporting was meant to pierce.

The chitchat got us through our entrées, and I resigned myself to the idea that this would be it, another little shot of false hope, a perfectly decent date, followed by a dwindling e-mail thread. Then, out of nowhere, as we were sharing a piece of almond cake, with the date all but over, he said he liked the way I talked.

"The way you use words," he said, "I like it."

Thrown off, once again, by his guilelessness, I didn't know how to respond.

His eyes were green. I rarely noticed the color of people's eyes, and found it implausible when it came as one of the first descriptors of a person in an article, as if from yards away people picked up the color of two dots in the head. But our faces were only about two feet apart, and he was looking at me with unnerving directness, and I saw that his eyes were definitely dark green.

"Did I say something wrong?" he asked.

"No."

He put down his fork and rested his elbows on the table. "I know it's too early to ask this," he said, "but do you have a boyfriend?"

Just like that the nattering in my head ceased. "Not at the moment," I said, monitoring his expression, wondering if my nonchalance had hid well enough the full answer: that I had never really had one, not for more than a few months.

"What about you?" I asked.

"Not at the moment," he repeated after me, smiling, as if maybe he had seen through me but didn't care.

The last thing I wanted to do was lurch onto the subject of past relationships. So I don't know why I said, "There's been someone, though?"

"We were in grad school together," he said.

What I detested most about my jealousy for other people's pasts was how it yoked me to Michael. In the solitary years since Bethany, he'd edged toward bitterness. I was determined not to let myself do that. Still, I couldn't help but picture Seth and his boyfriend drinking with friends in student apartments, sitting on the floor at parties holding hands, knowing without thinking about it that later they would be naked together in their bedroom, the flow of sex between them running into their work as well, which they would have shared, too. For Seth it was a memory now, and all the more glamorous for being just that—an assumption, like wealth to the heir.

"But that was a while ago," he said. "What about you?"

"It's been a while, too," I said.

He smiled again, broadly this time, as if we were already co-conspirators, as if my response were a seduction, not a cover. He was doing it again, making intimacy out of nothing more than his own passing pleasure. And just like that, he caught me up in it.

"I probably shouldn't tell you this," I said, "but I downloaded that song you played me. And I probably shouldn't tell you how many times I've listened to it, either."

He blushed. "You can tell me that," he said.

He slid his hand across the table and turned it open to me. The skin of his palm was damp.

"So," I said. "I have an apartment..."

"Really? How unusual."

"I mean—"

"Yes," he said.

I had grown used to sex as a short burst, a onetime thing, the pleasure keyed to the danger, but leashed by fear. It was easy when everyone did the same, exposing themselves for the quick high. Like the occasional seizure of an otherwise controlled body, flagrant but brief. But there was nothing flagrant about standing perfectly still in my bedroom with the lights off, letting Seth, in no kind of rush, unbutton my shirt, or in feeling the warm contour of his ribs with the tips of my fingers. The script called for speed and gruffness, for the porn-like boasting and debasement of locker-room jocks getting off on themselves and each other, that fantasy toughness meant to ward off exactly the confusion I was in now, unsure what to do and trying not to shake.

Seth leaned in bravely and kissed me on the lips. I drew him closer, as if to shield him from his own frankness, until we were hugging. There was still nothing to this. He could be anyone at all, and gone tomorrow. I knew that I should probably play it cool. But he wasn't playing it that way. For whatever unknowable and maybe even fucked-up reason, he wasn't sticking to his side of the line. It was strange to realize that we were kissing and half undressed but hadn't started the clock yet, hadn't set the pace toward coming. When I touched him I actually experienced what I touched. For once, each of his features—the little curve at the base of his spine, the slope of his shoulders—wasn't separated out by my camera's eye, exported into pornography, and graded for hotness.

I kept motioning us to jump ahead, to speed up, and he kept letting me know it was okay, that we could go slowly. When he stopped my hand going into his jeans, I had the urge to say, All right, already, let's not get reverential about it, but then his other hand brushed down my back, and I shivered.

It occurred to me that he might be less neurotic than I was. That he might know himself decently well. Which made me think that if we were going to fuck for the first time tonight, I should do the fucking, so things didn't get too out of balance.

Eventually, he got us naked and under the sheets together. And still we just kept kissing and running our hands over each other.

If only I'd had that third drink or a hit of pot, I might have been able to drift. But I was stuck in the moment. He began kneading my ass, but I leaned away from the touch and untangled myself, rolling onto my back.

He waited a few moments, then asked if I was okay.

"I'm great," I said.

"We don't have to do anything more. This is fine."

"I just need to keep it together," I whispered. I hadn't meant to say it aloud. But I couldn't reel it back in.

He turned onto his side, facing me, and rested a hand on my stomach. "What do you have to keep together?" he said.

He wasn't my confidant. I couldn't pretend we had any basis for that. "It's nothing," I said. "This is good."

"Yeah. It is. So is talking with you . . . What's up?"

"I'm usually not like this. Actually, I hate it when guys are like this."

"Like what?"

"Nothing," I said. "I'm not used to the slow thing."

"We can go faster," he said. "I'm just enjoying the ride."

A framed Ansel Adams poster hung on the otherwise bare wall facing my bed. I had tidied the dresser beneath it before going out, and my desk as well. This was the furniture I'd lived with since the year after college, and for all the years I had now managed to afford this apartment. Friends and dates had come and gone, admiring the light and the view. I had been glad for the security of their admiration. But seeing it through Seth's eyes, I was reminded how little I had done to make it my own. I hadn't wanted to interrupt the clean white lines or clutter the open space. Which had left it sterile. One of the thousands of adult dorm rooms in Manhattan, where credentialed children performed their idea of adult lives.

"It's ridiculous," I said. "To be telling you this. I don't know you. But what the fuck? I haven't felt normal since the other night. Since we met. You don't know anything about me. But I have a brother—an older brother—and he hasn't been with anyone for a really long time. It doesn't usually hit me like this. But he's alone—and I'm here. And I feel guilty. Really, though. I'm not usually like this. I don't think about it all the time, I promise. I'm sorry. I'm fucking this up, aren't I?"

"No," Seth said. "Kind of the opposite, actually."

I got hard again when he said that. I wasn't thinking about sex, but I was as stiff as I'd been all night.

"It's too early to say this, too," he said. "But I think you're beautiful."

He reached across me, put a hand under my back, and pulled me on top of him until we were chest to chest.

"I want to keep talking," he said. "But first I want to fuck you. Is that okay?"

For a moment I thought he was trying to divert us back into the safety of porn, putting on the uniform of machismo to get us out of this jam. But that would require speed—to gin up the scene and keep it moving—and he didn't speed up. He went as slowly as before, kissing and massaging, as if he'd walked out of some Eden of time, where no one had thought to even measure the stuff. He took me on my back, kissing me as he went, moving at such a gentle pace it seemed to have nothing to do with domination or control, or even orgasm. There was just the sensation of it.

A sudden, fierce pain pulsed at my temples and then let go.

I almost always role-played it, acting the stud giving it to the boy, or playing the shameless boy myself. But Seth wasn't playing. He didn't mutter anything in my ear, he didn't harden into self-regard. He kept his eyes open, his dick firm inside me, but the rest of his body almost lax, as if we were cuddling. It should have turned me off—neither of us being in charge—but the lack of a story set me afloat, leaving me light-headed and close to joy.

For the first few months we kept up the pretense of scheduling dates. It was a way to flirt, to be coy, as if one of us might say no. We'd choose a restaurant, or plan a meal, and at the end of the evening Seth would ask if I'd like to spend the night together, and I'd pretend to consider.

I kept waiting for him to disappoint me, by not calling or texting, or by calling or texting too much, but he didn't. Which left me trying to disqualify him on other grounds: his apartment was too gayly neat; there weren't enough books in it; he wasn't a political junkie; his voice got queeny with his friends; he watched sitcoms, liked animated movies, owned a cat named Penelope. But I actually found the tidiness of his apartment reassuring, and he did in fact read the news, if not all the polls. And when he bantered with his friends he seemed to be having fun.

I'd always pictured myself with someone serious and austere. Someone preoccupied by serious work. His remoteness would captivate me. He'd be handsome, of course, but unselfconscious about it. And he'd love me undemonstratively, with the matter-of-factness of authority. And then there was Seth, who held my hand in public, kissed me in front of his friends, and thought I should wear brighter colors. I'd been looking for a suit who preferred men, not someone who enjoyed himself.

I decided the way we'd met would catch up with us. One of us would get bored on the Internet and decide to hook up with someone else, just for fun, and there would follow an awkward coffee date and that dwindling exchange of e-mails I'd anticipated the first night at the restaurant. It would have been a kind of relief. To get back to normal. But the months went by and it kept not happening.

The journalists and political staffers I spent my days with were mostly single or divorced. They either slept with each other or dragged around convoluted stories of people in other cities who they were trying to figure something out with. On the road, we drank together in hotel bars. It was the communion of diehards I'd dreamed of being invited into four years earlier, leading into the Bush and Gore campaigns, and now had the assignment to join just as the early positioning and fund-raising in advance of the primaries were getting started. And yet whenever I traveled, I found myself making excuses to go to my room early to call Seth.

"I think someone has a boyfriend," he said when I phoned him for the third night in a row from Des Moines.

I could picture him sitting in bed watching a movie, under the clean pine shelves he'd built and installed himself, his knees raised up under the covers, laptop balanced on top of them, all his laundry folded and put away. I'd never been with a man long enough to yearn not just for sex, or not even for sex, but for the mere presence of him.

"I want to stop using condoms," I said.

"You make it sound like a heart attack."

"I'm serious," I said.

"I can tell."

Something about his even-tempered nature made me feel like a child, which infuriated me, and meant I had to stay with him to prove that I wasn't.

"Are you alone?" I asked.

"No, my other boyfriend is here, but he's very understanding."

"What if I thought that I might love you?"

"Now there's a question," he said. "What if, hypothetically speaking, you thought there was some possibility that you *might* love me? That's what you're asking? Like, what would my advice be?"

"Sorry, that's unfair."

"It's somewhere between unfair and charming, but we can go with charming."

I didn't know why I kept getting hard when he said things like that, but I did. I wanted to slap him.

"I think I love you," I said.

"Are you drunk?"

"No! I'm not drunk. I love you." Take that, I thought, waiting for his retort.

There was a pause, and then he said, "Can I ask a favor? Will you say that again when you get home?"

"Okay," I replied, grudgingly.

"Good. Because I love you, too."

I barely took in what he'd said, wanting so badly to keep going myself, to confess that this was the first time I had ever spoken these words to any man, that I was ashamed to be thirty-one and never have reached this point before, that I was afraid my loneliness was a leprosy, a disfigurement, which, if he ever saw it, would repulse him.

"Lucky me," I said, instead. "How's your other boyfriend going to take the news?"

"He'll be all right. I'll let him down easy."

Such lightness. It left me giddy. But right there, riding up the back of that swell of happiness—the thought of Michael. I saw him at his computer, filling out another dating-site questionnaire, trying to choose a picture, disliking every one. My brother—the perfect kill switch. So very reliable. The same switch thrown every time I reached the point of stepping outside myself.

I hadn't told Michael anything about Seth yet, though it had been six months already. Being single was something he and I had long had in common. Something to commiserate about. Celia was the one who'd been in relationships. Michael and I didn't want each other to be alone, but the fact that we were had developed over the years into a kind of solidarity. It gave us a means to be close. And to remain loyal, somehow, to the past. Part of me knew that this was a racket, that it fed on gloom. But I didn't know how to give it up. I could play down what was happening with Seth, suggest that it was still preliminary, and who knew what might come of it. I could even tell Michael that I was in love. He would listen to such a declaration with thirst, at least when he stopped talking about his own predicament long enough to hear it. But that Seth loved me back? That if anything he was the more affectionate? Of course Michael would never be less than polite about it. He'd say he was glad, and yet I would be cutting him off, leaving him more isolated than he already was. And what for, if I could just soft-pedal it, allowing him the sense that nothing had really changed?

One of the things that had recently made it easier to imagine telling Michael at least something about Seth was that after years of trying, he had finally gotten into graduate school. Albeit at the advanced age of thirty-six. We had thought it would never happen. My mother had fretted to Celia and me that he just made himself more miserable by applying fall after fall, only to reap another set of rejection letters each spring. But somehow he'd managed to persevere, and now he had done it. He said he didn't care about an academic career, he just needed to do his work, and that he would be happy teaching high school if there were no college jobs. It was a plan, at least, a way he might eventually support himself. My mother still helped him with his rent, wrote checks for his therapy, and ran down what little savings she had. Here, at last, was a solution. Only it turned out his stipend didn't cover everything. He would need to find work, and take out more loans. Because of his lousy credit he needed a co-signer.

"He'll be the one paying them back," my mother said when informing me she had already agreed.

"And if he doesn't?" I asked.

"What am I supposed to do? Tell him he can't go?"

She worried about him every day. Now, finally, he had good news. She couldn't deny him the chance. This left only the question of how he would get from Boston to Michigan. Michael driving a U-Haul for two days by himself to an empty apartment in a town he'd never been to seemed like a bad idea to all of us.

"He would never ask you," my mother said. "And obviously you're busy . . . but it would be such a help."

Before she suggested this, Seth had invited me to meet his family in Denver on the same August weekend that Michael was due in Lansing. I'd fantasized about having in-laws. A comfortable, accepting couple who would be delighted their son had found a clean-cut professional, and who wanted to welcome him into their family. Their comfortable, intact family. Seth's older sister, Valerie, and her husband, Rick, lived with their infant son just a couple of streets away from Seth's parents. Rick worked at the construction firm Seth's father ran. They were all, apparently, keen to meet me. I wanted very much to go with him, but if I could get Michael set up in his apartment and settled there, he'd have his new start. When I mentioned to Seth what my mother had asked of me, he said he understood. There would be other times, he said. I should do what needed to be done.

Michael and I left Ben and Christine's apartment on a sweltering day in the middle of August, the old Grand Am that I had given him years ago hitched to the back of the moving truck.

He was in bad shape. The preparations for moving and the prospect of leaving the place he'd lived most of his adult life had addled him. I had to repeat the simplest directions two or three times before he could process what I had said. Whatever meds he was taking weren't doing a very good job. I'd lost track by then of all the combinations he had tried. He talked about them when-ever we spoke, but they had blurred together in my mind.

On the highway I had to remind him to keep up his speed on the hills and when to use his blinkers. He'd always had a poor sense of direction but after we stopped for gas outside Albany, he couldn't even find his way back to the thruway. I lost my patience then, and told him to pull over and let me drive.

It took us another five hours in occasional rain to reach Ni-agara Falls. The quickest route to Lansing was through southern Ontario and back across the border at Port Huron. Niagara was an obvious place to stop for the night, and neither of us had ever been. I found us a motel on the Canadian side with a parking lot large enough to accommodate the truck and hitch, and checked us in on my credit card. There wasn't much daylight remaining, and I wanted to get down to the water to see about catching a boat out to the falls.

"I should stay here," Michael said.

We were both frazzled from the drive, but I couldn't stand the idea of not getting out for a walk.

"What if someone calls?" he said in a stricken voice. He sat perched on the edge of one of the beds, staring at the motel phone.

"What are you talking about?"

"I'm not getting any signal," he said. "They might try the landline."

"They? Who's they?"

He examined me in alarm, as if I were telling him to abandon a vigil for the missing.

"No one even knows we're here," I said. "No one has that number."

He heard my words but didn't seem to believe them. "You go ahead," he said. "I'll be here."

"That phone isn't going to ring," I said. "Get your jacket."

He hesitated a moment, tortured by the dilemma, and then he did as I said. I don't know what I detested more: his reluctance or his capitulation. They both infuriated me.

Out on the street, he trailed a few feet behind me, and I had to slow up to keep him at my side. We passed through hordes of tourists milling at the bins of trinket shops and gazing like deer into the caverns of sports bars. I hadn't expected much from the place, but I hadn't realized how ugly it would be, either.

We reached the passageway leading under the road and down toward the water, and joined the other latecomers being funneled into the lines of metal stanchions. Before long, we were through the ticket booth and onto a boat.

As it eased away from the shore, we climbed onto the upper deck, and the cliff came into view, and behind that the high-rise hotels. I headed toward the front, glad for the cooler air. A few minutes later, as we neared the falls and the boat nosed its way into the mist, people donned their clear plastic ponchos and we bobbed back and forth at the edge of being enveloped by the spray. We had seen this sight at a distance crossing the bridge from the American side, and I had thought, Yes, there it is, as pictured. But without the perspective of distance it was suddenly unfamiliar. A white atmosphere billowed around us like the depthless, blank white that people claim to see as death approaches. And high above this cloud, the huge lip of water tumbled downward, a perfect disintegrating line against the waning sky.

I had heard someone describe seeing the Himalayas for the first time, how they appeared like the limit of the earth, an edge beyond which there could be nothing but the emptiness of space. I'd never understood what they were talking about until now. I knew what I was seeing—what I was supposed to be seeing—yet

243

on that rocking deck, with the roar in my ears and the whiteness encompassing me, my points of reference fell away, and it seemed that I was gazing into the void.

It's worth it, I thought. Just for this, for a few moments of the almost sublime, even if I had to half talk my way into it, and allow myself the cliché of being impressed by Niagara Falls. I was in awe. And the vastness washed the frustrations of the day away, and I forgave Michael his worry and his fear.

When I turned around, I spotted him at the stern, not glancing upward but off the side of the boat, his glasses beaded with water. Everyone had raised the hoods of their ponchos, but this somehow hadn't occurred to him. His black hair was soaked flat against his scalp, and he was hunching his shoulders, as if that would protect him from the sky.

Just look, for Christ's sake! Look! I wanted to shout, but he wouldn't have heard me.

The boat began to chug in reverse, the prow reemerging from the mist. I walked back to join Michael. The other passengers were chatting with one another now, flipping through images on their cameras to see what they had captured.

"Amazing, right?" I said.

He nodded in a quick, automatic fashion, as if I had spoken in a foreign tongue and it was simplest for him just to agree.

"You're soaked," I said.

"Oh," he said. "I guess I am."

We reached the border crossing at Port Huron by midmorning the next day, and East Lansing by early afternoon. His apartment was a few miles south of campus in one of the graduate-student housing blocks set along a wooded cul-de-sac. The building was a two-story stretch of concrete, from the early sixties by the look of it, with stairwells at either end of a wide, second-floor walkway.

His unit had two rooms, a galley kitchen, and a bathroom, with white cinder-block walls and linoleum floors. Five hundred dollars a month, Internet and utilities included. Celia had done the research online, and she and I had agreed he wouldn't get a better deal even if he made a trip in advance. It would be the first place he'd ever lived on his own. I wished it were nicer.

"It's clean," I said, and he agreed.

We needed to unload the boxes and get the truck returned before we were charged for another day. The records took nearly an hour, and the books that much again, despite his having left most of both collections in our mother's basement. He had a futon, a chest of drawers, a desk, bookcases, a few lamps, and one of the old wingback chairs from the living room whose torn fabric my mother had pinned a cloth over. I asked him how he wanted the furniture arranged and he said he didn't know. I suggested the desk by the front window, and the bookcases along the rear wall, and he agreed. The boxes we left in stacks by the door and in the bedroom. When we were done, I followed him in the Grand Am to the rental lot on the other side of town. I'd reminded him as we were leaving that we needed to fill the tank before returning the truck, but he passed one gas station after the next, until I called him on his cell and told him again.

He turned off into a Speedway, and I parked at the edge of the lot to wait for him. He struggled with the gas cap, unable to open it. A minute went by, and then another, and still he couldn't manage the task. He didn't kick the truck in frustration. He showed no signs of impatience at all. He just stood there, failing at it. Until eventually he turned around and scanned the lot. When he saw me, he didn't wave me over or call my name. He remained by the capped tank, helpless and abdicating. Can't you do it for me? his expression asked.

"I'm curious," I said later, in a Thai restaurant in a strip mall near campus. "What would you have done if I hadn't been there?"

"I guess I would have figured it out," he said sheepishly.

"And if you'd been with Caleigh, you would have figured it out, right? You wouldn't have just stopped. What is that? Why do you do that with me?" He'd passed beyond his hyperarticulate, racing worry into a kind of fugue state, scared of the menu and the waiter and the food. "Why should it be different?" I said, jabbing the question at him, willing him to do better than this.

"I don't know," he said. "I'm sorry."

My phone rang—Seth calling from Denver. I told Michael I would be back, thankful for the excuse to get up and walk out, even if it was into the hot evening air.

"It's like babysitting," I said after Seth asked me how things were going. "Like taking care of an aging child."

"He must be glad you're there, though," Seth said.

"I guess. That's not how it comes out, but yeah."

I asked about his visit home. He'd spent the morning playing video games, and the afternoon at the mall. When we'd first started dating, each new discovery—that I didn't need to make weekend plans to fill empty evenings, that I had someone to talk to at the end of the day—had come as a revelation. The discoveries were different now. I could sense his mood in a phrase or two. I knew when he was worried about me, and felt guilty for it. These were their own kind of marvels, strangely reassuring as proof that Seth and I were, in fact, involved. Just hearing him describe his day with his family untensed me. Forty-eight hours with Michael and it was as if my own life had ceased. I hadn't returned phone calls or even responded to my editor's e-mails. Through the plate-glass window of the restaurant, I saw my brother waiting in front of the food that had now arrived. For a moment, I glimpsed him as a stranger might: a thin, unshaven man in black cotton work pants and a gray button-down shirt damp at the armpits. Pale-skinned, hair thinning, already middle-aged.

Seth was going on about a party he wanted us to go to the following weekend, and a friend he wanted me to meet, and I said it all sounded fine, without really listening, thinking instead of the picture of Bethany I'd seen on the desktop of Michael's computer when he opened it at the apartment, still there after all these years.

"You had a long day," Seth said. "I'll let you go."

"Can we talk before bed?"

"Yes, silly. Of course."

As soon as I reached the table, Michael asked what was wrong.

"Nothing," I said. "Why should anything be wrong?"

"I just thought something might be the matter."

"No," I said, scraping rice onto my plate, suddenly ravenous. "It was Seth. The guy I'm seeing. I've mentioned him to you."

"Is he okay?"

"He's fine," I said. "Everything's fine."

"You're dating him."

"Yes."

"That's good," Michael said. "How is it going?"

"Actually," I said, "it's going really well." I could have stopped there. But he'd asked. "To be honest, I think we might be in love."

His head moved fractionally up and back, as if avoiding a punch. "That's good," he repeated, more gravely this time. "I'm amazed you haven't been talking about it. I can't imagine not needing to talk about it. Given how frightening it is. You must be afraid he's going to leave you."

"Not really. I think we're good."

He squinted at me, trying to make sense of what I was saying. "Where did you meet?"

"Online. Last winter. He's from Colorado. His parents are still

247

there, still married. Apparently they want to meet me, which I guess is a good sign."

"Extraordinary," Michael said. "Has he been in therapy?"

"I don't think so."

"What do you guys talk about?"

"Whatever comes up, I guess. He's got good taste in music. You'd like some of the stuff he's played me."

More than telling him I was in love, it was telling him this that felt cruel. Michael's crushes had always run through music. This would make it real for him.

"He understands my work, too," I said. "When things come up last minute, or I have to leave town, he's good about that. You should meet him sometime."

"Sure," Michael said, gazing at the curries, which he still hadn't touched. He didn't lack an appetite. He just seemed to have forgotten how to serve himself.

"Here," I said, holding out a plate to him. "Eat."

And so we did, in silence.

"What courses are you going to take?" I asked, eventually.

This he was able to answer at length, listing subjects and texts, going into the critical orientations of the various members of the faculty and how they did or didn't comport with his own theoretical commitments. "I've read most of the first two years of the material before," he said. "I'd start my dissertation tomorrow, if they'd let me."

Seeing an opening, he started in on his perennial subject: slavery and trauma. I could never tell if he actually thought he was discoursing on all this to me for the first time, in which case the drugs had given him mild dementia, or if—and this seemed more likely—it didn't matter a great deal whom he was describing it to, he just needed to narrate it, over and over.

Earlier that summer the magazine had run my first feature in months. I had written a story about Wall Street bundlers who had begun to favor Democrats. My editor had cut some of the color I'd worked hard to get into the piece but not, for once, the implied criticism. It had drawn a slew of comments on the website and been reposted all over, making the marketing department giddy with excitement. Michael was on the list of friends and family to whom I had sent a link, people who didn't read the magazine and would otherwise never see my work. He'd been on that list for years. My mother subscribed, of course, wanting to see my articles in print. Celia usually sent a quick e-mail in response, as she had to this one. But from Michael, as usual, not a word. At home during Thanksgiving or Christmas, he would listen attentively enough if I was telling him about an assignment, but I had no sense if he ever read what I wrote, and, if he did, what he thought of it.

As the waiter arrived to clear our plates, I asked Michael about it. Maybe it was having finally told him about Seth. Or the fact that I had a flight back to New York in the morning, and didn't know when I would see him next. Or simply that the two of us hadn't spent this kind of time together in I couldn't remember how long, and I wanted to know.

He appeared confused by my question, and took his time answering.

"You've had advantages," he said. "The networks you've been a part of, the friends who've hired you." How did he know friends had hired me? Had I told him that? Had Celia? "The kinds of advantages most black people don't get," he added.

I'd been leaning forward in my chair, keen for his response, but I sat back in wonder now. I didn't think he had given my reporting a second thought. But no, he had it all worked out.

"And so that makes what I do illegitimate?"

"Not illegitimate. It's just part of the context. Not many black women report on politics for national magazines."

"Oh, come on. Is that really where we still are? Isn't that what you called 'bureaucratic multiculturalism'? Checking the box with a colored face?"

"That's a danger, sure. But maybe what's more telling is how you take the suggestion that the world isn't a pure meritocracy. Like it's an insult to your accomplishment."

"And it isn't?"

"Well. If it's an insult, think what that means: all the qualified people just happen to be upper middle class and white. That's a three-hundred-year coincidence."

"I'm asking you about the work I do, and you're giving me a lecture on affirmative action?"

His impassive eyes gave him the look of an ideologue trying not to sacrifice principle for sentiment.

"I read your piece," he said. "It was well done."

Maybe because I was tired, or because it had been so long since he'd offered me any praise, even this reluctant snippet caused my self-pity to well up in its warm, depressive sweetness. I worked as hard as I did, for so little pay, on articles and mini-articles and web teasers that passed into the ether almost as soon as they were published, ignored in favor of the cable-news bloviators, and yet still it turned out I was too privileged and establishment to satisfy my brother's politics.

"Thanks," I said, signaling the waiter for the check. "I'm glad you liked it."

Back at the apartment, he helped me assemble his futon, and we opened the boxes with the sheets our mother had packed, along with the pillows and blankets. He made up the bed while I put away the plates and bowls, and rinsed off the silverware. Then we unpacked his suitcases and set up his closet. I wished we could play music, something to make the rooms a little familiar before I left, but he had forgotten his speaker cables, so we worked to the sound of the fan in the window.

By the time we'd sorted all his belongings except the books and records, it was nearly eleven. I had an early flight from Detroit, and it would take us an hour and a half to get to the airport in the morning. I had booked myself a motel, and I drove us there in the Grand Am, along the empty streets, wanting more than anything for him to say something funny as we passed the gas stations and the darkened malls, something absurd to lighten the moment and release us both.

In the parking lot, as I handed him the car key, it struck me that I should have booked us both at the motel, so he wouldn't have to sleep in that apartment with no air-conditioning on his own. But it was late. It would take time for him to go back and get his pills, and I was exhausted.

Michael

I'd imagined it like the reading group with Caleigh and Myra: the camaraderie of a devotion to radical scholarship, an interrogation of the historical determinants of affect in black life, and perhaps some volunteers for the reparations movement. But to my shock it turned out that most of my fellow grad students subscribed to cable, went to the gym, and weren't certain yet what interested them enough to write about. It's not that they objected to my work, or didn't want to hear about transgenerational haunting, but it didn't move them. It was my thing, which was fine by them, though not a cause for urgency. Doubtless I came across as something of an odd quantity, being the only white man in the program and older than the junior faculty. Which isn't to say anyone behaved in an unfriendly manner, just that if there was a potluck, I didn't hear about it. No matter, I told myself, you're here to do your work.

That might have been enough, if I'd been able to consume books and articles as fast as I had those many years ago during the first reprieve of Klonopin. But pages of text appeared waxed to me now, covered in a film of distraction. By noon I'd have only a paltry set of notes, and acid in my stomach at the horror of all that remained unread. I kept putting off the duller course work to try to do my own, only to fall behind on both. In the evenings, on the phone, Caleigh tried to convince me things would improve, that I simply needed to adjust, while Mom suggested I would sleep better if I turned down the heat.

It hadn't occurred to me that living on my own would be different from living with Ben and Christine. I'd come to dread Ben reminding me IT'S THURSDAY, the day I spent in fear of forgetting to take out the garbage or properly clean the bathroom (I might use the wrong detergent and ruin the tile; I might miss a patch of mold and reap a silent resentment). There was none of that on my own now at Spartan Village. I took the trash out when so moved. Yet no one was in the other room watching *24*, eating slow-cooked legumes. No one affectionately mocked my frozen-enchilada dinners, as Christine had for years. I hadn't realized that her laughter was what made them honorable. I had lived most of my adult life with Ben, and later with him and Christine together, without noticing I was doing it, and yet I had never suspected that hearing the muffled edge of their conversations through closed doors and the toilet flushing upstairs had done so much to assure me that other people existed. In the new apartment the cinder-block walls cut off all sound of the neighbors.

Occasionally, on the walkway, I'd chat with the portly medical resident from next door, a soft-skinned, childlike man from Delaware who was doing a rotation at a pain clinic and complaining of having to treat nothing but refractory patients. Like the woman who'd gone to visit relatives in Chicago after her third spinal surgery only to be run down in the aisle of a Costco in a shopping-rage incident, requiring him, against his better judgment, to FedEx her a prescription for fentanyl patches, which she'd applied all in one go, causing her to miss the Detroit stop on her bus home, and sleep through to Toronto. They're dumpster cases, he said, other services don't want to deal with them, so they turf them over to us. Leading me, naturally, to wonder what kind of supplies he might keep in his own apartment.

As is the way of things, I was forced to take more Klonopin to get through the days. Dr. Bennet had written me for a decent supply to tide me over during the transition, but I'd run through it in a jiffy. Then I went through the batch that Dr. Greenman, my new shrink at the University Department of Mental Hygiene, had prescribed before a month had passed. The first time, she obliged me with an early refill, and she did it again a few weeks later, as any humanitarian would. But after my third request she began exhibiting signs of moralism, suggesting I needed to be more disciplined.

By then, the sweating had commenced. Night sweats were one thing. I was used to waking in soaked sheets; bedding could be laundered and the day needn't be lost. But sweating through my shirt before making it to the bus stop was a real drag. The temperature had nothing to do with it. Wind could be blasting off the steppes of Michigan and still my pores ran like broken faucets, my skin as slick as a clapped donkey in July. In seminar, I hesitated to raise my hand lest the stench of my underarm waft across the table. But I'd waited a long time to get here and I wanted to contribute, so I started bringing a washcloth and an extra set of clothes with me onto campus each day, to towel off and change before class.

The program was affiliated with a mentoring scheme for minority high schoolers, and with Caleigh's encouragement, I signed up to volunteer two afternoons a week. They paired me with a sopho-more named Jaylen. Our first task was to work through a review book for the state English test. But after ten minutes muddling through a Marge Piercy poem, I commented on his Juicy J T-shirt, and we got sidetracked on a discussion of the Memphis origins of crunk. I concurred in his judgment that Three 6 Mafia's "It's Hard Out Here for a Pimp" was a mainstreamed train wreck by an otherwise innovative crew, and that Juicy J himself bore much of the responsibility, given his brand-expansion ambitions. This was around the time that Oris Jay (aka Darqwan) finally got around to releasing another Sheffield bass record on his homegrown Tex-ture label, and I suggested that if Jaylen really wanted to give his thorax a shake he check out some British dubstep. Which I'm happy to say he did. By our third meeting it was clear I had more in common with him than I did with my fellow grad students. For one thing, we were both fifteen (at the level of the psychic), we listened to inordinate quantities of dance music, and as far as I could tell, we were both attracted to his English teacher.

I did my best dragging him through Abigail Adams's correspon-dence and *Newsweek* excerpts on paragliding, but at the bottom of the sessions we always circled back to what we were listening to. When I mentioned I had a subwoofer in the trunk of my car, he asked if he could hear it, and I ended up driving him home to the beat of a Torsten Pröfrock / Monolake workout from Ber-lin. Rolling through the streets of Lansing with him, I realized I hadn't had anyone else in the car since arriving in Michigan, and certainly no one to listen to music with. I rather appreciated the company. Unlike my family, he never asked me to turn the volume down. And really, what would I have done all these years with-out a monster sound system in my car? Where else, beyond the walls of a club, can you experience bass loud enough to wipe your

255

memory clean without complaint from the neighbors? Sound systems are what turn cars into escape vehicles, even if you've got nowhere to go. A drive to the convenience store is five minutes of that storm blowing in from paradise. I'll take the sneers of oldsters at intersections expecting gunfire. The relief is too rare to give up for civility's sake.

Jaylen was understandably wary of me, but excited to suddenly be a font of pre-releases for his friends, who couldn't believe he'd got his hands on a bin full of screwed and chopped tracks they hadn't even heard of. I didn't review much anymore (not wanting to write about Moby turned out to be a real professional liability), but the records and press releases still arrived by the bushel, adding to the stacks Alec thought I should be putting up on eBay. I started giving most of the non-dross to Jaylen. I'd fill a bag with CDs and the odd twelve-inch, and offer it to him when I dropped him off. I'm sure I went on too long when we happened upon a snippet of Wordsworth or a James Baldwin quote in his review materials, but he didn't seem to mind. You're weird, he said. How come you're not a professor? I told him that I was nominally in training to become one, but that I wasn't sure if the modern academy was sufficiently politicized for me. You should meet my mom, he said, she always votes. I'd seen his mother in their driveway a few times, and she'd offered a wave. Luckily her looks were not of such force as to arrest me at first sight, but I certainly had no objection to his suggestion that I make her acquaintance.

I appreciate you helping Jaylen, she said, when I brought him home one afternoon. I hope he's not asking you for all that merchandise you're giving him. That child is spoiled enough. I get it for free, I said, it's no trouble. So you're over at MSU, she said. I'm still working on my bachelor's over there. I keep saying I'll

finish in time so when he's getting out of high school we can graduate together, but we'll see if I make it.

Thank goodness that even at greater proximity she didn't trigger
in me the obsessional rush, tensing my gut or goading me into
telling her that I loved her. The moment had a gentler aspect. I
didn't converse with many people outside of seminars. Weekends
were empty—only phone calls, and always the apartment in silence when I hung up. Yet I didn't feel the necessity to romance this
woman. I only wanted to go into the house with the two of them
and share a meal. But then I heard Caleigh's voice saying, Flipper,
don't be a creep. So I kept it to pleasantries and took my leave.

When I raised my uncontrolled perspiration with Dr. Greenman,
she asked if there was anything I was particularly anxious about
at the moment. Like, say, the Feds trying to garnish my fellowship
checks for back taxes? Or your refusing to write me a script for
enough medicine to get by? Or that I waited so long for this
chance to get everything down, from George Clinton to the Fin-
land Station, from slave ships to Holocaust studies to the echo
of loss in the speed of a high hat, only to find my concentration
shot? But I didn't want to be rude. She was a basically sympathetic woman, in her wide-wale cords and cable-knit seasonals. I
believed her concern for my condition to be genuine, even if her
rectitude about prescribing controlled substances blinded her to
the fact that my need for them at this point was nothing more or
less than a way to make it through the hour.

What could I do? I began trolling for benzo equivalents on the
Internet, where people seemed to agree on the utility of kratom,
a quasi-opioid tea drunk by Thai fieldworkers that apparently
took the edge off in a serious way. The FDA hadn't gotten around

257

to banning it, so I ordered a pound and got started. It had no place in an aromatherapy regime, but neither did people with actual problems. Its effect was akin to strong coffee laced with high quantities of Benadryl. I consumed it every morning. That's how my days began: more Klonopin than the doctor ordered, a thermos of coffee, a mug of kratom, three or four legacy meds, a few hundred milligrams of whatever Dr. Greenman was pushing, followed by a hot shower. By November, I'd largely given up on my course reading, let alone any assignments past due, which made attending my seminars less relevant and even inappropriate. My mother would only worry if I told her, as would Celia and Alec. I talked to Caleigh about it, but she chastised me, saying that even if I didn't write brilliant essays, I needed to keep up with the work. This was my chance, she said. This was how I would find a job.

On Tuesday and Thursday afternoons, I did my best to gather myself with a change of shirts and an extra cup of kratom before driving over to the school to pick up Jaylen. The idea was that we meet for the first month in the safe space of the school and then, once trust had been established, we could venture out on our own. Mentors were asked to keep tabs on their mentees' academic progress, but we weren't required to limit ourselves to that. Mostly Jaylen and I drove around Lansing with the subwoofer.

I'd started playing him old-school stuff I thought he should know, music I hadn't listened to in years, Larry Levan garage mixes, Afrika Bambaataa, Neil Young, anything with an ache of the real. When I got to Donna Summer, though, he balked. You're just trying to mess with me, he said. That's fag music. To date, he'd struck me as a mild-mannered kid. As for his mother, on the spectrum of the politics of black respectability, she fell somewhere in the hesitant middle, of small enough means to preclude class pretensions but scared enough for her son to want him to toe a line she never had. Music seemed like their compromise, the thing she didn't try to control. He could visit the imaginary power of making his white classmates fear a black planet, but still turn the music off and get on with the business of getting on. But that masculine fantasy left no room for Donna Summer or Diana Ross or, for that matter, Nina Simone or David Bowie. They queered the pitch. Telling him that my younger brother was a respectable, middle-class homosexual didn't seem like it would do the trick. Instead, I played him the last twenty seconds of Summer and Moroder's "Our Love," where the synth begins to pulse and drip over the beat like chemicals made to dance, and I told him, There is no techno without this. It's the genealogy of what you already love.

When we got to his house, his mother, Trish, was just pulling in. I could offer you some coffee, she said, if you like. They lived in a one-story brick house with a front sitting room used only in the event of company. The couch and chairs were covered in clear plastic to protect the fabric, which I was glad for, relieved that my dampness wouldn't make a stain. On the glass-top coffee table was a bowl of dried flowers, russet and dusty pink. Jaylen sat uneasily on the far end of the couch from me, and rolled his eyes when his mother said she'd love for him to go to MSU when he graduated high school. He's already a Spartans fan, she said, so why not? Because I don't want to stay here, he said. She cast a chastising glance at him, then turned to smile at me.

Do you have your own kids, she asked, hopefully. Yes, I said, I have a son and a daughter. They're six and eight. Oh, that's just the best, she said, and laughed. By the time they get to this one's age they're nothing but trouble. Though he's better than his sister. She's already living at her boyfriend's and there wasn't no use trying to stop her. You must be run off your feet with those two, she said, and here you are taking time to help Jaylen.

They don't live with me, I said, they're with their mother in Chicago. I go there to visit them. I could feel Jaylen's eyes on me, but he said nothing. Well, at least you do that, she said, philosophically, at least you do that. Sweat flowed down my torso and I could only hope she didn't smell it. It's Jaylen's turn to make dinner, she said, he's doing tacos. You'd be welcome to stay.

After a few extra Klonopin in the bathroom, the scene became quite ordinary: the overhead light in the kitchen, the shredded Kraft cheese, Jaylen's dogging his mother for pestering him not to eat so fast. Even the conversation about what I studied, which usually confused people, seemed ordinary enough. When you live most days alone in a room with a tiger kept from pouncing on you by nothing more than your constant stare, being poured a cup of Pepsi can feel almost Christlike in its mercy. It seemed perfectly natural to tell his mother, when she asked, that I had grown up on the south side of Chicago in an extended, mixed-race family. Oh, Flipper, Caleigh would say later, and we would argue. But there I was, eating dinner with the two of them, and we were jovial.

Despite my repeated insistence, they wouldn't let me wash the dishes. They mistook it for a chore. They didn't know the pleasure it would give me, or what that pleasure would count for. But I was their guest, and so I desisted. It was already dark out, the early darkness of winter evenings, when six o'clock seems like midnight. Jaylen's mother turned on the outside light, and I thanked her for the hospitality on the way out to my car. Be safe out there, she said.

Driving back to the apartment, I wondered if it was the anxiolytics that had padded my longing with enough cotton wool to allow for a bit of glancing human contact without injury or fever, or if letting go a bit of the truth is what had helped me to reach that clearing.

What do you fear when you fear everything? Time passing and not passing. Death and life. I could say my lungs never filled with enough air, no matter how many puffs of my inhaler I took. Or that my thoughts moved too quickly to complete, severed by a perpetual vigilance. But even to say this would abet the lie that terror can be described, when anyone who's ever known it knows that it has no components but is instead everywhere inside you all the time, until you can recognize yourself only by the tensions that string one minute to the next. And yet I keep lying, by describing, because how else can I avoid this second, and the one after it? This being the condition itself: the relentless need to escape a moment that never ends.

I woke the next morning at five in soaked sheets and a panic. With water from the bedside table, I took my last Klonopin and went straight to the stove to put the kettle on for kratom. I did the yoga stretches Celia had taught me, and after that I sat upright in a hard-backed chair for five minutes trying to breathe intentionally, as it said to do in the pamphlet she'd given me on self-soothing. For some reason, when I finished I was still thirty-six, single, and about to die. I called Dr. Greenman for a refill but the secretary in Mental Hygiene said she was out for the day. I had run the morning routine but still the terror reigned. It was then that I checked my e-mail and read the message from the university saying that pursuant to a letter from the Department of Education about a previously undisclosed episode of default, they were putting a hold on the loan disbursement I needed for my rent and food.

When I managed to focus again on the screen, I looked up Dr. Greenman's home address, and drove to her house. It was a black-and-white Victorian with gingerbread trim and a bevy of shrubs clipped to the nines. She answered the door in a University of Wisconsin sweatshirt and a pair of burnt-orange wide-wales. The lenses of her glasses were big enough to serve demitasse off. Michael, she said, I don't see patients at home. You need to make an appointment through the clinic. I just need a refill, I told her, then I can get through the weekend and come in next week. We've talked about this, she said. I can't write prescriptions on demand, certainly not from my house. And if I'd taken a bullet to the groin, I wanted to say, you'd tell me to reschedule? Why don't I just bleed out on your hedge, and we'll call it a breakdown? But I couldn't be rude or unkind to her. Her affect remained warm, even as she sawed at the rope I was hanging from. Are you thinking of hurting yourself? she asked. Because if you are you need to go to the ER and tell them that I sent you. It was thirty degrees out, but I might as well have been weight training in Lagos for the river of sweat running down my back. Michael, she said, putting her hand on my forearm, as if I were a person at that moment, rather than a nerve, I want to help you, but I can't do it like this. If things get bad, she said. They are very bad, I said. I understand, she said. If things get worse, and you think you're in danger, you need to go to the hospital. I can't give you more of the drug, but I can meet you on Monday morning to discuss all this. We can come up with a plan. Right now I have my daughter with me, and I need to go back inside.

Caleigh was at work, and after half an hour of imploring me to just get in bed and watch *X-Files* reruns, she said she really, really had to get off the phone. Celia didn't pick up. Nor did Alec. I got my mother's machine but didn't want to leave a message that might upset her.

I don't know how long I stared at the picture of Bethany on my desktop screen before dialing her number. It might have been an hour. I examined the pixels of her teeth as I listened to her phone ring. Miraculously, after all her years of silence, she answered. She was saying hello, I was saying it's Michael and asking how she was, we were conversing. At long, long last. She had moved to Houston and finished college there. She had a job at a health club. I couldn't see her working at a health club, but she didn't sound as if she were dissembling. She asked about me and I said things were going okay, that I'd finally got into grad school and was trying to write. Are you going out with anyone? I asked, which of course I shouldn't have, period, let alone almost right away, but I had to know because if she was single and she had picked up the phone, then the vicious little engine in my chest idling at breakneck speeds might shut down long enough to let my eyes rest. You didn't call to ask that, did you? she said. No, no, I said, I'm just curious, I just want to know how you're doing. Okay, then, she said, if you say so. I'm engaged, actually. I think you'd like her.

The liquor store took my credit card with flying colors. Mostly the light amber of Cutty Sark and the shaking blue script of my signature. When I could be sure no one was looking, I sipped from the bottle in the parking lot, turning up the volume on Norma

Fraser's "The First Cut Is the Deepest" (is it self-pity when it provides no comfort?). Somehow I'd never become an alcoholic. Luck of the draw. But as a major CNS depressant, liquor has its advantages. It struck my reptile brain square on its diamond head. Booze—the ancient dimmer of fear and sorrow. The granny of all psychoactive meds, a blunt old hag toddling down out of the mountains with a demented smile and a club. World? she sneers. What world? And swings her cudgel at your skull.

Eventually a détente was achieved. The awful precision of things drifted off to one side. I drove around for a while, walled up in sound. About the music I had listened to since I was a child, my father had never said much. His own tastes were a mixed bag, baroque numbers he'd picked up in the Church of England, Elgar and the grand imperial fade-out, tossed in with Sinatra and Frankie Laine. But whenever "Bridge Over Troubled Water" came on the radio in the car, my mother would remind us that it had been one of his favorite songs, and it had often occurred to me that he had done something like that, laying himself down over the trouble he himself had become, so that we could pass on. I wondered how any of them—Celia or Alec or my mother—managed to live anywhere but on the lip of his grave, eyes pinned open, trying to look away. How were they not cold to the touch of anyone but those, like my father, like Bethany, who ended who you were by making you over again in their image?

There is just the one sequence: Stepping from the terminal at Logan into that furnace heat on the afternoon I arrived home from England with Peter Lorian, my undershirt soaking through before we crossed the parking lot, the glint of the sun on those car roofs, the blue sky and molten asphalt, all perfectly unreal and incredibly precise. Arriving at the house, seeing my mother with her arms open to hug me, her hugging me, my being impervious to her touch. Then watching the three of them cry in the living room, wanting to comfort them but not knowing how, sealed off and sure only of this: I left them here to suffer and now he is gone. The one sequence. Like a groove on a record cut too deep for the needle to climb out of. No matter what else is playing, this is always playing. That is the point of volume—to play something louder than this groove. The volume of speakers, or of obsession. The power of the sufficient dose.

The drizzle and headlights, the storefronts and street signs—they all ran into one another, softening things up. When I knocked on the front door of the house, it was Jaylen who answered. Hey, he said. We don't have the program today, do we? No, we don't, I said. And then, realizing I needed to say something more, I added, I just wanted to thank you for the meal last night, I was so glad to be here. No problem, he said, peering at me with some concern. My mom isn't home yet, if that's who you came for. No, no, I said, I just thought I'd drop by. Maybe it was true after all that I would never be with anyone romantically. That my anguish, which for a time had specialized in love, had once more become indivisible from the rest of life. In which case relief might come from elsewhere. Standing in front of me in the entrance, Jaylen was uncertain how to proceed. I'm sorry I don't have any records for you today, I said. That's all right, he said, you've given me a bunch. I can give you more, I said, many more. You need some kind of hood, he said. I looked up and felt the rain on my face. You're right, I said, I do. Is it okay if I come in?

He had a Technics turntable in his room set up on milk crates filled with vinyl. There was the requisite Tupac poster, and the one that I'd given him from Run-D.M.C.'s first album, with Simmons

265

and Smith in fedoras and tracksuits up against a brick wall. The bedsheets were still red Mickey Mouse. His schoolwork was piled on his dresser, his clothing on a beanbag, which he cleared for me to sit on. I picked something up yesterday you might like, you want to hear it? he asked. Please, I said, carry on. It was an Indochina remix of Kaci Brown's "Unbelievable." The original (hardly the right word) was a catchy, overproduced bit of Nashville hit-making, the kind of track that still gets called R&B though it's sung by a white teen from Sulphur Springs, Texas, and has neither. But Indochina (aka Brian Morse and A. Fiend) had stripped away the lip-gloss piano and session-music guitar, laying the vocals down over a four-to-the-floor beat straight out of 1979, but quickened to the pace of a Rotterdam gay night. I couldn't help but nod my head up and down, as Jaylen did, listening to this thoroughly unremarkable voice engineered to the vanishing point, and yet, when driven by the drum machine and lofted on waves of synth, still reaching the note that the heart pines for.

> It's unbelievable but I believed you
> Unforgivable but I forgave you
> Insane what love can do
> That keeps me coming back to you.

It's kind of gay, he said. I wouldn't play it at school, but it's got a kick, huh? Kind of gay? I wanted to say. Do you have any notion how many homosexuals sweated their asses off on the dance floor to make this soaring bit of derivative trash possible? How many died of AIDS, OD'd, or went broke on the way to that girl from Texas cutting a deal with Interscope to record a track that achieved its own unwitting ideal only when most of it was torn away by the people who really needed it? Any idea of how much eloquence was borrowed to pay that royalty? But it seemed like a lot to go into just now, and I felt as at rest as I had in a very long while, sitting in Jaylen's room with him, with the turntable and the records, talking about music. As if he were my friend and I was his. Yeah, was all I said, it's definitely got a kick.

He put on the Darqwan twelve-inch I'd suggested to him the day we met, "Rob One 7," a cavern of distorted bass filled with an assaultive drum line and haunted now and then by a laserlike phrase of keyboard. As good a sonic portrait of postindustrialism— or at least of unemployment in Sheffield—as one was likely to come across. Knowing his speakers weren't up to the task, Jaylen plugged in his headset and handed it to me while he flipped through a crate looking for what to play next. I slipped into the cavern and disappeared.

Here at last I could track the ghosts by ear, listening to them dance in the cut, the lost coming alive again in the vibrations of my skull, and through my whole body, which was free now to be nothing more than a tunnel, a passageway for the missing to travel back along, the music bringing them home.

Can I ask you a question? Jaylen said, when the track had ended. Sure, I replied. How come you told my mom you have kids? You don't have kids, do you? No, I don't, I said. I guess I just didn't want to disappoint her, she seemed to like the idea. But don't worry, I said, it's nothing romantic toward your mom, I just felt at home. I'm sorry if I let you down. The wall of the booze was beginning to disintegrate. I could feel it washing away and the dread rolling in behind it, lapping at the tips of my nerves.

You're strange, he said, cueing up another dubstep record, this one on a lower volume. He took a seat at his desk and scrolled through something on his phone. I should go, I thought. But the idea of getting up and leaving the house was terrifying. If I stayed here, in his company, I might knuckle through. They would cook dinner, I could eat with them. The overhead light, the grated cheese. It could be ordinary. My eyes started to twitch, as if I were caught in a waking dream. At the ER, they would think I was just a drug seeker.

The door opened and Jaylen's mother appeared. She looked across the room at me, prone on the beanbag, my body beginning to shake, and I could tell by the alarm on her face that it was getting late, that things were already far along, and that I would need their help.

Margaret

It's terrible how dry the ground has become. The brook is down to a trickle and the thistle and ferns along its banks look almost wintry. All of July and August it hardly rained, not even on the muggy days when thunderheads came through in the afternoon and lightning flashed in the distance. I had to water most evenings. It's the middle of October now and I'm still watering to keep the soil of the beds damp and the bushes from withering. Yet for all this, these last few weeks have been the most glorious weather, cloudless skies and temperate days, perfect for being out like this in the morning, and in the early evenings during the week, when I get home from work. The light is so clear in autumn.

In the meadow at the end of the street, the late-blooming asters have flourished despite the drought. The last snowy clusters run all the way up the slope to the verge of the woods. With your back to the road you get just a hint of wilderness, of what it would be like if none of us had ever come here. I used to avoid this section of my loop, it being the path John likely took. But eventually the avoidance became the reminder, and so for a long time now it has all been one, this place where he was, and I still am, the street and the field, alive with the change of seasons.

Around the yard lately I've been clipping back the red flowering branches of the euonymus, which was threatening to take over the driveway. There are bulbs to be planted, and beds to be re-soiled, along with the raking and mowing, which Michael has been such a help with. I don't have to ask him, he offers. We've taken all sorts of things to the dump which I wouldn't have been able to carry out of the bulkhead on my own: the tea chests in which we shipped our books back and forth across the Atlantic, full of old magazines; Alec's and Celia's high school belongings; a dorm room's worth of furniture Caleigh left with us ages ago. All of it good to be clearing out, given the situation.

We have breakfast together most days. He goes upstairs to his computer while I'm at work, and he's there at the house to greet me when I get home. I make supper, he does the dishes, often we watch a film before bed. The truth is I quite like having him with me again. He's a considerate person and always has been. He does talk about his predicament and his ideas at never-ending length, which means he's not always the best listener, but still, we're company for each other.

It was my friend Suzanne who recommended the real estate agent. She said Veronica was very pleasant and down to earth, unlike most of them, and that if I wanted, she would come by and have a look, just to see what the possibilities might be. I wouldn't be considering it if everything else I owe now didn't make it so hard to keep up the mortgage. The hospital's bill collectors are relentless. They call at all hours. They can be so unpleasant on the phone, as if we were criminals. And then with Michael not enrolled in his program, the loans I signed for him have come due, and there are those calls as well. I wish they would simply write. Then I could organize all the papers and take stock of them. I do hate not wanting to pick up my own phone when it rings.

I can't tell Alec about Veronica, or about the listing contract on my desk that she's waiting for me to sign. He'd stop me. And I don't want to bother Celia with all of it, not yet. It seems there might be seventy thousand or so left after everything's paid off, which is certainly more money than I've ever had at one time, and plenty to rent us an apartment. I would miss the garden, of course. That I can't pretend.

It was almost ten months ago that I got a call from Michael's doctor at the university. Michael had mentioned her to me, Dr. Greenman, and said that he found her sympathetic, which she certainly sounded on the phone. She said he had stopped a medicine too quickly, and that he'd been admitted to the hospital out there. It would be best if he took a leave of absence from school, she told me, and got transferred to a facility nearer home. Celia was the one who called her back and made the arrangements. Alec instructed me not to sign anything at the hospital here until he looked at the papers, but it all happened quickly, picking Michael up at the airport and driving him to that fortress of a building up on the North Shore. They wouldn't admit him unless I signed, so I did, which is why the bills now come addressed to me.

I drove up there to visit him almost every day, bringing him bags of pistachios, which he's always loved, and music magazines, and whatever toiletries he needed. His roommate was younger, in his early twenties, and pale as a sheet. He didn't seem to have any visitors of his own, so I brought nuts for him too, and pears, which he thanked me for in a whisper. Where his parents were, I have no idea.

At times Michael would be asleep when I arrived, and I would sit by the window with the paper, not wanting to disturb his rest. He lay on his stomach and side, his shoulder rising slightly with each breath. I hadn't watched him sleep since he was a boy. His hands and feet still had their little twitches about them, and he swallowed with a motion of his whole neck, and burrowed into his pillow. Before Celia and Alec were born, I used to stand over his bed and wonder at him: the mystery of his sleep, of his having a life separate from my own, sequestered in the privacy of dreams. A warm feeling, but lonely, too, because I loved him with more need than anyone I'd loved before, and when he slept I understood that he could leave me, and that eventually he would. At least in sleep he had a respite from bodily tension, the kind that had been with him from the very beginning, and which I had only ever been able to assuage briefly and in small measure.

I was younger then than he is now. Which makes the sequence wrong, being at his bedside like that.

None of the children, Michael least of all, would have wanted to hear that it happened to be almost forty-one years since I had taken the bus to Lambeth to visit their father in another north-facing hospital room. What do the dates matter? I could hear them asking, and I would have had no answer to satisfy them. They think it's simple of me, to keep track of time this way. I don't ascribe anything deep to it, I don't say it means anything in particular, other than that I'm sure I spend too much time thinking about the past. But it is a way to remain connected. Like visiting each of them if they move, so I can picture exactly where they are, which I do every night as I'm going to sleep, the images bridging the distance. Dates do the same. If I measure off the months and years, it is to link me to them, and back to them when they were children, and earlier still to when John and I were together before we were married, when everything was just beginning.

The reason, it turned out, that Michael was sleeping so much in the hospital was the new drug he had been put on. I don't remember the name of it; it begins with a Z. Dr. Bennet said it was an antipsychotic, but that I shouldn't be alarmed. Michael wasn't at all psychotic, he said, it was just that the medicine happened to be effective for anxiety as well.

272

When he first came back to the house, Michael did seem calmer. After a month or so I noticed he'd begun to put on weight. Good, I thought. He'd always been thin as a rake; it seemed a sign of health. But it kept going. He wasn't eating vast amounts of food—I don't cook vast amounts of food—but he got bigger by the week. In the last nine months, he's put on forty pounds, at least. He didn't remotely have a belly before but he does now. He's gone from concave to nearly barrel-chested. Even his eyes are set farther back in his head, encased in an extra layer of flesh. It's not right. His frame was never meant for it. This is the medicine they give to a man trying to regain his confidence? Together with all the other drugs, it's slowed his mind. When he talks, he pauses and halts, gets lost and trails off.

I do my best to bring him walking with me, especially if he's still in the house when I get back from work. Just fifteen or twenty minutes around the neighborhood at a decent pace to get him moving, not for the sake of his weight but because it's not good to be so sedentary. He usually says he'd rather not, and then I have to convince him. And on top of that persuade him that he doesn't need to bring his messenger bag, that black sack he can't be without. He's got half a pharmacy in there, along with books and papers. He treats it like a survival kit wrapped in a safety blanket. What if I need something while we're out? he'll say. On a walk? I ask. In the supermarket? It makes no sense. But each time I bring it up, it's as if I've never mentioned it before, as though he's never contemplated being without it and has to consider the risk anew. If I press, he relents, but I don't always, and so sometimes he walks beside me with the overstuffed bag slung over his shoulder like a deliveryman taking a stroll, and I wonder what people think when they see the two of us go by.

*　　*　　*

When I arrive back at the house, Michael's already made the coffee.

A few weeks after he left the hospital and moved in, I started having heart palpitations. I went to my doctor, assuming they were caused by the strain of his return. But the first question he asked was whether I'd been having more caffeine than usual. Unbeknownst to me, I had—triple the dose—drinking Michael's brew. So now I take just a third of a mug and add water from the kettle.

I tell him I'm meeting Suzanne for lunch later. Because my car is in the shop, I need to borrow his. "I could give you a ride," I add, hoping he'll want to come into the city. He goes once a week or so, to see friends, I'd like to think, but I don't interrogate him.

"Right," he says, the idea at least registering.

As we're finishing breakfast, Dorothy, from next door, appears on her front steps with her dog, Tilly, on the leash, which reminds me of the clippings from the paper I want to give her. She smiles and waves when she sees me coming across the yard with them.

"These are silly," I say, "but I've been meaning to leave them on your doorstep. I thought they might amuse you."

She thanks me, putting them in the pocket of her windbreaker, and we marvel at the glorious weather. I haven't gotten around to mentioning anything to her about the possibility of my leaving the neighborhood. I don't want to set everything in motion before I have to.

"How's Michael?" she asks in her usual cheerful tone, giving me a chance to say whatever I want, but keeping it light enough that I don't have to go into anything I'd rather not. I've always appreciated this about her, from the time she first moved into the neighborhood with her two children, soon after John died. She's not afraid to talk about anything, but she isn't insistent either.

After I tell her we're going into the city for the afternoon, she asks if we'd like to come over for stew later. I've eaten at her house umpteen times, and she in mine, but for some reason this morning her offer of dinner thrills me.

"That sounds wonderful," I say.

"Just knock, I'll be here."

As I turn back up the driveway, Michael's dreadful bumper sticker confronts me: *I HATE MY LIFE,* printed in big black letters on a white rectangle. He has no other bumper stickers—no flags or political slogans—just the rusted Pontiac emblem and *I HATE MY LIFE,* ludicrous and stark, there for Dorothy and anyone else who passes by to cringe at. I sometimes reverse the direction of the car, so that the sticker faces the garage, which Michael never seems to notice, but I can't do it every night.

I had to drive his car through the middle of town yesterday with that plastered on the back of it, everyone assuming the sentiment was mine. In the grocery-store lot, the bag boy could barely keep himself from laughing. It's absurd. And now I'm supposed to drive all the way to Boston.

I've had it. I walk into the garage, find the least ancient ice scraper on the shelf, and set to work. It's hard going, and I have to lean my weight into it, but the plastic edge does raise the sticker, bit by bit. I'm just about done with *HATE* when Michael sees me through the dining room window and steps out the front door to ask what I'm doing.

"What does it look like? I'm getting rid of this awful thing."

"But it's my car."

"That may be, but I have to drive it. And I'm not driving it with this on it. It's *ridiculous,* Michael. It's so *negative.*"

"It's a song. From the Pernice Brothers."

"It's perverse, that's what it is. Why in the world would you want to advertise such a thing?"

"You're worried about who's going to see it?" he asks, as if that were a bizarre concern.

"You don't hate your life, Michael. No one hates their entire life. It's juvenile."

He steps closer and glances down at the crinkled paper that hangs from the *MY LIFE* still adhered to the metal. Then, without a word, he takes the scraper from my hand.

I'm amazed by the assertion of his move. Shocked, even. I can barely believe it. He never does such things. I'm almost thankful. So what can I do but keep my sudden disappointment to myself when he steps past me and begins scraping away at what's left.

Driving along the pike, he stays in the right-hand lane behind a Hood Milk truck going fifty miles an hour. Alec would be whipping along, as if enacting some espionage fantasy, leaving me to grip the door; Celia would be in the middle lane; and Michael a decade ago wouldn't have realized how fast he was going, but now we remain stolidly behind the truck, and I say nothing.

We park on Boylston, near Copley, and he hands me the keys, saying he'll take the T back and get a bus home from the station. I tell him that if he lets me know where he's going to be, I can swing by when I'm through and give him a ride, if he's ready. He says maybe the record shop on Mass. Ave., but that I shouldn't worry about it, and then he walks off, the hood of his sweatshirt up over his head despite the plentiful sun.

At the restaurant, Suzanne is already installed in a booth, enjoying a glass of white wine. She's wearing a scoop-neck blouse and her red jade necklace, with her voluminous, dyed-black hair down over her shoulders. In all the years we've worked together, she's changed remarkably little. She's still forever on the make.

She hands me the wine list as soon as I'm in my chair. "What are you having?" she says. "It's on me today. I'm celebrating. Don't ask me what, I'm just celebrating."

The waiter, a conventionally handsome boy in his twenties, approaches.

"Do you ever do that?" she asks him. "Celebrate for no reason."

"Sure," he says, smiling gamely.

Right away, she starts in on gossip. The new library director's salary is apparently out of all proportion to what the rest of the staff earns; a member of the board is suspected of philandering with the wife of an Argentinian businessman; and the boy caught vandalizing the men's room turns out to be the younger brother of the previous vandal, which I'd already heard, but it serves up anew the question of the boys' stupendously wealthy and neglectful parents. I've never had Suzanne's talent for being scandalized. To be able to entertain oneself so fully is a skill of sorts. Particularly given the material at hand.

She's on her second glass of wine by the time we finish our salads, while I've barely touched my first. At work she's always whispering, her facial expressions tightly controlled, but in this half-empty restaurant, she gestures broadly, her eyes widening at the news she herself reports.

Eventually, in the lull of attending to her trout, she manages to inquire about Michael and the house sale, like small talk at an intermission. "What do his doctors say?"

"They hear about John, and that's it. They're convinced it's in the genes. Which I'm sure is part of it. But they didn't know them both. Michael's not his father. His father didn't spend so much of his time caught up with other people's suffering, the way Michael does with everything he reads."

"Misery loves company."

"How do you mean?"

"I'm an alcoholic," Suzanne says. "I suppose I've never said it to you flat out like that before, but it's not a surprise, right? Some people take pills. Some people go to church. I drink. Everybody's got something. I've known Michael a long time now. He's a tense guy. Doesn't have a lot of outlets. He suffers. What I'm saying is, it's *identification,* all that reading he does. It's what we tell the school groups when they read novels—see yourself in someone else's shoes. Right? There's nothing ambiguous about slavery. Plenty of misery there."

And with that, she shrugs, as if to say, *C'est la vie.*

When the waiter appears to check on us, she puts her hand on his forearm and says, "Be a darling, won't you, this Sancerre is just delicious."

I was hungry when I sat down, but I'm not anymore. "The fact is," I say, "I don't need that whole house, and if we moved closer in it would be easier to get to things. And better than shouting with Alec about money, and Alec shouting at Michael, which is all some families do."

"You're a good mother," she says. "Better than mine ever was. You're devoted to those kids."

"I'm not sure they see it that way."

"They should. Are you kidding? You could have been a train wreck, and who would have blamed you?"

Despite my protest, she won't let me split the bill. I'm still trying to give her cash as we walk back onto Dartmouth, where the wind has picked up.

"Don't give me any money," she says. "Just shop with me for a bit."

I can hardly decline, and it will give Michael longer before I go looking for him. I have to fight off her suggestions for a half dozen dresses and little bits of jewelry, after which she finally settles down and shops for herself. When we eventually say good-bye at her car, she makes me swear she hasn't been a bore, and that we'll do it again.

"About all that other stuff, I always thought your house was a little drab," she says, displaying her usual tact, her mouth still loose with wine. I shouldn't be letting her drive. "So don't worry about it. You'll do the right thing."

Leaves rain down across the wide path that stretches along the middle of Commonwealth Avenue. I pass women with strollers, and joggers out in the fine fall weather. Whenever it was pleasant out, this is where I came to read while John had his appointments with Dr. Gregory on Marlborough Street. In the cold or the rain, I would stay in the car, and wait. For someone else, besides me, to tell him that things couldn't go on the way they were.

I ran into him once, Dr. Gregory. At the cinema with his wife, a few months after John died. I wanted to hurt him. But we shook hands and he asked politely how I had been. It wasn't until much later that Michael began seeing him. I imagine he's still there, in that grand office of his.

When I reach Mass. Ave., I turn left, looking for the door that opens onto the staircase to the little record shop. I've been here once but forget which entryway it is. Up the block is the Virgin Store at the top of Newbury, and there in front of it, to my surprise, is Michael. He's standing on the corner, his messenger bag slung over his shoulder, handing out flyers to the people rushing by. He holds the papers out, forcing them to decline before passing. As if he's been paid to advertise some suit sale, or attract converts to a religious cult. The sight of it makes me flinch. Something is the matter. He's become confused somehow, unmoored.

I'm less than half a block away but still he hasn't seen me. I start walking toward him, to help him out of whatever trouble this is, and then I remember the pamphlets—the ones he keeps in his bag, with the picture of the black farmer tilling a field. That's what he's doing. He is handing out his pamphlets on reparations. Little booklets on the history of the slave trade for these Saturday-afternoon shoppers, who think they're being offered coupons and freely ignore him.

He's smiling as he does it, at each person, trying to establish a second of rapport. It's that deliberate, nodding politeness of his, apologizing for the inconvenience he's putting them through while imposing himself nonetheless.

I can't move. I want to stop him, to save him from being judged a kook, reduced to proselytizing on a street corner. But I'm the last person he wants to see. To be embarrassed by his mother fretting over him in public would only make it worse. I'm about to go, but he's seen me now and appears frozen, his hands down at his sides, his smile suddenly gone. He looks fixedly at me, as if suddenly there were no one on the street but the two of us. I must not cry. It isn't fair to him. I wave, and smile, and call out, "I'll see you later, then, I'm off," and I turn my back to him and retreat up the block.

Later, in the evening, after he has returned, the rain comes. It begins as a shower but soon the skies open and the drops drum fast against the roof and slap the windowpanes. I hurry around closing windows before the sills get soaked. Warm air floats through the screens of the vestibule and the back porch on this October night, as if carried in by a belated summer thunderstorm, one of those that never delivered its moisture back in August. On the dry ground, the water will run straight to the gutters, wasted. We need a soak, not a torrent. Twenty minutes later it is gone, swept away to the east, and there is only the sound of dripping branches, and the dark shining in the porch light.

One of the cable channels is showing *The Philadelphia Story*, which I haven't seen in years. I ask Michael if he'd like to watch it with me but he declines, saying he's going to head upstairs. It is such a pleasure of a movie, so stylish and light. You can't help but cheer for the drunken Cary Grant to get Hepburn back. They are meant for each other. I watch a bit, then a bit more, and soon it has carried me off into its gentle absurdity. It's already midnight when it ends. On my way to bed, I see Michael's light on under his door. Best to leave him be, I think, which is what I do, walking past without saying good night, in case he's fallen asleep reading.

It's in the small hours of the morning that I'm startled awake by a knocking at my door, and then the door opens and Michael stands there silhouetted by the sudden glare of the hall bulb.

"What *is* it, what *is* it?"

"I can't breathe," he says. "I'm suffocating."

My bedside lamp reveals a look of pure terror on his face. He comes to the foot of my bed, clutching his chest.

"Are you choking?"

"No, no, I just can't breathe, I can't breathe."

"Well, sit down," I tell him. Which he does, perching by my legs, his whole torso heaving. "Is it the asthma? Do you have your inhaler?"

"I'm not wheezing. I have to go to the hospital, you have to call an ambulance."

I get out of bed and put on my bathrobe. "It's all right," I say. "You're having an attack, isn't that right? You're worried. It's okay. Just keep breathing. Did you have a bath? I can run you a bath."

"No!" he says. "You have to call an ambulance."

"Michael! Come on now. You need to calm down. We're not calling an ambulance in the middle of the night. We can try Dr. Bennet in the morning. You're not going to the hospital."

He stares at me as if I'm casting him adrift in a storm. But what in God's name am I supposed to do? Drive him through the night? Or have sirens and lights in front of the house at four in the morning?

"There must be one of those pills that makes you sleep, surely. I can get it for you."

He shakes his head, as desperate and miserable as I have ever seen him.

"Come here," I say, sitting next to him on the bed, trying to hug him, though his body is stiff as a board.

"You're not going to help?" he asks.

"I'm not saying that. Stand up. We're going downstairs."

He follows me down into the kitchen. I turn on the lights, and fill the kettle, and get out the lemon and the honey, and from the cabinet in the dining room I fetch the Scotch that I never drink.

"I'm being crushed," he says.

I take a mug from the shelf above the sink, and make up the hot toddy.

"Why won't you call an ambulance?" he says.

I set the mug down in front of him. And then I sit in the chair beside him and I lean over and try again to hold him, listening to him tell me why the drink will do no good. And I tell him to sip it anyway. He says that he is going to die. I tell him that he isn't. Eventually, he picks up the mug.

He needs rest. A great deal of rest. And so do I.

Celia

On the way back up the hill, Paul walked ahead with Laura and the dog, and Kyle and I followed behind. The day was bright and clear. Through the gaps in the cypresses you could see across the mouth of the bay to the Golden Gate, and over the water to the slopes of the Marin Headlands. Little white sailboats crisscrossed the channel, and closer to the shore kayakers paddled, the waterway busy on a warm and pleasant Sunday.

Laura and Kyle had arrived Friday afternoon from LA. Her parents were taking care of their nine-month-old, giving them their first weekend off since her birth. They were appreciative guests, happy simply to be eating in restaurants or seeing a movie. The visit was good for Paul, too. They were his oldest friends, and a couple I knew well myself by now with all our visits back and forth, first to Boulder and then Southern California. It helped that neither of them had anything to do with the world of independent film, which meant Paul could share the vagaries of his periodic employment without the professional need to be relentlessly upbeat and bubbling with exciting projects. Once I had established my practice, he'd gone back to scriptwriting and line producing with enough success to keep at it, though still in a business that offered no security. In the presence of his college friends, the weight of all that lightened.

"I always forget how gorgeous it is here," Kyle said, pausing at one of the overlooks that opened onto the headlands and the ocean beyond. In the decade I'd known him his appearance had changed little. He still wore ratty jeans, a faded T-shirt, and a baseball cap over a thicket of dirty-blond hair, as if he'd rolled out of a dorm room bed, slightly hazy but in good spirits. "I guess we live on the coast, too, but you wouldn't know it."

I didn't much notice the landscape anymore. Or when I did, it was mostly to wonder how much longer we would be able to afford San Francisco. The tenuousness of remaining seemed the more present fact. But we were at least enjoying the outdoors more. It had been one of the reasons to get the dog, to spur us to take the hikes that we'd enjoyed when we first got here. We'd driven out of the city more in the last eight months, pressed by Wendell's pleading, than we had in years. It did all three of us good. I got a different kind of release than I did from sprinting, and Paul came home more relaxed than he ever did from the gym. And more likely, I noticed, to have sex. Which was good for more than just our love life. It calmed the worry, which I'd never quite rid myself of, that there was something lacking between us. A missing ease born of an insufficient trust. It didn't press on me the way it used to. But it was there still—the thought that we might not always be together. And that if it was going to end, I would be the one to end it. I knew it wasn't that simple, and that this idea served its own function, to regulate an older, more basic fear of mine that one day Paul, like my father, would simply vanish. Sex banished those abstractions. At least for a time.

"How are the two of you?" I asked Kyle. "Since the baby."

"We're good," he said. "I thought I'd hate having Laura's parents so close, but it's actually kind of great. Their whole freak-out mentality—the world as this ginormous danger, and how Laura would miscarry if she went jogging—they just dropped that stuff once the kid was born, which makes them a lot saner. And it's great for us. We're here, right?"

Saner. That was exactly how I thought of Kyle. He and Laura had married a few years after graduating with Paul. They'd moved to Colorado because they both loved to ski and hike. She'd helped to run a bakery for a few years, and he'd gone back to school for video-game design, which was what had eventually taken them to LA. Now he worked at a company where he smoked less pot than most of his colleagues and made enough of a salary that she could stay home, which she wanted to, at least for a while. I knew from Paul that they had their ups and downs, like anyone else, but their way of being in the world together was so full of ease, and so seemingly optimistic, I couldn't imagine them apart. At dinner the night before, when Laura had asked me how my practice was going, Kyle listened to my response as if I were a zoologist describing the behavior of primates. Therapy had never even occurred to him. It existed in a parallel universe. Which might have been one of the reasons I laughed more with him than almost anyone else I knew. The things that preoccupied me didn't enter his head, and that was permission enough to let go of them.

"What about you?" he said. "You still thinking about the kid thing?"

It seemed strange, in retrospect, that we had never told him or Laura about my abortion, given all our weekends together over the years, and how much else about our lives we tended to share with them. Paul and I had come back from that Bethany Christmas in Walcott still arguing about it, not because we disagreed about what should be done, but because I needed an acknowledgment from him, before I did it, of the depth of the inequity in what one contraceptive failure had cost my body as compared to his. A few weeks after I'd had the procedure, though, a kind of mutual forgetting settled over it, helped along by the fact that I told so few people, other than Alec and one or two friends. When the subject of children came up now, usually because of another couple having a baby, it was mostly an occasion to remind ourselves of how impractical it would be for us. And a reminder to me of how impossible it seemed that I should give that much more care than I already did to the people around me.

"I suppose we should try getting married first," I said, to my own surprise.

"That's not a requirement."

"No, but maybe it would do us good, to clarify things." Kyle turned back from the view over the water to face me with the kindly, open expression I always pictured him with, and which I found relieving, but also confusing, the way it offered no problem to hold on to. "I'm not complaining," I said. "I don't mean it to sound that way."

"You can complain about Paul all you want. You've been with him long enough. He's moody. I used to think he was going to stop hanging out with me because I was a ski bum and didn't read enough. But he's a loyal guy."

"You're right," I said, as we started again up the path toward the parking lot. "He is."

Next to the fountain that stood in front of the Legion of Honor, Paul was giving Wendell water from the little dish we kept in the trunk of our car. Laura stood beside them in her windbreaker, her hair tied in a ponytail, gazing contentedly over the city and the bay.

"Can't we stay for a week?" she said, as Kyle and I approached.

Though she'd always evinced the same easygoingness as her husband, I'd sometimes wondered if being laid-back was more of an effort for her, a thing she'd found in Kyle and successfully emulated rather than having been born into it. Though at a certain point it didn't matter. The emulation became the thing itself.

"Fine with us," Paul said.

I leaned down to pick pieces of bark and grass from Wendell's coat. He was a midsize black mutt, a collie mix, and rambunctious the way Kelsey had been, which had something to do with why I had favored him at the pound—that unaccustomed glee I'd felt as soon as we met him, a sense memory of Kelsey in the yard. He had that same eager spirit.

Once I had settled Wendell in the car, the four of us headed into the museum that stood in the middle of the park. I'd never liked museums on Sundays. They had a depressive air. Reminders of stultifying childhood outings, being told to keep quiet and stare at boring, supposedly important things. The strange loneliness of being together with your family. I had been saintlike in my patience compared to my brothers, who had quipped and mewled through those compulsory exercises like circus acts. At least as an adult, I'd shed the guilt I used to feel for not giving each and every work its earnest two-minute inspection, and allowed myself to roam freely.

I'd been through the collection before, and let Paul guide Laura and Kyle while I wandered into a visiting exhibition of an eighteenth-century German artist I'd never heard of. It began with a room of flouncy biblical scenes. Hovering cherubs and flowing gowns, a milk-white Christ at the tomb, surrounded by grieving women, God floating in the sky above the Annunciation. None drew me in. When my phone started bleating, a well-heeled older lady, the only other patron in the gallery, glanced at me in disgust before returning her attention to a friar bent in prayer.

287

Back in Massachusetts it was three o'clock. Sunday afternoon was not one of the many times that Michael usually tried me. I could do what, until the last seven or eight months, I'd always done. Interrupt anything I happened to be up to and respond to the latest emergency. Behaving otherwise still felt cruel. But in the spring I had flown back to see him in the hospital, canceling appointments with patients who needed their time with me, and whose fees I needed. I'd stayed two extra days to spell my mother's daily visits, and returned with a cold that lasted for weeks. After that trip, the way I had always been toward Michael gave out like an exhausted muscle.

I told my own therapist. I told Paul and Alec and even my mother. I said I couldn't do it anymore: talk to him two or three times a week for half an hour, about him and only him, a patient in all but name, listening to the deadening repetitions. Even if I understood, as he kept telling me, that being able to describe his state in the moment kept his panic at bay better than any drug.

I didn't stop responding to his calls. I just started waiting a few days before returning them. I held a bit of myself back. Knowing well enough that he was at the lowest point in his life. But that was part of it. The extremity of his situation. Where did it end? What level of need couldn't he surpass? However much his fate had weighed on me in the past, I'd never stopped to imagine that it wasn't my responsibility. I encouraged my own patients to see the limits of their obligation to members of their own families, but not myself. I knew full well, too, that talking to him once a week or every ten days left a greater burden on my mother. Alec, who had stepped back as I had, and at around the same time, speaking to Michael less often, understood it as well. We'd made a great effort to give him the chance of graduate school. But it had only led him back to us, worse than before. No one's capacity was infinite. I said that every week in my office. Now I believed it.

The next gallery was full of paintings on classical themes: robed gods in laurels arrayed in a tableau on Mount Parnassus; a nearly nude Perseus leading a horse; a scene of the School of Athens, with the brightly clad philosophers leaning over their books and tablets. I gazed blankly awhile at the last of these, attracted at least to the vivid colors. The show was hardly popular, even on a Sunday, and I could see why, given the stilted subjects and antique style. But it was enough for me, just then, that it didn't require anything of me.

Portraits of princes and aristocrats hung in the final, smaller room. Men in bright silks and brocade with ruffled collars and pendants adorning their breasts. Complimentary pictures for the men who'd commissioned them.

I took a seat on the bench to rest before heading back to rejoin the others.

The portrait in front of me had a different aspect from the rest: a man in his early fifties, simply dressed in a russet coat with a plain black collar and brown neckerchief. His wavy black hair hung down to his shoulders, with no wig or jeweled clasp to hold it in place. There were no tapestries or upholstered furniture in the background, just a featureless gray-brown, which focused all the viewer's attention on the face itself. It seemed to be by a different artist altogether. Not because of its darker palette and lack of finery, and not because it possessed any greater degree of realism. It was something more ineffable. I had the sense that this person had been alive. Not merely historically, like the other personages here, but alive in the way of experience. He'd been present to things which had marked him, and which were registered in the image. *Despondency,* I might have said, given the dark cast of the eyes and the unsmiling lips, but that didn't suffice. It hadn't been that simple. *Haunted,* I thought, but that wasn't right either. *Occupied* was more like it, inhabited by a thought not his own, a force not of his choosing, something he had endured over the course of years. When I stood for a closer look, I saw the label SELF-PORTRAIT.

The light in the picture fell on his wide forehead and across his nose, casting the right side of his face in partial shadow. His eyebrows were just fractionally lifted, not in surprise but in a kind of openness. As if the tension of anticipation had passed out of him. He was not an old man, yet no longer young. The eyes themselves were large, and black, and dead calm. They peered into me and into the past, to whatever it was that had brought him to such an unsentimental understanding of himself. An undeluded apprehension of things as they were. He was neither afraid nor heroic.

The longer I gazed, the more familiar he seemed: the brow, the full lips, the double chin. I saw it most in the expression itself, in that particular stamp of an inescapable fate. Some essence of my father was embedded in the painting, beholding me and seemingly on the verge of speech, the words already formed in the figure's slightly open mouth. I was listening as much as looking now. The utterance wasn't coming from any motion of the image, filmlike, but directly from him into me. He and I were together again, the facts, at last, irrelevant: that we hadn't saved him, that he hadn't saved us. He knew that it hadn't ended, that he still lived in Michael. I could say nothing in return. His presence was all there was.

We drove down through the Presidio to the marina, and found a restaurant with seating outdoors, and Kyle ordered us a pitcher of margaritas. I drank one before the food arrived, and another with my meal. Across the table, Kyle draped his arm over Laura's shoulders, and she rested her head against him, gazing through her sunglasses at the water. Apparently taken by the mood—the sun and the drink—Paul shifted his chair closer to mine and did the same, as coupley as he ever got in public. I drifted awhile in the comfort of the four of us there together, unoccupied.

Afterward we ambled across the road to the trail that ran along the back of the beach. This time when my phone rang it was Alec. I told the rest of them to go ahead with Wendell.

"Hey," he said, tight-voiced, yanking me in close right away. He told me how Mom had called him that morning in a state, how she'd been up in the middle of the night with Michael, how he'd wanted to call an ambulance, and how she'd had to talk him down. "And you know what else?" he said. "She's had a real estate agent in there. She's trying to sell the house. She says she doesn't know what else to do."

No space existed between the events and Alec's reaction to them. They were welded together.

"You agree we can't let that happen, right?" he said, sounding like a gambler in the hole with a weak hand. "We can't let her do that."

There had been an episode. This is why Michael had called. And now the charge of anxiety it had sparked was completing the family circuit.

"Well," I said, "you could start by separating your worries about money from Mom's."

"Wow," he said. "Okay, then. I guess you can pay for her nursing-home care out of your trust fund. Did you notice that I work in print media? From which, FYI, I'm about to be furloughed. So sure—we can separate out my *worries about money,* but you really think she should sell the house to keep funding Michael?"

The high school dramatist in him was alive and well. It's what had drawn him to politics in the first place, the performance and the rhetoric, an elaboration of the childish enthusiasm Michael and I used to mock him for. The deep familiarity of it collapsed the distance of the phone. He might as well have been standing next to me.

"We need to talk to her," I said. "You just told me. I don't know what I think yet."

"Fine," he said. "Talk to her. But you know as well as I do that it's not just about the house. The situation has to change. He's got to come off the meds. It's the only solution. He's got to get back to some kind of baseline, or he's never going to get better, he's never going to be able to take care of himself. He's drowning in that stuff."

Alec and I had debated this before, sometimes with Michael. When did the weight of all that medicine become worse than whatever lay beneath it? I didn't disagree with Alec that it might have already. But Michael had never seen it that way.

"I've been thinking about it all day," Alec said. "I called Bill Mitchell—"

"Bill Mitchell?"

"Yeah, about the cabin in Maine. I didn't even know if they still owned the place, but Mom gave me his number. It was a little weird, obviously, but fuck it. It's a place to go. I think he was sort of amazed I asked, but I didn't go into all the details. I made it sound softer, I guess, more Magic Mountain, but he got the gist. He stalled for a bit, but eventually he said that no one was using the place. The island house is all closed up, but the cabin's there. And he was okay with it. He just said fill the propane before we leave."

"Okay with what? What are you talking about?"

I'd come to a halt on the path, watching the three of them and Wendell step off the trail onto the sand and head diagonally toward the water.

"I'm talking about getting him off the drugs," he said. "Going up there with him. Getting him out of his room, out of that house.

Clearing his *brain*. What else are we going to do? What's the al-ternative? Just let her go bankrupt?"

I'd listened to plenty of his tirades about our mother and money, but this was different. His exasperation had a tender edge. More than angry, he sounded upset.

"Besides," he said, "I miss him. The way he used to be. Don't you?"

"You can't do it in a weekend," I said. "You can't just yank him off everything. It takes time."

"I know that. Which is why it has to happen soon. I'm getting this involuntary month of vacation. They're furloughing half the reporting staff. It's terrifying, actually. But there it is—time off, plus all the vacation I never took. When am I going to have that kind of time again?"

A handsome couple in Lycra shorts and matching tank tops jogged past me, earbuds in, hair nearly perfectly in place, muscles toned and slick. The kind of people whom Michael, in his bitter-ness, would despise.

"What if he doesn't want to?" I asked, beginning to picture it.

"I think he actually does—part of him. He's just afraid."

I knew what he meant. And he was right. I wished I had the money to send Michael off to some leafy clinic campus with nurses and massage and gentle yoga. The kind of program I some-times daydreamed of sending my own clients to. Maine in the off-season was hardly that. But it was time away. A step out of his immediate life, out of the constant emergency.

Maybe it was the looseness from the drinks at lunch, or the unusual course of the day, or even just my desire at that moment to be again with Paul and Kyle and Laura with their pants rolled up, playing in the shallows with the dog, but something allowed me to imagine what Alec was proposing actually coming to pass, and to sense what a relief that would be.

That evening, after we'd folded out the couch in Paul's office for our guests and said good night, the two of us got into bed, and Paul rolled up behind me, his chest to my back, snuggling as he didn't often do.

"They enjoyed themselves," he said. "Don't you think?"

I rested my neck in the crease of his shoulder and held his arms around me. "It's good having them here," I said. "I like how we are with them."

"As opposed to how we are without them?"

"You know what I mean," I said, squeezing him closer.

Wendell, the perfectly unconflicted hedonist, detected our affection from across the room and toddled over to get some for himself. He climbed onto the bed and tried to insert himself between us, and we chuckled and squirmed to fend him off with our knees, only to have him breach our defense, force his front legs into Paul's crotch, and collapse on top of us with a whimper. He settled at last for a spot beside me, where I could pet his flank, and there he quieted down.

"Did you always think you'd get married?" I asked.

"What do you mean?"

I waited for him to roll away onto his back, but he didn't. "Didn't you just assume it would happen?"

"Are you going to propose to me?"

"Don't tease."

"I'm not," he said, running his hand down onto my thigh.

"Yes you are."

"You don't want to get hitched," he said. "We discuss it every time we go to a wedding, and you talk about your patients' disastrous relationships, and how we still need to work on things. And then we go to Christmas at your family's, and Michael quotes us Kafka on marriage."

"Is that why you never proposed?"

"Says the feminist."

"Don't be mean."

He touched his lips to my neck, and then reached over me to pat Wendell on the snout. "I never thought you'd say yes," he said. "And I suppose it doesn't matter as much to me as it does to some people, the way it doesn't matter as much to you."

"I love you," I said.

"Likewise. Do you want to get married?"

"You're teasing again," I said.

He burrowed his head further down against my shoulder, burying his face in my back. And then, barely audible, he whispered, "No, I'm not."

Michael

REQUEST FOR FORBEARANCE

Dear Borrower:

If you are having difficulty making your loan payments and you have exhausted all periods of deferment and grace, you may be able to receive relief through the process of forbearance. In forbearance, your loan payments are temporarily postponed. Please note, however, that all unpaid interest will be capitalized, adding to your outstanding balance. If you are currently past due, submit this form as soon as possible, understanding that submission alone is no guarantee of approval.

Part I. Borrower

I request a forbearance to cover my outstanding balance of:
$68,281.11

To begin:
twelve years ago

To end:
upon the death of my successors

I am temporarily unable to make payments because:

"I had learned that a death had occurred that day which distressed me greatly—that of Bergotte. It was known that he had been ill for a long time past. Not, of course, with the illness from which he had suffered originally and which was natural. Nature scarcely seems capable of giving us any but quite short illnesses. But medicine has developed the art of prolonging them. Remedies, the respite that they procure, the relapses that a temporary cessation of them provokes, produce a simulacrum of illness to which the patient grows so accustomed that he ends by stabilising it, stylising it, just as children have regular fits of coughing long after they have been cured of the whooping cough. Then the remedies begin to have less effect, the doses are increased, they cease to do any good, but they have begun to do harm thanks to this lasting indisposition. Nature would not have offered them so long a tenure. It is a great wonder that medicine can almost rival nature in forcing a man to remain in bed, to continue taking some drug on pain of death. From then on, the artificially grafted illness has taken root, has become a secondary but a genuine illness, with this difference only, that natural illnesses are cured, but never those which medicine creates, for it does not know the secret of their cure."

—M. Proust, vol. 5, *The Captive*

My plan for the resumption of payments is:

As you well know from our correspondence, after years of training in the '90s, I was selected by the Department of Education to voyage on their first Student Loan Probe to Jupiter, as one of four debitnauts. We traveled for years, passing through nebulae of internships and retail, through the wake of an imploding technology boom, and on through the outer rings of bankruptcy, before finally reaching the planet's gaseous surface. Our hope was to make contact with the lost colony of the underemployed. What we found was distressing. In the early years, they had kept up their bonhomie, relying on peer counseling and the nostalgic rebranding of American canned beer. But their birthrate had dropped, and a persistent anxiety storm beginning in the early aughts had killed off the slackers, their priestly class, leaving them without a cosmology. Hopes of ever getting off-planet had dwindled, and the colony had renamed itself Fools of the Humanities. Our greatest surprise, however, concerned their weight. We'd expected a diet of burritos and helium. But to our astonishment, one provisioner, Eli Lilly, had remained in radio contact with them all along, and had been sending pallets of the atypical antipsychotic Zyprexa from a rocket pad in Kazakhstan. The colonists had been taking the drug for years. Their average weight was up to 280. Diabetes and dyskinesia were endemic. As one art history BA put it to me, When Christ asked for water on the cross, they gave him vinegar (whereupon, she might have added, he gave up the ghost). But really, another colonist asked, who *wouldn't* want major weight gain and a facial tic while aging and single? He spoke, I must confess, with some anger. He had been thin once, and even then had struggled to see himself as attractive. There seemed little hope of that now. Apparently, the company's shipments of the drug had ramped up not long before its patent was due to expire. Their representatives had begun pressing it on doctors as an off-label cure for everything from war trauma to stuttering, and it wasn't until several years later that its disastrous side effects were fully appreciated. Several colonists wanted to join the class-action lawsuit, but the rocket traffic was one-way. Empathizing with them as I did, I wished I could do something to help, yet all we had been given to distribute to them were forbearance request forms, which they quickly burned for heat. I returned an unchanged man.

In addition to the above-referenced loans, I owe:
The inalienable privilege of my race to the victims of the Middle Passage, a debt whose repayment has proven tricky to schedule, given the endless deferments, if not forbearances, and the way that the blood of slavery tends to run clear in the tears of liberals.

The sum total of my current assets is:
The knowledge that the psychotic violence of making black people black so that white people can be white runs through me as surely as it does through the bodies of all the jailers and the jailed.

Part II. Terms & Conditions

I understand (1) that I live with my mother; (2) that she is on the verge of selling her home to pay my debts; and (3) that my request for forbearance will never be approved.

I further understand: (a) That in the fall of 1803, along the coast of Mozambique, a Portuguese frigate named the *Joaquin* loaded 300 abducted Africans into its hold and headed south toward the Cape of Good Hope. (b) That a few days after departure, the people held belowdecks began to die. They died slowly at first, at an unremarkable rate of one a day, but after a month and a half, as the ship rounded the tip of the continent and began its Atlantic crossing, death became more frequent. For the next four months, the captives lay shackled in an airless dark, pressed against one another on a bed of their own excrement, vomit, pus, and blood, their bodies slick with waste putrefying in the equatorial heat as they woke chained to the corpses of strangers or parents or children, whom the crew eventually removed and threw overboard to the trailing sharks. (c) That by the time the *Joaquin* reached the Spanish port of Montevideo, 270 of the original 300 had died. Fearing contagion, the city surgeon ordered the ship back out to sea. With a storm blowing in off the pampas, the captain at first refused. But when the harbormaster threatened him with arrest and seizure of his ship, he relented and made for open water. Fierce winds quickly shattered the frigate's three masts and the ship nearly sank. Attempting to make it back to port, it was beached in the shallows of the Río de la Plata, where it remained for several more weeks while its fate was decided. (d) That the Spanish merchant who owned the ship wanted to auction the survivors to offset his losses, and sued the port surgeon for incompetence, demanding that his cargo be allowed to disembark. To resolve the dispute, city officials set up a commission of inquiry, and appointed five doctors experienced in the treatment of ailing slaves. (e) That observing that none of the officers or sailors of the *Joaquin* had died, the commission concluded, to most everyone's surprise, that the slaves had not died of infection. They had died from dehydration, and from what the doctors called *melancolía*. In the words of Carlos Joseph Guezzi, a Swiss-Italian physician, the loss of their homes and families, together with the conditions of their transit, had induced a "total indifference to life," "a *cisma*," or schism, that amounted to "an abandonment of the self." (f) That because this condition was deemed noncommunicable, the mer-

300

chant was free to bring his chattel ashore and sell them on the open market. And finally, (g) that during their passage, the captives aboard the *Joaquin* were often heard to sing.

Finally, I hereby certify that I don't pretend to know with any certainty why it is that I keep coming back to these scenes, to imagining these men and women and children chained in the rocking dark. While it would be most legible, and even palatable, to chalk it up to the theft of four hundred years of labor, to the profits of the trade that extend by corporate succession right up through to the bank that lent me the money to study the history of their own barbarism, it isn't economic reasoning or public justice that won't let me go. It's the withered bodies, the cries of the dying, the blood-soaked decks, that carnival of evil that each morning I try to medicate into the floor. The fact is that when I read the story of the *Joaquin,* I feel understood. Not in any literal sense—the comparison of my dread to theirs would be grotesque—but in the unrelenting terror, in that schism of the mind. Which is how I know now that the dead generations don't haunt down tidy racial lines, as if there were such a thing. The psychosis is shared. I was born into the fantasy of its supremacy. Others are born into the fantasy's cost. But the source of the violence is the same. The work I do is for no one's sake but my own.

Alec

The Mitchells' cabin overlooked an inlet at the bottom of St. George a half mile past Port Clyde, the last village on the peninsula. My brother couldn't believe I remembered how to get there without a map: right at the Baptist church, then out the little road that hugged the shoreline, dipping alongside a rocky beach and rising again onto higher ground, where the houses thinned out.

It wasn't the blue I remembered, but a light gray with white trim. The rest appeared more or less as I'd pictured it: the sloping yard, snow-covered now, the mound of boulders by the path, the aluminum gangplank that led down to the little dock, the flagpole and the blueberry bushes.

Across the street, farther up the slope from the water, stood a white Cape with a stack of lobster traps in the yard. There were a few more houses up ahead in the distance before the road vanished into the woods.

In the quickly fading light we carried the groceries we'd bought on the way up into the kitchen along with our luggage. Michael stood in the middle of the room, holding his messenger bag to his chest, while I went looking for the valves to turn on the water and gas. When I returned he hadn't moved, as if we were here on an errand, to drop a few things off, and would be getting back into the car. Asking him if he'd mind putting the food in the fridge seemed to break the spell, and he unpacked the bags while I carried wood in from the shed.

"You know how to light a fire?" he asked.

"Yeah, so do you. You've done it a hundred times."

"Have I?"

On the drive up I'd made a passing reference to some future point when it would be just the three of us, once Mom was gone, and he had looked at me in shock, as if the idea that he might survive her had never occurred to him. I nearly stopped the car to yell at him for being so out of it, for clinging to such a distorted view of reality, but I didn't want to start things out that way and I held my tongue, as I did now.

The cabin hadn't been renovated as far as I could tell, just well maintained. The dark wood floors were uneven but polished, the old floral-print furniture replaced with solid whites and tans. On the bookcases on either side of the fireplace were Mitchell family photographs: their two daughters at the ages we had been when we first came here, in bathing suits and life preservers, squinting in the sun, and later as teenagers and adults with boyfriends or husbands.

I told Michael to take the largest of the three eaved bedrooms upstairs, the one Mom and Dad had used, to give him the extra space, and I said he should go ahead and unpack his things, to settle in.

Over the last few weeks, Michael had agreed, reluctantly, to try what I'd suggested, but he drew the line at stopping the Klonopin, saying he would go off everything except that. Caleigh had encouraged him, which helped. So had my mother, who more than anyone else wanted for this to work but feared the difficulty of it for Michael. She had baked ginger cookies for our trip, and sent us off with apples and peanut butter and a bag of Michael's favorite potato chips, which he finished off with a beer as I made us dinner.

The night before, Seth and I had got into our first serious argument. We'd been seeing each other for a year and a half and through all that time had remained polite with each other, careful not to offend or disturb. It seemed like mutual care, mostly, a desire to protect what we'd begun.

He had put up with my travel schedule, right through to the election's dismal end. I'd been gone for weeks at a time and he hadn't complained. And when he needed to work on projects over the weekends that I did make it back, I didn't get after him about it. He even took in stride the news of my being furloughed by the magazine, hinting that we should talk about moving in together. And when my mother had called and told me about the real estate agent and the listing contract, and I said to Seth almost as soon as I hung up with her that Michael and I needed to go away, he said, Of course, I get it.

But when I was gathering my things in the apartment, getting ready to leave once more, and asked if he would do me a favor by booking me a ticket online for the train to Boston, he looked up from his computer, incredulous.

In a tone I'd never heard before, he said, "Do you have any memory at all how many times you said we'd take a trip together this week? After you were finally done. Does it even *matter* to you that you're going to use practically your whole time off with Michael, and none of it with me?"

"You think I should just cancel," I said. "After I arranged the place and persuaded him to do it?" He slammed his computer shut and walked into the bedroom. But I followed him, demanding an answer. "Is that really what you think? That I should just call Michael and tell him I decided to go on vacation with my boyfriend instead?"

"God forbid," he said. "But don't worry, I get it—no one has problems more important than yours. You've made that clear. And now you're going up there into the woods, all Robert Bly, to save him all by yourself. You're not as smart as you think you are."

Later, in the bathroom, passing the toothpaste, we slunk back toward each other. After turning out the lights, without saying a word, he fucked me quite hard, both of us knowing it would be bad to part for this long without touching. In the morning I promised to call him.

As I had suspected, we got no cell reception at the cabin. But the Mitchells had a working landline, which is what my mother called us on after supper, saying she just wanted to make sure we'd arrived safely and that the heat worked. She spoke to Michael briefly and then wished us a good night's sleep.

Along with the heap of books he'd stuffed in his messenger bag, Michael had brought a bunch of DVDs. We sat through two episodes of 24 together, a distraction I was glad for. He'd lost patience for anything slower than a Bruce Willis movie. It had to be action: car chases, galactic warfare, gangland slaughter. Luckily, next to the supermarket back on Route 1, I'd spotted a place that still rented videos, so I knew we wouldn't run out.

Before going to bed I told him he should do what we had discussed. He went upstairs and returned with his toiletry bag to the living room couch, where he rummaged through it and removed the orange prescription bottles, lining them up on the coffee table in what seemed an act of determined resignation. He set down five in all, plus the jar of kratom tea.

For years he'd insisted, like a child, that eventually a doctor would prescribe a pill which would give him the same relief he'd experienced the first time he had taken a drug. We had chastised him for believing this, for demanding such a purely external fix, and yet all the while we had wished for exactly that, for our sake as much as for his. To make the problem simply go away. That fantasy was over. That cure didn't exist. Every therapy, every drug, all the help we'd given—none of it had worked. So now there was no other choice. He had to be able to take care of himself. He had to get better. When my mother had called on that Sunday last month and told me she needed to sell the house, she had to have known that I wouldn't let her do it. Telling me was as good as saying she wanted to be stopped. And so I had stopped her.

"It's the right thing," I said, picking up his bottles with both hands.

"I'm not sure," he said, "I'm not sure."

For the first couple of days the hardest part for either of us was the lack of Internet. I hadn't been away from it that long in years. Nor had Michael. The absence of distraction left us irritable and bored. But that had been part of my idea for coming here, to disenthrall him from that constant, goading semi-stimulation which only fed his anxiety. To help bring him back to some kind of present.

After the countless hours I'd gorged on polling data and campaign gossip, scraping for angles in all that trash of information, I wanted to purge myself of it, too. Still, the first two evenings I couldn't help walking up the road to the one spot where I got a signal and standing there, shivering, as the headlines loaded. Michael had brought his laptop, but without new messages or updates from his myriad listservs to constantly anticipate and check, he hardly bothered opening it.

On our third morning I woke more rested than I had in a long time. Michael hadn't stirred yet. I dressed and went out into the yard, into the freezing air, and walked down the jetty to the dock from which we used to set out for the island.

Beyond the few boats still on their moorings, a bank of fog was moving in off the sea. I watched it slowly cover the spit of land at the mouth of the inlet, shrouding the fir trees and the granite shore, and then the whole end of the bay, covering the barnacled outcroppings where the cormorants landed and seals basked in summer, rolling slowly toward me over the water until I saw that it wasn't fog but snow, the flakes tumbling thick and silent out of the encompassing cloud, and I remembered that was how it had been up here when we were kids, seeing weather approach from a distance, a thunderstorm on the horizon, rain sweeping toward us like a curtain across the water, and how it had thrilled me, that enormity and power, how oblivious it was of us. I had an inkling of that again now, of that state of being wide open to time, not as a thing to use or waste, but as a motion of its own, an invisible wholeness made apparent by the motion of the world.

By the time the snow reached me, I couldn't see more than twenty yards, the rocks and the water and the boats all gone. When I went back into the cabin and saw my phone on the counter, I powered it off and stowed it in a kitchen drawer.

After breakfast with Michael, I made him walk the half mile with me to the general store. This became our routine, which he consented to more readily once he knew they sold doughnuts. In the afternoons we spent longer than necessary up on Route 1 restocking our food supplies and browsing every aisle of the video store, and in the evenings we watched one action movie after the next. Still, there were plenty of idle hours, and when Michael started having trouble sleeping, in what seemed the first sign of withdrawal, those hours began to gnaw at him.

"When is he going to stop that?" he asked me late one afternoon at the end of our first week, standing by the window in the dining room, peering over the embroidered half curtain.

All morning the lobsterman across the road had been chopping wood in his yard. He worked at a methodical pace, each gap long enough to make you think he was done. Until you heard another thwack of the ax, and the splintering of a log.

"When he's through, I guess."

"How old do you think he is?"

A loaded question, coming from Michael, who considered himself so ancient. He'd begun referring to these as "the winter years" of his life. Absurd on its face for a thirty-seven-year-old, droll, even, as a complaint about early middle age, though not the way he said it, with grim conviction.

As for the guy across the street, I'd noticed him a few times coming home in the late afternoons, and had watched him switch out the damaged lobster traps in the bed of his truck with replacements from the stack in the yard. He was some fisherman's son, not the old man himself. Thirty, maybe, with a build you could see through his thermal work shirts, and a dirty-blond crew cut. In the absence of Seth and pornography, I'd closed my eyes the night before and imagined him bending me over the hood of his Ford.

"I don't know, forty?" I said, for Michael's sake.

"No, no. He's not that old."

"Thirty-eight?"

Michael shook his head dismissively. "I always imagined I was younger than men like him. The way you imagine you're younger than your dentist. But I'm not anymore. He's married to that woman who drives the Bronco. She could be in her late twenties. They live in that house. It's amazing."

"It's a pretty ordinary house, actually."

"I don't mean the building. I mean he lives here in this polar vortex, surrounded by nothing but deer and a smattering of white people, and he's found a sexually attractive woman to live with him year-round. I find that shocking."

I couldn't help but smile. His voice was back. The speed of it, the acumen. He hadn't noticed it. But his halting forgetfulness was gone. He sounded almost like himself again. He even seemed to have more color in his face.

"I do give him credit for the bumper sticker, though," he said. " 'They call it tourist season. So why can't we shoot them?' I like that. No doubt he spends his spare time lobbying for an expansion of the welfare state, as well he should. But I wish he'd put a stop to that manual labor. The sound is harrowing."

He paced back into the living room, where I was reading an old copy of *Vanity Fair,* and scanned the room as if for intruders.

"How are you feeling?" I asked.

"Wretched," he said.

With no private clinic spa to help take the edge off, I started driving us to a gym I'd seen a little ways past the supermarket. It occupied a defunct car dealership, three walls of glass and a concrete backdrop enclosing a small field of secondhand Nautilus equipment. Up here in the off season it was as close as we were going to get to a regimen of something other than television.

Surveying the scene on our first visit—a woman in a terry-cloth tracksuit reading *US Weekly* on a StairMaster and a teen waif loitering by the free weights—Michael asked, "Where are all the muscle queens?"

Through music he had learned gay culture long before I had. The meaning of the Village People may have eluded me as a child, but it had never eluded him. I hadn't delayed coming out to him from any fear of rejection. If anything, being gay improved me in his eyes, placing me at least one step off the throne of patriarchy that he himself had so effectively abdicated. I just hadn't wanted to face the awkwardness of discussing sex with my brother.

Back then he had dressed so immaculately. All those English designer shirts of his, and the peg-legged trousers, and the dark suit jackets that hung so well on him, like a young Jeremy Irons done up to New Wave perfection. Once he returned from London, I'd never been able to keep up.

Now here he was on the treadmill in ancient gym shorts and a V-neck undershirt stained at the pits, straining under the weight he'd put on. He hadn't complained about his weight to me. He'd just commented in a way he never had before about how thin I looked, and I sensed his embarrassment at having had one kind of body his whole life, worrying he was too thin, and then suddenly having another, heavy not with muscle but fat. There was a perversity to it. Watching him struggle on the machine seemed like watching myself age in a sickly fashion. But at least here we could burn off a few calories, and another hour of the otherwise empty days.

Michael, however, was resolute that the workouts did him no good.

"No," he said flatly, when I asked him on the way back from one of our outings if he didn't feel just a bit more relaxed.

"Okay," I said. "But what is true is that you're taking one pill, not six. And you're not drinking the tea. The fact is, you're better than when we got here. You're more alive."

"Maybe," he said. "I don't know. Everything's shaky."

"Sure it is. You're waking up."

"You know it's not that simple. It doesn't change my situation."

"You don't have to think about that right now. We're stepping out of that for a while. Things'll look different when your mind's clearer. Which is why I think you should come off the Klonopin, too."

"I can't do that," he said.

"Yes you can."

"It's not what we agreed."

"It's what you want, though. When it comes down to it, right? You've said so yourself."

"Coming off that's what put me in the hospital."

"You were alone then. You're not now."

We were doing the right thing. He just needed to take off the last bandage. Like Celia said, the sedatives had walled his feelings in. And the higher the walls got, the more he feared what they protected him from.

But I didn't press the idea further right then. I needed to let it settle. I waited, instead, until we were eating supper that evening.

"It would take months," he said.

"I get that it's frightening—the idea of not having that particular drug anymore."

"It's not the idea, it's the chemistry."

When we'd arrived, he wouldn't have been able to even consider this. But here he was, considering it.

"Are you better now than the day you first took it?"

"Of course not," he said. His face was rigid with apprehension. But there was a pleading in his eyes. "You really think I could do it?"

"Yes. I think you can."

I'd bought us ice cream for dessert. We ate it in front of *The Bourne Identity*. In the final sequence, Matt Damon hunted snipers in the woods and fields around the country house where he'd fled with the woman from *Run Lola Run*. The Mitchells had

311

installed a flat-screen television with excellent speakers, and the crack of the rifle as Damon shot his attackers satisfied us both. Michael even smiled.

The next morning he asked if we should get rid of the booze in the house. He was afraid that he would resort to it if he tried coming off his last medication.

Without answering, I emptied the fridge of the beer and wine we had brought with us and poured each bottle down the kitchen sink as he watched. I rinsed them and took them out to the bins, and then I found a cardboard box and loaded the Mitchells' own liquor cabinet into it, and brought that to the sink as well. I was about to start pouring their bottles down the drain when it occurred to me it would probably be several hundred dollars' worth of alcohol to replace. Michael was still at the kitchen table, watching me.

"I'll take care of the rest of this," I said. "You should go listen to some music. You haven't been doing much of that."

I waited until I heard him open his laptop, followed by the tinny sound of synthesizers coming from his headset. Then I carried the box of bottles out to the shed and set it down behind the folded lawn chairs.

"We're clear," I said when I came back in. "You can give me the pills."

"You know I take them for a reason," he said. "I'm not an addict. It's not like I was fine before."

"I know."

"It's an illness," he said. "I'm not malingering."

"I never said you were."

"Dr. Bennet said he thinks I'd qualify for disability. He said he doesn't support it for most of his patients, but that he would for me—that my condition is that severe."

"That's what you want? To make it permanent like that? To get a subsidy for it? If you wanted that, why come this far? If it's all insulin for the diabetic, why even agree to come up here?"

"You told me I had to."

"No. I offered. And you agreed."

"You don't want Mom to sell the house. You think she should stop supporting me."

"That's true," I said. "But do you really think I don't want to help you? You always say talking about the anxiety takes the edge off, and that's why you're on the phone with Caleigh so much. Well, I'm here. You don't need a phone, you can talk as much as you need to. I'm not going anywhere."

He was trying his best to believe me.

My mother had promised to refrain from calling too often, but when the phone rang just then I knew it would be her.

"It's *very* cold up there," she said. "And you're getting another four inches of snow tonight."

Wherever I went, she knew more about the weather than I did.

"I'm mailing you some cranberry bread today, and I'm going to put in some cranberry sauce as well. I know you said you weren't doing a whole Thanksgiving dinner, but just in case. You might change your mind. How much longer do you think you'll be?"

She wanted me to assure her that Michael was all right. Whatever the content of her questions that was their purpose. I told her, as I had from the beginning, that I didn't know how much time it would take, but that she could go ahead and send her package.

Michael stayed on the line with her longer, describing his fitful sleep and his morning nausea, but telling her not to worry. He'd been freer of her at nineteen, living in Britain, than ever since. Sharing every step of this with her wasn't going to help, but I couldn't control them both.

Before Michael went to bed that night, I gave him three-quarters of his usual evening dose of Klonopin, which was two pills. I knew this drug was different. To come off it too quickly could be dangerous. It would take time. But we didn't have months to work with, which meant we just had to do the best that we could.

"It's all right if you need to wake me up," I said. "Just knock on my door."

He swallowed the tablet and a half in front of me and held his hand flat against his sternum, as if monitoring his breath.

I half expected him to revolt right away and demand the pills back, but his sleep didn't worsen that night, or the next few nights, through the end of our second week in the cabin, and so he agreed reluctantly to my suggestion that we cut back his morning dose, too. I kept the medicine bottle in my room and doled the tablets out to him like a nurse.

Usually when I traveled, Seth and I spoke every evening, but I had called him only twice thus far, which had pissed him off. Given how we'd parted, though, he wasn't going to offer me the satisfaction of showing it. The third time I called him, the night before he flew to Denver for Thanksgiving, he was as remote as ever, asking me civil questions and listening to my civil replies. And yet even this much contact with him made me bristle. I'd sequestered Michael and myself for a reason. It's how it had to be.

"I just need time," I said. "It won't last forever."

"You're the one who called," he said.

"I want to go away with you, and I want to meet your family. But I have to do this first."

"I know."

I couldn't blame him for his flat tone, or his disappointment. I asked dutifully about his week and who else would be coming for the holiday, but when our conversation petered out neither of us tried to revive it.

That night I heard Michael get up to use the bathroom several times, and when I went myself, the light was on under his door. He had to have heard me, to have known I was awake, but he didn't call out and I didn't knock. The next morning he was in a panic. He'd barely slept, and said his heart was beating like a jackrabbit's.

"You need to give me the pills," he said.

I didn't shout at him, I didn't tell him he was being irrational, I just said that the beginning would be the toughest, mentally, and that if he didn't sleep at night he could take as many naps during the day as he needed. He wasn't listening to me, though. He was too far inside himself. I handed him his coat and told him to come with me out of the cabin right away, before breakfast, knowing the cold would at least distract him.

It was on that walk that I noticed I didn't have to slow down anymore for him to keep up. I was the one trying to keep up with him.

The general store hadn't changed. It was a barn of a place, drafty, with high ceilings and creaking floors, built out onto the pier. Nearby was the dock where we used to tie our boat up to buy gas and supplies before setting out for the island, and opposite that a jetty where the lobstermen kept their skiffs. What had disappeared was the diner and fish fry next door, replaced by a pricier restaurant advertising "the Real Maine Experience," closed till spring.

I got us coffee and doughnuts and suggested we eat them at the counter. The longer we were out, the better. When we finished I convinced him to walk with me past the harbor to the other end of the village, and from there we went out the lane to the point, with its war memorial and the plaque to fishermen lost at sea. On the unprotected side of this spit of land the tide had washed the snow off the rocks, leaving visible clumps of gray-green seaweed.

Standing in the wind, looking out across the frigid water, I thought, This is absurd, our being up here alone in the cold. It's romantic nonsense. I'm probably about to lose my job. I need to be back in the city, hustling. And if I'm unemployed, how long will it take before I lose the apartment? Then what? Force a move with Seth before it's right? What good would all this be if it left me that far in a hole?

"We had a picnic here," Michael said. "Do you remember? Kelsey killed a lamed seagull. She finished it off. Strange. This is the first place up here I even recognize."

"She killed a seagull?"

"Well, Dad wrung its neck when she was through with it, but I think it was fairly dead. Celia objected on procedural grounds—that we hadn't taken it to a vet. It was definitely right here. It's vivid as all get-out, actually. Like it was a minute ago. I can almost hear it. Maybe this is what it's like taking hallucinogens."

"No, that's different."

"You've taken them?"

"In high school."

He nodded slowly, as if to say, That makes sense, though it still seemed to surprise him. That he had been oblivious to this episode in my social life.

"I guess we didn't talk much then, while I was away."

He said it as if it had never occurred to him before. It was a simple enough statement, an obvious fact, and yet I found myself, without warning, close to tears. I'd always wanted to hear

316

from him. To know what he was doing in London, or just to hear him talk. But whenever he called it was to speak to Mom or Dad about school or money, and we didn't say more than hello. He sent cassettes in the mail a few times, but the only words that came with them were the track listings and Post-it notes warning *This will slay you!* or *Beware!*

"You liked it there, didn't you?" I said, as we crossed back over the empty parking lot toward the village.

"I did. I fell in love with a woman named Angie. That was the beginning. It's odd, but when I say that, I can smell the perfume she wore. I can smell it in my head."

I smiled to myself. When had I ever taken a stroll with Michael and heard him reminisce? The veil between himself and the past was lifting.

At half his usual dose his sleep got worse. By the end of our third week he couldn't concentrate long enough to make it past the first few scenes of a movie, or even to pick out a DVD in the first place. He became fixated on the sound of the guy across the street chopping wood, asking me every few minutes, "Why does he go so slowly?"

But the bursts of memory kept coming. He had always said he had difficulty picturing our father, or much of his childhood at all. But now, along with his monologues about how he couldn't go through with our plan, how he would never be able to do his real work again, how he had failed and had no prospects, there were these fragments of the years gone by, which descended out of nowhere. They were questions, mostly.

"Mom and Dad never drank much, did they?" he asked, as if suddenly recalling a detail of an otherwise elusive dream.

They were just single moments at first. He asked if it was true that I had broken my arm falling out of a tree in the garden in Oxfordshire, and I said, Of course, amazed each time that he could have forgotten such familiar stories.

"And I drove with you and Dad to the doctor, right?"

"Yes."

"At the octagonal house—Dad, he told us stories."

"Yes" was all I could think to keep saying.

By the time I had lowered him to a quarter ration, his body began to ache. His muscles were seizing up from the loss of the drug's relaxant effects. I bought him Tylenol and a heating pad at the drugstore. And when he had a particular spot that was killing him, I kneaded his back with my knuckles through his hoodie, which he kept on no matter how far I turned up the heat.

I was working a kink in his shoulder blade as he stood braced against the frame of the kitchen door when he said, "You let the snake into my room, didn't you?"

I stopped rubbing. This wasn't just his voice returning. He was going all the way back now. As if he were a teenager again, talking to his younger sibling. The immediacy of the tone, the urgency of the question, as if it had happened only minutes ago, took me right back there with him, outside the door of his bedroom in Samoset, there on the landing.

"That night the snake got into my room, you let it out, didn't you?"

He had lavished so much of his attention on that creature. I had been forbidden by our mother to touch it. No matter how many times I asked. I was too young, she said. Michael would sit with it on the back steps, wearing one of Mom's tennis visors and a pair of her giant sunglasses, the snake coiled on the cutting board on his lap. "It's basking," he would say, "as we all deserve to bask." Kelsey would stand vigil with me, intent on the serpent creature, its scales glistening like polished tiles, its forked tongue darting out to test the air, its lidless black eyes milky calm.

"It was after we went to the landing with Dad," Michael said now. "After you jumped in the mud."

That day, the one he meant, I had asked on our way home from church if we could take the Sunfish out on the bay, but everyone in the car had claimed it was too cold and too late in the year. Except Dad, who said, "Why not?"

"Then take Michael with you," my mother said.

But Dad didn't check the tide schedule before we left, and when we got to the landing the boats lay tilted on their sides across the mudflats. It had always looked like ordinary mud to me, but we'd been told it was dangerous, a deep silt that a man had drowned in once. We stood directly over it, at the end of the stranded jetty. Dad was already drifting off, beginning to think about other things. If we went home, he would read the paper, there would be Sunday lunch, and then he would nap and I would see no more of him.

I don't remember thinking about it much. I just stepped off the edge, threw my arms up, and called out to him. He swung around in an instant and leaned down to catch my hand just as the slime reached my neck, saving me with a sudden strength.

When we got home, Michael wouldn't stop saying that I had done it on purpose, that it wasn't an accident.

And Michael's memory was correct. It was that night I waited until everyone's light was out, then snuck down the back stairs into the playroom and let the snake rush into the mesh bag Michael used to transport it. I carried it up and unleashed it through the crack of his door, watching it slither toward his bed.

"Why did you do it?" Michael asked now. "You little wheezer."

I nearly punched him in the neck right then, to punish him at last for all his mockery of me. But the urge broke almost at once into sadness, a sense of the utter goneness of that time. And then that, too, faded, leaving in its wake a wholly unfamiliar gratitude. For the fact that he had been my brother, and had let me hate him. For the fact that the five of us had been a family at all. And that Michael himself wasn't gone. He was coming back now, here with me, piece by piece.

As the drug left his system entirely, he began to hear things. He would come into the kitchen and put his ear to the speaker of the radio, bewildered to discover that it was turned off. He heard drums and synthesizers, he said, and the lyrics of entire songs. They went on for minutes at a time.

I found him in the living room examining the Mitchells' stereo, and later watched him listening at the window for a singing he heard coming from outdoors. I told him not to worry, that it was just a phase, his mind readjusting.

Then came the sound of buses, and doors closing somewhere in the house, and loud static. He stopped sleeping altogether. I kept expecting him to rest on the couch during the day, but his pacing became more relentless. He begged off going to the gym, saying he was too fatigued, and I couldn't contradict him.

There was no elegant way to do this. He was going to suffer.

He stayed in the living room mostly, and I stayed with him. I brought him food that he wolfed the first few bites of, as if starved, only to leave the rest untouched. More than panic, he seemed in the grip of fever. He begged me to give him back the pills. What point could there be in telling him that I had already thrown the rest away? It would only make him more frightened still.

I kept forcing him to take walks in the mornings, and again in the late afternoons, when the agitation was at its worst. I convinced him a few times to take off his hoodie and lie facedown on the couch, and for half an hour or more I rubbed his back and neck, telling him over and over to breathe. After a while his shoulder blades would unclench and his head would sink deeper into the cushion, and I'd think that he might at least doze off from exhaustion. But as soon as I stopped, he got up and paced again, asking if I heard what he heard, driven from room to room by something close to delirium.

It seemed as if whatever anxiety the drug had kept in check over the years had been stored up rather than eliminated, pooling like a dammed river in his head, and now the gates were open and the flood had arrived. There was nothing to do but wait for it to run its course. Eventually, his body had to tire.

By this time the rest of the world seemed distant. I had phoned Seth only once since our last conversation, and I'd done it in the middle of his workday, when I knew he wasn't likely to pick up, leaving a message rather than fully accounting for myself. I'd begun to let Celia's calls go to the answering machine, and my mother's as well. But then one evening Celia tried the cabin number again and again until I picked up.

"You promised," she said. "You said you'd stay in touch. Mom's been calling me every day."

I'd stopped giving them updates because I knew what would happen. Michael would tell them he couldn't keep going, and not being here to understand the progress we had made, they would decide to call a halt to it. Celia would shut it down.

"There's not a lot to report," I said. "It's hard. We didn't expect it to be easy, right? But you should hear his voice. You wouldn't believe it. He sounds ten years younger. He sounds alive."

When she asked to talk with him I could have made an excuse. That he was in the shower, or finally getting some sleep. We had come this far. What good could there be in going backward, in losing the ground he'd suffered to gain? But I hadn't slept much myself in the last few days, listening for him in the night, worrying as soon as I closed my eyes that the whole effort had been a mistake. At least if he spoke to Celia, the decision to keep going wouldn't be mine alone.

I went into the living room and handed Michael the phone, thinking, This is it, we tried.

He heard Celia out on whatever she had to say for a minute or two, then replied, "I just need to sleep. That's the thing. It's brutal, not sleeping. But Alec's here. He's trying to help me." Again he listened, and again he deflected her. "You shouldn't worry anymore," he said. "Any of you."

He could have ended it right then by complaining enough to her that she would command me to stop. But he didn't. He chose not to.

"He sounds like a wreck," she said, once Michael had handed the phone back.

"He's started remembering," I replied, going upstairs, out of earshot. "You always said that's what he needed to do, isn't it?"

"Alec, you're not going to solve his life for him in a month. This has to be the beginning."

"I know. That's what it is. But I have to see it through. Will you call Mom for me? Just tell her it's okay, please."

It snowed again the next morning, blanketing the road and the car and our footprints on the path. When the sky cleared and the sun came out, I told Michael we were going to walk in the opposite direction this time, away from the village.

There were only three more houses beyond the Mitchells' along this stretch, all closed for winter, their driveways blocked by the snowbanks the plow had left behind, their yards smooth white planes sloping toward the water. We followed the road into the woods, where the sunlight barely penetrated and the quiet was nearly complete. Michael hadn't been out of the house in two days, since he'd stopped sleeping altogether, and he seemed discombobulated by his surroundings. He neither lagged behind me nor sped ahead. Finally, his vigilance had ebbed, his attention growing softer. More than anything else, he seemed to be trying to find his bearings.

After a half mile or so, the road climbed into a rocky field that overlooked the bottom of the inlet. From here we could see across the open water to the island, a mound of dark green ringed by snow-covered boulders and a strip of granite at the waterline.

"That's the house," I said. "On the bluff." I had remembered the island as being much farther out, in a great expanse of sea, but in truth the distance was only a mile or two. "Do you see it?"

Michael squinted. "Where is it?" he said.

I pointed, guiding his head. His eyes were puffy, and practically drooping shut, even out here in the cold. He'll sleep now, I thought. I'll give him food and hot tea, and he'll sleep.

But he didn't. Not that night, and not the next, and not the night after that. On his sixth sleepless night I got up in the small hours of the morning to take a piss, and as I padded toward the bathroom, I heard the back door open downstairs, and then footsteps on the kitchen floor.

"Michael?" I called.

The footsteps stopped.

"Yeah?" he said, after a moment.

"What are you doing?"

When he gave no response, I turned on the hall light and went down.

He had taken a seat in the dark at the dining room table. I switched on the lamp on the sideboard and saw in front of him a juice glass and a bottle of Scotch.

"There's a song," he said. "It won't stop."

He tore the seal, uncorked the bottle, and, using both hands to steady it, poured himself a drink.

"Where did you get that?"

"You put it in the shed."

"But we agreed. You asked me to get rid of it."

He lifted the glass to his lips and took a large swallow. "I didn't mean to wake you," he said. "You should go back to bed."

I put on a sweatshirt that I'd left on one of the dining chairs, and sat at the table opposite him. Had he watched me take the box of booze outside? Or had he just figured I was too much of a skinflint to throw it away? It didn't matter now. One drink wouldn't hurt him.

We sat for a minute or two as he finished what he'd poured.

"Do you know?" he said. "I haven't had sex in six years. Six years ago—and that was just twice, with Bethany. Before that it was two years. Twice in eight years. I started writing pornography. Back in Michigan. Just for myself. So at least there would be something besides the Internet."

I didn't need to know this, I didn't want to know it. But I had said that I would listen, and so I did.

"It helped, actually," he said. "Making it personal like that. It was surprisingly effective. Just the writing of it."

"That makes sense. I guess."

"The good thing about some of the drugs—they amputated my libido. Which made it easier. It was a blessing, it really was."

"You said there was a song in your head, what song?"

" 'Temptation,' New Order. Just one line on a loop: *Up, down, turn around, please don't let me hit the ground / Tonight I think*

I'll walk alone, I'll find my soul as I go home. Their lyrics were never great. But that melody played on the bass line..."

"It's not going to keep going like this," I said. "It can't go on like this forever."

"You keep saying that."

"Because you're off it now. All of it. This is the trailing stuff. You've done it."

He rested his forearms on the table and leaned forward, lowering his head. "There's a limit, Alec. You don't want to think about it, but there's an ethical limit to what anyone should have to endure. You can't just negate that with sentimentality. With the idea of some indomitable spirit. That's a fairy tale. It's what people say about other people, to avoid the wretchedness. It's just cruelty by other means. Requiring a person to stay alive. For you. Dad, for instance. I never blamed him. I never did. He reached his limit."

"You're hearing music, Michael. It's going to pass. I can put on other music. We should have been doing that, we should have been listening to more music together."

"It's not that," he said. "I understand now why they deny people sleep to torture them. That's what it is—torture."

"You've had a drink. It'll take the edge off. You should lie down and close your eyes. The exhaustion's going to catch up with you."

He seemed to be laboring for each breath, his lungs trying to stretch the skin tightened over his chest. Again using both hands to steady the bottle, he filled the glass three-quarters full.

"That's not a good idea," I said.

He gazed at the plastic juice glass with its checkered print. "I shouldn't have gone back to England," he said. "I should never have left you all there in that house. Not that I could have stopped him. But I could have warned you. I could have been there."

"You wanted to be with your friends," I said. "You were in the middle of school. We got it, Celia and me, we understood."

"I couldn't stand being there. I had to leave. But that's the thing, that's the thing—I still dread it. It's already happened, but I still dread that it's about to happen—soon, right now...I haven't been a good brother," he said. "I'm sorry." He reached across the table and took hold of my upper arm, squeezing it tight, as he used to when I was little.

"Yes you have," I said.

I had never seen Michael cry. Not even when we were children. The muscles of his face unlocked. His whole jaw seemed to loosen, his mouth came open, his lips shook. In his glistening eyes there was a brightness. He looked new again. New and terribly sad. And I cried with him.

"I didn't know what to say when I came back that summer," he said. "You were all so upset. But I didn't feel anything. Nothing. I was blank. I kept trying, I knew I was supposed to feel something, and to help you, but I couldn't. And it was so hot. You remember? It was stifling. For weeks. And I just stayed in my room playing records because I didn't know what else to do."

"You were wearing wool," I said, and laughed. "You had on those gray wool pants and a blazer when you came in. You looked so different. Like a grown-up."

"I despise that house in summer."

"Celia and I—we were there together when Dad was sick. We saw everything, and I guess we—her, mostly—we made up some way of talking about it. But you were gone. I thought you'd been talking with Dad on the phone, that somehow you knew him better. I didn't know what to say, either. It wasn't your fault."

To have ever been impatient with Michael's suffering seemed suddenly callous. All the effort I had expended pretending our lives weren't much different, so that he wouldn't have to feel lonelier than he already did—it hadn't been for him, but for me. Because I had wanted so fiercely not to pity my brother. Not to pity him as I did now.

It occurred to me that I could kiss him. I could take him in my arms. He hadn't been touched like that in so long. I could help him. Not with the love he wanted, but with the love that was here. What harm could there be in that?

I handed him a paper napkin and he blew his nose. He took another sip of his drink. I just smiled. It didn't matter now that he'd begun to cry. He was finally opening, and letting go.

"Do you remember being up here in the summer?" I said. "Playing on the rocks, out on the island?"

"I think I read *Death in Venice*," he said. "Which Mom approved of for some reason. *The poet of all those who labor on the brink of exhaustion.*"

"Those phrases of yours—the ones you read aloud—that's why I started writing. I probably never told you that. It was because of you reading me those lines."

He sat up in his chair, confused by what I'd said, straining to understand it.

"You were so excited by the sentences, they were so satisfying to you. It was like listening to someone preach, the way you read them. I didn't know what most of them meant, I just heard your rhythm. And I wanted to be part of it."

"Really?"

"I tried to sound like that, whatever it was. To write something you might want to read aloud like that. It's not what I do anymore, obviously. But yeah, at the beginning."

"*The miracle of an analogy,*" he said, using the napkin now to pat the sweat from his forehead. "That's what Proust calls it. *On those rare occasions when the miracle of an analogy had made me escape from the present.* That's the only real life, the only thing that makes you know you're alive—the backward ache. That's what music is. The trouble—for me—is that at some stage I realized those miracles, those aches, they have a history. They're not private. The music's always about what someone's lost. That's what you hear, when it's good: the worlds people lost, the ones they want back. And once you hear it that way, you can't avoid it—that it's somehow about justice."

He emptied his glass a second time and placed it on the table.

"It's like water," he said. "I don't feel a thing."

"I never wanted to say this to you, it seemed too harsh," I said. "But whenever you started talking about all that reparations stuff, I kept thinking, The only reparations getting paid are from Mom to you. Like you were demanding she give you another childhood. For her to take care of you that much. Because you were angry about the way things went for you. And it just didn't seem fair. To her. And it still doesn't."

The freshness of his sadness had begun to recede, his expression becoming more distant. I couldn't tell if he was considering my words, or if he simply hadn't taken them in.

"You want me to have a life like yours," he said. "Like yours or Celia's. Someone to be domestic with, a profession, so that I'll be taken care of. Mom wants it too—for me. But that's what I mean about sentimentality, how cruel it can be. Because how can I ever not want those things when you all want them for me? And yet it's never going to happen. I don't mean that in a self-pitying way, even if I do pity myself sometimes. I just mean that isn't my life. People don't want to be loved the way I love them. They get suffocated. It isn't their fault. But it isn't mine, either."

"You can let go of that now, though," I said. "The childish, obsessive stuff. That's part of what you've been holding on to."

"You're not listening," he said, and lifted the bottle again, filling his glass almost to the brim.

"Why don't you take it easy," I said, and reached over to slide the glass away from him, off to my right. "I'm here, I'm listening. Finish what you were saying."

He stood slowly from the table, walked into the kitchen, and returned with another glass, which he filled and began to drink from. "I told you," he said, in a voice I didn't recognize, low and determined. "I have to sleep now."

The countless times he'd said this before, I'd heard it as a complaint. To be sympathized with, yes, but not so much as to alter my plan. But this sounded different. There was no more pleading. Instead, he was doing what he never did—asserting himself. I could have stopped him. I could have taken the bottle away, and the second one he had carried in and placed on the floor beside his chair, and poured them both down the sink as I had the others. But I didn't. I watched him drink that third glass of Scotch to the bottom, and another after it.

Did I know then what would happen—know without knowing?

At some point I stood up from that table and walked into the living room, where I scrolled through the music on Michael's laptop, and found one of the albums I remembered him playing for me over and over. "Come here," I called to him as Donna Summer's "On the Radio" began to fill the air of the cabin.

Michael didn't move at first and I called out to him again. Finally he raised himself and came in to perch unsteadily on the arm of the couch.

"Why are you playing this?" he asked.

What he had said to me a moment ago was true. I hadn't been listening to him, not for years. I'd wanted him to be better for so long that I had stopped hearing him tell me he was sick. For the first time I saw him now as a man, not a member of a family. A separate person, who had been trying as hard as he could for most of his life simply to get by.

I took both his hands, interlacing our fingers, and I swayed to the beat, which had kicked in now beneath Summer's pining voice. "Come on," I said, encouraging Michael with the motion of my arms to sway with me, and after a moment he did, to my surprise, reluctantly rocking his head from side to side, woozy and out of time but responsive nonetheless, his knees bouncing just a little to the beat.

How long had we both been ashamed? How long had he suffered alone?

I stepped in closer and, taking his wrist in my hand, guided his arm around onto my waist, and put my own on his, holding him to me. Gently, I pressed his head down onto my shoulder. And then the two of us leaned against each other, and danced.

I remember seeing the taillights of the lobsterman's pickup come on in the dark, and listening to the chug of its aging muffler as he backed onto the road and pulled away toward the harbor. That's how I know it was still nighttime when, instead of remaining awake with him, I left Michael downstairs on his own.

I saw that other bottle of booze on the floor beside his chair. And I must have seen the bottles of Tylenol, too. He had placed them on the dining table, next to the salt and pepper. I saw, and yet I didn't see.

I didn't mean to wake you. You should go back to bed.

That's what he had said to me when I came down. I knew he wasn't going to stop drinking. Not until he slept, no matter what it took, or how long. But still I left him there on his own and went back up to my room and turned out the light.

I slept until midmorning, later than I ever usually did, a thick, dreamless sleep. I woke calmly to the sound of dripping and saw icicles outside my window melting in the sun. Lying there in the bed awhile, I listened for the sound of Michael in the house but heard nothing other than the trickling noises of the thaw out in the yard.

I got dressed and was halfway down the stairs when I saw him. He lay on the couch, eyes closed, head tilted back, his legs stretched toward me. Below the edge of the blanket covering his legs, his splayed feet were visible. A dried streak of vomit ran from the corner of his pale mouth, down his cheek and onto his shoulder. The empty bottles stood on the coffee table beside him.

I knew right away that he was dead. And that I had failed him.

Yet still I hurried to the couch and knelt beside him, as if I could shake his body back to life. His hands were cold to my touch, his chin jutting upward at an unnatural angle, as if he were gasping for breath. Lifting his head off the pillow, I gathered it into my arms, and clasped it against my chest, rocking back and forth, weeping into his hair. Wake up, I kept whispering, please, please wake up.

I have no memory of how long I held him. Or of how long afterward I remained in the chair opposite, beholding his body, the brow furrowed, the eyes resting like stones in their sockets. Long enough to observe a square of sun creep down the wall, across a map of the bay, and onto his glowing form, before it slid onto the rug and vanished.

I had never understood before the invisibility of a human.

How what we take to be a person is in fact a spirit we can never see. Not until I sat in that room, with the dead vehicle that had carried my brother through his life, and for which I had always mistaken him.

I knew that as soon as I stood up, I would have to act. I would have to go into the world and seek help. But as long as I remained in the chair, in the silence, none of that could begin.

Celia

I didn't believe it. You never do, at first. The force of the need for it not to be true blots the truth out. Afterwards, there is a daze.

I remember, once Alec had reached me and I had left work, lying on the floor in our living room, with the green fronds of the palm tree out on the sidewalk swaying against the white of the clouds through the top pane of the window and the telephone wires sagging gently across the view, and not thinking of Michael, not yet.

Strangely, what played itself over and over in my mind wasn't Alec and Michael in the cabin and what could have happened between them, but a night almost two decades ago, back in Walcott. I had been out drinking with Jason and his friends in the field at the end of the brook path, sitting in the dark out in the meadow. Jason and I were still dating, despite my mother's worry that we did drugs together, and despite my having lied to my father, on the last day of his life, about breaking up with him. I had told my father that because I thought it would make things easier for him, to be able to tell my mother that he had succeeded, knowing I could hide the truth from them easily enough.

Jason had been awkward around me for weeks. He didn't know what to say about my father's death. That night he kept slipping his hand out of mine. He joked restlessly with his friends and the girls they had brought with them, even as they paired off and began making out on the grass. When the banter died down, I nudged him onto his feet and we walked up the slope toward the woods, where we lay down and began kissing. I wanted to feel his weight on top of me, but he stayed up on his elbows, letting only our lips touch. The hours with him that summer were the only hours in which I didn't feel drowned. I couldn't tell him that, though. He wouldn't have wanted to hear it.

I willed him to put his hand on my stomach, to nuzzle his face against my chest, taking us farther away. Instead, when he heard the voices of the others starting up again, he rose and sauntered back down the hill. I didn't follow right away. I lay there taking in the stars in the clear night sky, listening to the voices trail off, telling myself that what my father had done wasn't easy for Jason either. I needed to be patient.

When I got up and returned to where we had first gathered, they were gone—all of them. I crossed the meadow back and forth calling out to Jason in a stage whisper, as if I might wake someone. But they had departed, he and his friends, off to drink at someone's house.

It was as I walked home alone through the warm darkness of that summer night, in the nearly perfect quiet of our neighborhood, that I vowed never to let that happen again. Never to put myself in a position to be left by a man. It was one of those youthful promises you make to yourself and keep long after you stop recognizing what you are doing, or how it is distorting your life.

That's what kept coming back to me in the numbness of the afternoon after Alec's call: how deeply I had made that promise, and how long I had kept it, never being with a man who might leave me. Always maintaining that control.

A promise to oneself never to be left. What sleight of mind.

The radio station at BC, where Michael had DJ'd, aired a tribute show, playing the music he had championed. Alec, my mother, Caleigh, and I listened to it together in the living room in Walcott. Caleigh had come to stay with us at the house for a couple of days before the memorial. There were a hundred things to do, and Alec and I did more or less all of them, working together like the well-honed team we sometimes were. My mother, who never got sick, came down with a heavy cold. Her friends Suzanne and Dorothy brought meals to the house for us, and arranged the food for after the service.

It seemed to me the wrong time to announce my own news that Paul and I had decided to get married, which I'd been waiting to tell my mother in person at Christmas, but Paul disagreed and said she would want to know, which once I reflected on it seemed right—to give her that. The morning before we flew back to California, I found her upstairs in her bedroom, writing thank-you notes to the people who had sent their condolences. She cried again when I told her—for me, and for Michael—but I was glad that I had done it.

I gave myself a few days back at home before going in to see my clients again. It was hard at first. And it stayed hard for months. To sit there quietly, hands folded in my lap, listening to them elaborate on their troubles. An old impatience returned, the kind I had experienced when I started as a therapist: the urge to search for the moments in their past that contained the key to liberating them in the present. That's what I used to do, press for more and more family history, excusing it to myself as interest and attention, when really it was a distraction from the suffer-

337

ing in front of me, a desire to find the passage of experience that would explain their pain away. What good plot didn't offer that? A meaning sufficient to account for the events. But as time went on, I realized that my clients' lives weren't works of art. They told themselves stories all the time, but the stories trailed off, got forgotten, and then repeated—distractions themselves, oftentimes, from the feelings they were somewhere taught would damn them or wreck them.

It had taken me a long time to see how strong this desire for an answer was. I had to train myself to notice how it arose, and how to put it aside. Because if all I did was scour what a person said to me each week for clues, I wouldn't do her much good. I had to give up my own need to cure if I was going to stand any chance of shepherding her toward acceptance of who she already was.

I never did that for Michael. I never gave up my belief in a secret, a truth lodged in the past, which if he could only experience and accept would release him. I thought of it as that moment of his in the woods with my father and Kelsey and me. An awkward teenager living in a town he loathed, on a walk he didn't want to take, trudging through his unhappiness as adolescents do. And then through no will of his own, as we came to that clearing and paused, sensing all around him a malignancy he couldn't name, a violence he had to escape. A vision of evil.

When Alec told me what Michael had said to him on their last night, about feeling guilty for going back to England without somehow warning us, I thought to myself: Yes, that was it, the moment he needed to confess and let go of. As if it were that simple.

He'd sounded so desperate on the phone from Maine. And yet I hadn't said what I should have to Alec—that it had gone too far, too quickly, and that he had to stop it. I'd kept believing in the one catharsis. As Alec did, and my mother, in her own manner, and even Michael, who never stopped trying to want what we wanted for him. How could he? We're not individuals. We're haunted by the living as well as the dead. I believed that before. But now I know it's true. It's what he kept trying to tell us.

Alec

Seth's sister, Valerie, picked us up at the airport. I greeted her from the backseat as the two of us piled in with our luggage.

"So you exist," she said. "Welcome." She had the same fine black hair as her brother, only longer and with a slight wave to it, and the same dark green eyes. "Don't worry about Luke there," she said, "he's out cold." The head of the toddler strapped into the safety seat beside me rested back and away from his little body, a clear streak of drool leaking from the corner of his mouth.

Beyond the terminal and the car-rental lots, the view opened onto a flat and nearly empty plain, an expanse of scrub brush stretching either side of the highway. The low clouds of a winter sky met the outline of foothills on the far horizon. Valerie sped down the passing lane, cruising by trucks and utility vans as she and Seth chatted over the sound of hit radio turned low. After a while billboards appeared, followed by gasworks and factories, and mile after mile of single-story warehouses built along empty access roads. Eventually I could see trees and the beginnings of neighborhoods, the Denver skyscrapers still off in the distance.

Seth's parents lived in a large ranch house on a street of ranch houses set back on one-acre lots lined with cottonwoods. His mother met us at the door wearing a white blouse and a necklace of braided pink coral.

"There now," she said, placing her hand gently on my arm. "I finally get to lay eyes on you."

I'd expected a friendly reception from her, in particular, given what Seth had told me, but the warmth of it came as a surprise. She led us onto the sunporch, where she'd put out cookies and iced tea. In the yard beyond, a blue tarpaulin sagging with unmelted snow covered a swimming pool rimmed in white concrete. There were well-tended juniper hedges and a flagstone path leading down the middle of the lawn to a creek. All of it appeared to me as most everything had for the last many weeks, as a still photograph of a place now vanished.

Seth's mother and sister asked me anodyne questions about what parts of Colorado I had visited, and about the winter weather in New York, any topic other than my family. I answered politely, watching Luke roll on the floor with his grandmother's terrier.

Since Seth and I had met, I had wanted to come here and meet his family, but for the last two months it had been hard to want anything. It will be good for us, Seth had said, encouraging me. It's time. And so I had come.

After our snack, I went to nap in the room we'd been given on the opposite end of the house from his parents' room. It wasn't Seth's. He hadn't grown up in the house. It was a room meant for guests. Plush beige carpet, a chaise longue under the window, two sinks at a double vanity between two sets of louvered closet doors. I fell asleep as soon as I laid my head on the pillow.

An hour or more later, Seth woke me with a kiss on the forehead. He rubbed my chest and kissed me again on the lips.

341

"They want to take you to the mall without me. Is that awful?"

I had been terrified that I would lose him. That Michael's death and the blank state it had delivered me into would annul what we had begun. But he had helped me as no one else could have by insisting we go forward with finding a place to live together, even when it seemed for a few weeks that I might not get my job back. At my weakest moment, he had refused to doubt us.

"It's okay," I said. "I'll go."

His mother and sister and I drove for twenty minutes in his mother's ample Lincoln, through a wide grid of commercial strips whose intersections had long lights and generous turning lanes, the late-afternoon sun glinting off the columns of windshields.

"We didn't mean to kidnap you," his mother said. "But he's kept you to himself long enough, and I have to ask somebody what he likes to wear these days."

"You're earning major points," Valerie half whispered to me as we crossed the parking lot. "This is what she does with people she likes."

It was Saturday and the mall was full. Parents herded small children through crowds of dashing teens. Seniors ambled along the promenade. Salespeople in chinos and polo shirts smiled vaguely from the stools of jewelry carts. A janitor mopped orange soda from the white tile floor, while above and through it all played "Friday I'm in Love," one of the Cure's lighter pop ballads.

"I just want to know if he's as much of a neat freak with you as he is with us," Seth's mother said. "He practically alphabetizes his shirts."

In the Brooks Brothers, I limited myself to recommending mediums over larges and suggested Seth would probably want to

342

purchase his own jeans. When his mother pressed me to let her buy me a tie, I fended her off with Valerie's help.

We kept at it for an hour or so, through several stores, and then sat together at a Starbucks. They asked me more questions, venturing now onto the subject of my mother, and of Celia and Paul. I did my best to reciprocate, inquiring about where in Denver they had lived when Seth was a kid, and about Valerie's work as a guidance counselor. It was kind of them to be doing this with me, and I wanted them to know that I was glad for it.

By the time we got back to the house Seth's father and Valerie's husband, Rick, had arrived and were in the sprawling kitchen with Seth unloading meat from a cooler. His father was an older, rougher version of Seth, taller by a few inches, with a larger jaw and broader shoulders, and the mottled skin of a man who'd spent his life working outdoors. He had the same upright posture, the same way of gesturing with his shoulders, and he spoke in that clipped rhythm of Seth's, flat and quick. Their resemblance was uncanny.

He gave my hand a firm shake, introduced his son-in-law, and then asked me if I liked to grill. Rick stood a few feet off holding a platter of marinated steak.

"Alec wants to talk to us," Seth's mother said as she leaned down beside her husband to rummage through the vegetable drawers of the fridge.

"You're saying he can't make up his own mind?" his father retorted, as though I were not in the room. Seth smiled at me in mock apology but remained conveniently silent. Rick's expression suggested the better choice was to join them. Reaching over his wife's back, Seth's father grabbed me a beer from the top shelf, and the three of us walked out onto the patio together.

They had come from a meeting with a developer. A set of

permits for a condominium on the outskirts of downtown had been delayed, costing their firm thousands of dollars. They included me in their talk of the minutiae of contracting as though I were an old pro.

"I've been telling Seth for a couple years we need a designer," his father said. "He's got a job here anytime he wants it."

The burnished gold of his father's wedding ring and the gold face of his watch caught the light of the flames. I found it hard not to keep staring at him, the way he had planted himself in front of the grill, moving only his hands and arms as he flipped the slabs of meat with a fork, addressing his comments to the fire. I wondered how he saw me. What did he think of the man who slept with his son? Did my presence force him to imagine it? Had his wife instructed him to accept me? Had he ever desired another man himself?

At the dinner table he stood at the head and carved the steak into strips, arranging them on the plates his wife held out for him, making sure everyone had been served before sitting. As we ate, Seth reported on our plans for a trip up to the mountains early the following week, and Valerie and her mother made suggestions for places we should stop along the way. When Rick asked me what kind of work I did, Seth's mother answered for me, informing him that I wrote about politics. At that point a quiet descended on the table.

"If those congressmen sell themselves any faster," Seth's father said, "they'll be shipping their own jobs to China."

I laughed. And soon everyone was laughing, nervously relieved, Seth most of all. He slid a hand onto my knee under the table and squeezed it. I couldn't remember the last time I had let go even this much. His father, delighted with the response to his quip, began to opine on government corruption and shoddy foreign building materials, and the uncertainties of interest rates, until eventually his wife told him he was boring us and announced there was pie.

I imagined Celia rolling her eyes at the scene of Valerie and her mother clearing the dishes and disappearing into the kitchen to tidy and wash while the four men kept their seats. But then Seth got up to help them, leaving the three of us alone once again.

"Let's fix you a drink," his father said, signaling with a tilt of his head for Rick and me to go through with him into the den. There a leather-topped bar with brass edging and a mirrored shelf stood against a paneled wall. Darkwood beams ran the length of the ceiling. There were birch logs stacked in the grate of a raised hearth. At the far end of the room a brown leather sofa and chairs faced a flat-screen lit up by the vivid colors of a basketball game playing out in silence.

"Rick here is bourbon, and I think tonight I am too—what can I get you, Alec?" He rested his hand on the amber bottle as he awaited my answer, the underside of his link bracelet touching the leather of the bar's surface.

"Bourbon's fine," I said.

He palmed ice into the tumblers and poured three generous drinks.

"Cheers," he said, looking me in the eye for the first time, just for an instant, and offering a small nod of the head, as if allowing me still further into the circle of his acknowledgment. Rick did the same when I glanced at him, and the three of us clinked glasses. It was a simple, male gesture, this little close-lipped dip of the chin, the eyes meeting ever so briefly. I'd given and received the nod a thousand times. It was what remained, I suppose, of tipping your hat. But I'd always experienced it as more than that. As a forswearing of an implicit threat of violence. A sign, between men, of disarmament.

"Cheers," I replied, aware of the closeness of their bodies to

345

mine—Seth's father's big frame, Rick's barrel chest and thick legs. These two men I had only just met were granting me an unspoken acceptance, giving me that minimal respect of belonging with them. But only in the narrowest sense. I'd earned the right in their eyes to be treated as a man. As a participant in the basic competition among all men.

Just noticing this, not letting it pass as an ordinary fact of meeting strangers, unclenched something in me. A fist in my gut. A bracing against attack.

I tried listening to their talk about suppliers and the housing market but I couldn't focus on their words. I saw their lips and eyes move, their weight shift, and as I watched them I understood clearly and for the first time that this was the reason part of me had come to loathe Michael. His refusal to be like other men. His refusal to compete. To live in the grip of that fist, the way I always had, and the way these men did. And I glimpsed what I had never allowed myself to admit before, which is that somewhere in me lay a hatred of my father, too, though for the opposite reason—for playing the game but being too weak to win it. A hatred I'd kept hidden from myself as a boy but never let go of, and which his death and my pity for him had prevented me from owning up to all these years.

"But on the whole," Seth's father was saying, "it's not a bad life."

Rick, as seemed to be his role, agreed with his father-in-law.

Behind me I heard Seth's footsteps and a moment later he was standing next to me, our circle widening to admit him.

"Sethy," his father said. "Get yourself a glass." He topped off all of our drinks and poured one for his son.

As the four of us raised our glasses, his father once again gave me that quick nod. But I didn't play my part this time. Returning the gesture seemed too small a response, and too cold. It was a kind of acting—a kind of life—that had led me, without my realizing it, to despise the men I loved.

Instead, I put my arm over Seth's shoulder and said to his father, "I want to thank you for having me here. I love your son very much."

Margaret

I find it remarkable how time works its way into a place. And thus how blank of time new places can be. This ceiling, for instance, here in my bedroom in the morning light of September. It means almost nothing. It is new, like the light fixture at its center, and the double-glazed window that the light comes through, and the louvered closets either side, which have so much less in them than the ones in Walcott ever did. All of which is right, and really as it should be.

After great pain, a formal feeling comes—

Those quotes Michael carried with him everywhere on sheaves of paper in his messenger bag turned out to be declamations, mostly, about the lasting evils of slavery. But there were others, too, on music and art, and life more generally. A few of which have stuck with me since I read through them last winter, in the months after he died. They were like notes to us that he had written but never delivered. Or delivered by speaking them only after I had stopped listening.

The Nerves sit ceremonious, like Tombs—

That is how it was for a time: abstract. Moving through tasks at a great remove. Meeting with Veronica, the real estate agent.

Tidying the house for the prospective buyers she brought around to view it. The hardest, of course, was going through Michael's things. Discovering from the pile of correspondence with his creditors, and his handwritten lists of the status of each loan and the amount outstanding, how he had tried right up to the end to manage his debts.

It took Alec less than a day to dispense with them all, except the one that I had cosigned. It required nothing more than a death certificate.

And then there were his records, in the gray milk crates along his walls, in boxes in the study and Alec's old room, all around the edges of the basement, too—thousands of them. I have no room for them here in the new place, but we weren't about to throw them away, so they sit in storage until we find them a home, where hopefully they can be kept together, and played.

In the new bathroom, the tiles are grouted a perfect white. The medicine cabinet is a perfect mirrored rectangle reflecting the snowy-white walls. I took baths before, but now there is only this glass stall shower, which the water beads on, catching any light in the room.

Are you sure you want to move? Alec asked, over and over.

I did consider staying, a while longer at least, mostly for his sake. Because he tried so hard to allow me to keep it. But I couldn't live in those rooms anymore.

Here, I walk to do my shopping, or along the wooded path around the reservoir. The neighbors have had me in for meals. I'm getting to know the mail lady. Best of all, Dorothy is only five minutes away. A few months after I moved, she told me she'd had enough of the suburbs and wanted to be closer to Boston, for concerts and museums. We see each other at least twice a week, for which I couldn't be more grateful.

After showering and dressing, I tiptoe past the guest room

and hear Celia and Paul beginning to stir. Paul could have stayed with his mother on the night before his wedding, but he and Celia wanted to be here together. I cross the dining room and close the French doors quietly so Alec and Seth can keep sleeping there on the foldout.

I baked the muffins yesterday afternoon, I just need to warm them in the oven, slice up the fruit, and start the eggs. I offered to do a larger breakfast, at least for their friends Laura and Kyle and for Paul's parents, but Celia said there was no need. Once my sister arrives from her hotel, the six of us will eat around the old dining room table that I brought with me, along with most of the other furniture that would fit. (Alec wheezes here as well, and says maybe it wasn't the mold in the basement that forced him to wear a mask, after all, but something in the rugs.)

"Let me do some of this," Paul says, coming into the kitchen in sweatpants and a T-shirt. He takes a melon from the counter, and a knife from the block.

"It's all right," I tell him, "I've got it." But he's found a cutting board already and starts in.

Despite the many Christmases he has spent with us, I've rarely spoken to him on his own, Celia or the others always being around. We did talk more when they had me out to San Francisco back in March. He was as attentive as I've ever seen him, to me and to Celia, making meals and arranging outings. I suppose some parents would worry about their daughter marrying him, given the financial instability of the sort of work he does, but I could never drum that up in myself, and I certainly can't now. I'm just glad for the fact that the two of them have decided to make the commitment, and glad to remember how well he got along with Michael, how he always laughed at Michael's antics.

On one of those outings, walking on Stinson Beach while

Celia played with the dog ahead of us, I found myself telling Paul how I wanted Dr. Gregory and Dr. Bennet and Dr. Greenman, and the people who'd invented all those drugs, imprisoned for what they had done. I hadn't said it like that to anyone before. Even to myself. And he took it in stride, saying that he understood.

He hands me the melon and I slide it into the bowl with the apple and the berries. "Really," I say, "you should go and do whatever you need to, I'm fine."

Seeing me infrequently, he is still solicitous of the grieving mother in a way that those nearer by no longer are, now that it's getting on toward a year. For them, Michael's death has been absorbed into the everyday.

I listen to the four of them moving about the house as I set the table and get started on the eggs. It's the first time they have all been here together. I've been looking at the forecast all week, keeping my fingers crossed, and so far the prediction of a clear day is holding.

After Penny finally appears, we gather, and I wait until everyone has been served before helping myself to a little fruit. When Alec instructs me to eat more, Seth glances at me almost beseechingly, as if trying to apologize for my son. Until a few months ago, I'd never met a companion of Alec's. He's been unfailingly polite, and, like Paul lately, speaks to me as if I'm in imminent danger of falling apart. He seems terribly young, though he is only a few years younger than Alec. His mother sent the nicest card about Michael, which, having never met me, she certainly didn't need to do, and I wrote her back, saying I hoped we would meet one day.

For so long I worried Alec would never find anyone, given the difficulties of that world, and how tightly wound he is. Perhaps if he'd had his father's acceptance it would have calmed him. I'm just his mother. I can't pick and choose among his qualities, which he has always known, and so my acceptance means less. But he and Seth have moved into a new apartment together now, and I think he is happier than he wants to admit.

He is so committed to his guilt. He needs Michael's death to be his fault. It's what keeps his brother alive for him—that connection. As though, as long as he still has a confession to make, Michael will be forced one day to return in order to hear it. Without that prospect, there is only an ending.

This is the thing I have discovered: Michael's being gone doesn't mean we stop trying to save him. The strain is less but it doesn't vanish. It becomes part of our bewilderment, a kind of activity without motive, which provides its own strange continuity.

Penny and I listen as the four of them chat away about who's coming this afternoon, about the music for the ceremony and their plans to go out with the friends who will still be in town tomorrow night. My wedding was more formal, of course. My mother composing and sending out the invitations, most of them to my parents' friends. The formal dinner a week in advance for John's parents to meet mine. Fittings with the dressmaker, a meeting with the minister, the rehearsal at the church. John was patient with all of it, and bristled less than I did at the strictures of the costumes and the production. But none of that is necessary today, and it would make no sense for Celia.

When the vans arrive, they all help unload things into the little backyard that I share with the condominium on the other side of the building. Luckily, the couple who live there don't have much interest in gardening and were happy to hear that I did. There's been only one growing season so far, but I have cleared a few things out and planted a bit. I wish it were bigger, especially today. I did offer to pay for something larger, but Celia said no, this was fine, just family and a few close friends, not a year of planning and expense. She did at least let me buy her dress, a

352

knee-length, powder-blue silk with a white collar and cuffs, and a pair of shoes to match.

And the flowers—I was permitted to organize the flowers, which Penny helps me arrange on a table by the back fence and down along the four short rows of folding chairs. There should be more for me to do besides this, but it seems they have thought of everything.

Around noon Caleigh appears with rented speakers and a stereo, which she sets up on the little screened-in porch off the kitchen. She's helped by Ben and Christine, with whom it's been such a comfort to me to remain in touch this year. Caleigh wouldn't let me pay for her ticket from Chicago, where she lives now, though I suppose there is no reason I should have, besides how glad I was when I heard Celia had invited her and that she would be coming. She looks much as she always has, elegant and slender, and as shy as ever. She said she would stay on with me for a few days, so we can go to the storage unit and sort through some of Michael's records (she knows more about them than any of us). I've put aside whatever papers he had with her name on them, and a stack of their reparations pamphlets as well, for her to keep. She smiles her way nervously through introductions to the other guests as they gather in the yard.

In their one feint to tradition, Paul is kept from my bedroom while Celia puts on her dress and arranges her hair. I do what I can to help, buttoning her up from the back, fixing the clasp of her necklace, things I haven't done for her since she was a child.

She is thirty-six, my daughter. By her age, I had given birth to all three of them. They were already running across the yard in Samoset. It's not that I want that for her, or even that I want grandchildren, necessarily, though all my friends do have them by now. I simply want her to be happy.

"Do the earrings go?" she asks.

They are little pendants of blue glass suspended in silver wire, and I tell her they are perfect with her dress.

She looks not at me but at herself in the mirror.

"If your father were here, he'd know what to say. I'm sure I should be saying something to you—on a day like this. I should have said all sorts of things, over the years."

She glances at me, then back to the glass. "There are probably things you could have said," she allows.

Though she never wears makeup, today she's decided to apply a pale lipstick, which she does slowly and exactly, before dabbing her lips with a tissue.

"You know what I used to hate?" she says. "The stockings at Christmas. I didn't hate them. But they aggravated me. And the Advent calendar. All those little rituals, no matter how old we got. It seemed like you were avoiding reality, just being naive."

"I'm sure I was, I—"

"Mom—listen: I don't think that anymore. I see these women and their partners or husbands, people with kids. They're falling apart—money, or mental health, or whatever it is—and they don't know what to do. They're desperate. You were trying to keep our world together. To keep things the same. I get that now."

"It's incredible how you take care of all those people. I don't know how you do it."

"You took care of us," she says. "You did your best."

I hug her, so as not to cry. "Well, Paul's very fortunate. I do know that."

She lets herself be hugged. "I envy you sometimes," she says over my shoulder, "with the weather and all those dates you remember, enjoying all of that, those little things. I thought that was naive, too. But you're lucky. It's good you can enjoy it."

Before I can take in what she's saying, the door opens and Alec

354

saunters in, half displacing us from in front of the mirror in order to adjust his tie.

"The crowds have gathered," he says. "They await you with bated breath."

I don't know what is funny about this, except it's the sort of thing Michael would say, parodying the moment. And that, perhaps more than anything, is what makes me laugh, which causes the two of them to smile, and then start laughing themselves, about nothing at all, it seems.

Soon I have to wipe my eyes, I'm laughing so hard, and I tell them, "Oh, come on now, we have to hold ourselves together."

"Why?" Alec says.

The service itself is brief. I walk Celia down the narrow aisle. Two of their friends read short poems. Kyle leads them through their vows. At the end, everyone claps and the newlyweds point their guests to a long table, where champagne glasses have been set out. The white tablecloth is bright in the full sun. The light dazzles the wine as it's poured. Ben and Laura and Caleigh make sure everyone has a drink in hand. After a while, Alec taps his glass, the conversation quiets, and he gives his sister a toast their father would have been proud of.

It is quite warm and people begin to sweat, their foreheads glistening as they chatter and laugh, enjoying themselves on a beautiful afternoon. And though I know I shouldn't be looking backwards, that I should be here in this moment, I can't help it that all of this—the garden with the drinks, and the sun, and the people in a buoyant mood—carries me back to the day I went to the house on Slaidburn Street, off the King's Road, taken along to a party by a friend, through a low-ceilinged hallway and onto the little square of lawn at the back, where I saw John for the first time, standing in his pin-striped pants and shirtsleeves behind the dining room table they had carried out onto the grass and covered with what looked like a folded bedsheet. He was mixing gin and tonics, and after he had made me one, he stepped around that table to drink his own with me. To begin our first conversation. With such politeness and such care.

It's a day I recall not in sadness, but in wonder at all that followed.